GLOWING PRAISE FOR CHET RAYMO AND THE DORK OF CORK

"A POWERFUL AND LOVELY NOVEL....It's not uncommon to come across a book that touches your heart, or another that engages your mind. It is uncommon, though, to find one volume that does both. This novel does that beautifully."
—*West Coast Review of Books*

"THE READER WILL ADMIRE RAYMO'S COMPLEXITY OF PLOT AND THE SIGNIFICANT QUESTIONS HE POSES IN THIS NOVEL. He will also come away from *The Dork of Cork* touched and smiling after the character Frank Bois, who, in almost every way, is an Irishman larger than his 43 inches."
—*USA Today*

"EMOTIONALLY SATISFYING...FULL OF BEAUTIFUL LANGUAGE...Raymo seems to have an equal gift for character, story, and language; an equal gift for the exterior and interior aspects of his tale."
—*Los Angeles Times*

"A SPARKLING READ...the quest of a poetic-minded dwarf child of a beautiful, sexually attractive mother who may (or may not) be able to perform miracles. Very Irish, very extreme, very good."
—**John H. Mitchell, author of *Living at the Edge of Time***

more...

more...

"[A] REASSURING AND ENJOYABLE GARP-LIKE
NOVEL...Raymo knows how to apply astronomy and
physics to the human condition in a fun, naturalistic way."
—*Cleveland Plain Dealer*

"ENCHANTING...a coming-of-age novel and
philosophy textbook...deftly sketched."
—*Kansas City Star*

Also by Chet Raymo

A Geologic and Topographic Profile
of the United States

365 Starry Nights

The Crust of Our Earth: An Armchair Traveler's Guide
to the New Geology

Biography of a Planet: Astronomy, Geology,
and the Evolution of Life

The Soul of the Night: An Astronomical Pilgrimage

Honey From Stone: A Naturalist's Search for God

Written in Stone: A Geological History of
the Northeastern United States

In the Falcon's Claw: A Novel of the Year 1000

The Virgin and the Mousetrap: Essays in Search of
the Soul of Science

THE DORK OF CORK

CORK

✦

CHET RAYMO

WARNER BOOKS

A Time Warner Company

Grateful acknowledgment is made for permission to reprint from the following: "Never Give all the Heart" and "The Lover tells of the Rose in his Heart": reprinted with permission of Macmillan Publishing Company from *The Poems of W. B. Yeats: A New Edition*, edited by Richard J. Finneran (New York: Macmillan, 1983). "Leda and the Swan": reprinted with permission of Macmillan Publishing Company from *The Poems of W. B. Yeats: A New Edition*, edited by Richard J. Finneran. Copyright 1928 by Macmillan Publishing Company, renewed 1956 by Georgie Yeats. "Parting": reprinted with permission of Macmillan Publishing Company from *The Poems of W. B. Yeats: A New Edition*, edited by Richard J. Finneran. Copyright 1933 by Macmillan Publishing Company, renewed 1961 by Bertha Georgie Yeats. "The Circus Animals' Desertion" and "An Acre of Grass": reprinted with permission of Macmillan Publishing Company from *The Poems of W. B. Yeats: A New Edition*, edited by Richard J. Finneran. Copyright 1940 by Georgie Yeats, renewed 1968 by Bertha Georgie Yeats, Micheal Butler Yeats, and Anne Yeats.

Warner Books, Inc., 1271 Avenue of the Americas, New York, NY 10020

 A Time Warner Company

Printed in the United States of America

First Trade Printing: April 1994
10 9 8 7 6 5 4 3 2 1
Originally published in hardcover by Warner Books

Library of Congress Cataloging-in-Publication Data
Raymo, Chet
   The Dork of Cork / Chet Raymo.
      p.   cm.
   ISBN 0-446-67000-6
   1. Title
PS3568.A928D6   1993   92-50529
813'.54—dc20   CIP

Book design by L. McRee
Cover design by Jackie Merri Meyer
Cover illustration by Thomas Woodruff

We must not look at goblin men,
We must not buy their fruits:
Who knows upon what soil they fed
Their hungry thirsty roots?

—*Christina Rossetti*

All dreams of the soul
End in a beautiful man's or woman's body.

—*W. B. Yeats*

1

Begin with beauty.

Clouds part to reveal the moon already contained within the shadow of the earth. Not typical clouds for this part of the world. In Ireland we are used to smothering blankets of gray, or wet sheets of moisture flapping in the wind. We are used to racing clouds, scudding in from the Atlantic to shred themselves on the razory limestone steeples of the city, especially at this time of year, when, if we are lucky, we might get one uncloudy day in ten. Tonight the clouds are heaped in cumulus billows, almost tropical except for their gloomy pallor, and moving with a stately calm, exposing in their passage broad gaps of black night.

I write in my journal: *6:03 p.m. Clouds part. Moon fully eclipsed.*

The moon has shed her luminous dress behind boas, so to speak, behind boa fans. Now the clouds are swept aside and there she stands, starkers, flushed a spooky pink by light refracted through earth's atmosphere. I applaud. It was, you see, a perfect show, all the better for having been concealed in the initial stages, a teasing performance. Alone at my garret window in Nicholas Road I laugh out loud and clap.

But I also get down to business. *Southern highlands: pink marble veined with gray. Mare Imbrium tinged the color of tea.* I estimate the color of the moon at midumbral stage on Danjon's scale: $L = 3$, I decide, *pearl pink, features obscure, yellowy rim to the shadow.* Tomorrow I will send my observations to Dunsink Observatory in Dublin. Their usefulness will depend upon how many other observers in Ireland had an unobstructed view of the moon at totality. Perhaps I was lucky. Perhaps Cork City was front row center. Perhaps only for me did the moon swerve her concealing fans.

But even if my observations are unique in Ireland, they will have only marginal scientific value, glanced at by the Dunsink staff, then filed away in the observatory basement in a box labeled "Eclipse Observations, Amateur." Eclipses of the moon are not particularly rare. They are, however, rare enough to draw me to my garret window and cause me to fill a dozen pages of my astronomical notebook with descriptive notes (*tinged the color of tea*: I like that). And predictable. Rare, predictable, and therefore interesting. Like the appearance of a comet. Or a conjunction of planets. Or certain hereditary diseases, such as genetic dwarfism, that express themselves in succeeding generations with grim mathematical regularity.

Amateur. One who loves. Loves his moon in pink eclipse, loves his drop o' drink. I pour myself a tumbler of port—or, I should say, another—the last sediment-filled dregs of a generic vintage purchased at a high street shop for £4.50, pungent, acidic, guaranteed after a half bottle to make me slightly ill. I hold the glass up to the window and view the moon through it. The disk disappears, like one of those red-ink pictures in a child's playbook that becomes invisible when viewed through a sheet of red plastic. Clouds glide in the port-filled glass but the moon is gone.

Alone. Alone at my spidery window with the moon doing her cloud-fan trick. A dog barks in the cul-de-sac. Bats squeak and dive among the chimneypots. I have my astronomical journal. My glass of port. An agreeable hint of stiffness between my legs. And now, again, that tingle in the spine! Even as I watch, the moon edges out of the earth's shadow into sunlight, an eyelash-thin sliver of radiance. I write: *An eyelash-thin sliver of radiance.* I note the time.

I pick up a dusty paperback from the garret floor by the moon-filled window, Zola's *Nana*. It has lain there for years, with others of its kind, but now, for no particular reason, I pick it up, blow off the dust, turn it in my hands. The spine is naked, the cover missing, the pages dog-eared. I open it, moisten my fingertip, and turn a page or two. Certain passages—the text is French—are underlined or marked with checks in the margins. I riffle the pages with my thumb and something as friable as a pressed flower flutters to the floor, a slip of newsprint torn from a newspaper, powdery with age. At the top of the printed story is written—in a schoolgirl's practiced hand—"*de le Cork* Examiner, *Cork, l'Irlande, 24 juin, 1946.*"

Cobh. *A stowaway French girl, age 16, was today put ashore at Cobh from the American troop ship USS* California. *According to Emigration Officer Mr. Jack Kelly, the girl boarded the ship at Le Havre together with approximately 800 American soldiers being shipped home. She apparently had the cooperation of some of the soldiers in boarding the ship and in evading ship's officers. She was discovered as the* California *entered Cork Harbor for provisioning. Kelly gave the girl's name as Anne-Marie Coupeau. She carried no passport, nor any possessions other than the clothes on her back. During an interview with port officials the girl managed to slip away by climbing through a lavatory window. She is still at large. The authorities at Cobh wish to reapprehend Miss Coupeau so that she can be questioned further and returned to her home. Kelly appealed to the public for information on the girl's whereabouts. She is about 5 feet 5 inches tall, with short dark hair and green eyes. She was wearing a blue dress and black pullover at the time of her disappearance. "The girl is pretty," Kelly said. "It is easy to see why the lads gave her a hand up."*

There are two errors in this report. The girl's name was Bernadette Bois, not Anne-Marie Coupeau, and she carried two things more than the clothes on her back. In the pocket of her dress was a copy of Zola's *Nana*, the very copy I hold in my hand. Here on the flyleaf is her signature together with the date *5 mai, 1946*, and, on the title page, stamped in red ink, *Fravel et Fils, Libraire, Fleurville*. Fleurville, on the Normandy coast, was the girl's home. In her womb she carried the germ of a male child, no more than twenty-four hours old at the time of her interview with Jack Kelly, a single fertilized cell, but soon to fission—two, four, eight, sixteen—directed in its flawed flowering by an aberrant gene.

Dwarf. Not an easy word to say, even more difficult to write. An ugly word. But a writer is committed to telling the truth. The truth is this: Bernadette Bois's son is a dwarf. The technical term for my condition is achondroplasia. Trunk normal, limbs shortened because of a disturbance of the bone-producing cells in the growth plates of the long bones, large brachycephalic head, sunken nasal bridge, stubby hands and feet. Normal intelligence. Normal sexual functions. Normal life expectancy. The malformity is genetic, an autosomal dominant trait the geneticists call it, which means that the aberrant gene might have come from either parent. I was conceived on a government-issue mattress on a lower deck of an American troopship steaming cautiously (for maverick mines still drifted in the waters south of Ireland) toward Power Head and the entrance to Cork Harbor. My father was a crew-cut, khaki-clad American GI who had survived the battlefields of Europe and now felt himself even more uncommonly lucky when the pretty French girl pulled him into her body. ("I do not know which of the *garçons militaires* was your father," she said to me, "but all of them were *beaux* and all of them were kind.") He came before he had time to stammer what he felt were the required words of endearment. He filled her up with endless miles of waving wheat, buttermilk skies, and purple mountains' majesty, and in that irrepressible rush of American goodness, one wildly thrashing sperm raced to her waiting egg, bearing (so she led me to believe) the damaged gift of achondroplasia.

I am forty-three years old and forty-three inches tall. Balding, square-jawed, thick lipped. My ears are florescences on the side of my head, my nose might have been struck a blow with a hurley, my spine has a twist that I must consciously correct by turning my body to the right. As compensation for these physical deformities, the Irish state is pleased to award me seventy-seven pounds per week. With the leisure afforded by that sum, I spend my time filling my head with all manner of knowledge. There is a chair at the Cork City Library that is mine alone. I haunt the bookshops of Lavitt's Quay. I live in the same flat in Nicholas Road into which my mother moved with her infant child in the autumn of 1947, the upper floors of a terrace house owned by Elizabeth Brosnan. The house remains as it was when my mother moved in except for the numerous books that line the walls in tall, unstable piles. The garret too is filled with books, most of them mine but some formerly my mother's.

Amongst these myriad volumes is one of my own authorship.

Here on my desk are the printed galleys of the book that has been my occupation for the past half-dozen years and now comes to fruition: a work on the night sky, descriptive and poetic, with a generous lacing of personal history (and Bernadette's story too), soon to be published in a first edition of twenty thousand copies by Penguin. I am told that this is a substantial number of copies for a first work by a new author. Also untypical is the publicity planned for the launching. There will be trips to London, television interviews, meetings with the press. The publisher has planned these exhibits to parade my deformity. It is because of my deformity that the publisher has such confidence in the marketability of my book (we are dealing here with the undeniable commercial value of the grotesque, the monstrous, the side-show freak). But—we shall see. I am anchored to my solitude. I hunker down among my boxes of books. I heap them more closely about me, as if building a bunker. I watch, apprehensively, for each piece of mail that Elizabeth Brosnan slips beneath my door, looking first not for the addressee—*Frank Bois, 14 Nicholas Road, Cork, Eire*—but for the orange imprint on the reverse—*Penguin, Ltd, 27 Wrights Lane, London.*

Nightstalk. That is the title of my book. Three

hundred and twenty-seven pages of words, my own, cast unforgivingly into type. On the first of those pages is the dedication: *To Jack Kelly, for the stars*.

4

      Jack Kelly stepped from the redbrick Port Authority Building into summer fog. *Gunpowder fog*, he thought, *still thick with the stench of war*. The harbor was crowded with ships from the Cobh quays to Ringaskiddy and Haulbowline, some at anchor, others gliding soundlessly through cotton-wool mist: British minesweepers waiting for brighter weather to resume their dangerous harvest in the mine fields south of Ireland; coasters chartered by the Dublin government laden with coal, grain, and salt for citizens weary of wartime rationing; ships the color of the North Atlantic—wartime, ghost-ship gray. Jack remembered the harbor as it was before the war, bright with billowing spinnakers in rainbow colors, white sails filled with the golden light of evening, scarlet steamship funnels inflating perfect balloons of pungent blue smoke, yachts with fittings of polished brass and varnished mahogany, pennants, burgees, ensigns, flags. Gone now. He pushed his greatcoat collar up against the chill. A southerly wind came up from the sea, past Roches Point, the forts, and Spike Island, dead-ending against the limestone buildings of quayside and the whitewashed houses heaped upon the hill. He stood on the fog-slicked steps of the Lusitania Memorial and counted the vessels at anchor, comparing them against a list he carried in his head. The ships rose and fell silently on the swell. *The flotsam of war*, he thought. He winced with regret.

The *California* was gone.

Gone, thought Jack. He was a large man, thick limbed but not fat. His skin was translucently pink and blue veins stood out on his cheeks and the backs of his hands. Thinning red hair flew out in wisps about his crown and his chin tended toward jowly, but he carried well his thirty-seven years. Lines at the corners of his mouth betrayed a tendency to smile, but now he was somber, his mind on the ship that was steaming past the Old Head of Kinsale toward the open Atlantic, and on the passenger it had left behind.

Again today a reporter from the *Examiner* had been around to inquire about the girl. Her story, the circumstances of her flight—a young girl, eight hundred men—had caught the attention of an editor. *No, she had not been found. Yes, the Gardai had been notified. Yes, she had been trying to get to America. Yes, attempts had been made, unsuccessfully, to locate her parents through the authorities at Le Havre. No, he did not know how many of the American lads had been part of the scheme. No, he did not know if disciplinary action had been taken against the soldiers, or even if the girl's accomplices had been properly identified.* The reporter scribbled notes and departed. Jack arranged the pencils on his desk, first by color, then by length. Then by color again. He rubbed his thick pink hands briskly together and looked at the empty chair where the girl had sat. He would be required to write a report describing her escape. His superiors would not be pleased. They would say that he was lax, that the girl's evasion of custody was typical of his inattention to detail.

I am not inattentive, thought Jack to himself, as he jiggled his pencils into a new arrangement.

The stowaway girl spoke no English, but he'd a bit of French. He had questioned her gently.

"*Comment vous appelez-vous?*" Her cottony dress clung to her knees, violets on an azure field. Her green eyes swam about the room, alighting nowhere.

"Anne-Marie," she said at last, shrugging nonchalantly.

"*Nom et prénom?*"

"Coupeau."

"*Quel âge avez-vous?*"

"*Seize ans.*"

"Where is your home?" he asked. "*Domicile?*"

She looked briefly into his eyes but said nothing.

Clerks from other offices clustered at the doorway, whispering. The bold, pretty girl who called herself Anne-Marie Coupeau was a bit of a celebrity. She slouched forward in her chair, heels spread wide on the lowest rung, knees together, elbows on her knees, chin resting on the knuckles of her hands. He thought: *She does not take any of this seriously. It is as if she were a school child waiting at her desk for the bell that will dismiss class*.

Jack himself had six daughters, the oldest nearly the age of the stowaway. He sympathized with the

girl's parents, their daughter gone missing, presumably without revealing her destination. He had
telegraphed inquiries to Le Havre, without satisfactory response. And there was something else that
had occupied his mind during the hours since Anne-
Marie Coupeau made good her escape, something
about this willful girl who apparently thought nothing of boarding a ship with eight hundred young
men, something he had seen in her recalcitrant
green eyes. He could not put her out of his mind.
He pulled his cloth cap from his pocket, slammed
it onto his head, and felt ashamed.

Bernadette Bois pulled shut the lavatory
door and waited briefly to make certain she was
alone. She easily pushed open the window, but
there were wrought-iron bars beyond. She studied
the obstruction, then stripped off her sweater, took
the book from her pocket, and dropped sweater and
book through the bars. Pulling the toilet's chain to
disguise the sound of her scramble, she dragged
herself up onto the window's sill and squeezed
through the bars. She fell to the pavement in a passageway behind the Port Authority Building,
scraping her shin on the sill and bringing a fall of
redbrick dust down onto her dress. Waiting outside
the lavatory door, Jack Kelly heard the gurgle of
water from the overhead tank and, embarrassed,
moved farther down the corridor.

She was not at all certain where she was. Somewhere in Ireland. Not in the city of skyscrapers and lights where she had hoped to disembark. A gray place. Not warm, though the height of summer. From what she could see from where she stood by the wall at the back of the Port Authority Building, a place of dustbins and puddles. But it was *hers*. She commanded it immediately. She wriggled into her sweater, brushed brick dust from her skirt, and stepped into the quayside streets as if she had lived there all her life.

I allow myself some measure of invention. Much of what I know about Bernadette's first months in Cork I learned from Jack Kelly or from the diarylike notes that she sometimes made in the margins of her books. I have a few photographs from that time, printed on cheap postwar paper. With a magnifier I examine a snapshot of my mother taken by Jack a year or two after her arrival at Cobh. She poses on a quay, Albert Quay perhaps—yes, there is the Customs House in the background— saucily on a balustrade, legs crossed Betty Grable—style, skirt hiked up above her knees. She is thin, apparently happy, and young. Her hair is swept up in a kerchief. There is a pram.

Wait. The pram comes later. For now—*she wriggled into her sweater, brushed brick dust from her skirt, and stepped into the quayside streets as if she had lived there all her life*. Two months later she spoke passable English and lived in Cork City. She took a room in a boardinghouse in the Glen Ellen Road and lived by her wits, taking work where she could find it. She folded clothes for a laundry in Blackpool, polished brass hardware and name plates for a bank in the South Mall, cleaned lavatories for the nuns of St. Monica's Convent. She lived on bread, fruit, and tea, and warmed her tea on a tiny primus stove provided by her landlady. She wore the same blue dress and black pullover every day because those were all she owned. On Saturday evenings she rinsed out her dress and undergarments in a galvanized bucket of cold water drawn from a tap at the back of the house and sat shivering naked under her woolen blanket as the wet clothes steamed dry beside her one weekly fire. By then she knew that her body had lost its rhythm, and began to fantasize that the father of the child would somehow know that his seed had taken hold in her womb and come to retrieve her—and the child—to America.

But of course he did not come.

Then, in Patrick Street, she passed the man who had conducted the interview at Cobh on the day she was put ashore from the *California*. She was in her eighth month of pregnancy and no longer the thin impertinent child who slouched forward on the chair in Jack Kelly's office lying about her name, giving as her family name that of the heroine of her book. Now her belly bulged outward and her shoulders were thrown backward to balance the weight of the child.

Jack passed without recognition, then stopped and did a turn. He hurried after her and caught her up by touching her arm.

"You?" he asked, withdrawing his hand. His fingers had gone taut and tingly as they might in a hot bath.

She pushed the collar of her pullover (stretched to accommodate her swelling body) up about her cheeks.

"Ah, 'tis you," he said. "The girl from the *California*."

It was her green eyes that he had recognized.

He took note of her body, the pallor of her face, and the transformation of her eyes—yes, that was it, no longer liquidy but jade, no longer dreamy but still defiant.

He thought awhile and said, "I'll not turn you in."

Instead, he took her into the Cock and Swan and treated her to shepherd's pie and a pint of cider. She greedily devoured the meat dish and quaffed the cider as if she had been drinking it all her life, when in fact it was her first. When she had retrieved the last crumb of flaky crust with her moistened fingertip, she turned to her benefactor and smiled sweetly. She had not yet spoken a single word to Jack Kelly, but he *knew* as he placed a shilling on the marble counter that he would become her lover.

But not yet. There were other things to attend to first. There was the impending birth. It was Jack who obtained a willing midwife, pretending to be the baby's father. And when the child was delivered, he did not flinch in his loyalty to the girl from the *California*. He was there at her bedside, holding her

thin wet hand, when the midwife pulled from Bernadette's womb the unfortunate child, a squashed sort
of thing with legs and arms disproportionately small
compared to the torso, like sprouts budding from
the eyes of a potato. Ears like crushed cabbages.
Nose smashed. The child seemed to be all head.

"Great God," said Jack Kelly.

He saw the fright in the face of the girl who was,
after all, not much older than his daughter. He took
the infant from the midwife and held it against his
chest. He cooed. He sang a song about angels and
infants. And when the midwife had tidied the room
and tucked my mother securely between the sheets,
he gave her a half-crown and sent her away.

"'Tis a lad," he said, beaming into the imploring
eyes of the exhausted girl. "And look at the size of
the turnip between his legs, a fine big root of a thing
from a black-earth hill."

Jack's wife, Effa, had borne six children in
as many years. Jack loved them all. He loved especially Emma, the eldest, fourteen. Emma was religious, sometimes distressingly so. She went to
early Mass every morning at St. Colman's Cathedral,
and then again later with her class at school. She
possessed, he imagined, a kind of prescience ("She
knows things," he said to Effa), and he accounted
it to her devotion to the saints. She wanted to be a
nun. Try as he might, Jack Kelly could not see the

sense of it, but he held the girl's hand, stroked it, nodded his head and said, "I'm sure you'll be happy."

"Oh, Da," said Emma, "I do love Jesus so."

And Jack replied, "Of course."

But he was thinking of Bernadette (for by now the girl from the *California* had revealed her true name) and of the pale tautness of her body as she sat beside him on the bed next to the cot where the sweet-tempered stump of a child contentedly snoozed.

"I should go soon, Da, to the convent at St. Bridget's, to be a postulant," said Emma.

"And do you not think you might ever want to marry?" asked Jack. "Have children? A family?"

"Da, please! We have been through all of that. I don't like boys a'tall. They are mean and silly."

He looked into her moist eyes and loved her more, sorry that such goodness would not be appreciated by a man, but grateful too that she would not throw herself away on someone mean and silly.

I am not unfaithful, Jack thought to himself.

He came to Bernadette's room every Sunday afternoon. He told his wife that he took long walks out to East Ferry, across to Midleton by Tom Roche's boat, then back through Carrigtohill and Foaty Island, as in fact had been his habit, but instead he took the train into the city and walked to the house in Glen Ellen Road. He sat with Bernadette on the edge of the bed in her small damp room and listened to her stories, which seemed remarkably many and complex for a girl so young. She told him of her childhood in France, of the exploding mine that exterminated the children of Fleurville, of her own miraculous survival, of her mother's bizarre religious devotions, and of her father's death at the hands of the Germans. She told him of her flight from Le Havre, and of giving herself to the young soldiers in the hold of the *California*. What she never spoke of was the deformity of her child. She seemed to take no notice of it. She reeled endless stories into Jack's ear, all the while tickling the soles of her son's tiny clublike feet as he lay beside her in the bed. When she spoke to the child, it was not with baby talk but as she might speak to an adult—as she spoke to Jack.

"What will you name the boy?" asked Jack.

Bernadette shrugged. "He is an *américain*. He should have an *américain* name. Like Bill or Tony."

"But he is also French," said Jack, who could not bear to think about what had happened aboard the USS *California*. "He should have a French name. Jean. Or François."

"François," said Bernadette. "I'll call him Frankie."

With an infant to nurse and care for, Bernadette could not work, and without proper papers she could not apply for the dole. So Jack Kelly gave up the mustard-slathered beef sandwich and pint of porter he was accustomed to take for lunch each day and gave the money he saved to Bernadette ("For the child," he said). His Sunday walks along the untarmacked byways of Midleton and Carrigtohill grew longer. He sat on the unmade bed in Bernadette's room and listened to stories he had heard twice or three times before because he was in love with the green eyes of the storyteller. On the first Sunday of August 1947, with the temperature soaring into the seventies and sunlight streaming through the single ungenerous window of Bernadette's room, the girl from the *California* stood up from the edge of her bed and placed Frankie in his cot. She came and stood before Jack Kelly, who sat as he was accustomed, with thick pink hands clinched upon his knees. She looked at the blue veins in his cheeks and the fret of tiny lines at the corners of his mouth. And grasping the hem of her blue dress with violet flowers she pulled it over her head.

Jack closed his eyes in astonishment, and when he opened them, she was holding out her hands to him. She drew him up from the bed and helped him remove his clothes—jacket, vest, tie, collar stud, collar, links, shirt, shoes, garters, socks, trousers, undervest, shorts—which she dropped in a heap on the floor. *I am not untidy*, thought Jack. He felt the sunlight burning like a blacksmith's iron into the small of his back and his skin flush crimson. He stood half-paralyzed at the thought of what was about to happen. He let his eyes rise slowly from the floor up along the curve of the girl's calves and thighs. He marveled at the firmness of her belly and her breasts. When his ascending inspection reached her face, he blushed.

And Bernadette, who did not own a looking-glass, admired herself in the full-length mirror of Jack Kelly's eyes.

8

*

Silence. That is the first thing I remember about the stars. The huge overarching silence, like a thick duvet that muffles every sound.

Jack Kelly led me to the top floor of the house in Nicholas Road, to a garret used for storage. He carried an electric torch to guide us through the gloom. At the back of the garret a gable window opened onto the sloping roof of Bernadette's kitchen. Jack prised open the window. He set me down in darkness and removed my shoes, small brown boots especially cobbled by a shoemaker in the Douglas Road. He removed his own shoes. He put his finger to my lips.

"Shush," he whispered. "Your mother mus'n't know. She will worry with her boy on the roof." We held our dusty breaths and listened for Bernadette's *shuffle-shuffle* as she moved between the sitting room and kitchen below, in her stockinged feet, two thick pairs of woolen socks. But of course we heard nothing. I stared at the open window, my heart in my mouth, and seeing the stars reflected in my gaping eyes, Jack said, "Don't be afraid."

I wasn't afraid. The window framed the stars of Lyra and Cygnus. Bright, beckoning stars, swimming in a sea of light. The window was the entrance into another world. What lay beyond the window was not the same *outside* that I entered through the door of the house, the door that led into Nicholas

Road. Outside the garret window there were no trams with unmanageable steps, no shops with sweets in tall glass jars on unreachable counters, no kindly people offering the dwarf child beggar's mites of pity. None of that. The window was a passageway to silence. To solitude. And to beauty.

Jack squeezed his large body through the frame, turned, and lifted me onto the roof. We sat on the slope of the kitchen roof with our backs against the garret slates. We were sandwiched between two black planes—the slates below, the sky above. The sky! So luminous with stars. Like sparkling water flowing over black rock. A vast endless cascade of twinkling light. And silent. Utterly silent. As if I had cotton in my ears. All of those stars, that cascading river of light, and not a sound.

Jack took bits of the silence and shaped it into words, whispering. He named the stars: Vega, Deneb, Altair. He traced the patterns of the constellations. He told me stories of birds and fish and of Orpheus with his lyre. "Albireo," he said, and the name of the star was like an incantation. He might as well have said "abracadabra." Words ignited on his tongue.

"Stars blow up," said Jack.

Stars blow up. For the first time in my life I understood what words are made of. They are made of silence. Later, in school, one of my teachers did a demonstration with an electric bell suspended inside a glass jar. The bell was set clanging and then the air was pumped out of the jar. The bell went silent, its clapper swinging soundlessly like a boxer throwing punches at a pillow. As I sat with Jack on the roof of my mother's kitchen looking up at the stars it was like that, like the bell in the vacuum. Stars exploded in utter silence. My heart, too, beat as wildly as the clapper of the bell, but there was no sound.

I was six years old.

9
*

Those star-filled nights with Jack on the roof of Bernadette's kitchen came later, long after Jack and and my mother had ceased to be lovers. During the summer of 1947 they met on Sunday afternoons in the damp little room of the boarding-house room in the Glen Ellen Road with water seeping in murky floods through faded floral wallpaper and a single south-facing window sipping at the sunlight when there was any to be had. Jack sat upon the bed and listened to Bernadette's interminable stories. She described for Jack everything that had happened since his last visit: things seen on the street, words exchanged with shopkeepers, noises heard in the night. And when she had exhausted the particulars of her own life, she told him the stories she had read, in those days usually the novels of Colette, *Claudine at School, Claudine in Paris, Claudine Married, Claudine and Annie*. Jack imagined she must have memorized every word. He was not interested in any of this, neither her own trivial day-by-day experiences nor the adventures of Claudine. But he listened. That is, he *truly* listened, nodding in assent, gasping with surprise, shaking his head in disbelief. He was not bored. He watched her eyes, green, bright, enthusiastic. He watched her mouth shaping the words. He sat on the edge of her bed admiring her beauty and listened with unfailing contentment to her endless catalog of jab-ber.

When the hour approached that Jack must leave to catch the last train that would bring him home in time for a plausible completion of his Sunday "walk," he and Bernadette removed their clothes and crawled between the sheets. She reveled in the heft and security of his big-boned embrace, his brooding kindness. She teased him into a kind of unfocused bliss, moving her hands unashamedly to every part of his body. Jack never ceased to be astonished by her lack of inhibition, by her unflag-ging appetite for novelty. Her youthfulness was like a drug, lulling his awareness of the unseemly differ-ences in their ages.

Jack was a fastidious adulterer. Before he left the house in Cobh for his Sunday "walk," he always dropped a few sweets for Bernadette into his pocket along with his sandwich. He patted his inside jacket pocket to ascertain the presence of the packet of condoms he purchased each month from an enter-prising first mate on a coaster working between Cork and Swansea. When he disembarked from the train at Glanmire Station he always took a different route to the room in the Glen Ellen Road. And, later, on returning home, he never failed to tell Effa of the things he had seen on his walk—a heron by the slip at East Ferry, curlews at Foaty Island, a tiny firecrest that preceded him along the East Ferry Road, flitting through the hedge just five paces ahead. Jack was a methodical man, methodical in his infidelity, methodical in his lies. He did not wish to hurt anyone, least of all Effa.

Effa was a Kerry girl, handsomer and darker than Jack, with hair like a tangle of sturdy black sewing thread. He had met and married her during an early posting to the emigration office in the port of Fenit near Tralee. She had borne him six girls in six years and it was Jack who said no more. With that decision (necessary, he felt, for the orderly advancement of his career and the financial security of his family) their coital relations had ceased, to the dismay of both partners. Contraception was never discussed.

Nor would he hurt the girls. The girls were his life. Emma, the eldest; bright Sarah; Una and Orna, the twins; gay Caitlin; little Deidre—all with their father's wispy red hair and translucent skin. Several years after Deidre was born Jack decided to impose order upon the chaos of the household. He ascertained each girl's favorite color. Emma, violet. Sarah, yellow. Una, red. Orna, blue. Caitlin, green. Deidre, pink. He purchased a two-quart tin of Dulux enamel in each color and painted their beds and dresser drawers and chairs at table. He asked his wife to dress them accordingly. Effa sensibly baulked—she considered the scheme a silly example of Jack's obsessive need for order—but when the girls begged their mother for clothes in *their* colors, she gave in. On washing day the kitchen table was piled with clothes in rainbow colors. "My Rainbow," Jack called the girls.

It was Emma, the eldest, who finally guessed. It was Emma who followed her father to Cork City on the seventeenth Sunday of his affair with Bernadette. It was Emma who tagged along unseen as Jack walked to the house in the Glen Ellen Road. It was Emma who waited for two hours on the front stoop of the house. It was Emma who at last climbed onto the roof of the coal bunker at the side of the house, tearing her plum-colored stockings and acquiring coal-dust smudges on her violet skirt. It was Emma, weeping for her carelessness, who peered in at the dusty window of Bernadette's room.

When twenty minutes later Jack emerged from the boardinghouse, he found his daughter sitting on the doorstep, eyes swollen, the bib of her dress blotched with tears. She would not meet his gaze, nor did he wish it.

He sat beside her. He tried to take her hand in his, but she wrenched it from his grasp. Her nails tore at the backs of her hands and drops of blood speckled the gray stone steps. He reached down and smudged the drops with the flat of his thumb as if to erase them. His body felt empty, like a skin shed by a snake.

"'Tis a sin," she blubbered.

"No," he said, for he felt no shame for the thing itself. "'Tis a sin to be found out."

"'Tis a mortal sin."

Still he did not grasp her meaning.

"Emma," he said. "Dear Emma. How can I explain to you? It is not what you think. It does not mean that I don't love your mother. It does not mean I don't love you. What—" He did not know how to continue. He did not himself understand. Perhaps it meant all those things.

"I'll go to Hell," she said.

And she looked at him, her eyes full of terror, her hands twisting in her lap, the nails tearing at the backs of her hands until her dress was smeared with blood.

"You?" He did not understand. He thought she might feel guilty for spying.

She banged her fists against the step.

He said, "You did what you thought best. You were trying to protect your mother."

He fiddled with the knot of his tie. He noticed a tiny spot of blood on his vest. He began to think of the train that would soon be leaving Glanmire Station. He began to wonder how they would answer to Effa.

"I saw it," said Emma, wretchedly. "Oh, Da, I saw it."

10

What Emma had seen through the dusty window of the boardinghouse on Glen Ellen Road was a naked girl, hardly older than herself, astride her father, moving upon him as if she were riding a horse. The girl's white breasts were cupped in her father's big pink hands.

It was the *seeing* of their lovemaking that she understood to be her sin. She had *watched*, a moment longer than was necessary to ascertain her father's betrayal, not with curiosity but with an acute paralyzing pain. It was as if she had been *forced* to watch by some wicked spirit within herself.

Jack only dimly understood his daughter's distress. He did not grasp that merely *seeing* a thing—a thing for which the girl bore no personal responsibility—might be perceived as sinful. But Emma felt it. She knew that her sin was unabsolvable, that it could no more be erased from her soul than the scar of a burn might be excised from the skin. She *knew* that those few moments at the window had removed forever the possibility that she might be a nun.

"You mus'n't tell your mother," said Jack. "There is no point in hurting Effa too. 'Tis bad enough that I have hurt you."

Emma looked into his eyes and flopped her head like a rag doll from side to side. Her hair flew up in coppery wisps about her head.

"You must stop," she whispered.

He thought she meant that he must stop his affair with Bernadette, but it was to herself she spoke, remembering.

"I will," he said. "But you, in your turn, must not tell Effa."

"I cannot now, ever."

And again he misconstrued her meaning. But in misconstruing, he was reassured.

12

Jack knew then that he had entered Bernadette's bed for the last time. He had made a promise to his daughter. The promise could not be broken. But he would not abandon the French girl and her damaged son. That was another promise he would not break, a promise implicit in loving her. He would find a way to regularize their relationship so that it need not be a secret from Effa. And somehow he would use his connections in the Immigration Service to make legal Bernadette's residency in Ireland, and that of her son.

These thoughts occupied his mind as he and Emma returned to Cobh on the 5:15 train. The engine moved tardily out of Glanmire Station. It crept past Tivoli and *clack-clack*ed through Cobh Junction with the mournful rhythm of a dirge. Or perhaps the journey just *seemed* slow, an unconscious adjustment of Jack's psychological clock, a backward pressure on the hands of the clock in anticipation of his encounter with Effa.

He was not distracted by conversation with his daughter. She rode next to him in silence, looking neither to the left or right. As the train rattled along the causeway to Foaty Island, he pointed out cormorants feeding; she refused to look. When he tried to pat her hand, she snatched it away. She had wrapped her left hand in her kerchief, and the scratches on her right hand she covered with her left. With both hands she sought to hide the flowery brown stains in the lap of her dress.

When father and daughter arrived at the house in Westview Terrace, Effa knew at once that something terrible had happened, but she had the good sense not to ask what it might be. She waited for Jack or Emma to be forthcoming. Emma retired immediately to her room (she alone of all the girls had private space, a gable room on the third floor). Jack went into the garden and began fussing with his telescope, a Scott & Boland four-inch reflector that he used to conduct his surveys of the night sky. When Effa came out and stood beside him, he said, "The declination knob is sticking."

He went to the toolshed to fetch his screwdriver.

"Just tell me that Emma is all right," said Effa finally, as Jack fiddled with the declination control of the scope, dismantling the gear casing and nervously dropping the retaining screws into the grass.

"She's fine," he said. He was on his hands and knees, looking for the lost screws. He spoke into the ground. "She's fine. She fell and scraped her hands, that's all. I met her as I returned from my walk and helped her home."

Effa watched as Jack scuttled on all fours, away from her, to a place where the screws might never be. She said: "I know you are lying, Jack Kelly, but I'll not press you to tell the truth."

"The girl's fine," he mumbled.

But Emma wasn't fine. She did not emerge from

her room for a week. She tossed her blood-smeared dress and all her other violet garments out the window onto the dustbins in the back garden. She took her remaining clothes from the violet dresser and heaped them against the wall. She removed the bedclothes from her violet bed and slept on the floor. And there, amidst the clutter on the floor of her room, dressed only in her white cotton nightdress, she pecked at her meals.

It was Effa who finally made it clear to Jack that Emma would not return to her bed as long as it was painted violet.

"What color does she want?" he asked.

Effa went up to Emma.

"Black," she said, returning.

Jack went out to the high street and bought another tin of enamel, Midnight Black. The girl removed herself from her room, huddling in a corner of the kitchen, while Jack changed the color scheme. He painted the bed, the dresser, the bedroom chair. He painted slowly and deliberately. It was like obliterating a rainbow.

13

At least once each month, from the time I was six years old to the age of ten, Jack Kelly took me onto the roof of the flat in Nicholas Road. The stars were hooks on which he hung his stories. And what a body of lore Jack possessed! Star legends from the Greeks, Romans, Egyptians, and Babylonians. African star tales. Norse and Celtic stories. The sky did not seem deep enough to contain them all.

"Look, Frankie, look at that star there." He took my hand and led my pointing finger out along the arching body of Andromeda to a star in Perseus.

I looked. By now I knew the major celestial guideposts. "Mirfak?" I asked, pleased that I knew the name of so nondescript a star.

"No, Frankie. Back, closer to Andromeda, the second brightest."

I saw it.

"'Tis the Demon Star," he said, and I took a shiver from his body, as a small tuning fork vibrates in resonance with a larger one.

"The Arabs called it Al Ra's al Ghul, the demon's head. That's where we get our own name for the star, Algol. The Romans called it Gorgoneum Caput." He tapped his temple.

I knew the story of the Gorgon. "'Tis the Gorgon's head," I whispered. "The Medusa."

"They say that if you look at that star for long enough you'll turn to stone, just as the monster Cetus turned to stone when Perseus took the Gorgon's head from the bag and dangled it before its eyes."

We huddled closer, our backs against the cool slates. The sky was pricked with stars. All of them seemed monstrous.

"Well now, everyone thinks the Medusa was ugly," said Jack, "and that it was her ugliness that turned folk to stone. But that's not so. Ah, she was beautiful, no doubt about that, one of three beautiful sisters. Their vanity it was that angered the gods and caused Zeus to change their hair to serpents. The Medusa's hair was snaky, sure enough, but her face and her figure were as pretty as your mother's. She was wondrous beautiful. And terrifying too. Beautiful and sinister. And why do you think, little Frankie, that such a lovely star has an evil reputation?"

I didn't know. I waited for Jack to tell me.

"'Tis a variable star. The star changes brightness every two days, it does."

He made the variation of the star sound magical, miraculous. But he also explained the geometry of eclipsing binaries, moving his pink fists in circles, one about the other, until he was sure that I understood how it was that one star could intermittently block the light of another.

14

Beautiful and sinister. Jack thought I didn't understand. But I understood. I was eight or nine years old, but even then I understood how beauty and hurt get jumbled up together. Even then I had seen how long are the shadows that beauty casts.

When Bernadette heard Jack's knock on the door she knew that everything had changed. With the first rap of his knuckle on the oak boards she knew that she would never again huddle against the secure pink warmth of his body. She also knew that she now possessed his affections more securely than ever before.

She opened the door to see a wretched man.

Jack said nothing, but entered the room and took his accustomed seat on the bed. He looked about at the dark stains on the walls, at the bed's rusty iron spindles showing three or four layers of chipped enamel, at the tiny primus stove precariously perched on the windowsill next to two pink teacups, and at the tiny stunted feet of the infant in the cot.

And at Bernadette, who was wearing the dress in which he had first met her, the cotton dress with purple flowers on a field of blue. He saw in her eyes that she already knew what he had come to say.

"You are beautiful," he said, and sat upon his hands.

"I will miss you, *mon bel homme*."

"Ah, you have not seen the last of me at all," said Jack.

But Bernadette knew that. She knew that Jack was in her life to stay. It was their lovemaking she would miss, the Sunday rituals that led to a few moments when the plainness of the room was invisible, when the smells of paraffin, grime, and damp were over-whelmed by the lusty exudations of Jack's body.

"Collect the child," said Jack Kelly, "we'll be going out."

He stood. He placed her shawl upon her shoulders. She wrapped the child in its blanket and lifted him from the cot. (Do I remember? No, it is impossible. I was much too young. Then why do I see it so clearly, the gray wool shawl against Bernadette's pale cheek, the weariness in Jack's eyes?) For the first time they walked together from the boardinghouse into Glen Ellen Road and down the hill to the River Lee.

They promenaded along the quays. She told him stories—of her childhood in Fleurville, France.

From the chalk-filtered water of the public fountain in Fleurville's market square rises a statue of the third-century martyr St. Victor. The limestone saint seems to walk on the surface of the pool. The townspeople call him *le homme aux pieds mouillés*, the man with the wet feet.

From the town square roads lead east, west, and south. If today you were to take the western road out of the old quarter of the town, you would quickly find yourself in an unbroken strip of petrol stations, tire shops, supermarkets, and fast-food restaurants that merges at last with a similar tawdry commercial strip reaching out from St-Jean-sur-Mer seven kilometers away. But you need not go that far. One kilometer from the fountain of the wet-footed saint an inconspicuous signpost on your right directs you to the ruins of L'Abbaye de St-Victor, now enclosed by a mass of prefabricated corrugated-iron buildings in which is manufactured the sweet herb-based liqueur known worldwide as Victorine. Beyond the abbey and La Maison Victorine (a name too elegant for the untidy assortment of buildings it describes), reaching from the St-Jean-sur-Mer

Road to the cliffs by the sea and mostly built over with identical suburban houses, is the twelve-acre tract of rich chalky land that was the farm of Albert Bois.

Imagine the town, the western road, the ruined abbey, and the farm as they were in the autumn of 1942: contrails of Allied bombers high overhead, a *tump-tump*ing of antiaircraft batteries along the coast, dust and smoke of the German convoys or patrols that race through town, the gray-uniformed usurpers of the *hôtel de ville*, the swastika-emblazoned flag that flies from the mast at the *hôtel* entrance. Erase this overlay of war and Fleurville and its environs in 1942 might be any town of rural France in any century, excepting the last few decades of our own.

It is late afternoon. Seven children lie belly-down in the grass at the edge of the sea cliffs on Albert Bois's farm. Six boys and a girl. The girl is Bernadette. She is twelve years old.

A large, black, spherical object rests in the sand on the beach below. It has come in from the sea on the morning tide. A squad of German soldiers constructs a barbed-wire barricade around the object, as if they were making a pen for a somnolent but dangerous beast. They work methodically under the direction of an officer who sits on the concrete sea wall with his back against the cliff. The officer is smoking.

When the stakes have been driven deep into the sand and the wire strung, the soldiers post a sign and go away. Of the seven children, only one has the courage to scramble down the cliff to read the sign. When she returns, she tells the others what she has read. *Achtung! danger! vous voilà prévenu!*

16

In the occupied towns of the channel coast a curfew prevailed from sundown to sunup, but in the summer of 1942 patrols to enforce the curfew were insufficient and people in the countryside went about their business, which at harvest dragged late into the evening hours. No one noticed when, by prior arrangement, seven children met just after dark in the woods on Albert Bois's farm.

It was the Thing they had come to see.

They ran through the fields to the clifftop where they again flopped down on their bellies with their chins on the edge of the cliff. On the dark foreshore below, the Thing lay quietly breathing in its wire cage. The tide licked its black belly.

"Come and see," said Bernadette.

She scampered down the steep path to the shore. Her companions followed, frightened, unsure.

They gathered at the wire barricade, peering in at the Thing as if it were a panther at the zoo. Their breathing—slow, rhythmical, unified—matched the pulse of the tide. A westerly breeze came up, blowing warm dry sand against their bare feet. The sea was gray and empty. High above, contrails crept toward the heart of the Reich, catching the last rays of twilight.

"It's a bomb," guessed one of the boys.

"Bombs have fins."

"And pointy noses."

"It's part of an airplane."

"Or a submarine."

"Maybe it's American."

"It must be valuable. The Germans want it."

"It's probably empty. If it weren't empty, they would have taken it away."

"It's not empty," said Bernadette.

They looked at her in wonderment, the solitary girl. Her arms were thin and white. Her green eyes blazed.

"It looks empty," they said.

"It's not empty."

Bernadette imagined that she could *see* inside the Thing. She saw something dark and gelatinous like the guts of a fish. She saw something foul. "It's not empty."

Their eyes moved from Bernadette to the Thing and back again. They were frightened of the Thing, and they were also frightened of Bernadette. They were frightened by her confidence—and by her intuition, which seemed infallible and dangerous.

The oldest boy, Charles, moved along the wire toward Bernadette, letting the wire slip through his partly closed fists, loosening his grip to let each barb pass, until his hand touched hers, their hands side by side on the wire.

"Easy enough to tell," he said. He kissed her on the cheek, a kiss so brief she thought she might have imagined it.

Then he picked up a stone and threw it.

*

The galvanized wire went through their bodies like razors, followed by a hurricane of shrapnel. Parents and soldiers gathered up the pieces in wicker baskets. No one had the heart to separate limb from limb. Even the Germans wept.

When the townspeople arrived at the beach, they found the girl wandering dazed. Her dress had been blown from her body but she was not scratched. Of the six boys not a piece of flesh could be found bigger than a forearm, but the girl was unhurt. In her two hands she still held a six-foot strand of barbed wire.

*

Bernadette's survival was accounted a miracle. That she bore the name of the visionary of Lourdes confirmed the opinion of the townspeople that she possessed special powers. They came to Albert Bois's farm to gawk across the fence at the thin green-eyed girl who had been so favored by the Virgin. They placed flowers at the farm gate, flowers from their gardens or from the roadside. They waited outside the schoolhouse to catch a glimpse of her. They followed her in the streets of Fleurville when she came to church or market.

Their constant surveillance frightened her.

A German film crew came to make a newsreel. The mine had been British. The killing of the six children and the "miraculous" escape of the girl was effective propaganda. They filmed her barefoot in the farmyard feeding the chickens and in the schoolroom with six empty desks. They filmed her at the funeral of the boys, standing near the six pathetic coffins, which contained randomly sorted parts of bodies, and at the gaping crater in the sand, not yet, after seven days, erased by the tide.

People from the Fleurville region began to hope that Bernadette's miracle might be catching. When she walked into the town, strangers stepped out from cafés and bars to rub medals, chaplets, holy pictures, and missals against her dress. They brought children afflicted with tuberculosis or chronic colic or asthma and pressed them to her. Terrified, she touched them, as her mother insisted, and then ran behind the house, where she furiously wiped her hands on her dress or scrubbed them with soil from the garden. She was nauseated by the illnesses of the children she was asked to touch—the coughing, the scabious skin, the involuntary jerking of head or limbs. Old men with rheumatism or psoriasis begged for bits of her clothing that they might apply them to their bodies. Her mother took to cutting up Bernadette's outgrown dresses into ten-centimeter squares that she sold to the supplicants for twenty-five francs.

No one guessed that it was Bernadette who had led the boys to the mine.

Bernadette knew two things. She knew that she possessed a power. She had *seen* the interior of the mine, had seen it as clearly as if the thing were made of glass. And she knew that the gift of vision that enabled her to penetrate the mine was not divine but physical, that it stemmed from within her own body, from dark cavities beneath her belly. The proof was clear. The vision had been visceral, bloody. Her body, too, had begun to bleed. And when she removed her shift at night she saw that her breasts had begun to swell.

Bernadette's mother, Anne-Marie, was a small wiry woman with sunken temples, aquiline nose, and thin lips firmly pressed together. She had long been given to bouts of depression. As a young woman she had been beautiful, delicately sketched, so to speak, in aquarelle, but life on Albert Bois's farm had hardened her features and clouded her eyes with a gloomy hopelessness. Now, with the affair of the exploded mine, her life was again transformed. She brightened, took an interest in life; she began, in effect, to tend the shrine of her daughter's reputation. With the proceeds from the sale of the cloth squares she employed builders to construct a replica of the Lourdes grotto near the farm gate on the Fleurville–St-Jean-sur-Mer Road. A sign posted at the shrine indicated that rosaries touched by Bernadette were available for sale at the door of the house, along with the ten-centimeter squares of cloth from Bernadette's clothes. Madame Bois was not avaricious. It did not occur to her that she might be exploiting her child. She was convinced of the girl's special blessings. She did what she did for the glory of God, and if there was in it some measure of financial reward—well, no one blamed her.

Albert Bois was not pleased with the goings-on that occupied his wife and so frightened his daughter. The supplicants and curiosity seekers at the farm gate attracted the attentions of the Germans, whom he despised. The miracle-mongering smacked of superstition or hysteria. But Albert Bois did not doubt that Bernadette's survival was somehow connected with a special gift. He had sensed her prescience on many occasions. As a young child she had often addressed herself to thoughts in his mind that he had not yet expressed. She would say things like, "Papa, you should bring in the hay today, it is going to rain." And Albert Bois would look at the sky, and test the direction of the wind, and listen to the wireless, and there would be no sign or prediction of rain. He would leave the hay on the ground, and twenty-four hours later it would be sodden.

Albert Bois did not doubt his daughter's gift.

Bernadette no longer played with other children. She abandoned her former haunts in the fields, in the woods, and on the shore. She became solitary, seeking out the quietest corners of the house and barns. She remembered the touch of Charles's hand in the instant before the mine exploded, and imagined that she remembered the pressure of his lips on her cheek. And she began to read.

19

Solitude. Solitude and books. These were constants of Bernadette's life and these I inherited. Like my mother, I am a solitary bibliophile. I do not go out in daytime except to the library or the bookshops on the quays. I cannot bear the pitying eyes of people on the streets. When I walk, I walk at night. I walk when the streets are mine alone. I walk when the city is blanketed by stars.

I walk especially on nights when the moon is full, hanging low on the southern hills. I strike out into the countryside south of the city or west along the Lee. I walk all night, returning home only when the stars fade and the moon sets. The countryside is transformed by moonlight. Distances dissolve. Moonlight compresses miles and miles of scenery into painted flats like stage sets. Each bend in the road is a card turned over in a game of chance; I don't know what I will find—a rush of wings, a pair of eyes, a skittering beast, a vole, a badger. I see with my ears. I listen to the teachings of hedgehogs, the oracular pronouncements of woodcocks, the fox's silky poetry. Country roads by moonlight are a spectral world of flutter, scuttle, and slink. When the moon is full I do not waste it. I walk in its pearly light and no one pities my stumbling gait and made-to-order boots.

20

An envelope slips in at the door. From my chair at the desk I see the familiar imprint: the orange penguin in its oval. I do not go immediately to fetch it. I continue working, glancing occasionally at the envelope on the floor. Or I stop working and stare at the envelope as a cat might watch a cricket, mesmerized.

I am leaking away.

At night my body leaks into the bed; I wake to damp-spotted sheets. My ears discharge onto the pillow. My handkerchief is wet with mucus from my nose. Even my pen leaks into my shirt pocket, staining my chest with splotches of blue ink. For forty-three years I have contained myself within a membrane of solitude. The contract with Penguin has punctured the membrane. Each envelope at the door is another pinprick. Soon I will hemorrhage.

21

Young Bernadette Bois, spared by the bomb that dismembered her companions, discovered in her solitude the novels and stories of Colette. She saved her pennies to purchase slim volumes at Fravel et Fils, Libraire. She did not bring the books home. Her mother would have taken them from her. Her mother would have said the books were *interdits aux enfants*. Her mother would have considered them *impropres*. Instead, Bernadette took her books to church.

She read the works of Colette while sitting on the back bench of Fleurville's parish church, the church of St. Victor. When the *curé* entered the sanctuary she hid her novel under her coat and replaced it with her prayer book. No one wondered that she should be there. No one wondered that she should spend so much time in apparent prayer. She was, after all, La Bernadette de Fleurville.

The first of Colette's novels that she read was *Le Blé en Herbe*. The story was a door. And a mirror. Vinca and Philippe. Seashore. Shrimp nets. Bare feet upon hot sand. Awakening love. With a pencil from her school bag she underlined certain passages: *"In the crevice of that rock,"* Vinca whispered over his shoulder, *"beauties, such beauties. Don't you see their little horns."* Such sentences were poetry. And the scenes of consummation—of Philippe and Madame Dalleray, of Philippe and Vinca—these she puzzled over, reading the story again and again, letting her imagination expand to fill Colette's suggestive voids. At night she rehearsed the puzzles in her bed.

And so with the other books. When she felt she had exhausted a volume, she returned it to the shop, recovering a part of the price toward her next purchase. Soon the proprietor began to set aside books that she might choose to read. "Look, Bernadette. See what I have for you today. Colette's *Gigi*."

Or *The Cat*. Or *Claudine at School*.

Once, as she sat reading in her usual place, a young German officer entered the church. He went to the front of the sanctuary and lit a votive candle. She watched him from the shadows. He turned. His eyes were intensely blue. He blessed himself, touching his fingertip to his gray tunic as delicately as a dragonfly touches the surface of a stream. He glanced briefly at the figure huddled in the back pew. Then he walked to the font at the sanctuary door and dipped his fingers into the holy water.

22
*

The first vegetables of the season—lettuces, peas, and spinaches—were coming to maturity when the Germans came to build their motor depot. They requisitioned ten acres of Albert Bois's land and paved it over with tarmac and gravel. They plowed his vegetables into the earth.

Albert Bois watched disconsolately as the bulldozers savaged his farm, his vegetable garden, his field of oats. Bernadette watched too from her bedroom window, curled in the window seat on plump pink cushions, arms about her knees, gently rocking. She watched the heavy camouflage-colored machines rearrange the earth. She watched the garden's green give way to mud and gravel and camouflage netting. She watched the grotesque wire fence go up to enclose her father's desecrated fields, topped with spirals of razory wire. Then the trucks arrived and took up their positions row by row.

Each day after school and on weekend afternoons she retrieved her current novel from its hiding place and went to the bench at the back of the church.

She was waiting.

On June 4, 1944, she came to her father and said, "Papa, tomorrow the Americans will come."

Albert Bois considered the weather. He considered the wind and clouds. The weather did not seem sufficiently settled for an invasion. The Americans and English would never risk a channel crossing except in settled weather. Nor was there was any special activity on the road that might indicate German apprehensions. But he had learned not to doubt his daughter. He touched her cheek. He smiled.

The next morning Bernadette and her classmates were ordered from the school to take their places with the other townspeople in the village square. The square was ringed about with armed soldiers. The *curé*, the mayor, and ten other men chosen at random stood in a line by the fountain. A German officer spoke in French; it was the blue-eyed young man who had blessed himself in church. His message: *Tires of trucks in the motor depot had been punctured during the night. Twelve hostages would be executed in one hour's time unless the guilty person or persons were identified.* The officer gazed mournfully at his watch. The townspeople, including the hostages, looked to the clock on the gable of the town hall. Soldiers and townspeople waited in silence. Rain showers swept the square with sheets of fine spray. When one minute remained within the designated hour, Albert Bois walked into the square and threw a cobbler's awl at the commandant's feet.

Bernadette's teacher moved quickly along the line of students to put his arm about her shoulders. The eyes of the townspeople shifted from Albert to Bernadette, as if they expected a miracle—an animated statue, a spinning sun, soldiers turned to salt or stone. Bernadette neither moved nor wept. She closed her eyes and let her spirit drift out of her body. She felt herself ascending. She left her body standing in Fleurville's town square, a hollow plaster saint in a line of schoolchildren who had all begun to weep.

Albert Bois was made to stand in the fountain of St. Victor. Water poured in over the tops of his rubber boots, anchoring him heavily to the floor of the basin. He stood erect, his shoulders thrown back, his brown arms crossed defiantly on his chest in startling contrast to the androgynous passivity of the limestone saint. When he fell, blood pumped furiously from the clean hole between his eyes. It was as if the bullet had punctured a boiler in full steam.

Bernadette's presentiment had been a day too early. The Americans came on the sixth of June, not the fifth. The punctured tires had been repaired.

23

Jack Kelly, as the Americans say, cashed in all his chips. He knew exactly what he was doing. He knew that he was surrendering any chance for promotion. He knew that if he acted aggressively on behalf of Bernadette, then when he had achieved his goal, the little volume of space he had created for himself within the crowded warren of the civil service would collapse upon him like a tent whose poles have been suddenly removed. He acted with a full knowledge of the consequences. He used whatever influence he had at the Department of Internal Affairs to regularize Bernadette's presence in Ireland, blustering when necessary at those functionaries of lesser rank who might help him, and standing cap in hand before those higher officials who greeted his importunings derisively over half-spectacles while tapping their pencils impatiently on their desks.

And he confessed himself to Effa.

In the dark of night when he heard her wakeful breathing beside him in the bed, he blurted out the whole story, as to a priest through the anonymous gloom of the confessional. She was caught unawares. She knew he had done something foolish but had not suspected this. Tears accumulated at the corners of her eyes, but in the darkness he could not see them. He lay there on their marriage bed as stiff as a corpse. Splinters of light from a motorcar on the West Cliffe Road slipped across the ceiling and down the wall, quick as an autopsist's scalpel. His breath knotted in his throat. He listened; for what? For words of absolution, for the prescribed penance. Time passed. Neither of them spoke. Nor did they sleep. They lay side by side unmoving in the bed and the house made night sounds—sibilant hisses, groans, snuffles—about them. With first light Effa rose, before Jack, as was her custom, to put the kettle on the stove and riddle the grate.

It was not in Effa's nature to punish Jack. No apologies or recriminations passed between them. She accepted his word that the affair was over. If, as he insisted, he was to continue his alliance with the girl ("She has become my responsibility," he said at breakfast, staring forlornly into his tea), then he must bring her to the house. She must see who it was who had been her rival.

Effa was an improbable woman. Her generosity to Jack was measured out in proportion to the gravity of his betrayal. She accepted his confession, processed it, and tucked it away in some subbasement of her soul. On Sunday afternoon Jack brought Bernadette and Frankie to the house on Westview Terrace, as casually as he might have brought a niece or cousin. He did not tell Bernadette that Effa knew of their affair. It was, he said, a new start. Bernadette was frightened, but Effa welcomed her. Effa took Bernadette into her home. She prepared a steaming pot of tea, opened a Christmas tin of biscuits, baked fresh scones. She dandled Frankie on her knee. The five youngest daughters of the house played with the infant as if he were a doll, tickling and cooing and tapping together his tiny fistlike feet.

Emma was not to be seen.

Bernadette sat numbly on her chair, her teacup clutched in her two hands to keep it from rattling on the saucer. She lapsed into French when she was required to speak—*oui, madame; non, madame; s'il vous plaît*. The domestic drama in which she found herself playing an unknown role was puzzling, foreign, vaguely terrifying, like a comic opera or puppet pantomime. Jack, Effa, and the flame-haired girls entered, exited, nodded, spoke, smiled, laughed, squabbled, picked up the baby, and put the baby down as if following some imperfectly memorized script, glancing from one to the other, uncertain of their cues. At last Jack stood up, rubbed his pink hands briskly together, and indicated that it was time to return to the city. Bernadette snatched up Frankie and fled from the house as if it were afire.

"Jesus Mary and Joseph," said Effa to Jack. "How could you have done it? She is only a child."

24

Early morning. A mug of tea steams on my desk next to the packet from Penguin, still unopened. It will be, I know, a first proof of the jacket of my book: the title, the cover art, the flap copy, *the photo*. More puncture wounds in my dwindling store of confidence. There will be other leaks. Other bloodlettings. The stove struggles to life, sucking its arterial oil, hissing and groaning like the tuning-up of a distant orchestra. I settle into my chair beside the stove with the current issue of *New Scientist* and turn to the astronomy pages. On the radio, RTE 3 offers for its morning concert Haydn's *Creation*.

Silence. A chord, C-minor, somber, out of nowhere. Fragments of music. Clarinet. Oboe. A trumpet note. A stroke of timpani. Chaos. Hushed, the chorus sings, *And the Spirit of God moved upon the face of the waters. And God said, Let there be light.* Voices whispering, *And there was light.* A sunburst! A brilliant fortissimo C-major chord. Blazing out like a packet bomb tossed through the window, rattling the dusty teacups hanging on their rusty hooks, shaking the spiders from their corner webs. The stove takes its direction from the radio, coughs bass phrases and emits high-voiced pings as the cold night-metal stretches and yawns. The kettle whistles. *In splendor bright is rising now the sun.* The music celebrates creation from nothingness. Order from chaos, every atom in its place, nothing broken. The chorus flings stars into the room. Galaxies fall hissing onto the hot stove. On my desk a cream and yellow packet crumples under the weight of the music, like a newborn planet afflicted with too much gravity.

25

*

The jacket bio is reservedly brief: "Frank Bois lives in Cork, Ireland." What were my publishers to do? They would have preferred: "Frank Bois, a dwarf, lives in Cork, Ireland." But my condition is hardly relevant to the book, which is after all about the stars, about the night sky, about distances of space and time that stretch far beyond the abbreviated dimensions of my achondroplasic limbs. Yet the publishers know that my stature has a currency, a specie of exchangeable worth. They know—it is their business to know—the value of the apparently miraculous coexistence of intelligence and deformity, wine from water as it were, loaves from stones. A photograph! Yes, that's the ticket. A photograph on the jacket. A full-page back-of-the-jacket photograph. The Tom Thumb intellectual. The pipsqueak oracle. They flew their man to Ireland to take the picture. Unannounced he appeared at my door, young, tanned, bleached hair tied in a ponytail, open-necked floral shirt and soft linen jacket, bestrung with cameras, meters, film bags.

"Hi. I'm Tony."

"Ah, Tony, yes. Hello. I'm Frank Bois."

"Thanks."

"You're very welcome," I replied, not quite sure why I was being thanked.

Where? Where to shoot? Of course, where else but in this room, the troglodyte's burrow, the troll's fouled nest. A background of books piled helter-skelter, charts and maps in disarray, the big acrylic star globe sitting in its soup-bowl stand, and the desk—the desk where the deed was done. *Yes, yes*, said the man with the cameras, bleating like a lamb as he danced about the room, peering through his viewfinder, arranging and rearranging papers on my desk, tacking things up on the wall and taking them down again, tripping over boxes. In the end he left things as he found them, pushed me into place by the desk and snapped away through innumerable rolls of film, turning his cameras this way and that, crouching, veering, stretching, as the little motors that advance the film pathetically whirred.

I would be less than honest if I did not say that I am pleased with the outcome. The photograph takes up the entire reverse of the jacket. It accomplishes its purpose. The desk looms at my shoulder, immediately establishing my height (the star globe rising behind like a full moon). The crushed nose, the square head, the disproportionate limbs: all there. And yet there is a kind of dignity. I have *the look* of an intellectual, a poet, my blunt chin propped on the rolled collar of my black pullover, my arms folded thoughtfully across my chest, my corduroy trousers sagging cavalierly about my ankles. Yes, indeed, this is a person who might have something to say. Looking at the man in the photograph I see much to admire. For the first time in my life I find myself—how should I put it?—not handsome exactly, but interesting, darkly attractive, and—dare I say it?—raffishly sexy.

Of course, the early reviewers of my book will

have only bound galleys, not the jacket. But the photo will be included in the publicity kit, so as the reviewers read, the diminutive author will fix them with his pleading eyes. Pleading for what? Honesty? Critical integrity? Or charity? The pulled punch? Good Oxbridge liberals all, the reviewers will be inclined toward generosity but will not want to seem pitying. Some will sin on the side of harshness, pretending they honor the author by not blunting their critical knives, others will sin on the side of sentimentality. They will search (as did my publishers) for some delicate, indirect way to evoke in their reviews the author's abbreviated proportions without actually using the forbidden word. They will become acrobats of the euphemism.

Yes, the photograph. How do I say this without seeming vain, or worse, the victim of self-delusion? This person on the jacket, is it not possible to, ah, to imagine him as—as *desirable*? The eyes are gentle, romantic even. The heart that beats in that solid torso is normal sized and bursting with love on offer. There is a perceptible bulge in the corduroy trousers. And now, as I study the jacket photo, I see the tiny print in the margin: *Photograph by Tony Hanks*. I laugh. So that's what he said. Yes, thank *you*, Tony. You pulled off the impossible. You satisfied the publicity mavens at Penguin, Ltd, Wrights Lane, London, and you stroked the hungering ego of the writer in his den.

26

If you go to Fleurville today you will find a brass plaque affixed to the public fountain commemorating the execution of my maternal grandfather: *Albert Bois, 1903–1944, Héro de la Résistance* (I am informed of this fact by the *Michelin Green Guide to Normandy*; the plaque, the ruined abbey, and the Maison Victorine are the town's only claims to fame). The townspeople of Fleurville were forbidden by the German commandant to remove the corpse of Albert Bois from the fountain of St. Victor. His body remained there, crumpled face downward in a pool made red by his blood, slowly bloating and contaminating a considerable part of the town's water supply, emitting at last a mephitic stench that drove people from their homes and shops, until that sunstruck day in mid-June when the Germans packed up and ran before the advancing U.S. Fourth Army. And that is where Anne-Marie Bois claimed her husband, folded on his knees, his ballooned torso buoyed by water, his thick black hair streaming on the verminous pool like a lacquered Japanese fan. The limestone saint who stands above the pool had acquired a nick in the knee where the bullet emerging from the back of Albert's head had ricocheted.

Bernadette's mother retrieved her husband's corpse from the fountain and began her descent into madness. With liberation to attend to, Fleurvillians lost interest in La Bernadette de la bombe. No one came to the shrine near the farm gate. No one reached out in the street to touch religious tokens to Bernadette's dress, or asked the girl to place her hands on pocked skin or goitered necks, or came to the door of the farmhouse seeking patches of cloth. Anne-Marie Bois took her relics into the town, to the square fluttering with Tricolors and Stars and Stripes, hawking rosaries and mementos from a basket hung over her arm, but found no takers. The miracle of the exploded mine was forgotten, erased from consciousness like other distressing events of the occupation. Madame Bois grew paler, her features more birdlike, her feathery hair awry. Her prayers became frantic and morose. Townsfolk pitied her or scoffed. Bernadette, embarrassed, kept to her bedroom, except for an occasional foray to Fravel et Fils, Libraire, for the romantic stories that had become her only reality. On 25 August, as General Charles de Gaulle led the victorious Allied armies down the Champs-Élysées, Anne-Marie Bois came quite literally to the end of her rope.

I have all of this at second hand from Jack Kelly. It is part of the interminable saga of her past that my mother recounted to Jack during the sexually intimate stage of their affair, as a kind of foreplay, she chattering, he listening, until the sheer tedium of the oft repeated monologue created a mutual tension that could only be relieved by orgasm.

On a scaffolding of anecdote supplied by Jack I construct my story: A sultry evening, late summer 1944, the air still heavy and blue with the heat of afternoon. Purple clouds are heaped on the western

horizon. From somewhere west or south of Fleurville comes the distant *tump* of thunder or gunfire.
Bernadette in her room reinvents, as every solitary
child must, the art of self-pleasuring. A sound. Her
mother on the stairs? Bernadette tenses and pulls
the blanket to her chin. She waits, hears nothing
further, and drifts again into her dreamy ministra-
tions. Sleep. A night of agreeable dreams (". . .
*beauties, such beauties. Don't you see their little
horns?"*), waking occasionally to a room made
milky by moonlight, her body floating in a tropical
sea, a grotto made luminous with algal phosphores-
cence. Morning. She rises, splashes water on her
face from the porcelain basin, and briefly considers
the face of the fourteen-year-old girl that stares
from the mirror. Still in her white nightdress she
goes downstairs. Her mother is not at the stove,
nor in the yard. Bernadette sits at the table and
breakfasts on bread and curds. She goes to make
coffee but the kettle is empty and the stove is cold.
She begins to be puzzled. With perfect clarity she
sees her mother's face, the popping eyes, the drib-
ble of blood from the nose, the purple crease below
the ears where the rope has scrunched the skin like
a hessian sack.

It wasn't Bernadette who found her mother hanging from a rafter in the kitchen shed, a toppled stool
on the floor with chickens pecking at the leather
shoe that had fallen from the suicide's foot. Anne-
Marie's body was discovered by a neighboring child
who had slipped into the shed to steal an egg. When
the police arrived at the farm, they found Bernadette

huddled in a corner of her room, in her white night-gown, with a book beside her.

27
*

  Oh, yes, almost certainly Bernadette inherited her mother's tendency toward madness. All her life she had a way of selecting only those elements of reality that she wished to face; the rest she simply ignored. My dwarfism, for instance. She coped with it well enough; she was resourceful in obtaining the special shoes I was required to wear and in altering clothes to fit my stunted frame, even in obtaining a special disability allowance from the state (once Jack Kelly had sorted out our legal status). But my condition was never discussed, never consciously acknowledged. Her ability to deny what was broken or ugly was her refuge for sanity.

  In certain ways Bernadette could be counted remarkably sane. She harbored no conscious guilt, never worried about tomorrow, never looked back to yesterday. She took life's trials and pleasures as she found them, as if they were episodes in a novel she was reading. Consider, for example, the circumstances of my conception, that multiple copulation in the hold of the *California*. It is easy to say that Bernadette Bois was dangerously naive to have offered herself so heedlessly to several young men (how many? God knows). It is easy to be repelled by the thought of those scrub-faced, crew-cut,

khaki-clad kids taking turns in her thin white arms.
But I am confident there was no conscious promis-
cuity on her part. The young soldiers had helped
her. They had smuggled her aboard a ship destined
for America (the very name of the ship evoked sunshine, orange trees, and Hollywood). The boys were
"*beaux*" and "kind." She was not coerced. She had
fun. Fun. Such a crisp word. So innocent. So American.

She had few options. Upon the death of her
mother she was sent to live with her uncle's family
near Le Havre. I know almost nothing of the months
she spent in that house; it was one of the realities
she closed the door on. Those months were almost
certainly unhappy. She had no family or friends that
she cared for. Her uncle appropriated the monies
from the sale of the Fleurville farm; Bernadette got
nothing. When she saw a chance to make another
life, she took it.

She never looked back. Once she had made up
her mind to do a thing, once she crossed a threshold, that was it. No hindsight. Never. She met some
American soldiers on final leave in France, kids not
much older than herself. She was pretty. Her head
was full of fancies. She was one of Colette's young
heroines, and they were her rescuers. *All* of them.
She thought them beautiful. What were their
names? Chip. Rusty. Danny. Names like that. American names. When she took off her knickers and
jacked up her skirt, it was not she who blushed and
stammered but the soldiers, caught as they were
between reticence and an unbelieving appreciation
of what they perceived as their sudden good for-

tune. The green-eyed girl in the blue dress was their ticket to—to what? The episode in the hold of the *California* would be one of those stories they would tell and retell to their "buddies" for the rest of their lives, a one-off wartime miracle that would never happen again.

When Jack Kelly came into Bernadette's life, she welcomed him, too, and never gave a thought to the fact that he was married. It did not occur to her that their affair was for him anything more than it was for her, an episode in a story, a turned page. And when he ceased to be her lover—that was another page turned. Now he was her friend, a substitute for the affectionate parent she had never had, a grandda for François. The sexual thing she simply put out of her mind.

Jack came often to our flat in Nicholas Road. He sat in the chair by the pink-tiled hearth (the chair I am sitting in now) and listened to her stories. She was working as a sales clerk at Cash's. She described each customer, each transaction. Like Scheherazade, she had a thousand and one stories, but instead of spinning them out over as many nights, she packed as many as she could into one sitting. Sometimes the three of us went for walks on the Lee quays, and Jack taught me the names of seabirds as Bernadette chattered. Perhaps it was to escape her stories that Jack first took me to the roof of Bernadette's kitchen to show me the stars. Bernadette did not come onto the roof, just Jack and me. And sometimes he took me with him to his house in Westview Terrace in Cobh for a look though his telescope.

The first thing I saw through Jack's telescope was the planet Saturn. A cocked hat. A ring of gold. I moved my eye from the telescope to look at the starlike dot in the sky, then back again to the telescope. A ring of gold, a dot, a ring of gold, a dot. It was a kind of magic. I didn't yet understand the principles of magnification. I had only Jack's word that the haloed object in the telescope was the same as the white dot in the sky. The object I saw in the telescope seemed to have its existence *inside* the instrument, like one of those scenes inside a hollow Easter egg that one views through a tiny hole at the opposite end. For many nights after looking through Jack's telescope, when I closed my eyes to sleep I saw the planet looking back at me, a lidded eye. *Do you see the shadow of the rings on the face of the planet?* Jack had asked. I did not, or perhaps I did not understand what it was that I was looking for, but his words stayed with me. *The shadow of the rings. The face of the planet.* They were magical words, full of enchantment. I lay in my bed and examined the planet in my mind's eye, questioning it as the wicked queen in Snow White questioned her mirror, asking *Who's the fairest one of all*?

And there was something else about those visits to Jack's back-garden observatory. The girls. Caitlin and Deidre, Jack's and Effa's youngest. They were in their middle teens; I was six or seven. I was their pet, their doll. From the moment I arrived at the house in Westview Terrace, they tickled, coddled, teased. They lifted me into their arms and pressed my face into their sweet-smelling hair, scented with lavender and rose, perfumed clouds. They tousled *my* hair. They covered my cheeks with kisses. And later in my bed I would stare into Saturn's lidded eye winking out of memory, and wonder that life should offer such moments of unqualified pleasure. I had fallen in love. With the beauty of women. Their hair, their skin, their mouths, their eyes, the way they moved, the enfolding perfection of their limbs.

I cannot remember at what age I first understood that I was different. Not just different—for I suppose I had always known *that*—but *excluded*. I had been sheltered by my mother's solitariness, and by the unqualified affection of Jack's family, from—from what? I am not just *different*. I am repellent, odious, loathsome. I am of the race of monsters that aberrant genes visit upon the earth, the intellectually normal but physically misbegotten, the hunchbacked, harelipped, clubfooted, port wine stained, albinotic. I am their king, a prince of disfigurement.

I am Caliban. For, you see, Prospero and Miranda were no different from the rest of the physically correct; when they looked upon Caliban, they saw not just the misshapen body but also moral degeneracy and intellectual paucity. It did not occur to them that their ill-formed servant might be capable of thought and love, that he might possess a fondness for poetry or music, that his mind might range the higher elevations of abstraction. Nor did it occur to Miranda that Caliban might long for the intimacy of her arms with a *not unnatural* love; if he desired her (Prospero tells us as much), then surely it was with a brute's lust, foul's need besmirching fair. Caliban, as perceived by Prospero and his daughter, is a prick without heart, but Ferdinand—ah, pretty Ferdinand, with his dangling sword, is made chaste by the fairness of his form.

Nothing rankles more bitterly than this, that I am forever cut off by my deformity from the race of Mirandas. I watch them in the street. First, in the morning, the schoolgirls, in blue, green, or gray skirts with jackets and woolly stockings in matching colors, a flash of red tie at the throat, books bundled against their pubescent breasts, hair streaming down their backs. Next, the shopgirls and secretaries in short skirts and high-heeled boots, their hair showery and stylishly disheveled or cropped boyishly close, their bodies asway within their clothes. Then, the mothers with their prams, preoccupied, self-assured, bundled up in thick coats or heavy sweaters, but underneath their skin is redolent with suds and talc and kitchen odors. Finally, in the afternoon, in Merchants Quay or Patrick Street, the affluent matrons from the northern suburbs, voluptuous symphonies of silk, tweed, and wool, desultory, honey-tongued, vaguely lascivious.

Women are seldom out of my mind. I cultivate what my Christian Brother teachers called in Irish *peaca súil*, sins of the eyes, because no other sins are available to me. Once, passing late at night through Smith Street, I saw a woman that I took to be a prostitute, young, in short leather skirt and black stockings, knock-kneed but pretty in a doe-eyed, scatter-brained sort of way. Her image stayed with me, haunting my thoughts. Or rather, it occurred to me that she might become more than a thought. Was not my money as good as the next man's? Might not a prostitute be less squeamish than other women concerning my physical aberrations? I had no moral aversions to paying for sex. What I lacked was courage, the courage to ask. A week passed, then two. The thought of purchasing this woman's attentions took a deeper hold on my mind until I felt—how shall I put this? the distinctions are both subtle and crucial—I felt a kind of *love* for this person I had only briefly glimpsed. I had no idea what a prostitute might charge for her services. I returned to Smith Street with four crisp tenners folded in my pocket. She was not there. Nor the next night. On my third visit I found her, leaning in desultory fashion against a bollard, legs crossed, chewing gum. She was less attractive than I had remembered, but there was no turning back. It seemed a fair bargain: I would accept her gum chewing, and she would overlook the fact that I am forty-three inches tall. I approached her. I looked into her eyes, my palm dampening the notes in my pocket.

She said, "Be gone, ye little dork."

29

I am in this city but I am not of it. Neither of my parents was Irish. I was about to say that I brush shoulders with people who are only nominally my countrymen, but of course I do not; my shoulders brush against their hips, their hands, their arses. I am an alien from another planet set down into their city. I don't speak their language. My English has a French nasality. My idioms are those of novels, foreign magazines, scientific periodicals. I shun their public places. When I go for a drink, I frequent the pubs near Albert Quay, dockworkers' pubs, shadowy and tough. The customers in these places are burly men, with fuck-filled speech, their overalls unbuttoned to their bulging bellies. I like them. I like their surly brusqueness. I sit at the rears of their pubs with my Guinness or glass of port and I am left undisturbed. There is no ridicule, no pity. I seem to belong near these foreign ships manned by humans from every port: glistening blacks, chattering Asians, swarthy Mideasterners, tight-lipped Poles, blond Norwegians. They take me in their stride. They accord me no more notice than they do to the rats that scurry ashore on hawsers. I credit them this. These crewmen and dockworkers are not infected, like the rest of the city, with too much *normality*.

And St. Fin Barre's too. I am at my ease in St. Fin

Barre Cathedral. In winter, when darkness comes early, I go there for evensong. I sit in the shadows at the back of the north aisle and listen to the splendid voices of men and boys and to the great booming chords of the organ. The music billows into the vaults like smoke from a smoldering fire, curling up into the clerestory arches and rising in the choir to the feet of Christ Triumphant. In this city of Roman Catholics there is a certain welcoming anonymity in the Protestant cathedral. Yes, my fellow worshipers forgo sitting near me, yet they have the grace to let me be *invisibly* present, as if I were a lost soul drawn by the music into the warm margins of their faith (probably, they imagine, a stray Catholic, for surely only that tatty genetic stock could have thrown up my distortions). I say "fellow worshipers," but I do not come to the cathedral for worship. I come for music. I have sat on that hard bench in those twilight shadows for nearly forty years, and I have learned to love the entire repertoire of English sacred music: Stanford, Purcell, Batten, Dyson, Hollings—their names and music are as familiar to me as the stars and constellations. Such praise! These Anglo-Protestants don't grovel before the Creator hat in hand like the Roman Catholics. Their music is exuberant in nature's praise. The music of St. Fin Barre's answers the silence of the sky, rattles the bars of the terrestrial cage and shouts *We are here*. Outside on the pinnacle of the sanctuary roof is the gilded Resurrection Angel, his multiple trumpets aimed at the darkness like telescopes, blasting a plea to the silent stars. *Wake. Wake. Take notice!*

But of course the sky does not wake. There is no open grave, no resurrection. Only silence. We live and die in the cage. Music, at least, gives the living grace.

Bernadette Bois was raised a Catholic but left her faith in France. She left her faith in the fountain of Fleurville's central square at the feet of St. Victor. Despite Jack's plea she would not allow her child to be baptized. Just once, while pregnant with François, she went to the Catholic church in Dunbar Street. At communion she approached the altar, a glass box containing a marble statue of the Dead Christ, supine, naked but for a loincloth, marked with the wounds, and—the head lolling to the side—reposeful and sad. She began to shake. The place was pungent with scents of incense and wax. Above the altar another naked Christ hung by his hands. She closed her eyes and saw blood curling and curling in cold water. When she opened her eyes, the priest stood before her with the host in his hand. The priest's face was fat and pink, and tufts of black hair exploded from his nostrils. *Corpus Christi*, he whispered. She took the host into her mouth but could not swallow it. Gagging, she ran from the church to the bank of the River Lee and vomited over the railing into the algoid waters.

Then she found St. Fin Barre's.

The spired Protestant cathedral rises geologically from a limestone terrace on the south bank of the Lee, like a mass of stalagmites in a cool limestone cave. Inside, too, the cathedral is like a cave, silent, empty. But beautiful: gray limestone, red marble, polished brass. An aged sacristan hoovered the choir stalls but no one else was about. She circumnavigated the high altar and found the church to be a repository of stories. Pulpit, lectern, brass gates, choir stalls, bishop's throne, windows, and the ceiling of the sanctuary, all decorated with angels, demons, princes and princesses, stern fathers, fairy godmothers, good magicians, necromancers. She wanted to know the stories. At the back of the church she found a booklet describing the cathedral's interior and exterior decorations. The cost was one shilling, and a slot was provided in a wooden box to receive her money. She did not have a shilling. She dropped a penny into the box and took the booklet, resolving to make up the difference when she could.

The baptismal font was the most beautiful thing of stone she had ever seen, red marble supported on columns of green marble rising from a white marble slab, the entire thing affixed to an octagonal base of stone. Round the lip of the font she read the inscription inlaid in letters of gleaming brass: *We are buried with him by baptism into death.* What could it mean? She had been taught that baptism was a new birth, the beginning of a new life as a child of God. But these words? *Buried into death.* It was like a riddle.

The next day Bernadette went to a bookshop on Lavitt's Quay and bought an Old Testament, a battered volume no bigger than her hand, in exchange for three French novels, and began to put the stories together with the stained glass and sculptures of the cathedral. She began where the Testament began, with the windows in the north aisle. The expulsion of Adam and Eve from the Garden. Cain and Abel sacrificing. The death of Abel. Abraham and the three angels. The sacrifice of Isaac. Moses and the burning bush. Moses and the brazen serpent. And so on. She committed these stories to memory, and when her son was old enough to listen, she told them to him. As other parents took their children to a puppet show or zoo, Bernadette brought François to St. Fin Barre's. She stood him under the arching portals and told him the stories of the tympanums and soffits. Among the carvings in the arch of the central portal, there is one of an astronomer with his telescope. *It is Jack*, she said, and her son was astonished that Jack should be carved in stone with kings and queens.

31
*

On Sunday evenings, after Jack had departed for Cobh, Bernadette took her son to evensong in the Protestant cathedral. She sat with him on the back bench, in the shadow of a thick limestone pillar, her feet propped on the kneeler. She did not pray or participate in the songs and responses. What she liked was the music, the lights, and the colors of the vestments. It was not at all like the Roman church, so full of morbidity and self-denial. Here there was an element of suspended disbelief, a theatrical fiction, and she—in her passive way—was a player. She understood (instinctively, not consciously) that the entire point of the Anglican service was a compromise, a matter of having of one's cake and eating it too, a theology scrubbed clear of any cosmic responsibility, roses without thorns, a glossing over. And that suited her fine. So baptism was *into death*: yes, get the dreary stuff out of the way right at the beginning. Put it out of mind. Make music. Tell stories. The Anglican service (as she understood it) was a work of art, all romance and burnished detail. Like a novel by Colette.

She held her son's hand. His stumpy little legs stuck straight out from the bench. And that's where Roger Manning found her, sitting in the brassy shadows, the organ booming a nave-filling fugue. She was aware of his presence without actually seeing him—fidgeting there by the back wall, hands clasping and unclasping behind his back, toe nervously *tap-tap*ping under the hem of his cassock—and the thought of his anxiety pleased her.

He was curate of the cathedral, an ordained priest of the Church of Ireland, in his early thirties, tall, thin, saucery black eyes, pale skin, and dark hair that slicked down across his forehead. He entered the church one Sunday evening through the public door and— Well, there she was, sitting with the child, half-hidden by the limestone pillar. He stood with his shoulders pressed against the notice board by the table with the postcards and booklets and watched her throughout the service, having fallen instantly in love with the back of her head, and waited, waited for her to turn round. When the last reverberations of the organ collapsed into stony silence and the sacristan extinguished the altar candles one by one with a silver snuffer, she stood, turned, and the Reverend Roger Manning was smitten by her beauty.

And indeed she was beautiful. Can the boy who was only four or five years old be counted a reliable witness? My memory is sharp, even from that tender age, and I have photographs that confirm my memory. She was in her early twenties. Her skin was porcelain and her eyes a memorable green. Her hair was self-cut, chopped off with borrowed scissors, engagingly ragged. She dressed in the French way: cotton dresses that clung to her body, a chiffon scarf wound round and round her neck, dark stockings, and fabric shoes held to her feet by thin elastic straps. She was not at all like the fussily attired Anglo-Irish women in bulky tweeds and laced thick-soled shoes who occupied the forward pews. She was unlike anyone Roger Manning had ever seen.

And the child. The child was disconcerting, worrisome, vaguely repellent. But that too was part of the virulence of his malady. He wondered at the out-of-nowhere *otherworldliness* of this strangely beautiful girl accompanied by a dwarf child. They might have been concocted by the Brothers Grimm.

And Roger Manning? Roger Manning was in exile.

He had been sent down to Cork from Dublin, where a promising career had been abruptly truncated by a clumsy and unconsummated affair with the wife of the dean of St. Patrick's. To be fair, it was not Roger who initiated the liaison, and had it not been for his scruples, the thing might have gone further than it did. As it was, the *amour* was laughable: frantic kisses in the dean's study, some ineffectual groping in the sacristy, and once, when they thought the dean was celebrating Eucharist in the cathedral, Roger had his pants down about his knees when the aggrieved husband arrived at the vestry door to collect his spectacles. Fortunately for Roger, the details of the attempted consummation were something of a blur for their shortsighted appraiser, but enough was apparent to cause the bright young curate to lose the confidence of his dean. If the dean had arrived with his spectacles affixed to his nose, Roger Manning might have been exiled to the wilds of Donegal or Mayo rather than to Cork.

It was not the first time the young curate had been pursued by an older woman, or even by a married woman; there was something about his clerical good looks and head-in-the-clouds demeanor that women found irresistible. Nor was it the first time he found himself susceptible to their importunings. But Roger's involvement with women was one of bemused experiment rather than passion; he never ceased to be astonished that women found him attractive. In a curious way, he felt that to spurn their advances might represent a *slackness* of his Christian service.

Bernadette was different.

As she left the cathedral—after waiting for others of the congregation to depart—he nodded a greeting. She seemed, he imagined, vaguely aware of his presence. She moved quickly out the door, dragging her dwarf child by the hand, and although she did not *avoid* his eyes, her expression betrayed no reciprocal interest. This pattern of failed communication continued week after week (for now he took care to ensure that his own services were not required in the sanctuary). If he had known that she too now sometimes fantasized about his thin white hands and black eyes, his infatuation, already debilitating, might have proven fatal. Once, in Mercier's Bookshop, she saw a book of Yeats's poetry with the author's portrait as frontispiece (it was the well-known painting of W. B. Yeats by his father), and she thought it resembled the young priest. She bought the book, an expensive hardcover, going without tea for a week to recover the cost, and devoured it at a single sitting. Of this, Roger Manning knew nothing.

One Sunday evening in October he followed her home, down along the quays, up Abbey Street past the Red Tower, into Nicholas Road. He stood in a doorway across the street from her house and watched until the light went on upstairs. He was conscious of the absurdity of the situation: a priest skulking in the shadows like a pervert or a thief. He was nibbling well-gnawed fingernails and wondering what to do next when a policeman making the rounds appeared before him.

"Evening, Reverend?" inquired the officer, who

recognized the curate of St. Fin Barre's; it was more a question than a greeting.

"Good evening," murmured Roger Manning. Knowing some further explanation was required, he stammered, "Visiting the sick."

And then scuttled off like a rat discovered by a sudden light. It was *he* who was sick and he knew it.

32

As Roger gnawed his nails and anguished, and Bernadette imagined a dozen satisfying conclusions to an unbegun affair, I sat with my mother in the back bench of St. Fin Barre's and looked up to the twelve night-stained windows of the clerestory, each window representing a sign of the zodiac. By day the windows were as bright as the stars themselves, but in darkness the colors of the glass became pale and terrestrial, and I began to long for the occasional Sunday evening when Jack would stay in the city until darkness and take me onto the kitchen roof.

On those nights my mother went alone to evensong, with her volume of Yeats's poems clutched to her breast, and Jack took me on a tour of the real zodiac. His wealth of star lore was inexhaustible, and for every constellation he had a dozen stories.

"There are eight and a half animals and four and a half humans in the zodiac," said Jack. "Can you name them?"

I tried, remembering the Gemini twins and the half-man half-horse Sagittarius, but forgetting that Pisces is plural.

Jack's stories of the sky were lessons in history, geography, and science. Maths too. He taught me circles and degrees, the geometry of spheres, the factoring of time. I might as well have been a Zulu child tutored by an elder of the clan, or a Navaho boy in the company of the tribal shaman. What I learned from Jack on the roof of Bernadette's kitchen would be about the only schooling I would get. Bernadette had no great willingness to send her son to school, and she did so only when badgered to comply with schooling regulations by the education authorities. When I found myself in a classroom, I was deliberately uncomprehending. I avoided the companionship of other children. I sulked. I defied the earnest efforts of my teachers to instruct me. With good reason they thought me retarded (and with bad reason, too, for they were quick to equate my condition with stupidity). My sullenness cast palls of despair across entire classrooms, so that soon my teachers cared little whether I came to school or not. At home my mother read aloud from *The Wind in the Willows, Peter Pan, Winnie the Pooh*, as much for herself, I believe, as for me—and to practice her English reading skills for more grown-up works. I was wide-eyed at her powers of fantasy. With Bernadette, as with Jack, I was eager to learn, and I far outstripped my classmates in the breadth and depth of my knowledge.

The walls and windows of St. Fin Barre's were another text more jam-packed with knowledge than any of the books I found at school. In medieval times, when books were scarce, the decorations of cathedrals were important instruments of learning, as in even earlier times the starry sky was a text for young scholars. Both texts—cathedral walls and starry sky—were opened to me, by my mother and Jack Kelly.

33

The curate of the cathedral nibbled his fingernails and pined as he watched the pretty young woman in the back pew whispering stories to her dwarf child.

He did not even know her name.

Why did he not simply introduce himself, begin a conversation, ask her if he might show her the treasures of the cathedral, invite her on a tour of the episcopal palace, take her to dinner at a nearby café? A simple, direct approach. As natural as breathing. But for Roger Manning none of it was simple, direct, or natural. It was, in fact, vastly complicated. Inexplicably so, given his usual ease in the company of women. On more occasions than he could remember it was they, yes, the women, who initiated intimacy, startling him with the earnestness of their advances and making him wonder what it was about himself they found attractive. He was naturally unselfconscious. The only mirror in his room was a fish-eye shaving mirror that made his cheek look fat, his eye bulgy, the stubble of his beard coarse and prickly. Of his perfect white teeth, red lips, and dark lashes he was oblivious. He was— like the man Bernadette thought he resembled—a poet, although not a good one. His verses were inclined toward awkward, bisyllabic rhymes. If asked about the sheaf of papers he carried in his hand he was likely to blush and stammer and stuff the verses into the pocket of his cassock, an unaffected modesty that made him even more attractive. He had not, in any of his relationships with women, been *in love*. He was simply drawn to them the way a leaf detached from a tree is drawn to the earth. He was astonished by their attentions. He had been trained to minister. He did not feel sinful.

But the girl in the back pew at evensong—whatever it was he now felt, he had not felt it before, and because it was new, he feared it. He fixed his eyes on the elliptical curve where the dark cotton of her dress met her neck. What he felt was—well, not Christian. That is to say, it was not the same muddle of curiosity and priestly service that he felt when eager Anglo-Irish women undressed in his presence, rituals that mimicked in reverse the vesting ceremony of the priest before Eucharist, each garment carefully removed and folded to the murmur of prescribed endearments, seductions as chastely performed as if they were legislated by the Book of Common Prayer. No, not Christian. His evensong visitor stirred something pagan, idolatrous. He felt sullied and vaguely guilty, but more intensely *alive* than he had ever felt before.

On this night she was alone, without the child, therefore more approachable, and he practiced what he would say when she rose to leave. He rehearsed a dozen opening gambits, all of which seemed awkward, inadequate. As the great organ in the transept pumped out the last thundering chords of Hollings's Trumpet Minuet, Roger Manning's tongue went fat and soft in his mouth, and when she passed him on her way to the door he was able to manage only a labored smile that was really more of a wince. She fixed him briefly with her green eyes and a fist closed on his heart. When he recovered sufficiently to take a decision, he followed her into the cathedral yard, but she was gone.

He looked up into a vast Byzantine mosaic of stars.

34

In *Nightstalk* I have changed Roger Manning's name to Arthur Whelan, and I have made him fair not dark, but I dare say he will have no trouble recognizing himself if he reads my book. I acknowledge in a prefatory note that whatever persons appear in my story have been given fictitious names. Manning must be close to seventy now. He is parson of a run-down parish in the Midlands—Ballymahon, I believe—having slipped (for reasons I will disclose) even further down the ecclesiastical ladder. Every Christmas I receive his card, always with the same message: *Greetings of the season, I think often of your mother, Roger Manning.* A few years after his banishment from Cork, he published, un-

der a pseudonym, a volume of erotic verse dedicated with admirable frankness *to Bernadette Bois*.
He sent her a copy before her death, inscribed simply *Roger*. I open this little book, entitled *Gargoyle*,
and read at random: *She touched his manhood with
desire, setting his tame heart afire, in glittered
night.* Poor Roger. He takes as his central image, if
I understand him rightly, one of the four gargoyles
above the portals of St. Fin Barre's, which represent,
in the words of the cathedral guidebook, "the conflict and triumph of virtue in the soul of the Christian." In each of the carvings virtue is symbolized
by a beautiful woman slaying a monstrous vice.
Over the leftmost door of the cathedral, Chastity
subdues a ruttish goat, from whose crooked mouth
gushes runoff from the roof.

Manning's book of poems is one of the sources
for my account of his affair with Bernadette.

It was with some misgivings that I included Roger
in *Nightstalk*, but of course it would have been impossible to leave him out, since he was so intimately
a part of my young life, and I suspect that he might
rather enjoy inclusion. His present posting is so
remote and depopulated of parishioners that his
bishop has very likely forgotten that he exists, and
in any case the events I recount happened so long
ago that few of those who know him are likely to
make the connection between the Arthur Whelan of
my book and the real Roger Manning. If *Nightstalk*
has attracted the enthusiasm of my publisher, it is
because I have leavened my meditations on the
night sky with a generous measure of personal anecdote, including a sprinkling of spice drawn mostly

from my mother's life; for some of the spice I owe Roger a debt of gratitude.

But if it were not for Bernadette, Roger Manning's obsessive infatuation might never have amounted to more than weight loss, sweaty palms, nibbled nails, and addled thoughts. It was Bernadette who took—so to speak—the goat by the horns. She was nothing if not resourceful. One warm September dawn Roger turned from the altar at Communion to discover the source of his affliction sitting in attendance, her dwarf child by her side. He was so shaken by her presence that he left out great blocks of the service, to the consternation of the other members of his tiny congregation, all women, who glanced worriedly and reprovingly from one to the other. Bernadette would not have known what parts of the service had been excluded for she knew little of the ritual to begin with. She sat far back in the nave, and when she was not watching the celebrant perform the eucharistic rites she was reading from Yeats:

> *For everything that's lovely is*
> *But a brief, dreamy, kind delight.*
> *O never give the heart outright . . .*

At the appropriate moment in the ceremony she went to the step to take communion, and when he looked into her green eyes, made liquidy by candlelight, the wafer shook so violently in his hands that he could hardly direct it to her mouth.

After Communion he hurriedly divested and rushed to the rear of the cathedral, where Bernadette was sitting in her usual evensong place, smiling sweetly.

"I—usually—that is—yes—the day is—will you breakfast," blurbled Roger Manning.

"Yes," replied Bernadette.

"There is a coffee shop on Sullivan's Quay."

"Yes," said Bernadette, "but first I must take Frankie to school."

He walked with her to the school in Evergreen Street, where she deposited her son.

"We can have coffee at my flat," she said. "There's no point wasting money at the café."

She took him to the flat in Nicholas Road. She put the kettle on the hob. Then she removed his clothes, starting with his shoes and ending with his clerical collar and dickey. She pushed him back flat onto her bed, tied his hands to the bedposts with his black stockings, slipped out of her panties, and without removing her dress, climbed upon him. Roger Manning and the kettle came to a boil at the same time.

35

An envelope slips under the door. The familiar cream-yellow envelope with ovaled penguin. I make tea. I slice a scone and slather it with butter and jam. I drop a tape into the cassette player, Purcell's *Ode on St. Cecilia's Day 1692.* I poke up the fire on the grate and add two peat briquettes. I go to the machine and restart the tape. I gather up the tea things and pile them in the sink. I add another briquette to the fire. I collapse in my chair with my teacup and scone. I get up and restart the tape once again.

Triumphant trumpets and timpani. A dance of trumpets and strings. A somber adagio. A razzmatazz allegro. The bass intones, *Hail! Hail bright Cecilia*. The envelope prickles on the floor. *Hark each tree, its silence breaks*, the bass and alto sing. I retrieve the envelope. *Hark, hark, hark, hark*. I slice the cream-colored paper with the butter knife. *'Twas sympathy, 'twas sympathy*. I read the note my editor has clipped to two photocopied pages. "Read the good one first," she writes. "The other fellow doesn't know what he's talking about."

This is it! The first reviews of the bound galleys of my book from library and bookseller journals. One is good and one is bad, but which is which? I hold a review in each hand. I do not want to read the unfavorable review. Not now. Not until I've had a stiff drink. Or two. I carry the reviews downstairs to my landlady. Elizabeth Brosnan is ninety years old. She is sitting by the fire reading the *News of the World*. ROYALS IN LOVE NEST SCANDAL, the headline blares.

"Here are two reviews of my book," I say. "Have a look and tell me which is the favorable review."

She takes the two sheets, one in each hand, crumpling their margins fiercely between fingers and thumbs. She glances back and forth from one to the other, reading bits and pieces, and hands me one of the sheets. I fold it up and put in in my pocket. I toss the other onto her fire.

Handy Paige is the only literary agent listed in the Cork telephone directory. It is a year ago to the day since I walked into his reception room with my manuscript in hand. He is a tiny, bristly man, in his sixties, with piercing black eyes and nervous hands that flutter about his face like pestering insects. He stood up to greet me, inspecting me over half-spectacles, pleased (if I interpreted his expression correctly) for the rare opportunity to look down upon someone smaller than himself. His hand came crawling through the air like a scuttling crab. I shook it.

"I would like you to look at my manuscript," I said.

He squinched his face skeptically and pushed his specs up his nose.

I added: "It's—uh, sort of poetic, and scientific. Meditations, so to speak, on the night sky."

He drummed his fingers on his lips.

"No, that's not quite right." I corrected myself. "It's about the stars. The universe. Astronomy, you see."

He gestured to a pile of manuscripts on his desk. "Junk, all junk."

"*This* is not junk," I assured him.

I placed the thick envelope into his hands. He shuffled it quickly onto the desk as if it were a hot dish.

"I bring the stars to earth," I said. "Or maybe it's the other way round."

He plucked a hair from his ear, examined it, flicked it over his shoulder.

"No, no, no," Handy Paige complained. "You can't sell any of that." He was trying to put me off. "It's all sex and romance these days. Fukkin' sex and romance. That's what sells. Catherine Cookson stuff. Give me thrusting gents and big-bosomed broads, I can sell it. Give me—what did you say? stars?—give me stars and you give me nothin'."

"Have a look at it," I insisted. "My address is on the envelope."

He looked me up and down. A glimmer of interest flicked across his eyes. He was no fool. He knew my physical stature might elicit the interest of a publisher even if my book was junk. The little finger of his right hand twisted in his ear. He screwed up his lips. He shrugged. He frowned.

"I know people in London," he said, as if to himself. He showed me to the door.

Three days later a note came in the mail. *Twelve percent*, it said. *Not a penny less.*

Handy Paige got his twelve percent. Twelve percent of a £10,000 advance. I'll give this to him, he was right about knowing people in London. Handy Paige's nephew lives with a Penguin editor, my editor, Jennifer Down. Not many weeks later, Paige showed up at my door, grinning from ear to ear, hands buzzing excitedly.

"Yer on the pig's back now, Bois. They fukkin' like it."

"Who?"

"Penguin. Fukkin' Penguin L-T-D."

"You're kidding."

"Ten thousand."

"Ten thousand what?"

"Ten thousand pounds. Sterling. Half now, half when you've made some changes. Yer a rich man, my little friend. Yer the richest fukkin' dwarf in Ireland."

37

The favorable review is folded in my pocket, folded ten times over, like a roll of bank notes thick against my thigh. I try to concentrate on Purcell. The music of the spheres. The harmony of the wondrous machine. The altos sing, *In vain the am'rous flute and soft guitar jointly labor to inspire wanton heat and loose desire*. I think of Jack Kelly in the tiny back garden of the house in Westview Terrace, of a summer night, expounding on the Lyre. "The Lyre is the most important constellation in the sky," he said. "With that instrument Orpheus could make stones weep. He caused the trees to pull up their roots and dance."

I listened. Listened to the stars. The grass wet with dew. A warm breeze from Africa sweeping up the hill, leapfrogging garden walls. Lilies and dahlias bending in their beds. And the scents of Jack's daughters, lavender and rose:

> . . . *wanton, wanton, wanton heat*
> *and loose desire.*

Roger Manning lay in his narrow bed and tried to pray, his night clothes buttoned up to his neck, his hands clasped on his chest. He muttered a medley of remembered Psalms, *My God, why have you deserted me? How far from saving me the words I groan!* He tried to compose himself, tried to pray, *O Lord.* Squeezed his eyes shut. What's this? A light comes on, brilliantly white, a focused spot. A white director's chair in a circle of light. A woman rises from the chair and turns to face him. It is Bernadette. Her white silk dressing gown slips from her shoulders.

Dear God almighty, always the same. Always, his prayers slipped imperceptibly into fantasy. Kneeling at his bedside, at Eucharist, at evensong— Standing with the choir in the sanctuary singing *The Lord is my shepherd, he makes me lie down in green pastures*, and . . . impossible! . . . there in the niche behind the pulpit is Bernadette, dressed as a *shepherdess!* She beckons with her crook. Or visiting the ladies at St. Edna's Nursing Home. They are sitting in a circle and he is reading from the

Testament, the Sermon on the Mount. *Blessed be, blessed be* . . . his eyes glaze over. One of the women winks . . . *my God* . . . it is Bernadette, in shawl and gray wig. Demurely, she looks down to the ball of knitting in her lap. He follows her eyes.

Yes, of course he felt guilty. Not for the sex with Bernadette, but for the *enjoyment*. He was having, frankly, the time of his life. Pleasure fell like manna from heaven. There had been no courtship, no declarations of love, not even a seduction, unless you count their unacknowledged mutual appraisal at evensong a kind of seduction. She was leading him into unreconnoitered territory, a crazy erotic landscape, bizarre, Gallic, labyrinthine, fun. It was his *powerlessness* that worried him, his abstractedness, his sense of drifting from reality. He was frightened by the way she read his mind, anticipated his every thought. He knew that he was sinning, but he could not quite put his finger on the nature of the sin.

Bernadette had talked herself out. With Jack Kelly she had exhausted the reservoir of gabble stored up during the long silence following the deaths of her father and mother. She had no more time to waste on chat. She knew now that she would die young and she knew precisely *how* (once, in her bath, she saw the circumstances of her death, felt the water congealing about her limbs, green, algoid, opaque). There was no point in thinking on it; she had taught herself how to live in the present, and she was prepared to construct whatever present she desired.

Roger was the person she had been waiting for, her co-conspirator, her accomplice. She liked his dreamy eyes, pouty lips, and the firm whiteness of his body. He was tender, poetic, uncomplaining, a ready participant in her games. What she did not want from Roger was romance. If he showed up on her doorstep with flowers, she crumpled them in her hands and spread the petals on the bed where they would make love. If he took her to dinner— candlelight and wine—at the Huguenot restaurant in French Church Street, she spent the time stroking his trousered leg with her bare foot under the *nappe*. Her impatience with conventional courtship was disconcerting to Roger, who was, at heart, a romantic. He believed in wooings, sweet nothings, soft endearments. He knew that sex without love did not last, and he wanted his affair with Bernadette to last.

But Bernadette saw no reason why sex shouldn't last. It was simply a matter of imagination. If a novelist, such as Zola or Colette, could sustain a lifetime of creative invention, then so could she. Besides, she knew there was no need for her relationship with Roger to last forever. Forever was not part of her world.

On Ash Wednesday, 1955, the citizens of Cork posted shamrocks to the States to be worn on St. Patrick's Day, including shamrocks for Ike, the President. A light snow was falling. Bernadette went to St. Fin Barre's for evening service. She was not interested in the liturgy, only in the pageant of colors, movements, sounds. She liked the music, the vestments, the chant of Psalms, the numbered hymns.

She liked especially the modulated voice of the celebrant, the deliberate motion of his hands, the way his right hand unfolded like a flower to illustrate a point of the sermon, then curled back against his chest like a sleeping animal—so theatrical, so consciously acted. She didn't participate in the singing. She did not take Eucharist. She did not stand or kneel. She sat in her usual place at the back of the nave. She watched and listened as her lover celebrated the beginning of Lent.

The Reverend Manning read from the Epistle of Paul to the Corinthians: "Do you not know that in a race all the runners run, but only one gets the prize?" His eyes were cast down. He did not look at his flock, nor at the woman at the back of the church whose eyes were raptly fixed on the speaker. "Run in such a way as to get the prize," he exhorted his congregation, raising his eyes to the vault. He put his hands prayerfully together and touched the fingertips to his lips. "I do not run like a man running aimlessly. I do not fight like a man beating the air. No, I beat my body"—he thumped his fists to his chest, once, then paused—"and make it my slave so that, after I have preached to others, I myself will not be disqualified from the prize."

Later, he came to her flat. A candle burned by the bedside table. Frankie was asleep in the little room under the eaves.

"You are *beau*," she said.

"And you are *belle*."

"I watched you in your—what do you call it, your garment?"

"Alb."

"I watched you in your alb. I wanted to undress you."

"There?" he laughed.

"*Certainement.* In front of the bishop. There in the choir. In front of all those little boys."

He smiled.

"*Les jeunes choristes,* they are so pretty in their red dresses with white *chemisiers.* I tried to imagine Frankie—Frankie with the boys."

"He would have to be baptized," said Roger.

"Frankie sings beautifully."

"Nevertheless, he would have to be baptized."

Roger had other misgivings too as he imagined Frankie in the choir—that stunted little body in the midst of so much beauty. He was ashamed.

"There is no reason that Frankie could not be baptized, if you wished it," he said quickly.

Bernadette was silent.

Then she said: "Today in the streets everyone had ashes on their foreheads. Why do you not use the ashes?"

"It is an ancient Roman custom," he replied, "and has much to recommend it. But we believe it does not fit in with the words of Christ when he said, *When you fast, do not look somber as the hypocrites do, for they disfigure their faces to show men they are fasting.* It was in the Gospel today, you remember. *Put oil on your head and wash your face.*"

"Take off your clothes."

He was no longer surprised at her sudden whims. He followed her instructions, carefully folding each garment and placing it on the bedside chair. At last he stood before her naked.

"This is how I imagined you in church," she said.

"I'm afraid the service would have ended in a bit of a stir."

She went to the hearth and took a handful of ashes. Without a word she began to paint his body, first his face, then his chest and upper arms, his belly, his buttocks and thighs, with swirls and chevrons and stripes of ash.

She stood back and admired him.

"*Sauvage*," she whispered. "*Carnaval*."

"It is too late for *carnaval*," snuffled Roger Manning, shivering with cold. "Lent has begun."

39

Frankie was *not* asleep in his bed. He couldn't quite hear what was being spoken in the room below, but he knew that Roger Manning was with his mother. He crawled out of his bed and went through the window onto the kitchen roof. It was the first time he had done so alone, the first time without Jack Kelly. The slope of the roof, which had previously seemed almost flat, now seemed precipitous. The guttered edges fell away into yawning chasms. The slates on the steep pitch above the gables were slippery and rattled under his hands. From afar off, city sounds rose as from an infinite gulf: the *clack-clack* of wagons, the laughter of people in the Douglas Road, the bells of Father Matthew's church. When he leaned back to look at the stars, he was swept by vertigo, by a sense of slipping off the planet and falling into the sky. Without Jack's great body to anchor him, he felt that he must tumble into space.

The sky was moonless and inky black. Tarnished silver clouds scudded from west to east, and in the gaps he saw the stars, glimpsed in snatches as from the window of a moving train, as he had seen the birds in Lough Mahon from the train racing between Cork and Cobh. The stars seemed countless and strange. He recognized nothing of what Jack had taught him. Then he fixed upon one star brighter than all the rest. Drawing his knees up against his belly, he struggled to identify it. He searched his memory for what Jack had taught him about the brightness of stars, their altitudes, and their seasons. Then he smiled. It wasn't a star at all, but a planet. From its brightness he knew it could only be Venus or Jupiter. But it was too high in the sky for Venus; Venus could only be nearer to the sun. It was Jupiter! And now the other stars also became recognizable. Jupiter was in Gemini. And there to the west, the stars of Orion's belt. Taurus. The Pleiades. Sirius and Procyon. Caught in the flickering shutter of the clouds.

He had put it all together *by himself*. He knew he had done something irreversible, that having fetched these things up out of his head, he would have them forever.

On Easter Sunday, Jack came to the city with Effa and the youngest girls. They stopped at the flat in Nicholas Road with a gift for Frankie: a dog, three weeks old, a springer spaniel, the offspring of Jack's own bitch Cassiopeia. The boy named the puppy Canis Minor.

Bernadette said to her son: "*Tu deviens responsable pour toujours de ce que tu as apprivoisé.*"

Frankie frowned. He didn't like it when she spoke French.

"It means if you keep the dog, you will be responsible for it. It is from a book, *Le Petit Prince*. By an airplane pilot. It's about a boy who comes to the earth from a planet out in space."

She watched a drizzle of mucus flow from the boy's nose. He wiped it on his sleeve.

"If you keep Canis Minor you must feed him, clean him."

"Read me the book," pleaded Frankie. The dog curled dozing in his lap. The boy buried his runny nose in the puppy's ear.

The next day Bernadette went to Lavitt's Quay and bought a copy of *The Little Prince*. An English translation. Her son could read it to himself. She wrote on the title page *Tu auras, toi, des étoiles qui savent rire! Bernadette Bois*, and gave it to him.

He looked at the front cover, then at the back cover, then at the front again. The front and back were the same: A yellow-haired boy with a red bow tie on a planet only twice as large as himself. Two tiny volcanoes, some flowers, stars. He turned the book in his hands, getting the feel of it. Then he opened the book to the first page and saw a flock of birds lifting the boy into the air. And he saw the words that his mother had written there.

"What does it mean?" he asked, pointing to the inscription.

"*Étoiles* means 'stars,' " she answered. "*Rire* means 'laugh.' You will know what I have written when you read the book."

The boy read the book a dozen times. He read about the rose, the sheep, the fox, the snake. He was especially interested in the Prince's planet, a world in perfect proportion to his own small frame. He could circumnavigate that world in twenty paces.

She had quoted the fox: *You alone will have stars that can laugh*.

It will seem strange that my mother in-scribed herself in my book *Bernadette Bois*. Wouldn't other mothers have written *I love you, Mammy*, or *To my darling Frankie, Mam*? Of course. But Bernadette was not a typical mother.

There was nothing maternal about her. No mothering, no pampering, no mollycoddling. She provided me with clothing and food, but I was expected to dress myself, clean myself, feed myself. No instructions, no parental guidance. I simply came to know that if tea needed to be made, then it was I who must boil the kettle. She never said, *Frankie, it is time to bathe.* I took my cues from her own habits or went unbathed. She never criticized or gave advice. If I was laughed at by my schoolmates for mismatched socks or inappropriate gear—tees in winter, woolen trousers in high summer—she paid no mind. If I said, *They laughed at my trousers*, she shrugged. If my trousers or sweater developed a hole, she did not mend them but instead threw them away and sooner or later she somehow managed to buy replacements. She was not a repairer. If a thing broke or went tatty, it was discarded. Sometimes she included me in her activities—she often took me, for example, to evensong at St. Fin Barre's—but usually she came and went on her own, leaving me in the care of Mrs. Brosnan, who was no care at all. My mother treated me, from the cradle, as if I were an adult, as if I were her sibling perhaps—no, not a sibling, but a cousin or a friend. She was indifferent to my schooling; I went to school or stayed home as I pleased. Usually, I stayed in my room and read my books. I was content to be alone. I think she was grateful when Canis Minor came into my life. The dog relieved her of any lingering obligation to provide affection. From the dog I received a wet, generous, uncluttered love.

My mother's casual parenting was just what I

needed. She never pitied or made concessions to my deformity. She armored me with self-reliance. She fed my intellect without regard to the deficits of my body. By sparing me a mother's love, she conditioned me to solitude. There was the fair chance that I had inherited her own stubborn independence, quite separately from the mishmashed tangle of genes that was mine alone; and, it's true, I did prefer the coziness of my room to the busyness of the street or playground. And of course she knew that my achondroplasic body would isolate me more completely than even the walls of my room. It was inevitable (she supposed) that I would be alone.

Solitude is a gift. And an art. Solitude was Bernadette's gift to me, and my art perfected it. It was solitude that led me to the sky, to those vast empty spaces, those yawning infinities of silence. By the time I was nine or ten years old I had begun to go beyond Jack Kelly's tutelage into a night of my own devising. I kept a diary, a diary of the darkness, a diary of the hours from sunset to dawn. And when I was old enough to go about on my own, I left my perch on the kitchen roof and struck out into Cork's dark hinterland; and when I returned to the house after a night of tramping country lanes, I wrote down what I had seen. I have kept my diaries faithfully for more than thirty years. They are here now, in a pile on the floor beside my desk, more than a hundred notebooks scribbled full with my crabbed hand. These notebooks are my bank, my treasure, the savings of a lifetime, not pound notes or gilt-edged securities, but comets, meteorites, bolides, auroras, eclipses, conjunctions, occultations, zodiacal lights, moonbows, sunrises and sunsets of special color or distinction. For a long time I had the use of a fine telescope given to me by Jack Kelly, but I seldom used it. I never found the need to do so. The riches of the sky that are available to the unaided eye are plentiful enough to keep me occupied, especially in a country where the sky is overcast so much of the time. I persevere. I wait and I am rewarded. There are special moments in my diaries tagged with red stickers on the edges of the pages (the stickers came from Jack), moments of special grace, sky-gifts given and greedily collected. I choose a notebook at random and open it to a red-tagged page: 12 July 1963, a new moon no more than 25 hours old suspended in a brassy sunset, a wisp of gold leaf eyelash thin, a thing so rare and fine that to see it only once would justify a lifetime of watching. Another notebook: the nova of autumn 1975 in Cygnus, which I recognized in the sky even before I heard it announced on the radio, a new star of the second magnitude, the first bright nova of my lifetime, perhaps the last, a brilliant feather plucked from the swan's tail, a night of wild excitement and fevered watching. And another: the delicately beautiful Comet West in early March 1976, dangling by its tail in a blue-pink dawn. And another: the spectacular auroral display of September 30, 1961, the valley of the Lee tented in Technicolor pyrotechnics.

Antoine de Saint-Exupéry's Little Prince lived on a planet scarcely larger than a house. One evening just by moving his chair he was able to watch forty-four sunsets. Forty-four sunsets in a single day!

Here in Ireland we are lucky to see forty-four sunsets in a year. When I read the episode of the forty-four sunsets (I was eight years old), I knew that I had found the story of my life. *One loves the sunset when one is sad*, said the Little Prince to his pilot. And, yes, that is true. Solitude and sadness are like two hands pressed together, palm to palm. Once on Merchant's Quay I saw two dwarfs, a man and a woman, walking hand in hand, their faces radiant with affection. In this city there are others like myself, other achondroplasics with whom I might seek companionship, even love. But I cannot. Jack's daughters, Orna and Caitlin, saw to that, on those Sunday afternoons at their house in Westview Terrace, Cobh, with their laughter, their downy skin, and hair perfumed with the scents of their baths. I was in love, already, *at that young age*, with the beauty of women. I am not beautiful, God knows, but I will settle for nothing less—a colossal arrogance. I cannot change. I was nurtured, like Yeats's sailing moon, *in beauty's murderous brood*.

Down the path of self-hate lies madness, the madness of Anne-Marie Bois and of her daughter, Bernadette, a madness perhaps harbored in the DNA, a fatal twist to the family code that leads inevitably to depression and despair (dear God, what a mess of genes I was given). I will leave undescribed the unsavory anticipations of madness: the masturbatory rituals, the voyeurism, the port-soaked dreams. My sins, whatever they are, are terrestrial; I escape into the sky, dogged by desperation, afflicted by the sadness of sunsets, longing for something I cannot have. The sky is my asylum. I catalog and measure.

I count and plumb. I watch and wait. A hundred star-filled notebooks lay in a pile on the floor by my desk, flying their triumphant red flags. A hundred diaries of the solitary hermit nursing his madness on the sane solicitude of stars.

43

Emma Kelly left school and home at the same time. She cleaned out her desk in the convent school on Spy Road. With the other children she scrubbed her desktop with soapy water and thick-bristled brush, carefully removing all marks of pencil or ink and those patches of built-up varnish into which she had carved strokes and curlicues with her thumbnail. She bleached away ink stains from the linoleum beneath her desk, and when she had finished, she went into the lavatory to scrub the smudges from her knees. She took the brown paper covers off her textbooks and removed the inked words from the edges of the closed pages with sandpaper provided by the nuns. She placed the books in the appropriate pile on the table by the window. Her pen, pencils, ruler, and prayer book were dumped into her bookbag. She did not say good-bye to her teacher. Once she had dreamed of becoming a nun, perhaps having a classroom of her own. Those dreams were dashed by an image glimpsed at a window, a blemish of mind unacceptable to Christ.

Emma returned to her parent's house in Westview

Terrace and went to her room. When she emerged, she had exchanged her blue school pinafore for a plain black dress, black coat, black stockings, black shoes. She placed an envelope on the table in the reception room and, without a word to her mother or sisters, left the house. She carried her school bag, but now it contained two apples, two shillings, a hairbrush, a change of underwear and stockings, three issues of *Modern Screen* magazine, and a much-read copy of Thomas à Kempis's *Imitation of Christ*. Fifty minutes later she was knocking at the gate of the convent of the Sisters of the Annunciation in Douglas Road, Cork.

Emma did not ask for admittance as a postulant. She asked for a room and a job and was given both. The job, as a kitchen maid, paid ten shillings a week. The room was tiny and windowless; it had once been a kitchen pantry. The walls of her room were painted institutional gray, with horizontal unpainted stripes where once there had been shelves. The room contained an iron bedstead with clean linen, a wooden box (*Jaffa Oranges*) for storing her belongings, and another overturned box (*Kenya Tea*) at the head of the bed for her candle. The sparseness of the room suited her, and she resisted any efforts by the nuns to provide further amenities. From half-five in the morning to half-eight in the evening, she assisted the cook preparing meals for the nuns. During the free hours of morning or afternoon she went to the chapel, or stayed in her room and read the movie magazines that she kept hidden under her mattress. On Saturday afternoons she went to the cinema—the Palace, Pavilion, Savoy,

Ritz, or Lee. On the last Sunday of every month and at Christmas she visited her family.

Of the ten shillings paid to Emma each week for her services, she spent one shilling on Hollywood magazines, ten pennies for each of two visits to the cinema, ten pennies for sweets, five pennies toward her monthly visit to Cobh, and the rest she hoarded away in a biscuit tin that she kept in her Jaffa Oranges box. On more than one occasion—on *many* occasions—young men came to sit next to her in the dark cinema or tried to chat her up in the queue or asked her to join them in the loges. She spurned them all. She sat alone at the front of the theater while other afternoon patrons clustered in pairs in the back seats or in the loges, smooching and smoking. When she returned from the cinema, she read Thomas à Kempis. She tried to model her life on the life of Christ, making allowance for the fact that there were no cinemas in the Holy Land at the time of Christ. She did not complain about the long hours of her work, or the darkness and dampness of her room, or the dreary simplicity of her convent clothing. All of these she embraced and offered up to Christ. She contrived mortifications of her body—placed pebbles in her shoes or cinders in her bed, drank her tea cold and without sugar, pricked her palms with pins—and then dashed off to the Palace to watch Humphrey Bogart and Katharine Hepburn drag a boat through the leech-filled swamps of Africa, all the while stuffing her mouth from a bag of sweets in her lap.

She was not interested in young men, except abstractly. Jesus was the only male presence in her thoughts. She kept holy pictures of *The Good Shepherd* and *The Sacred Heart* tucked between the pages of her movie magazines: small, garishly colored pictures, gilt edged. On the back of the pictures were printed ejaculations—*Sacred Heart of Jesus, Have mercy on us*, that sort of thing—and the indulgences, say, three hundred days subtracted from her time in Purgatory for each recital. Emma imagined Jesus in the guise of a movie star, blue-eyed Jeffrey Hunter in *King of Kings*, perhaps, or young Richard Burton as the Roman soldier in *The Robe*. Sacred and profane became mixed up in her mind until her thoughts at chapel and at the Palace or Savoy became a muddle of dreamy ejaculations and moving holy pictures, a celluloid Jesus and Technicolor saints, pebbles in her shoes and chocolate-covered candies melting in her hand.

Hidden away in her tiny room—her chrysalis—she had become quite pretty, tall and willowy, with skin of translucent clarity, a figure both thin and pleasantly shapely (bouts of fasting and bags of sweets), and a tangled nimbus of coppery Kelly hair. She turned men's eyes, though they were deterred from flirtation by her unfocused way of drifting through the world without being part of it. In cinema darkness her cheerlessness was easily mistaken for sultriness, and her soft gray eyes became focused by the flickering image on the screen. Slouched in her chair, her shoulders hunched forward, her lips moistened with candy and glistening in the dusky celluloid light, she was an irresistible quarry for men on the make, but whenever a lad slipped into the adjoining seat she removed herself to another chair without acknowledging his presence.

A psychologist might say—oh, would *certainly* say—that Emma had sublimated her sexuality in religion, that the pricking of her palms and the cinders on her sheets were a way of gratifying appetites that could not be consciously acknowledged, and that a traumatic glimpse of her father having sex with a girl of her own age had caused her to become abstracted from normal desires and fulfillments. But that easy analysis would be false, or at least simplistic. Emma had been intensely religious from the first day she went off to school. At the time of her First Communion, at age seven, she had caused a crisis in her family by declaring herself unworthy to receive the Body of Christ. Alone among the six Kelly girls she showed no interest in boys. Of all the girls, she was least concerned with clothes, dolls, pretty things. All of this came before the shocking incident on the coal-shed roof. It is probably best to say that her religious devotions and self-mortifications were a *parallel stream* to a sexuality not yet fully awakened—Jesus Christ and Jeffrey Hunter striding side by side down the convent corridors of her mind.

The Annunciation Convent in Douglas Road is no more than a few hundred yards from the house in Nicholas Street where Bernadette Bois lived with her son. Occasionally, mother and son passed Emma in the street. Bernadette always greeted Emma, but Emma made no reply.

"She looks like Orna," said Frankie, after one of these encounters.

"She is Orna's sister."

"Why doesn't she talk to us?"

Bernadette shrugged. "She prefers to be by herself. That's why she lives alone instead of with her parents."

"Does she not like us?"

"I think she wants to be alone."

"She's pretty," said Frankie.

Oh, indeed, she was pretty, and eventually she turned up on our doorstep to become a resident ambassador from that household of pretty red-haired girls.

44

On the Eve of St. John's, June 23, 1956, Emma Kelly had seventy-six pounds in a biscuit tin that she kept in her Jaffa Oranges box. She was twenty-four years old, and in her own mind and in her own way a bride of Christ, not a nun exactly, but a hanger-on to the cloister, a silent participant at the fringes of the professed life, often asked to become a postulant but persistently refusing. She was a daily communicant at the South Chapel, slipping away from the convent kitchen as soon as breakfast's washing up was done and returning in time to begin preparations for the midday meal. She listened to the reader at the nuns' meals. In her room she read Thomas à Kempis over and over until she had memorized every word. During quiet evening hours she went to the convent chapel and prayed her beads, a dreamy recitation of repetitive prayers. The chapel was close and dusky, lit by the purgatorial glow of votive candles and redolent with scents of beeswax, brown soap, and ammonia. The beads slipped through her fingers. Time passed. She was neither happy nor unhappy. She was content.

St. John's Eve fell on a Saturday. The next morning Emma went to the Jaffa Oranges box to fetch her Sunday dress. The biscuit tin was gone. The seventy-six pounds was gone. All of her savings for seven years had vanished.

Tearfully, she reported the tragedy to the cook. The cook took Emma by the hand and led her to the superior of the convent, Sister Columbanus. Sister Columbanus gathered up Sister Edna and hurried with Emma to the ex-pantry behind the kitchen.

"Where did you keep the money?" asked Sister Columbanus.

Emma pointed: "In a Jacobs Biscuits tin." She had stopped crying. Her eyes were red and puffy.

Sister Columbanus fussed about in the Jaffa Oranges box, turning out Emma's few possessions— her weekday dress, her stockings, her underwear, her tiny hoard of toiletries, her hairbrush. When the inventory was complete, Sister Edna returned the items to their place.

"It was not wise to keep such a sum of money in such a place," said Sister Columbanus.

"Why?" asked Emma. "No one comes here but me."

Sister Columbanus did not answer. She removed the candle holder and Thomas à Kempis from atop the Kenya Tea bedside box and handed the two items to Sister Edna. She tipped up the box and looked underneath. There was nothing. She stooped to look under the bed. She lifted the mattress and removed *Photoplay, Silver Screen*, and *Cinema News*. She did not hand the magazines to Sister Edna.

"These aren't appropriate reading materials for a convent," said Sister Columbanus.

"But I'm not in a convent," whispered Emma. "I'm in a pantry."

"They are not appropriate."

"They are cinema magazines. There is nothing wrong with cinema magazines."

"Then why are they hidden under your mattress?"

Emma did not know why she had hidden the magazines under the mattress. She was sorry she had done so.

"My money," she whimpered.

"We shall have to keep looking for your money. It wasn't wise, you know, to keep such a sum in such an insecure place. You should have given it to me for safekeeping."

"Shall I call the Gardai?" asked Sister Edna.

"I think not," replied Sister Columbanus. "The money might turn up. Perhaps Emma has misplaced it. Or forgotten that she spent it. It would not be desirable to have the police come to the convent. What would that look like? It is best to keep the police out of it."

"My money," whispered Emma.

"Her money," said the cook.

"Her money," said Sister Edna.

Emma left the convent. She packed her things into the Jaffa Oranges box and left. The cook slipped a crumpled pound note into Emma's hand, wiped Emma's eyes with the hem of her apron, removing her tears, adding flour. The flour made Emma's eyes look less red.

"Where will you go?" asked the cook.

Emma shrugged. She knew where she would go, but didn't say.

"If you need help, you can always come back here," said Sister Edna, who had come to the kitchen to see Emma off.

"Perhaps you should go to your parents," said the cook. She placed buns and jam into Emma's box.

"Pray for me," said Sister Edna.

Emma left the convent by the gate into Douglas Road. She walked around the corner to the house in Nicholas Road and knocked at the door. Bernadette was not home. Bernadette was working. Ten-year-old Frankie answered the door.

45

Jack Kelly told me the story of the Herd-boy and the Weaving-girl. A star story from ancient China. Where Jack learned it I do not know. Vega is the Weaving-girl, and Altair is the Herd-boy. The two lovers became so lost in their attentions to one another that they neglected their duties to Heaven.

To remedy this unacceptable state of affairs, the gods separated the lovers with a celestial river, the impassable barrier of the Milky Way that flows between the two stars in the summer night. But the gods were not without compassion. Once a year, on the seventh night of the seventh moon, at the height of summer, the lovers are allowed to meet when a bridge of birds briefly spans the stream of stars.

I was the Herd-boy; Emma was my Weaving-girl. The river between us was more than the difference in our ages; it was the gaping, unbridgeable gulf between brokenness and beauty.

Bernadette welcomed Emma into our house but made it clear to the girl (who was two years younger than herself) that the arrangement was temporary and only to last until Emma could find accommodations of her own. As it turned out, Emma was with us through the summer and into the autumn of 1957, while I poured over astronomy books and Bernadette pursued her dalliance with Roger Manning. My mother urged her unpaying boarder to find work, but Emma was timid and frightened. She stood forlornly outside commercial premises with signs in their windows soliciting barmaids or kitchen girls, but could not gather up sufficient courage to go in. *Soon*, she said to Bernadette. "Soon" stretched into August and then into September.

Emma took my bed in the garret room, and I was removed to a cot mattress on the floor under the eaves. I did not mind surrendering my bed. I was pleased to have Emma in my room. She was not like her younger sisters; she was neither playful nor affectionate. She seldom spoke. But she did bring into my room a *presence* as provocative and sweet as a lingering perfume.

I watched her from my bed.

Pretending to sleep, I watched, and—oh, yes, I knew exactly what I was doing. I was ten years old, but my voyeurism was calculated. I forced myself to stay awake until Emma prepared herself for bed. I arranged myself on my cot mattress with the blanket pulled over my head and a tiny round fold contrived in the blanket's edge, so that when she came into the room and lit the candle, I would seem to be fast asleep when in fact I was watching through the fold, like an astronomer with his eye to a telescope, across a Milky Way of candlelight. It was not her nakedness that I waited to see (Emma was uncommonly modest; she slipped into her nightdress before removing her vest and knickers), but the rituals themselves, the retirements and awakenings, the ballerinalike movement of her limbs, the creasings and the foldings of cotton or silk, her bare feet on the splintery boards, the aureole of hair on the pillow, her slim white hands clutching *Silver Screen* magazine in the murky light. She was my Weaving-girl, and I waited, all that long starry summer, for my bridge of birds.

46
*

Dear God, what hope ever was there for a child nurtured on Emma's sweet diffidence? What hope for a kid who was beginning to realize, this time with ruinous clarity (in some sense he had always known, even from that moment when his squashed little form emerged into the midwife's waiting hands), that he was fundamentally, structurally, architecturally different from other children. And set apart by his difference from Emma's unreachable beauty. From Orna and Caitlin. From the girls in the street, the girls of his own age: Mainin, Kathleen, Bridie, Pauline, Joan, Marcella. Oh, yes: the stars. He had the stars. They were unreachable too. I retrieve from my tumbled pile of star-diaries (here on the floor next to my desk) a student's composition book from that time, filled with the ten-year-old's childish scrawl. I open it to August 1957. The entry is marked with a red tag. And in the margin, an explosion of exclamation marks! Bold underlinings! It was the summer of the Perseids.

Every morning I rose in the darkest hours of the night and looked out the window. If the sky was clear, I climbed out onto the kitchen roof with my blanket. I wrapped the blanket about me. I watched and I counted. On 7 August I counted twenty-three meteors. The next three nights were cloudy. Then, on 11 August, I observed seventy-six meteors in the course of a single hour! Seventy-six bits of a lost

comet plunging into the earth's atmosphere, igniting streaks of burning vapor. It was a night of wild
joy. Among the most intense pleasures of that night
were two bolides, massive meteors that burned with
fiery colors—yellow, orange, green—brilliantly in-
candescent, disintegrating at the end of their luminous tracks in starbursts of gold. All of this is
recorded in the boy's diary. Perhaps memory is not
reliable—thirty-three years have passed!—but the
enthusiastic scribbles in the diary suggest that 1957
was a banner year for shooting stars.

As dawn erased the last meteors from the sky I
scuttled across the roof to return to my bed, dragging my blanket, and stopped at the window. Emma
was at the washbasin, her nightdress down about
her waist, splashing water on her breasts and shoulders. Her back was to me. What did I see? A flow of
hair the color of the dawn. Shoulder blades like
nascent wings (and between them the soft brown
rectangle of a cloth scapular). The deep declivity of
her back. A glimpse of coccyx where the nightdress
hung about her hips. Is the image reliable? Can
memory be trusted? Three decades have passed. I
close my eyes, *willing* neural circuits to click, syn-
apses to ignite. And, yes, I *see* what the boy saw
then. The image has been carefully processed,
folded, and stored away, laid up like a special garment, a baptismal gown or a wedding dress, in tissue paper, dusted with moth flakes, tucked far back
in the darkest closets of the brain. I unfold the memory. It is as fresh and bright as yesterday.

On that morning I put away the things of the child.
It was not a sexual awakening, although that was

part of it. There was nothing in my heart that morning but tenderness, a tenderness that overflowed the bounds of Emma's beauty to fill the world. I lay on the roof of my mother's kitchen and the city filled up around me, filled up with tenderness, like a summer haze rising from the River Lee. It was as if something had clicked in my brain, a switch thrown from boy to man. I saw that I was different, *and that I would always be different*. I understood that I would always be a watcher, observing beauty as through a telescope, as removed from the possession of what I saw—of what I saw *as desirable*—as I was separate from the galaxies and stars.

I would like to use the phrase *religious experience* for what occurred on that morning of Emma's quiet ablutions. I recognized a certain *fitness* to the world, an *appropriateness* that had nothing to do with justice or mercy. There was something in the juxtaposition of her proximate *almost touchable* beauty and the infinite untouchable beauty of the streaming Perseids that—how shall I say this without sounding pretentious?—I understood that whatever exists is good, not by the measure of any individual person's happiness or sorrow, *but by merely being*. Since that morning I have often felt sorry for myself, but I have never felt punished by a negligent or malicious God. I knew from the moment I saw Emma at the basin that my future happiness or unhappiness would only be found within myself.

If I discovered that morning the kernel of a faith that has sustained me (with a supplementary measure of drink) throughout my life, then Emma was the Paraclete. When she had dressed and departed, I entered the room through the window and examined the residue of her presence—the scented soap still wet with froth, the damp towel that had touched her skin, the concavity in the white sheet on the bed where she had slept. I had found a religion, such as it was, and the object of my rapt attention—as *wholly other* as any Barthian divinity—was beauty.

47

No affection passed between Emma and myself. She neither gave nor invited intimacy. Unlike her younger sisters, who accepted my deformity (and perhaps even saw it as vaguely endearing), Emma—if I am not mistaken, perhaps I am unfair—was offended by it. Her standard of male beauty came straight from Hollywood: Montgomery Clift, Tyrone Powell, Charlton Heston. On the wall above her bed (my bed), close to her pillow, were pinned two pictures, one from a movie magazine, the other from a church calendar, Robert Taylor and Christ the Good Shepherd—the same doe eyes, the same dark curls, the same pouty lips with just a hint of a smile. These were her icons of perfection. I simply didn't fit. I was the broken child, the hobbled elf, a prying, sniffing hop-o'-my-thumb lurking in the verges of her handsome world.

But between us a certain commerce did ensue, and the intermediary was Canis Minor. Emma adored my dog. The dog adored Emma. If she and

I entered the house at the same time, the dog stood shaking indecisively between us, like Balaam's ass, until it seemed it would shake itself apart. I wasn't jealous. The dog was my go-between. I cuddled it, petted it, stroked its silky hair, invested it with my tenderest affections, then watched it run into Emma's arms. She held Canis Minor in her lap, tickled its chin, pressed its snout against her breast, and back it came to me bearing an ineffable envelope of her exudations. The poor animal never knew what a burden it carried as it bounded back and forth between us, exuberantly panting and wagging its tail.

Meanwhile, Roger Manning did not know what to do about Bernadette Bois. He was quite stricken by her. On more than one occasion the words *I love you* almost slipped out of his mouth into her ear. She did not invite such declarations. She seemed decisively content that their relationship should be sexual only. She never whispered words of endearment, except to that part of him that was beginning to seem as if it must forever have a separate life. If she spoke to him directly—to *him*, Roger Manning, the man for whom the sexual apparatus were mere attachments—it was always by way of a provocation. It was, he decided, a *very* strange relationship.

It occurred to him that they might marry. It oc-

curred to him that he and Bernadette and Bernadette's dwarf son might move into a terrace house
near the cathedral and live happily ever after. God
knows, he had nothing against the sex. Sex with
Bernadette was—well, quite splendid. But he imagined a more settled life. Pints of milk on the front
stoop. Mozart on the gramophone. Peeling spuds
at the kitchen sink while Bernadette stirred the pot
at the stove. Soap and stockings and toothbrushes
in the lavatory and the folded *Irish Times* in his
place at table when he came down for breakfast. He
imagined all of this and it seemed desirable.

There was *one* problem: He could not imagine
how he might introduce Bernadette to the bishop.
By now half of Cork knew of his attentions to the
girl. The relationship, if not proscribed by church
law, was at least irregular. He would have liked to
bring Bernadette to the bishop's house and put
things right. But he could not. It wasn't that Roger
was a snob. Quite the contrary. He was proud of
Bernadette. No, the problem wasn't Roger; the problem was Bernadette. She did not want to meet the
bishop. She did not want to meet *anyone*. And God
knows what she might say or do in polite company.
She was, thought Roger Manning, a loose cannon,
a loaded gun; one never knew when she might go
flying off the rails.

For one thing, there was the way she dressed.
Like a French schoolgirl. Dark dresses and woolly
pullovers. Cotton scarves. Black stockings and cloth
shoes. So—well, *bohemian*. So *just short* of re-
spectable. Mind you, he liked the way she dressed;
her dress was modest, childlike even. Yet one was

always aware of the body *under* the clothes. He never tired of looking at her, in the cathedral, in the street, in the café. And he noticed how she caught other men's eyes. She always seemed about to doff whatever she was wearing. And of course that was the problem. It was well and good for Roger to imagine Bernadette slipping out of her clothes, or even perhaps the poor jealous fool in the street, but what about the bishop? What, for God's sake, would the bishop think?

And her atheism. She professed no faith in a transcendent being. She was—what? A witch. A *good* witch, certainly, but a witch. A sorceress. A caster of charms and spells. And *he* was a priest of the Christian church, a minister, a server of sacraments. Most importantly, he was a theist. Or was he? Maybe he didn't believe in God at all. Maybe he was merely trapped by the *habit* of belief, addicted to the security and *sensibleness* of his faith. Why else was he such a willing acolyte at her witch's sabbaths? No matter how you looked at it, there was a conflict of faith, and it was difficult to see how it might be resolved in the conventionality of the domestic hearth and marital bed.

Roger longed for respectability. Respectability with Bernadette. Yet he could not imagine how he might disentangle himself from those decidedly unrespectable (and immensely pleasurable) erotic games that Bernadette was so endlessly capable of contriving. He was, he considered, on the horns of a dilemma. All at sea. At wit's end.

He resolved, despite her protests, to introduce her into society. Into *his* society. But he would be cautious. He would nudge her ever so gently toward conventionality, toward the house with the bright kitchen, the tidy parlor, the feathery marital bed. He would take her to the home of his friend Hans Scrieber, the professor, the physicist, the foreigner, the agnostic nonconformist. Scrieber was a socialist, perhaps a communist, a man of unconventional acquaintances—artists, scientists, even (Roger Manning suspected) homosexuals. His house was a place of lively, irreverent repartee. Scrieber would not think Bernadette odd. Scrieber's wife, Greta, and child Hilde would not think Bernadette odd. The people that Roger had met at Scrieber's home were themselves all a bit odd, each in his or her own way. Yet, Scrieber's house had all the attributes of domesticity. A cozy cottage in the countryside. A carefully tended garden. A child. It was the perfect venue to enter into society with Bernadette.

Roger wrangled an invitation to dinner, for himself and Bernadette. But he made two miscalculations. He was not yet aware that Bernadette's father had been killed by Germans. Hans Scrieber had fled his native land at the time of the Austrian *anschluss*, disgusted with Hitler and Fascist politics; nevertheless, he was German, and further distinctions Bernadette was neither willing nor able to make. Nor was Roger aware of Scrieber's satyric compulsion to bed every woman he met.

49

It was Scrieber's idea to invite Emma to Inishcarra. Roger had mentioned Bernadette's unpaying houseguest.

"Bring her along," said Scrieber.

"Bring who along?"

"Emma. The other girl."

Roger was doubtful. From what he knew about Emma, she might be even more unreliable in company than Bernadette.

"Do. Oh, do," insisted Scrieber. "It will be charming. One can never have too many young ladies around."

Hans Scrieber was forty-six years old, but fit and vigorous as a man half his age. He bicycled five miles back and forth each day to the university. Weekends he tramped in the mountains of West Cork and Kerry. During extended holidays he often returned to his native Alps for serious climbing. He was not tall, but his body was straight, thin, and as taut as a violin string. A photograph taken at the time of the dinner party shows glistening black hair combed straight back from a spacious forehead, piercing eyes magnified by thick rimless glasses, elegant nose, thin lips, jutting chin. Altogether a commanding physical presence. Also, a captivating lecturer and a brilliant astrophysicist. Had it not been for the war and his German nationality, he might have won the Nobel Prize for his work on the physics of stellar interiors. It was still a possibility.

Ireland was a comfortable place for a German expatriate to spend the war years. Scrieber had been grateful when the offer came from Prime Minister De Valera of an academic posting at either Dunsink Observatory or University College Cork. He chose Cork because of its nearness to mountains. His teaching responsibilities were minimal—one course of studies each term in astrophysics— allowing ample time to pursue his theoretical research. He was particularly involved at that time in the evolution of stars to the red giant stage at the end of their lives. Although contented with Ireland and the Irish, he felt somewhat isolated from other physicists who were working on similar problems. Now that the postwar situation on the continent had returned to normal, it was rumored that Scrieber might return to Germany—to Göttingen or Berlin. His Irish colleagues were reluctant to lose the stimulus of his forceful and creative mind.

It was not easy for Roger Manning to convince the two women to attend the soirée at Scrieber's. Bernadette acceded only to Roger's sad-eyed pleading. He wooed her to Inishcarra with a handsome morocco-bound volume of Yeats's poems. On the flyleaf he inscribed, quoting Yeats, *I thought of your beauty, and this arrow, Made out of a wild thought, is in my marrow*. She yielded. Curiously, Emma was interested in the invitation—perhaps because Roger made Scrieber's milieu sound vaguely Hollywoodish—but protested that she had nothing to wear. At Roger's urging, Bernadette took Emma to a shop on North Main Street and bought her a frock, a floral print with white lace collar. As for herself, Bernadette had no intention of wearing anything other than her usual attire.

For all his longing for conventionality, Roger was pleased to arrive at Scrieber's house with these two unconventional women. Even their sullenness enhanced their airs of unconformity, a welcome bohemian antidote to Roger's own Church of Ireland *properness*. He basked in their sulkiness, their unaffected beauty. But he was nevertheless on edge, like a terrorist holding a finely triggered bomb. The other guests included a portly, cigar-smoking English theoretical chemist and his anorexic spouse; a tuxedo-clad Irish poetess (Greta's friend); a bearded young fellow of unspecified occupation in Tyrolean gear. Roger noted that everyone except his own two companions seemed to talk at once. The conversation hummed chaotically about his ears; he could hardly catch the drift of it. Continental politics. The "red scare" in America. A novel called *Magister Ludi* by someone named Hesse. When he thought he had found the thread of the conversation, a snatch of German threw him off.

"Your charming girls must sit at my side," said Scrieber to Roger as the company retired for dinner.

Bernadette slipped into a chair at the foot of the table, as far away from Scrieber as possible, and refused to budge, but Emma was guided by her host to the place on his left. She clenched her hands against her white lace collar and gazed blankly at the bewildering variety of glassware and utensils arrayed in front of her. Her eyes were rimmed with shadows, gloamings of sadness that Scrieber found irresistibly attractive. She was pretty in her gape-eyed innocence.

"And what's your *passion*?" asked Scrieber, fixing her like a butterfly to a board with his steely blue eyes. He used the French pronunciation. His hand rested on the table close to her breast.

Roger held his breath and stared into his plate.

Emma's lips quivered. She was suddenly struck by the *paltriness* of her life. Words came creeping toward her tongue from the darkest corners of her mind, only to shrivel in the dryness at the back of her throat.

"Ah, the wine," said Scrieber, turning suddenly away, releasing her. "So hard to obtain a good Austrian wine." He displayed a tall green bottle to the company. "I have this sent down from Dublin. It's superb." He laughed. He had left her dangling at a precipice.

The net had been thrown, the pin pressed home. Scrieber had infected Emma with a germ of fear, and fear, as we all know, is curiously akin to desire.

The other people at the table—the chemist and his wife, the poetess, the Tyrolean—have no relevance here. Their chatter is the backdrop against which we observe Bernadette's pained silence and Emma's dull shiver of fright. With labored gaiety Roger sprinkles flakes of chat into the conversation, like confetti onto a passing parade. The unrelenting tremor of his legs has caused his stockings to sag about his ankles.

There is one last element of the story to put into place amidst the tinkle of cutlery and china, the clank of empty wine bottles being tossed into dust-bins, the soapy hands and tea towels of washing up. With a finesse no one has noticed, Hans Scrieber has maneuvered Bernadette alone into the reception room. His thin lips form ever so unctuously into a smile. His eyes become bluer even as she watches. With his long patrician fingers he touches the back of her hand.

He says: "Can I see you sometime?"

His accent is German.

Bernadette musters her one syllable of the evening, a syllable as hard and brilliantly cut as diamond.

"*Non.*"

50

I am a connoisseur of stars, those glittering celestial lights, night's flickering candles. My book—the anxiously awaited book, the book that even now is perhaps making its way toward Ireland, the book of sad and deliberate night-psalms that bears on its jacket a photograph of the reclusive author—is about stars, stars that tinkle in night's desert like little bells. Hans Scrieber also concerned himself with stars (and he too has made his way into *Nightstalk*, though subtly disguised). I own a copy of one of Scrieber's books: *Nucleosynthesis in Normal Stars and Stellar Evolution.* It is dense with equations. Perhaps no other physicist knew as much about what happens at the cores of stars as

Scrieber. He was the wizard who unraveled the secret of a star's burning. As far as I know, Hans Scrieber never actually looked at stars in the night sky. For one thing, he was desperately nearsighted. And although a vigorous outdoor man, he was strictly a daytime naturalist. The night frightened him. The *unboundedness* of night, like the unboundedness of the sea, oppressed him. When darkness fell, he pulled the shades and lit the lamps. The jaundiced light of tungsten suited his nocturnal intrigues, those endless, precisely executed seductions that he believed were essential to his intellectual creativity.

He would not let Roger Manning's attractive companions get away. The naïveté, silence, and youthfulness of the two women had affected him deeply. Manning's girl, Bernadette, had made it clear that not much was to be expected in *that* direction. But Emma—yes, Emma was *just* possible. What was it that William Blake said about sexual love springing from spiritual hate? Hans Scrieber correctly apprised that Emma had been wounded. He would enter her through the gaping sore of her self-hate. But first he must bring her into his home so that the psychological tension of the conquest would invigorate *every* aspect of his life, charging even his mathematical equations with that spark of divinity that made the interiors of stars obey the commands of his mind.

Greta Scrieber was a willing accomplice to her husband's adulteries. No, perhaps *willing* is too strong a word. But certainly she had become accustomed to her husband's infidelities. She had taken several lovers of her own (of both genders) when sexual intimacy had ceased with her husband. From the earliest days of their contentious union he had lectured her on the "pathetic inadequacies of bourgeois marriage." Yet a bond between them somehow endured. For her part, the bond was based on respect for her husband's intellectual brilliance. The Scrieber Instability, the Scrieber Proton-Proton Cycle, the Scrieber Function were part of the international canon of astrophysics. Students studied these things in every university, *her* husband's creations; she basked in reflected glory. Hans Scrieber, for his part, admired his wife's sensibleness—and her *staying power*. The more he abused her loyalty, the more tenaciously she clung to him. There was nothing whimpering or soft about her attachment; she held on like a bulldog to an antagonist's leg, with bared teeth. His marriage, for all of its tensions and instabilities, provided the refuge he required when the time came to *end* an affair, for end them he always did. It was the *conquest* that electrified his mind; once the conquest was achieved, the galvanizing pressure subsided. Then—then his marriage provided a handy rationalization for retreat and repositioning.

At her husband's suggestion, Greta approached Roger Manning with the proposal that Emma come to Inishcarra as a mother's helper, to mind Hilde and assist with household chores. This Roger dutifully conveyed to Emma through Bernadette. Bernadette foresaw the risk, but Emma *was*, after all, an adult capable of ordering her own life, and Bernadette was not her keeper. Moreover, the Scriebers' offer of employment seemed the only practical way to get Emma out from underfoot. As for Emma, two pounds a week for her services seemed a handsome sum that would again open the doors of the dusky cinemas of Cork.

51
*

     A knock at the door, the *thump-thump* of officialdom. It is the postman with a package too large to fit through the slot.

It is not the first time I have opened the door to this man. He looks over my head, deliberately, then, glancing down, pretends to discover me. *Ah*, he says. *Ha*, he laughs. And then: *So* there *you are!* He hands me the padded envelope.

"From London," he says. "Imagine that!"

I close the door. On the postman. On the billows of effluent-scented mist that roll up from the River Lee. I close the door on the wide world, throw the bolt, click the latch, and take my package upstairs to my chair by the fire.

The package might as well contain a bomb. It will explode my life to kingdom come. It will blow out the walls of this dark little flat in which I have lived with reasonable happiness for forty-three years. Blow my cover, my camouflage, my concealment. When I pull the tab that seals the thick brown envelope, the walls of the house will be exploded outward and I will be discovered, naked, bandy-legged, prick in hand. But the writer's ego is such that I am willing to sacrifice everything, even happiness, for some measure of acclaim.

I turn the package in my hands, enjoying its heft. I recognize Jennifer Down's handwriting, the familiar cobalt-blue ink. Her script is large, open, generous—*Frank Bois, 14 Nicholas Road, Cork, Éire*—not at all like my cramped and stingy scrawl. The book is thicker, heavier than I imagined it might be.

I place the package on the chair and make tea. Then I put the teapot into the sink and pour myself instead a tumbler of port. It is a very good port, ten years old, black as bramble and thick as honey. From the advance for my book, this has been my one extravagance: Cockburn's best.

At last I pull the string across the top of the envelope and the book slips into my hands. Purple-black, the color of a dear port. Pale yellow letters—*NIGHTSTALK An Astronomical Pilgrimage FRANK BOIS*—set against a Renaissance chart of the constellation Virgo, the virgin's languorous nude body faintly etched onto a field of deep night, a sheaf of wheat in her hand, each star wreathed in a gloriole of light. Jennifer's cream-yellow card is clipped to the jacket, and in her hand, *Frank, It's a book! And a handsome one at that*.

I turn the book. On the reverse, the photograph: the minuscule night pilgrim in his roll-collar sweater.

It is a bit of a shock to see him there. He is almost the same person I see in the mirror but not quite. There is something more, something that is the creation of the photographer, Tony Hanks: a seamy, self-confident intellectuality, the stuff of Sunday-newspaper magazine supplements, *A Room of One's Own: an interview with Irish writer Frank Bois*, that sort of thing. The star globe looms at the author's shoulder like a fortune teller's crystal ball, a necromancer's plaything. The books, the scattered papers, the eccentric dishevelment. I stare, astonished. Is this person me? This person whose image is affixed to 327 printed pages? Perhaps this person in the photograph is, after all, the *real* me, and the person I see in the mirror—that stump-footed little man stewing in his sorry juices—perhaps *that* person is the fiction, the creation of the warped fun-house mirrors of the author's mind.

It was at Jennifer Down's suggestion that names in my book be changed. I had written *Nightstalk* as a straight-up memoir of a lifetime of experiencing the night sky, and the personae of my original manuscript bore their own names: Bernadette Bois, Jack Kelly, Roger Manning, Emma Kelly, Hans Scrieber, all the rest. But Jennifer Down was worried, I suppose, about the legal situation, the possibility of libel; some of these people are still alive. *It works better if the personal anecdotes are fictionalized*, she insisted, and so I changed the names, some of the venues, bits and pieces of the scenery, and added a disclaimer. Only the narrator keeps his given name: Frank Bois, the blasted blastula, stunted from parturition, drunk on beauty, seedy pornographer of stars.

I open the book at random and read: *At the age of ten I was sent to the Christian Brothers school in Cornhall Road. At my mother's request, but grudg-*

ingly, I was excused from religious instruction. While other students were drilled on the articles of their faith, I was banished to a tiny room near the brothers' refectory, a room with no window. A chair and a desk faced the wall. There is nothing fictional about this episode. It is *fact* that the school was in Cornhall Road and it is *fact* that the godless boy's place of exile was windowless. The boy was far happier in solitary confinement than in the classroom. He did not then, nor would he ever, become a willing participant in the rituals of the school—the classroom conspiracies, the cloakroom banter, the sports-ground games. Other students made friendly overtures. They proffered invitations. They teased him sportingly, not meanly, about his size, and tried to include him in their fun. He felt condescended to, pitied, and kept to himself. The boy's seclusion was self-imposed. He was a voluntary exile. Nature had spawned him of the race of teratoglyphs—centaurs, hippogriffs, unicorns, rocs. He was hatched by a serpent from a cock's egg. He was not meant to live among ordinary boys and girls.

In the eyes of his teachers, the redoubtable Christian Brothers, the boy was—*I was*—doubly cursed. I was unbaptized and a dwarf. It was hinted that the two afflictions might be related, that my stunted stature was caused by Original Sin, and that the blemish might be washed away by baptism. I was wise enough not to take these hints to heart. I had no faith in the power of water to relieve me of my deformity. I entered upon adolescence with a hopeless *idée fixe*: my transformation, if it came at all, would be by the power of beauty. Call it, if you wish, the Frog Prince Syndrome, call it pathetic, but take my word for it, it was agonizingly real.

I will never forget the moment I realized that night has a *shape*. I was sitting at my solitary desk in that windowless room near the brothers' refectory. In a classroom down the hall my classmates were reciting the Seven Gifts of the Holy Ghost, or some such flummery. At the top of the desk was a circular hole that had once received an inkpot. With my thumbnail I absentmindedly scratched two lines into the varnish, two tangents to the hole that met in a vertex, two intersecting lines that touched the circumference of the hole like the sides of a wizard's pointy cap. I looked at the two lines and I said aloud, *That is the shape of night*.

Night is the shadow cast by the earth. Because the sun is bigger than the earth the shadow is cone-shaped. Earth wears night like a wizard's cap. When Brother Dolan came to fetch me for maths, I showed him my discovery. *You were meant to be practicing your script*, he said. From that time on—until the publication of my book—I kept my night-thoughts to myself.

A simple discovery—old varnish, a thumbnail, a circular hole meant to contain an inkpot, a child sunk up to his chin in the quicksand of solitariness. Here is what I read in the premier copy of my book, freshly printed on crisp paper, still scented with odors of the bindery, page 156: *Every object near a star wears a cone of night. Near every star there is a ring of cone-shaped shadows that point into space like a crown of thorns. The sun's family of nights includes the shadows of nine planets, several dozen moons, and an army of asteroids. Every particle of dust in the space of the solar system casts its own tiny pyramid of darkness. The sun bristles with nights like a sea urchin prickly with shadowy spines.*

53

I pour myself another tumbler of port. It is half-eleven in the morning and already I am slipping into a slough of intoxication. My book—hot off the press—lies abandoned on the floor. I am pondering instead an advert in last Sunday's *Observer* color supplement for a line of mail-order swimwear. *Create a Sensation on Vacation. Fresh from California with a Riviera Feel.* A model in a purple and black tank suit, cut high on the hip. Stunningly pretty. Wet hair falling across her shoulders. Dry sand on her hands, hip, and thigh.

Handy Paige knocks at the door.

He has received *his* copy of the book.

"It's a fukkin' beauty," he exclaims as I open the door.

He waves the book under my nose as if it were a bouquet of flowers I was meant to smell.

"A beauty. A fukkin' beauty."

"I'm glad you're pleased."

"Pleased? Yer fukkin' right I'm pleased. This little book is goin'ta make me rich. It's goin'ta make us both rich!"

I indicate my tumbler, offering him a glass of port. He pushes it away.

"I've heard from my nephew, the kid who lives with Jennifer Down. He says they're going *all out* on this one. All the big stores. W. H. Smith's. Waterstones. The works. Piles and piles of books. Special displays. That sort of thing. The fukkin' works."

His hands flutter like startled pigeons.

I sink morosely into my chair. The purple-and-black—clad beauty lies on the armrest. *Sizes mixed with pleasure. Just ask.*

Paige stands in front of the fire, wriggling his backside toward the heat.

"We've got to get you out on the hustings, man. We've got to get you *over there*. Ya can't sell books sitting on yer arse in Cork. People don't buy a book, they buy a concept. *You're* the concept, Bois. The sex-crazed poet dwarf. We gotta sell a concept."

"I'm not 'sex-crazed,' Paige." I glance at the swim-suited beauty.

"Listen, Bois, I don't give a fuk about your private life. I don't give a fuk about *reality*. I sell books. I've got twelve percent of yer lovable arse."

"I have no desire to leave this flat, Handy. And I certainly don't intend to go to England."

Paige raps me on the knees with his copy of my book. He dances from one foot to the other.

"It's too late for that, Bois. Too late to crawl back

in yer hole. I sold this thing. Ya owe it to me. Fer Chrissake, man, you owe it to yerself."

I am suddenly depressed by the emptiness of the tumbler. I am depressed by my swimwear princess.

"OK, OK."

His black eyes blaze, expelling sparks into the gloom.

"OK. So you don't do it for me. You don't even do it for yourself. You do it for art. This is *art*, Bois . . ."

He waves the book like a revolutionary flag.

". . . art. You don't create art and then bury it in the back garden. Art is meant to be seen. To be *read*, Bois. Meant to be read. You get out there and sell *art*. I'll take my twelve percent. We're both happy."

I shrink in the force of his badgery heat, sink deeper into my chair. I long to fill my empty glass but haven't the conviction to rise.

"Leave it to me, Bois. I'm in touch. I'll take care of everything. You're the fukkin' genius. I'm the businessman. Just leave it to me."

He grasps the book in his two bristly hands and shakes it under my nose.

"Piles," he says. "Piles and piles of books. Posters. Autograph sessions. The works."

My head is in my hands. *The 1990 Riviera Swimwear Collection. Dynamically different, the talk of the press.* Handy Paige lets himself out the door. The sex-crazed poet dwarf pours himself another drink.

Fairies. Fairy hills. A boy and his dog.

It is midafternoon on the day of Paige's visit, one of those wretched damp gray Irish autumn afternoons, sodden cotton wool piled against the windows. Handy Paige's agitations of the air have stilled. The fire in the grate has settled into a heap of yellow ashes. The scuttle is empty. An empty bottle leans drunkenly against the fender.

The author considers himself. By any standard this day should be one of celebration. His book, long in the making, has been accepted and published by a prestigious house. The publisher intends to make the book a success. It is a handsome thing, done up smartly on good-quality paper. A fetching jacket, eye-catching. On the reverse, a photograph of the author, not unhandsome.

So why this enormous feeling of collapse? Why at this moment of triumph does he feel like a gutted fish? The frog prince trapped in his clammy skin, warts and wrinkles, bulging eyes, anus caked with excrement and mud. Look! There, at the corner of his eye, moistening that sad glutinous globe, a tear.

A boy and his dog. Out along the Douglas Road, past Donnybrook, up into the hills where today sprawls the airport. Honeysuckle and bramble. Blackberries fat as plums. Foxglove and montbretia. Warm sun. Canis Minor threads the hedges, loping through fields, splashing in ditches, scaring up rabbits and magpies. A liss. In the middle of a broad pasture, a fairy fort, an ancient earthen wall, a grass-crowned O. The boy takes a seat on the circular mound, the dog lies panting in his lap. He has heard in school of fairies taking babies from their cradles, boy babies especially. Taking them away to the fairy hills, feeding them on fairy food, including them in fairy revels. The boy wished himself snatched. There was a risk, he knew, to body and soul; the danger is greatest, his teacher had said, for an unbaptized child. It was a risk worth taking. He did not believe in fairies, but if at that moment the fairy hill had opened up, inviting him to enter, he would have rushed in. He would have given up the world of sunshine and honeysuckle, foxglove and montbretia, for fairy transmutation, to be made into a thing of proportionate limb, fair, elfin, beautiful. Never to come out again except at night. Except by starlight.

The memory—the memory of that day on the fairy liss seeps up out of the past as if from some spawn-dark pool, reminding me of certain lines from Yeats. I lift myself out of my chair and rummage through the tumbling piles of books in search of my mother's morocco-clad volume of Yeats's poems. Yes. Here on the flyleaf is Manning's inscription. And here are Bernadette's notes and glosses, slashes, exclamations, checks, underlinings. One can almost see her pricking at the words with the nib of her pen, digging out the meanings, plucking for herself little garlands of voluptuous sound. I follow her winding path through the pages and find the verse I'm looking for, the terrible truth-telling lines that my mother has wreathed in a double gyre of dots, setting them off from all that comes before and after:

> *The wrong of unshapely things is a*
>   *wrong too great to be told;*
> *I hunger to build them anew and sit on a*
>   *green knoll apart,*
> *With the earth and the sky and the water,*
>   *re-made, like a casket of gold.*

55

Greta Scrieber came to Nicholas Road in her Ford motorcar and took Emma Kelly to Inishcarra. Greta understood that she was bringing an offering to her husband. By the time the car turned into the Coachford Road at Victoria Cross, she had misgivings. She had reached a conclusion: Emma was pathetically, dangerously naive.

The girl carried her belongings in a tattered leather case with a broken strap, borrowed from Mrs. Brosnan so that she would not go to Inishcarra bearing her possessions in a Jaffa Oranges box. She sat stiffly in Greta Scrieber's motorcar with the leather case on her lap, her hands fiercely clutching the handle, the broken strap held earnestly in place. She wore the floral print dress with white lace collar that she had worn to the Scriebers' dinner party. In the leather case were her one other dress, undergarments, stockings, a nightdress, toiletries (but no cosmetics), *The Imitation of Christ*, a paper-clipped pile of Hollywood pinups, and three dog-eared copies of *Silver Screen*.

She was remarkably pretty, not in a glamorous way, but with the prettiness of youth. It occurred to Greta that Emma was more a country child than city girl. Or she might have been a postulant fleeing the convent. Yet, there was something else about the girl that was— What was it? There was a *knowledge*, an unspecified experience, a sexual vulnerability. Greta Scrieber could just detect it, casting sidewise glances at the girl as the car hurtled along the banks of the Lee. It was—yes, it was in her eyes, and in the way she held her body, hunching her shoulders forward so as to minimize the fullness of her breasts. Even her skin seemed to radiate an unnatural heat, like a piece of metal repeatedly bent. Greta knew that her husband would see it too. Perhaps he had already seen it. Of course. Yes, of course he had seen it. He would have *known* that Emma was seducible. Otherwise he would not have risked rejection. He would have been assured of success even before he requested that the girl be brought into his house.

If it was not eagerness for sexual experience that Greta detected in Emma, then what was it? She was not certain. But there was no denying that this splendid girl possessed a *depth* and a capacity for love that had not been plumbed. Against her better instincts she found herself envying her husband.

The house at Inishcarra is tucked into a glen by

the River Lee and overhung by mossy oaks, gnarled pines, and sycamores. Two monkey-puzzle trees stand like sentinels at the gate. The garden was then bright with Greta's floral displays, put out in German rather than Irish fashion, in marching ranks of blossoms. Behind the house a path led through a green lawn to the bank of the Lee, where chalky water purled in pools of sedge and cress. Emma's bright room looked out upon the lawn through billowy chintz curtains. Her bed and dressing table were skirted in the same pink fabric and a sky-blue carpet covered the floor. On the dressing table lay a vanity set—comb, brush, and hand mirror—trimmed with mother-of-pearl. Above the bed hung a framed reproduction of Degas dancers.

Greta Scrieber stood at the door of Emma's room, watching the girl take in her new surroundings. Greta: forty-two years old, short dark hair in Louise Brooks bangs, smart trousered suit, pink Egyptian cotton shirt, a man's black silk tie; no longer sexually intimate with her husband but devoted to him, confident of his incomparable intellectual gifts, enchanted by his worldly friends. When Hans Scrieber travels to international conferences, it is *she* who accompanies him, not whoever is his current mistress. It is *she* who sits at his side among his brilliant colleagues, *she* who understands and discusses with impressive confidence the technical intricacies of his work, *she* who orders his life, sustains the conditions of his creativity, and receives in return a kind of loyalty that is deeper and more enduring than sexual union. Although her own erotic needs are neither as intense nor as constant as those of her husband, she has ample opportunities among their unconventional friends for satisfying her desires. She stands with her arms folded across her body, one hand beneath the open jacket of her suit, her chin resting on the back of her other hand. She watches Emma explore the room—timidly, tentatively, touching the curtains, stroking the mother-of-pearl–backed brush, dragging her finger as through water across the soft pink coverlet of the bed. Greta knows what will ensue. The exquisite psychological drama. The slow excitement of tension, the erotic charge that will build in the house like static electricity. The deceptions. The allurements. The subtle cruelties. The dénouement. What she does not know is how or with what degree of integrity Emma will survive her husband's artful *divertissement*. Emma: Twenty-six years old, of child-like demeanor. Taller than Greta, tall and whispery. Skin with a pale ceramic glaze, hair a tangle of coppery fire. Her dress is not stylish, nor does its color (Greta observes) suit her complexion. She is startled by the beauty of the room. Mrs. Scrieber has placed flowers—asters and cornflowers—in a cut-glass vase on the bedside table. The bed has two pillows, one encased with frilly lace, the other tucked carefully below. The dressing table is topped with mirror glass; another oval mirror hangs above. She turns and turns on the blue carpet and smiles, blushing at her employer. She is attracted by the room. She is troubled by the room. It is prettier than she deserves. Her tattered leather case sits on the floor by the dressing table, its broken leather strap lolling against the carpet like a speechless tongue.

She wonders if Greta is waiting for her to unpack the case, to put her things into the wardrobe. She lifts the case onto the bed but does not open it. She smiles. She sits on the bed next to the case; then, wondering if she should have removed the coverlet before sitting on the bed, stands. Her eyes sweep the floor of the room, round and round, finally fixing upon Greta's shoes, brown leather with dark tasseled laces, guarding the threshold of the door.

Emma was treated as a member of the family. Her room was on the same floor of the house with the bedrooms of Greta and Hans. She shared their bath. She sat with them at meals. Mornings she prepared Hilde for school and walked with the child to the National School in the village. During the day she helped Greta with the gardening or went shopping in the village with Greta's list. At three o'clock she met Hilde at school and walked her home. If the day was fine they pottered in fields or pools along the river. Hilde liked Emma. Emma liked Hilde. Hilde and Emma became friends.

On Saturdays Emma took the bus to Cork and attended the cinema.

Hans Scrieber was not impatient. He didn't rush his conquest. He was working on a thorny problem of nucleosynthesis, the forging of heavy elements in the hot interiors of stars. It was a problem of enormous consequence, for the elements that displayed themselves in the sun's spectrum and their relative abundances offered an unparalleled opportunity to confirm or deny his theory of stellar evolution. If he was successful in his calculations, and if they were consistent with the observed solar spectrum, the Nobel Prize would be his for the taking. For this work he needed the tonic of a prolonged seduction, his equations must be made to vibrate to the same frequencies as his heart, the two things must come to a conclusion at the same time. It was a matter of pacing, of rhythm. The charge must be carried slowly, as by the belt of a Van de Graaff generator, until the voltage will be increased no further and there occurs a powerful discharging arc of sustained brilliance.

He began with small things. A wildflower—a forget-me-not or a violet—handed to her when he returned from his walk, delivered with a mock Teutonic bow and a smile as thin and slippery as a butter knife. His masculine things—razor, strop, dark musky soap, heavy talc—carefully arranged on edge of the bath (he imagined her there, languid in the hot water, his things, like talismans, infiltrating her consciousness). A slight pressure of his fingers upon her hand when he took from her a book, newspaper, or serviette. Exactly the proper amount of wine in her glass, no more or less than he knew she would drink. And of course, at every opportunity, he entered her—silently, lubriciously—with his piercing blue eyes.

Two weeks passed and Emma demonstrated no response. She was oblivious to his presence. She was happy. The dark circles around her eyes, the shadowy unhappiness he had found so inviting, had vanished. Hilde—the offspring of one of Greta's affairs, not his own child—occupied her affections.

Toward Scrieber Emma displayed only distracted formality. He placed a bright ladybug on the back of her hand, holding her thin cold fingers in his own; she brushed it away and withdrew her hand. He removed a gorse spine from the sole of her foot, working at the swollen flesh with a sterilized sewing needle; his heart raced; he felt his penis extend with satisfying force against his leg; Emma was dreamily absent.

His work too had bogged down. The equations had become intractable, like clay hardening before it had received its form. He found himself unable to concentrate. The air in his study was heavy, stale; it was impossible to take a breath. His wastebasket was filled with false starts, crumpled yellow sheets of mathematical notes that led nowhere. He did not require consummation, it was too early for that. But it was essential to know that he had successfully implanted the germ of desire, that his blandishments had taken hold. Of this he saw nothing.

When she was away to Cork, he visited her room.

In a leather case on the floor of the wardrobe he found the cinema magazines. And the snipped-out photographs of Hollywood stars. And the holy pictures: St. Martin, Francis of Assisi, Christ with gaping heart. And a thin book. He sat on her bed and read Thomas à Kempis.

56

Hans Scrieber received his Nobel Prize. It was in all the papers. The 1968 prize for physics: "For sustained and highly original contributions to our understanding of stellar processes." Put simply, Scrieber explained starshine. It was Scrieber, more than any other physicist of our time, who made us understand why the universe is luminous with light. It was *his* intelligence that was the equal of the galaxies. When one considers that all of life, all intelligence, depend upon the energy of stars for their creation and sustenance, then one gathers the significance of Scrieber's work.

It is a great mystery that nature is conformable to the human mind. Why should the laws of nature be written in the language of mathematics? Einstein explained the mystery this way: the goal of mathematics is to create beauty, and the only explanations we are willing to accept are those that are beautiful. But how does this explain the ability of a mathematical theory to predict what has not yet been seen? Scrieber's equations were created out of Scrieber's mind to describe nuclear processes that occur at the cores of stars, yet they make predictions—exact, quantitative predictions—about the relative abundances of elements in the universe (how much carbon, oxygen, iron, and so on), and when we look at the observational evidence, we find agreement with the theory. Scrieber had his own explanation for this curious congruence of mind and nature: in the throes of creativity he participated with the God-head, entered *into* the mind of God as it were. He never doubted that the sheets of yellow paper upon which he performed his calculations were as literally instruments of revelation as the stone tablets that Moses brought down from Sinai. This is not to say that Scrieber was religious in any conventional sense; he laughed at the naïveté of Christian believers, and at the naïveté of his pretty quarry as he sat on her bed reading her book of exhortations to the Christ-like life. Scrieber's God was abstract, mathematical. Scrieber's God was identical with the *plan of creation*. At his Nobel acceptance speech in Stockholm he said, "The physicist has no higher responsibility than to interpret God's *essential being*." He referred to the image impressed upon the medal of the Swedish Academy of Sciences, which he received along with the Nobel medal: Nature portrayed as the goddess Isis emerging from clouds, the veil that covers her face being gently lifted by the Genius of Science. It had been his honor and pleasure, he told his audience (which included the king and queen of Sweden), to lift a tiny corner of Nature's veil, revealing her divinity. These remarks were met with thunderous applause.

By the time Hans Scrieber received the Nobel Prize, in 1968, he had returned to Germany, and two years later he was dead of stroke at age sixty-one. Reminiscences of his life have been numerous in the scientific literature, and at least one major biography has appeared. These public documents have helped me to reconstruct that part of his life which overlapped my own. But I have also tried to see the events of that time through Emma's eyes, for it was Emma who had played a crucial role in my own appreciation of the stars—that small epiphany that occurred long ago on the morning of the Perseid meteor shower—and she will have a further role to play in the life of young Frank Bois, a role that requires that I follow her relationship with Scrieber to its infelicitous conclusion.

In *The Imitation of Christ* Scrieber found the key that would unlock Emma's psychological armor and allow him to enter her mind. He was excited by this sudden revelation, and his seduction took on new urgency. He had made a mistake, it had cost him time. He had played to her as the gallant, the romantic, the cavalier flirt, and she had not responded. Now he must play another role— that of the saint. He must come to her as Christ came to Teresa of Avila, in tongues of flame, anointed, seraphic. There must be in the seduction something solemnly liturgical. He must *absolve* her of her innocence and baptize her into the *goodness* of sin.

But first he must establish his omniscience. He invited her to join him on his daily walks. She demurred. He insisted. Not overtly but in so many words he evoked his authority as her employer to persuade her to accompany him. This made him resent her just a little. It was not in his nature to *force* a seduction. It was not elegant. It was like using brute numerical methods to integrate a difficult mathematical formula when a simple substitution would do the trick. But he was impatient. He had wasted time. An important conference was approaching at which he hoped to present a completed theory for the carbon-carbon cycle in stars. The problem of springing the beryllium gap stymied him. He must move quickly toward a resolution.

He walked with her along the River Lee toward Dripsey. She was like a child at his side, like Hilde. Her nearness energized him, made him feel youthful and articulate. She pushed the sleeves of her cardigan above her elbows and the whiteness of her forearms filled him with pleasure. He talked. He spoke of flowers, their colors, their times of blossoming, their devices for pollination. He spoke of cross-fertilization and self-fertilization and the botanical advantage of the former over the latter. He gently tore apart blossoms and showed her the reproductive organs, the tiny sacs on slender stalks filled with golden powder, the pistil with its roughened summit upon which pollen is deposited, the ovary harboring minute seeds. He took from his pocket a folding magnifier and let her examine the details of this wonderful machinery. As she did so, he bent to let his cheek touch her mass of coppery hair, becoming drunk on her scents. His speech was full of words she did not understand: circadian, cleistogamous, dicotyledon, gymnosperm, Linnaeus. But there were other words that pleased her: quicken, nectar, doctrine of signatures, flower-clock, sleep of flowers. There was a soft music to his speech, obscure yet pleasing. Certain of his phrases made her smile. *Silky sails. Barbed fruits. Nodding blossoms.* He quoted Shakespeare: . . . *tongues in trees, books in running brooks, sermons in stones, and good in everything.*

And he spoke of his work, his theory of stars. He unfolded for her the life cycle of stars as if he were displaying the sexual organs of a flower. He described wildly beautiful nebulas filling the spaces of the galaxy, glowing with the hot pink light of hydrogen, where stars are born. He described the whirling dust, the gravitational collapse, the ignition of thermonuclear fires, the terrible weight of self-gravity that sustains the burning, the wind of neutrinos like an invisible spiritual force flowing outward from the massy core, then the swelling, consuming planets, and the star's fiery death as a supernova. His eyes blazed behind thick spectacles, intensely blue in the summer light. As he spoke, he moved his slender fingers, rubbing the tips together, as if the elements of his story were tangible objects he held in his hands. She understood none of it, none of this web of physics and chemistry that he spun over her. What she did understand was that he possessed a kind of magical influence over the universe. And for the first time she looked into his eyes, desperately puzzled, seeking the source of his baffling authority. That was her mistake: looking

into his eyes. She should have fixed her gaze—
as she had done before—on his watch fob, or the
cufflinks that danced near the ends of his coat
sleeves, or the pointy toes of his elegant shoes.
But she looked into his eyes, briefly. She felt dizzy,
dazzled by his knowledge, bewildered by her own
ignorance. She was stricken by the godlike *certainty*
that she saw in his eyes and by the unworldly beauty
of his speech.

He began to use phases he had taken from
Thomas à Kempis. *Beauty is within. As from a living
fountain. Love all men who truly love.* Tiny threads
of words, taken out of context. He wove them casually into his speech as he sat with Emma at the
breakfast table or as they pottered about in the
kitchen, making tea, washing up. *We often do not
realize how blind we are*, he would say, quoting the
medieval mystic, and the words sounded vaguely
familiar to her and reassuring.

One morning when Scrieber had bicycled to the
university and Greta was pruning the lonicera at the
bottom of the garden, Emma went into his study.
The study was "out of bounds," not only to Emma
but also to Greta and Hilde. The proscribed room
was on the ground floor of the cottage, off the dining room. French doors opened from the study onto
the garden, but these were always closed and covered by drawn curtains. The window that opened
onto the river was also darkened.

She thought, *It is like a church*.

Scrieber's desk was at the center of the room.
There were many bookcases and a side table with

a gramophone. She turned the record that lay upon the turntable so that she might read the label: Janá-ček, *Intimate Letters*. And books. So many books. She drew her finger along the spines of the volumes on one shelf. Servien, *Probabilité*. Eddington, *Mathematical Theory of Relativity*. Shrödinger, *Space-Time Structure*. Weber, *Die partial Differentialgleichungen der mathematischen Physik*. The words were resonant but meaningless, like the incantations of a magician, or the words used by the priest at Mass. On the floor were neat piles of scientific journals—*Physical Review, Annalen der Physik*—with slips of different-colored paper protruding from their pages. She sat in Scrieber's chair and placed the palms of her hands on the polished mahogany of the desk. She moved the swivel-chair backward, and forward again; it glided silently on the dark carpet.

Emma Kelly clicked on the green-shaded desk lamp and felt the warmth of the bulb on her hand. Her face, too, flushed warm, though her body shook with chill. His fountain pen lay on a yellow pad. It was a thick instrument, as thick as her thumb, jade green, with a gold band like a wedding ring at the bottom of the cap. The pad was covered with mathematical notations, strange squiggles and hieroglyphs, carefully inscribed in brown ink. Sheaves and sheaves of the yellow paper were set to either side of the desktop, right and left, in neat piles. From the back of the desk she lifted a small leatherbound notebook and riffled through it. The writing was in his hand, but in German, words she could not read. On the last page she found a list of paired initials, each followed by a date, and of these the last were *EK* but without a date.

Emma took to her bed. Her body shivered as with fever, but when Greta took her temperature it was normal. In the evening Hans came to her room. He sat on the edge of her bed and wiped her forehead with a cool damp cloth.

"May I bring you tea?" he asked.

She shook her head.

"A glass of cool milk?"

Again, no.

Her radiant hair, splayed against the pillow, was like the corona of the sun in eclipse, made to glow by the unnatural warmth of her body. Her eyes had retired into shadows.

"Let me feel your pulse," he said, tenderly but with authority.

She withdrew one bare arm from under the blanket and offered him her hand. Beads of moisture stood upon her skin. Her pulse was high.

"You pulse is normal."

She did not remove her hand from his grasp.

"You must let me become your lover," he said, matter-of-factly, as if he were telling her the time of day.

58

I am tempted to say "the rest is history." The morning after their first lovemaking she found a love note on her pillow. Other notes followed. He presented her with a paisley-covered paper casket containing scented soap and eau-de-cologne, and this she emptied and used to store her growing bundle of amatory declarations. He wove about her a web of beautiful words from which she found herself unwilling or unable to escape. His words and his body were all the same—hard, luminous, blinding, as when in a cinema she turned and looked backward into the brilliant eye of the projector. She closed her mind to any thoughts except the inevitability of his nightly arrival, the *tap-tap* at her bedroom door. It was always the same. He wore his moiré dressing gown and brought her some small gift—flowers, a copied verse, ribbons, a bottle of scent. He touched her cheek. He took her hair into his hands and kissed her forehead, cheeks, and mouth. He removed his gown and he was naked. When he came into her, she felt both pleasure and pain. That what they were doing might be sinful, he cleverly disguised. He made their lovemaking seem—how shall I say it?—*sacramental*.

She did not know it, but a date had been added to the final pair of initials in Hans Scrieber's red notebook.

The red notebook was available to Scrieber's biographer, but the initials *EK* are not explained in the great physicist's biography. Let me here unravel the mystery, add the details that Scrieber's biographer was unable to discover. Throughout the autumn months of 1958, Emma Kelly was Scrieber's mistress and the binding knot of the curious ménage in the cottage at Inishcarra. Emma understood—vaguely, without admitting it to herself— that Greta was a party to the liaison. Greta often came to Emma's room, early in the evening, after the three of them had taken coffee in the parlor. She brushed the girl's wispy hair one hundred strokes with the mother-of-pearl–backed brush and tied it with ribbons. Or she brought Emma one of her own exquisite nightdresses, purchased in Paris or Berlin. Or she sponged Emma's back and shoulders with cool water and dabbed her with scent. All of this, Emma knew, was by way of prelude to a visit by Greta's husband.

Certainly, Emma was exploited by a man more sophisticated, more experienced, and more intellectually *agile* than herself. And yet, as the consummation was achieved, one would not say that Emma thought of herself as a victim. She did not think of herself much at all. She merely *existed* in a suspension of willfulness, as if enveloped by the assuasive darkness of a cinema auditorium. As Scrieber caressed her body, she *watched*, as if outside of herself, as if her perceiving self hovered above the bed like a guardian angel, and—yes, this is the striking thing, the thing which muddies the moral waters— she thought herself beautiful. Her eyes—or rather the eyes of that watching other self—followed

Scrieber's hands as they made their delicate explorations of her breasts, her belly, and that tangle of coppery hair at the base of her belly, *and found pleasure in what they saw.* When he entered her, she found herself silently speaking ejaculations—*Jesus, Mary, Joseph, pray for me; Sacred Heart of Jesus, I place my trust in Thee*—not because she thought to invoke divine intervention, but because these familiar utterances were the most natural things that came to her lips.

59

Hans Scrieber experienced a period of intensified creativity such as never before. Between September and November of 1958 he produced three remarkable papers that would be mentioned with particular enthusiasm in his Nobel citation. Not only did he solve the intractable problem of the beryllium gap in stellar nucleosynthesis, but he also produced startling insights into the synthesis of trans-ferric elements in supernovas, and he calculated expected neutrino fluxes from sunlike stars. This latter work was of special significance. It offered for the first time the possibility of experimentally exploring nuclear processes taking place at the core of the sun.

In mid-November Scrieber went with his wife to a conference in Boston whose subject would be precisely the neutrino question. They sailed on the Cunard line from Cork Harbor, leaving Hilde in Emma's care at the house in Inishcarra. While the girl was at school, Emma went into Greta's room and removed a small photograph of Hans. This she carried in the pocket of her dress as she moved about the house. There was no urgency in her activities. She poked at the fire. She washed up the tea things. She removed the tea things from the cupboard and washed them again. She tidied. She straightened the curtains. In the afternoons she catered for Hilde. Vaguely, without fully framing the thought, she imagined herself the mistress of the house. When she found Greta's own belongings lying about— a woman's magazine, black stockings, a piece of jewelry—she covered them up or hid them away. She closed the door to Greta's room and kept it closed. One night she slipped into Hans's room and slept in his bed.

The Schriebers returned just at Christmas, which was not celebrated in the Inishcarra household.

Emma waited for Schrieber but he never came. At meals he was formal, preoccupied. His eyes had grown smaller behind his glasses, his smile thinner. He treated her with kindness, but without intimacy. There were no presents, no love notes. He spent long hours at the university, and when he returned to Inishcarra he retired to his study. She took care to wear her prettiest frock, to brush her hair, to bathe with the heather-scented soap he had given her. At night she went naked into her bed, as he had requested, and clutched the blankets to her chin. She listened for the sound of water running in his bath, for his footsteps in the hall, for his *tap-tap* at the door. He did not come.

In the first week of January there was snow. It lay upon the ground for two days and made a crystal fairyland of the garden. Hans and Greta stood at the dining room window admiring the beauty of the outdoor scene. Emma knew herself excluded.

That afternoon Greta approached her.

I have gone on at some length about the goings-on at Inishcarra because those events connect with my own life in several important ways.

Firstly, there is the thematic relevance, the painful apposition of brokenness and beauty. When I reflect upon Emma's fate, I think of Leda in Yeats's poem "Leda and the Swan":

> . . . *the great wings beating still*
> *Above the staggering girl . . .*

It is a poem that my mother elaborately annotated in her *Collected Poems*, not because she identified with Leda, but because she was determined to avoid Leda's fate. *She*, Bernadette, would not be a victim. She would put on swan feathers, she would pare *her* beak; she would not be used. But Emma—Emma was not Bernadette; she had neither Bernadette's resilience nor self-esteem. What the two women shared was beauty. And hurt. The hurt experienced by Bernadette during the last years of the war became the source of her strength. The hurt dealt to Emma at Inishcarra empowered her—

. . . Being so caught up,
So mastered by the brute blood of the air . . .

—to one cruel act of violence.

Then, there is Scrieber, the star prober, the man whose imperious intelligence refused to merely watch. Where he saw beauty, he took it as his right. No galaxy was too remote to be probed by the quickness of his mind. Mathematics was the instrument with which he ravished the stars, shaped them to his will, penetrated to their very cores. Because of Scrieber's forceful presence in the margins of my life, I have read his works, both the popular works on stellar processes—the Pearson Memorial Lectures, for example, that he delivered to the American Academy of Sciences—and the technical papers, insofar as I was able to penetrate the dense mathematics. I read these works as I might read about travels to distant lands; they did not change my immediate perceptions of the stars, but they created a broader, richer context for my meditations on the night.

And, lastly, there is Emma, who eventually returned to Nicholas Road, having walked the six miles from Inishcarra clutching her unclasped leather case like a baby in her arms (so fiercely had she pulled the latch strap tight, the thing had come loose in her hand). Canis Minor was wildly pleased to see her. And I too was glad for Emma's return, though it would mean giving up my bed again for the pallet on the floor. I was worried, however; we were all worried, even the dog. Emma had changed. Yes, she was still silent, still moody, but now her eyes, instead of being dreamily unfocused, were sharply fixed, as sunlight is focused by a burning glass. I watched her from my pallet, with the bedding folded about my head, as she prepared herself for sleep. I was chilled by the hard edge on her desultory beauty. The *déshabillé* that previously had stirred a vague exhilaration now evoked an unnamed fear.

Emma's scatterbrained charm was gone. It was as if wires had been pulled out of the cerebral circuits that link mind and action. Bernadette saw it. Bernadette recognized that Emma was poised for an act of violence, but could not quite bring the thing into focus. She imagined that Emma might do damage to herself, or to me. When she left for work, she insisted that I go to school, and forced me to take up my despised seat in the classroom of the Christian Brothers school in Douglas Road. After school I was forbidden to return to the house until Bernadette herself arrived at half past five, so I walked to Albert Quay and watched the freighters unload their bulk cargoes.

Emma neither spoke to us nor joined us at meals. She sat on the edge of her bed with the sheets grasped fiercely in her fists. Once, in the middle of the night, she got up from her bed and crouched in a corner of the room, her arms wrapped about her knees, staring into darkness. I woke, but I could not watch. I pulled the blanket over my head and wept.

61

Bernadette blamed herself for the tardy specificity of her vision. When it finally came into focus, she was waiting on customers in the kitchen-wares department of Cash's. At first she couldn't quite make it out. She thought that what she saw was the wet mat on the floor of the bath, or grass in the back garden after rain. She closed her eyes and tried to concentrate, while customers waited impatient and puzzled. She stared into the pool of intuition that was in her so fecund with images.

And saw the ears like floppy rags.

You become responsible, forever, for what you have tamed. If only my mother had refrained from giving me that little bit of wisdom, written as her inscription in *The Little Prince*, for ultimately it hurt more than anything else. It was me, after all, who tamed the dog. It was me who fed it, bathed it, took it as my companion on long walks into the hills. It was at the foot of *my* bed that Canis Minor slept.

So where was *I* when Emma pushed the dog into the rainwater barrel in the back garden? I was sitting on a bollard on Albert Quay watching clamshell derricks unload potash from a Hamburg freighter. It was Bernadette who found the dog, when at last she understood her intuition and rushed home from

Cash's. She looked first in the bath. Then in the garden.

Emma was gone.

I did not blame Emma for what happened to Canis Minor. I blamed only myself. Yes, it was unreasonable to take that guilt upon myself. Emma's act of violence could not have been anticipated, certainly not by an eleven-year-old boy, but the calculus of guilt is never reasonable. I was stricken by the *wrongness* that I should have possessed the dog's affection in the first place, for by then I knew I was born an outcast from the world of love. I looked at the sodden, lifeless animal on the garden pavement, retrieved from the rain barrel by Bernadette, and knew I had failed to protect what I had tamed.

Emma had taken a pound note from Bernadette's room and gone home to Cobh. Two days later she was admitted to Our Lady's Psychiatric Hospital in Cork, across the river from the university. Poor Emma. I do not believe that she was mad, although she was diagnosed as psychotic and locked away. If she seemed detached from reality, it was only because she had never known reality, or at least not much of it. Her knowledge of the world had been imparted to her by Hollywood and the church, the one steeped in fantasy, the other in myth. Scrieber had wormed his way into her tiny store of reality and used up what substance there was. When he pulled out, she collapsed like an empty sack. We will never know what distortion of love caused Emma to fix her catharsis upon the dog, but that act of violence removed from her heart the anger she carried away from Inishcarra. Just once, my mother went to visit Emma at the hospital. I went too. What we saw was extraordinary. Never had Emma looked more beautiful. She wore a gray institutional dress. Her marvelous coppery hair had been cropped short, shorter even than Bernadette's, so that it seemed no more than a warm radiance framing the pale features of her face. Her eyes were like—may I use an astronomical image? it is wonderfully accurate—her eyes were like the moon in eclipse. If, as Effa Kelly once said to me, the eyes are windows of the soul, then Emma's soul in her sweet detachment was more beautiful than ever.

One autumn night many years ago I turned my binoculars onto the full moon. It was a spontaneous gesture; I did not expect to see anything special. I was startled to see a flock of geese move across the bright disk. To observe the birds against the moon seemed a remarkable coincidence. Later, I learned that full-moon watching by organized groups of amateur ornithologists was one way the nocturnal migrations of birds were studied in the days before radio tracking and radar. My lunar geese, it turned out, were not so special after all.

Saint-Exupéry's Little Prince took advantage of the migration of a flight of wild birds to make his way from his small planet to the earth. As a boy, I dreamed of going in the opposite direction, of hitching myself to a flock of birds and making my way from the earth to a more welcoming planet, a Little Prince sort of planet more in proportion to my stature. The geese that I saw silhouetted against the moon were only a mile or so away, hundreds of thousands of times nearer than the moon, but the impression was strong that I had caught the birds far out in space, beating their way across the starlit gulf that separates the earth from its satellite. Only a little imagination was required to imagine those moon-bound geese dragging along behind them an eleven-year-old boy intent on escape.

I included the incident of the moon geese in my book. It is used by the *Times* reviewer for her lead. Yes, reviews of *Nightstalk* have begun to appear. Each Sunday morning for the past three weeks I have walked to the newsagent by Trinity Church to collect the *Times* and the *Observer*. I bring them home and place them in a pile by my chair. The pile is now half-a-foot thick, but the newspapers remain unread. I am afraid of what I might see. It is Handy Paige who shows up at my flat with the *Times* review. Quite a big one, all of page four of *Sunday Times Books* (excepting a quarter-page ad for a new novel by Morris West), and includes the author's photograph. We are not told who Penny Howth might be, but to her I owe the first appreciation of my novel to appear in the popular press. From among her charming mishmash of quibbles and exhilarations, my publisher will surely find the requisite number of marketable blurbs.

"Silly bitch," says Handy Paige.

"What do you mean?"

"Just what I says. She doesn't like the women in yer story."

He jabs his finger at the page of newsprint as if he were spearing peas with a fork.

" *The women in Mr. Bois's memoir are strangely abstracted from reality. They seem to incorporate elements of male adolescent fantasy.'* What the hell does that mean? Jaysus Mary and Joseph."

"Oh, she's right," I say. "Bernadette and Emma *were* abstracted from reality. I have described the two women exactly as I remember them. The memory is inevitably filtered through the boy's imagination. To have described them in any other way wouldn't have been true to the boy's experience. Anything else would have done harm to the truth."

"So, right. One of the women is your mother, right? *Your* mother. And Penny Hoosit doesn't like her. Sounds to me like she wants you to rewrite history."

Handy is so agitated the newsprint begins to disintegrate in his hands.

"No, Paige. She's right. What she says rings true."

"Whadaya mean 'rings true'? She's wrong! You want ta sell books, right? If she doesn't like yer book, she's wrong. Plain wrong."

I remove *Sunday Times Books* from his hands and smooth it on the desk.

"Would you like a cup of tea?"

"Jaysus, Bois. Do I look like the sort of bloke who drinks tea in the morning?"

I am trying to read the review; Paige hammers on the desk.

"And what else?" he blurts. "She says the book is a memoir trapped up as fiction. She says the book is *sentimental*. What the fuk is 'sentimental'?"

"Look, Paige, stop carping. The review is overwhelmingly positive. I like the way she begins with the episode of the geese against the moon. I like what she does with that image. It's a very perceptive reading of my book. And she may be right about her quibbles. I never wanted to change people's names, that's Jennifer Down's idea. The charge of sentimentality may be accurate also. As for the portrayal of the women, how is the author of the book supposed to know *anything* about women? Show me the woman who will give me the time of day. Ask Penny Howth if she will come here and sit with me by my fire. Just sit here and talk. With my squabby little legs sticking straight out in front."

"Fer Chrissake, Bois, stop feeling sorry for yerself. This is a book, it's not some fukkin' piece of yer soul. It's goin' ta make it or it's goin' ta sink. I want yer book to make it. If yer book makes it, we both make money. I make money. You make money. If ya've got money, Bois, who gives a fuk if ya've got a one-inch dick?"

"I don't have a 'one-inch dick,' Paige. That's part of the problem. My 'dick' is longer than my legs. So to speak."

Paige rolls his eyes and plows his fingers through his hair. His shoulders shake. He slams his fist into the review. The desk resounds and trembles.

"We're in the *Times*, Bois. We're off to a good start. We're going to London next week. Sign books. A launch party. A fukkin' *launch* party. I've a couple of interviews lined up. An' I'm workin' on more. I got it all worked out with Miz J. Down herself."

He reaches into his inside coat pocket and slaps an itinerary onto the desk.

"It's all here." He jabs.

I cringe.

"That's it, Bois. Pull yer pants up. If anyone says somethin's wrong with yer book, fuk 'em. I've been in this business for thirty years and take my word for it ya don't get anywhere bein' a molly. You're gonna go over ta London and act like ya own the place. Piss on their socks. Jaysus, man. Jaysus Mary and Joseph, I finally get a book a publisher likes and what do I get for an author. A *dwarf*. A fukkin' dwarf who hasn't got the balls to get out of his chair. But we can make that work to our advantage. We already *have* made it work to our advantage. It's the fukkin' key to our success. We'll put ya right up there at the front of the dwarf parade. The fukkin' king of the dwarfs. Just shape up."

He grabs up a copy of *Nightstalk* and thumps the photo on the reverse with his hairy knuckles.

"Pull yer pants up, Bois," he says. "We'll go to London and give 'em a sumthin' they'll never forget."

63

This is the *Times* reviewer's last paragraph: *It would be a shame if this book achieved success only because it is a courageous account of what it means to live with an emotionally crippling deformity. Frank Bois's beautifully crafted memoir deserves acclaim by any standard.*

64

Roger Manning stood motionless before his congregation, his head bowed reverently, his hands clasped together on his chest. After a dramatically prolonged pause, he lifted his eyes and said: "Evensong in St. Fin Barre's Cathedral, slight thing that it is, makes a contribution to something much larger, infinitely larger. That larger thing is the worship which is this minute being offered up to God by Christian people throughout the world, on every continent, in every time zone. The words of the service may be spoken in many languages, but they are the same, our common prayer. They proclaim the wonderful works of God in history, and the goodness of nature."

He paused and let his eyes drift about the nave of the cathedral, somnolently, just above the heads of the congregation. He glimpsed Bernadette, in the second-last bench, half-hidden behind one of the massive limestone pillars. And he saw just the top of her son's head.

He tapped his lips thoughtfully with his finger, then looked directly at the parishioners.

"The words of the service are complemented by the music of the cathedral choir. It is *beautifully crafted* music . . ."

He carefully enunciated the words.

". . . which the choir and the organist offer on our behalf. You might have noticed . . ."

He glanced over his shoulder.

". . . that the highest part of the cathedral is directly above the choir. Not above the sanctuary, but above the choir. It is here that our voices of praise and service rise up to God. The musicians offer on behalf of the people the most perfect music that it is our power to make. We all participate in hearts and minds."

He tapped his lips again, his other arm clinched about his waist under his black stole. He closed his eyes. He rocked gently on the balls of his feet. Then he turned briskly, flaring his surplice, and swept back to his place in the choir.

"Did you notice that your mannerisms in church are exactly those of the rector," said Bernadette later.

Frankie had been sent to his room upstairs. The boy was asleep, or perhaps reading. Roger lay on his back in Bernadette's bed. She sat astride him, her legs scissored beneath her, running her finger lightly along his naked body from his Adam's apple to his groin.

His eyes had that soft unfocused look they always had when he removed his glasses. She smiled.

"I suppose you are right," he said. "I never thought about it before."

"I love your body," she whispered.

"It's probably a natural thing for a curate to mimic the more experienced priest. It's not a conscious thing. I don't do it deliberately."

She said: "Even the voice. So solemn. Like listening to the BBC on the radio."

He laughed.

"Like play-acting."

He laughed again. "It *is* play-acting, I suppose. But that doesn't make it less important. All religious worship is a kind of play. There is no human activity more gracious than play."

She ran her finger along his erect penis.

She said: "Ireland is such a Catholic country, Roman Catholic, I mean. So few Protestants. Did you know there were more people in the choir tonight than in your congregation. Doesn't it all seem rather hopeless?"

"That's why I am happy in what I do," he answered.

She puzzled her brow.

He said: "It is because it is so hopeless that it is important. If half the Roman Catholic churches in Cork fell down, it wouldn't make any difference. There would still be just as much Roman prayer, just as much Roman ritual. But *my* voice matters. We are few. What I said tonight about history and nature is important. That is the difference between *our* voice and the voice of the Roman church. We affirm the *goodness* of the world. Roman Catholics emphasize the sinfulness of nature. We praise the Creator. They praise the Redeemer. It is important to affirm the difference. If it is hopeless, so much the better."

Bernadette bent forward and snuggled her face into his neck.

"*Joli,*" she whispered. "So hopeless and so pretty."

He wanted to say that he loved her.

Two floors below, Mrs. Brosnan snoozed by a faltering fire. One floor below, my mother made love to Roger Manning. I could hear their muffled voices, although I could not make out their words. I heard the creaking of their bed, like stress in some distant part of a ship on which I was a passenger. See, here in my diary from that time, the boy's description of their amorous noises: . . . *like a creaky ship*.

The diary, drawn from the sprawling pile on the floor by my desk, is a student's exercise book. I turn the pages, looking for clues to the man I have become. I barely recognize the boy's script, neater then than now, showing the influence of endless penmanship drills imposed by teachers on those unhappy occasions when I was forced to school— circles round and round, zigzags up and down, on ruled paper, endless solitary drills in place of the lessons the other children had in history, geography, and literature. My teachers assumed I was retarded, and they had reason enough to think so. I seldom spoke, even when spoken to. I refused to answer questions, though almost always I knew the answers. I simply sat, preferably at the back of the room, miserably mute. But there was something more, which had nothing to do with my silence or unsociability, something I have spoken of before: the assumption on the part of my teachers that a stunted body must necessarily contain a stunted mind. So while other students ciphered or recited, I was drilled in script. Not with a pen, as if with so sharp an instrument I might do damage to myself or to others, but with a big blunt pencil, on ruled paper, round and round, up and down. I didn't mind. I welcomed drill. It obviated the need for participation in the normal business of the classroom and allowed me to listen. What I heard, I learned. Only for catechism lessons was I retrieved from penmanship drill and forced to participate with the class (this was before my escape from religious instruction at the Christian Brothers school). I might not have an educable mind, my teachers assumed, but I did have an immortal soul. Even Hottentots, pygmies, red Indians, and golliwogs had souls. Only a *little* soul, perhaps, a dwarf-sized soul in keeping with the size of my body, but a soul that needed saving. And so I was asked to fold my arms and listen quietly as the other students committed to memory a catalog of virtues and vices, a vast unwieldy calculus of sin and a numerology of salvation. Exactly what was this "soul" that needed saving

I wasn't sure. Like most children of that time who were taught in Catholic schools, I imagined the soul as a circle, for that was how it was presented in the catechism. A pure white circle for a soul in the state of grace. A splotchy circle for a soul besmirched by venial sin. A black circle—as black as the ace of spades—for a soul damned by mortal sin. I carried such a circle somewhere inside my body, as I might carry a coin or keyring in my pocket, and I imagined it to be about the size of an old penny. Where inside? Not the head. Nor the breast. That little disk was implanted below the belly, near the root of my penis, tangled in the tendrils of my fantasies, buried in an adolescent's burgeoning sexuality as a leprechaun might bury a coin among the roots of a tree.

My religious instruction was canceled out by Bernadette's example. When I told her of the things I learned at school, she laughed. She did not dwell upon sin or salvation. Whatever existed was good, and she closed her eyes to anything ugly or evil. Alone in my garret bedroom, rain thrashing the slates, I heard from below the creaking labor of their love and I imagined a great bright splash of rain-wet goodness spilling off their bodies. Unfortunately, the goodness that enveloped Bernadette and Roger on their groaning bed did not easily translate up the narrow staircase. While my mother and her lover gathered milk and honey, I lay on my bed in the dusky garret, lapsed in fantasies, privately darkening the penny-sized disk of my soul.

It is all here in the boy's diary. The creaking bed. The rain on the slates. The rain turns to wind-driven sleet and clatters against the dusty panes of the little window that looks out upon the night. Somewhere out there beyond the stinging gray of an Atlantic storm, a myriad of stars shimmer in their blue auras. Planets puff with spores. Galaxies respire. The boy is a part of it. Look, here, at what the supposedly retarded child has written in his diary: *Everywhere, the world burns with life's flame.*

It was not difficult to guess what was in the package. The package was long and roughly cylindrical.

"It's a telescope," I said.

"Ha," said Jack Kelly. "Let's just see."

He laid his burden on the floor by the hearth and took out his pocket knife. He cut the twine that held the heavy brown paper in place. Bernadette and Roger Manning watched. When the paper was folded back, the barrel of the telescope was revealed, and next to it the folded tripod.

"Sure, 'tis yours, me boy-o."

My eyes became as big as the lens of the scope.

"'Tis yours. If it's OK with your mother."

I looked to her. She shrugged and smiled.

"But sure, *it's yours*," I pleaded. I did not wish to take Jack's telescope from him.

"Not anymore. I'm being transferred to Rosslare and I don't want to drag it along. I'm fed up with Irish skies. Too many clouds. And besides, I'm getting too old to sit out in the cold. It makes my bones ache. My girls haven't shown any interest in the stars. So Effa says, 'Give it to Frankie.' "

I placed my palm on the shiny red metal tube. The turning mechanisms were iridescent in fine films of lubricating oil. The wooden legs of the tripod had been polished to a luminous sheen.

I lifted the tripod and stood it on its unextended legs. Jack lifted the tube and showed me how to mount the telescope in its cradle.

"But . . ."

The thing seemed too grand to be mine.

"No 'buts,' " said Jack. "You can use it on the roof, but be careful you don't come crashing down into your mammy's kitchen."

He winked at Bernadette.

"We will miss you, Jack," she said.

"I'll miss you too, my Bernadette. You gave me something finer than any telescope. Look at this heart, Roger"—he thumped his big chest with his fist—"still burstin' with love for her."

"We're both lucky," said Roger Manning, somewhat flustered. He shifted from foot to foot. He savored Jack's domesticity. He wished it might be his and Bernadette's.

Jack patted my head. "You can use the telescope to discover a comet," he said. "Comet Bois–1959. The boys up at Dunsink will be green with envy."

"And Emma?" asked Bernadette.

"We are taking her with us. She's a wee bit better. They put the juice to her—"

He tapped his forehead.

"The other girls are drifting away. Effa will be glad to have Emma about."

Roger said: "Write to us, Jack. Especially let us know how Emma is getting on."

I wanted to speak. I wanted Jack to know how much I appreciated his gift—this marvelous glistening instrument. And the stars. The stars, too. He had given me the stars. I remembered the generous contours of his body as we sat on the roof looking at the night. I remembered the tackiness of the tar on summer nights and the coolness of the slates against our backs. I remembered the huge pink nets of his hands that he threw out to catch the constellations. Those caught stars fluttered in his hands like captive birds. And the stories—the stories that he wound about me like an endless string. And Emma.

My mouth moved. My face labored to speak.

67

If you look closely at Tony Hanks's photograph on the jacket of my book you will see a bit of the telescope—the eyepiece end of the tube—sticking out from behind a pile of books on the floor, just to the left of the author's legs. It has been lying there since 1972 when it was knocked off the roof by a gust of wind. The objective lens is shattered and the optics are knocked askew. With the money I make on the book I will have the instrument restored. Jack Kelly is dead. A restored telescope will be a kind of memorial.

I am not a telescopic observer. I prefer the night

as it presents itself to the naked eye or to binoculars. But Jack's instrument gave me much pleasure in the years before the rogue wind did its damage. The day the telescope came into my possession, I took it to the roof and pointed it to the place on the horizon where I had seen the moon rise the previous night (what I saw is all here in my journals). When the moon came into view, it rose night side first. The unlit side of the moon was above the horizon for almost a minute before I was aware of its presence. Then, quite suddenly came a scintillation of light on the crest of the distant hills, the deeply shadowed dividing line between lunar day and night, filling the eyepiece of the instrument with a glorious golden glow. It was like the rising backdrop of a stage set, a feat of theatrics suitable for an opera. Straight up out of the ground came the screen of light, miraculously magnified by the telescope. The Sea of Serenity. The sunlit peaks of the Haemus and Caucasus Mountains. A line of craters—Plato, Archimedes, Ptolemy, Tycho. As the full circumference of the moon's bright limb broke free of the horizon, I glimpsed the dark blemish of the crater Grimaldi. The whole spectacular show lasted but a minute. The rising had seemed long and ponderous, but it was almost instantaneous. The telescope had slowed time as it fattened space. When the rising was over, I took my eye from the scope. The moon shriveled to a dot of light and time quickened. I slumped back against the slates of the pitched roof, exhausted and afraid. The moon had risen like the Lady of the Lake from dark water, like

Titania from enchanted sleep—majestic, confident, golden, magical. I wanted desperately to share what I had seen. But with whom?

There was no one.

Roger Manning longed for domesticity. He was thirty-four years old. His eyeglasses grew thicker year by year. His hair was graying. His shoulders ached when he slept. He had developed a tic in his cheek. He was in love.

Early in his career he had been ambitious. He had imagined himself the dean of a cathedral or even a bishop. Certainly he possessed the requisite intelligence and suitable gifts of eloquence and oratory. He presented the lean good looks of a man on the rise, a man who might grow portly and gray with considerable distinction in a bishop's palace in Dublin or Armagh. But, regrettably, there were *the women*. Wives of parishioners. Unmarried spinsters. The spouse of the dean of St. Patrick's. Stumbling blocks. Why, he wondered, did they find him attractive? Even now the wife of the cathedral organist had taken to lingering in the sacristy as he divested after services. He recognized the signs of a calculated seduction. The softly lidded eyes. The immodest smile. The gratuitous compliments. Before, in Dublin, he would have toyed with her, leading her toward him, backing away, juggling with fire as it were, dancing on the precipice. Stumbling blocks. He didn't seek them. They unaccountably appeared in his path. And he had stumbled.

Now he found himself in love. With a woman who was in every aspect of character and dress an unsuitable complement to his ambitions. Wrong by class, wrong by education, wrong by religion. An unmarried woman with a son who was a dwarf. Bizarre. Unexpected. The ultimate, final, crashing stumble.

But, more remarkable, he was *glad* to have stumbled into Bernadette's world. He no longer felt ambitious. He no longer imagined the weighty heft of the episcopal ring on this finger, no longer dreamed of the throne and crozier. What he dreamed of now was Bernadette. And of a tiny parish in a provincial county. A glebe house. A garden. An occasional poem dashed off for the county newspaper. He would be chairman, perhaps, of the local historical and archeological societies. Take long walks with his wife along country lanes. Purchase a dog for the boy, a springer spaniel. Domesticity. Rural bliss.

And, oh, yes, the sex too.

But how? How would he bend her to his plan?

He must make her see what *he* saw. He must make her see the *desirability* of it all. Why should she work for a pittance as a shop girl when she could share his cozy ecclesiastical living? And the boy. The boy would be a man soon, presumably out on his own. Who would *she* have then? The answer was obvious. She could have *him*, Roger Manning, rector of St. Nowhere's. The two of them as happy as ducks in a rose-covered rectory.

He must make her see it.

Roger Manning moved out of his bachelor digs on the cathedral grounds and took a stylish flat in Sunday's Well, on the third floor of a stately house overlooking the Lee. Three big rooms with carpeted floors. Bright windows. A kitchen with a fridge. A tiled bath with a curtained shower. And behind the house, a substantial garden shared with the other tenants, a green lawn rising up the hill to a trellised gazebo. The rent for the flat was half his salary, but his needs were few and his savings were considerable. He fixed the place up to a high standard. Bought new linen. Potted plants. A framed reproduction of Van Gogh's *The Sunflowers*. A gramophone that played 78s, 45s, and the new 33⅓s.

When all was in readiness, he brought Bernadette home.

She followed him cautiously up the stairs, stepping to avoid rectangles of pooled light on the landings. The door to the flat was fitted with little panes of glass from top to bottom and covered inside with a lacy curtain. He turned the key in the lock and pushed open the door.

"Entrez," he said proudly.

"Merci." She bowed to him and stepped inside onto plush carpet.

"Très doux!" she exclaimed.

"Très doux, vraiment. Pour vous."

She sat on the carpet and removed her shoes and stockings. Then she turned and turned.

"It's like grass."

He watched, marveling, as she wandered through the flat. His dreams of domesticity took leaps and starts in his heart. She fingered through his stack of gramophone records. She ran her hand along the spines of the books on the shelves. She opened and shut the fridge door, once, twice, three times. She bounced on his bed.

"Do you like it?" he asked.

"The bed?"

"No, silly, the flat."

She shrugged. "It's yours."

Yes, he wanted to say, *but it can be yours, too*.

"Yes, but it can . . ."

"Shush!" she said. She looked into the bath.

"Bernadette, I . . ."

The words stuck on his tongue. He moistened his tongue and tried again.

"I . . ."

She pulled back the curtain of the shower. It was the first *real* shower she had ever seen, the first shower that wasn't just a spray nozzle stuck on the end of a flexible hose. And in its own enclosure, not in a tub. It was unheard of.

"Bernadette, I . . ."

"Get in," she said.

"In?"

"Into the shower."

"Why, for God's sake?"

She took him by the sleeve and pulled him into the tiled surround.

"Bernadette . . ."

"*C'est magnifique.*" She drew the curtain.

"What are you doing?"

She turned the tap.

A spray of cold water fell upon his face.

"For God's sake, Bernadette. We have our clothes on."

"Mais oui, comme il faut." She laughed and threw her arms about him, kissing him on the mouth.

He pushed her away, blinking behind his wet specs.

"I can't see," he sputtered.

Her hands were pushing back his streaming hair. His starched clerical collar had gone soggy.

"I can't see."

She was kissing him. She pulled on his shirttails. His fantasies of marital bliss were gurgling down the drain. When their mouths parted, his tongue at last found its speech.

"Marry me," he pleaded, eyes closed, lashes plastered on his cheeks, water dripping from his nose.

Bernadette had no intention of becoming a parson's wife. But she did enjoy visiting Roger's new flat. She *especially* liked Roger's new flat when Roger wasn't home. She liked taking showers. She liked wearing Roger's silk dressing gown. She liked sitting on the plush carpet in the bright reception room listening to Roger's collection of records—Rachmaninoff, Tchaikovsky, Chopin, Debussy. She devoured volumes of poetry from Roger's bookshelves while listening to *Claire de lune* or *The Moonlight Sonata*. And when Roger came home from his various priestly chores, she liked to make love on the plush carpet with a Beethoven symphony booming in their ears.

It wasn't quite what Roger had in mind. Bernadette never entered the kitchen. She never tidied the flat or watered the plants. She left her clothes scattered wherever they fell, and his clothes too. And—this he found most distressing—she always departed at night, no matter how late the hour, walking home alone through the city from the north side of the river to the south side, from Roger's elegant flat overlooking the Lee to her own rather shabby place in Nicholas Road.

No, it wasn't quite what he had in mind.

The worst part of it was, he didn't know where he stood. She recited romantic verses gleaned from his books but never spoke her own words of affection. Sitting naked on his bed, she read from Yeats:

> *He. That bird . . .*
> *She. Let him sing on,*
> *I offer to love's play*
> *My dark declivities.*

Romantic, yes, but she never did she say *I love you*. She never even spoke his name: Roger. Just those two syllables would have consoled him. *Roger, I am going home. Roger, pass the scones.* No, it was always, *I am going.* Or, *Pass the scones.* It's true, she had a way of touching his mouth with just the tips of her fingers and smiling into his eyes that struck him with a giddy paralysis. But she also had a disheartening way of avoiding any acknowledgment of his *importance* in her life—or of his *permanence*.

He was a kept man. A kept man who paid the rent for his own keeping. When, on that first day in the new flat, he had asked her to marry him, she had laughed. She stepped out of the shower and stripped off her soaked dress and undergarments. He stood in the downpour watching her through water-flecked spectacles as she toweled herself dry, distressed that his proposal had been dismissed so blithely, astonished at her beauty, disconsolate and ecstatic by turns. She was an enigma. It was not that she was complicated. On the contrary, it was her simplicity that baffled him. She seemed to live only on the surface of things, only in the moment, and if there was a person inside her lovely shell who needed love, then he could not find her. What Bernadette gave to him was both more and less than he wanted. He was inextricably caught in a trap with exits open and unguarded on every side.

There was also the matter of the rumors that had reached the dean's ear. The oblique reprimands. The exhortations to decorum. There was the strong possibility that he would be assigned to his eagerly imagined rose-covered cottage at St. Nowhere's as punishment for his indiscretions, but *without* the one person whose presence would make his exile desirable. Still, all of this might have been borne but for the arrival of the American.

Bernadette was away when he arrived on our doorstep. He was tall, gangly, loose. Blue eyes. Dirt-blond hair, thin on top, scraggly at the neck. A beak for a nose. Prominent chin. And a smile that exploded from ear to ear. His body slumped and jerked and stretched and collapsed as if he were a puppet on invisible strings. His limbs seemed to be articulated in such a way that they could flex in every direction. As I opened the door, his legs suddenly folded under him like the legs of a card table. He shrank by half. He was looking me straight in the eyes.

"Hi, li'l feller," he said.

Yes, that's exactly what he said, *Hi, li'l feller*, like in an American movie.

"Hi, li'l feller. Who sawed off your legs?"

It was impossible to feel hurt in the face of his ingenuous grin, that cheek-to-cheek keyboard of shining teeth. I laughed.

"I'm lookin' for Miss Bernadette Bois."

He pronounced it *boys*.

"My mother is working. She'll be home at the lunch hour."

His legs were still folded under him. He wore bleached-out jeans and an open-necked shirt with wide lapels. A zippered traveling bag lay on the floor by his side.

"And when would that be?"

"One o'clock."

"And would you mind if I just wait here for her? I've traveled a long way to see her."

No. The American visitor was *not* my father. The truth is even stranger. So strange that when Jennifer Down read my account of the American's visit in *Nightstalk*, she wrote in the margin of the manuscript *Makes demands on the reader's credulity*. My rebuttal was irrefutable. What happened happened. Fact is indeed sometimes stranger than fiction, and if truth strains credulity, then so be it. The American stayed in my book, but with a made-up name.

His real name, I soon learned, was Terry Klout ("My friends call me Terrycloth"). He was a bank clerk until he packed in his job to come abroad. He told me lots about himself as we waited for my mother. By the time Bernadette came through the door, Terry and I had become good friends.

As she entered, his eyes widened. I watched him: he gaped, admiring. She was twenty-nine years old and never prettier. She wore the yellow-striped frock required of all Cash's shopgirls. She carried a string bag containing a pint of milk and a bottle of Fairy Liquid. He sat on the edge of the hearth, appraising her. When at last he caught his wits and sprang to his feet, he towered over us.

"Miss Bois, M'am, my name is Terry Klout."

Bernadette said nothing. She placed the milk and washing-up liquid on the table.

"I'm an American. From Missouri."

He said *Mih-zur-uh*.

Bernadette said, "Yes?" She stood with her back to us, avoiding Terry's eyes.

"Well, M'am, it's kinda hard to say why I'm here."

"Yes?"

"I saw you once. Just after the war. On a ship, on the *California*."

Bernadette was silent. Then she said, "You were one of the . . . ?"

"No, M'am. I wasn't. I was too frightened. I just watched. I reckon you were the prettiest thing I had ever seen."

If the sudden appearance of Terry Klout after thirteen years strained Jennifer Down's credulity, my mother was no less surprised. And not a little worried.

"Why are you here?" she asked cautiously.

"That's what's hard to explain."

"Try."

"Well, M'am, you see, after the war—after I saw you, after we tried to help you get to America—after that, I mean, I went home, to Decatur—to Decatur, Missouri. I went home and I married my high school sweetheart, the girl I had gone out with in high school, and we had two kids, two sweet little girls, Lisa and Charlene. Lisa's the oldest but Charlene's smarter. Both girls are blondes like their mother. I worked—in the First Citizens Bank, nothing important, just a teller, although, well, sometimes I helped with loans. And on weekends I raced motorbikes. I was as happy as a . . . Then Marcia— that's my wife, her name was Marcia . . . *is* Marcia, I mean, she's still Marcia—took a job at the White Castle making burgers. You know, those little—"

He made a square with his thumbs and forefingers.

"—twelve cents?—"

He struggled. I laughed.

"—just to help out while the kids were in school. We didn't really *need* the money. I didn't want her to work, I told her that, but she was bored just sittin' around. Or that's what she said. Anyway, she wasn't at the White Castle three weeks when she ran off with the manager. One day she up and said, 'Terry, I'm going to live with Tobin.' Just like that. Came right out of the blue. Took the kids, too."

I couldn't help but laugh again. There was something hilarious about the way he recounted these improbable American events. I laughed. Terry didn't seem to mind. He shifted uncomfortably from foot to foot. He was as limber as a rubber man. His bones were elastics.

"There weren't anything to stay home for. So I quit my job, sold my car and my cycle—got more for the cycle than for the car—and came to Europe. Just to bum around, I guess." He laughed. "I know I'm a little old to be bummin' around. It's like somethin' the kids do."

"Yes?"

"Oh. Yeah. Well, I mean—when I got to London, I started remembering you. I guess I had never really forgot. Like I said, you were the prettiest thing I had ever seen. And I had never seen . . . I was a young kid then, but you were even younger. I had never seen . . . Anyways, I never forgot."

He reddened. The hair on his arms, I noticed, was yellow.

Bernadette was wary. "How did you find me?"

"Well, I left London and came to Cobh. That was

the last place I'd seen you. Then I came here to the city and looked through the newspapers at the library. I found a story about you being put ashore. And about your runnin' away an' all. The story gave the name of a guy, an immigration guy. Look, here's the story, I made a copy."

He unfolded a photocopy.

"Jack Kelly, his name was. I tracked him down. He's at a place called Rosslare. Anyways, I found him. At first, he wouldn't tell me anything. But I could see that he knew where you were. I mean, it was in his eyes. His eyes were all smiley sort of. So I just kept on badgerin' him and finally wore him down."

He grinned. I looked at Bernadette. Her eyes were narrow and skeptical, but I could see that she was reassured by Terry's smile.

"I just wanted to see what had happened to you," said Terry Klout. "I knows it sounds crazy, but I just wanted to see."

71
*

In my book I give Terry the name Calvin Jones. I don't know why, it just seemed a good Protestant Midwestern sort of name. The Calvin of my book doesn't have an unusual nickname, not like Terrycloth; he is just Cal. And I made him come from Kansas, not Missouri. The only thing I know about Kansas is what I read in the *Wizard of Oz*. It is flat, I guess, and mostly farms. And tornadoes.

In my book I painted a picture—in words, that is—
of Calvin Jones out there on the prairie racing
around on his motorcycle, stirring up huge clouds
of dust, roaring down flat gravelly roads with corn
as high as an elephant's eye stretching away for a
hundred miles and great dangerous thunderheads
heaped up on the horizons. Maybe it's not like that
at all. Maybe when my book reaches America—if it
does reach America—Terry will laugh at how I got
it all wrong. For all I know, Kansas and Missouri are
as different as day and night. But Terry won't have
any trouble recognizing himself. Of that I'm sure.
The Calvin Jones of *Nightstalk* is the real Terry.

Terry's appearance at our door after thirteen
years doesn't strain *my* credulity. I can understand
his motivation perfectly. I am forty-three years old
and I remember with photographic vividness a few
moments at the age of ten when I watched from the
attic window as Emma Kelly bathed at the basin. I
have described what I saw—the dawn-struck aureole of hair, the curve of spine plunging to that shadowy declivity where her nightdress fell about her
hips, the bare feet on the splintery boards of the
floor. I fell in love at that moment and I have been
in love ever since, not just with a disembodied *ideal*
of beauty, as I once imagined, but with Emma. I
have not seen her for—what is it? thirty-three
years—but if she walked in the door right now I
would love her no less than on that meteor-streaked
morning in 1957. So I can appreciate how Terry
Klout might nurture a memory of Bernadette for
thirteen years, a memory of a girl whose favors he
had not accepted, perhaps because he alone of all

those young men on the *California* was unwilling to take her casually. He had fallen in love with the girl they sought to help.

Images can lodge themselves in the mind with a tenacity that not even emotions can have. *Nightstalk* is a catalog of images, celestial and terrestrial, pure visual experiences. It was a visual image, I'll wager, that stayed in Terry's mind—like one of those amazing seeds that remain fertile for a thousand years in a pharaoh's tomb and blossom when exposed to water and light—so that even if he was not consciously aware of why he decided to "bum around Europe," it was the image of Bernadette that drew him here. At sixteen she had been, as Terry said, *the prettiest thing he had ever seen.*

She was no less pretty now. And when she walked in the door where Terry and I awaited her return, his face lit up with a fierce awakening. I recognized, even then, what it was.

It was love.

72
*

Terrycloth liked me. I mean, he *really* liked me. My mother accepted me—yes, that's the word, she *accepted* me, as she accepted the air she breathed and the food she ate. I was a *given* in her life, as much a part of herself as her own limbs. Jack Kelly loved me in a kindly way, a generous grandfatherly way, and his love was important. But Terrycloth—Terrycloth *liked* me. He was the only person in my life who liked me for what I am. He enjoyed my company. He wasn't at all nervous about my deformities. He wasn't oblivious of them, either. He joked about my size. He called me "li'l feller." He teased, but not meanly. His joking gave me confidence at a time when I was struggling to understand the huge *injustice* of my affliction. *Hey, li'l feller*, he'd say, *let's go get a brew*, and he'd take me to a pub. I'd scramble up onto a bar stool and he'd sit down beside me, a Guinness for himself and a lemonade for me. He wasn't the least bit concerned when other patrons cast curious glances in our direction, wondering who was this gangly American with the dwarfed Irish boy. Their eyes expressed surprise, revulsion, disapproval, as if, in violation of Irish hospitality, I had *imposed* my ugliness upon a guest. I know that one need not be mean spirited or uncharitable to react with aversion to my presence in a public place; it is an unconscious, protective reaction, an instinct to exclude from one's territory the alien, monstrous, and threatening. People do not wish to be reminded of the damaged potential of their race, and those of us who bear the germs of deformity are held accountable. We are expected to hide ourselves away, as if seclusion and isolation will allow the flawed germ line to wither. Even the most kindly and unprejudiced persons reflexively cringe in my presence. They might not know that they do it, but I know, I see.

Terry didn't cringe. Terry laughed. *Pug*, he called me. He'd squash my nose with the flat of his thumb and wink. *Ya got a face like a bulldog*, he'd say. We talked "man to man." He told me about his "shit-kickin'" motorcycle, "a big mean Harley-D," and about his automobile with "dual carbs" and "chrome pipes." I did not know exactly what dual carbs were, or chrome pipes, but the machines sounded exotic and wonderfully American. In those days there were few cars in Ireland, even in the city. Terry's stories of dirt-track drag races and highway joyrides at ninety miles per hour made me feel like a real hot-rod American—gunning engines, burning rubber, choking on the blue stench of partly burned hydrocarbons, with prairie sunlight glinting from polished chrome.

In turn, I told Terry about the night sky, about things I had seen—moon bows, shooting stars, conjunctions, auroras. He listened. He was interested. *Jeez*, he said, *I never saw any of that stuff*. He had lived under prairie skies all of his life, huge cloudless skies that rested on the horizon like an overturned bowl, and he had never looked at the stars. I was twelve years old, I lived in a city, mostly under clouds, and I had seen more than him. I showed him my diaries—the notes, the sketches. *Jeez*, he said. He liked me. We were pals.

But I knew *why* we were pals—the lanky American and the dwarf child. Terry was courting Bernadette. So it all came down to beauty after all.

For a month he lived in a boardinghouse near the railway station and came every day to visit us. When Bernadette was at work, he played around with me, and when Bernadette was at home, he folded himself into the chair by the fire and waited. Waited and watched. His eyes never left her. I don't think it occurred to him that he might be intruding himself into our domestic arrangements, or that he might be unwelcome. He watched and grinned, those corn rows of shining teeth stretching from horizon to horizon. Bernadette went about her business, and Terry waited and watched and cracked jokes with me. She pottered in the kitchen and half-listened to his stories of dirt-track triumphs drifting in from the reception room. At ten o'clock in the evening she would say to me, "Time for bed," and off we went to our respective rooms. She did not say good night to Terry, or good-bye. She left him sitting by the smoldering fire. He let himself out and walked across the two arms of the River Lee to his boarding-house in Lower Glanmire Road.

"Miz Bois," he said one Sunday morning, "do you mind if I take Pug-face here for a ride on a bike?"

She shrugged, as if to say *Do what you please*.

He had rented a big British machine, a Triumph 500 I think it was. It was parked in front of our house, in the Nicholas Road. When we went outside, the bike was surrounded by a crowd of kids.

"OK, urchins, move aside," said Terry good-naturedly. "Splitsville. Vamoose. Time for us men to go for a ride."

He kick-started the machine. It came to life in a deafening roar. He slung himself across the saddle and I climbed up behind. Again and again he cranked the throttle, racing the engine. The kids plastered themselves against the walls of the houses. Pauline was there, and Bridie, and Marcella.

"Hang on, Frankie," Terry shouted. I wrapped my arms about his waist.

He dropped the machine into gear and the big Triumph leapt forward, tires squealing, street dirt flying, to the top of the hill. Terry turned and thundered back down the hill toward Douglas Road. A face appeared at every window. The kids watched in wonder. We turned into the Douglas Road and roared off toward the south. I buried my face in Terry's jacket. I was sublimely happy.

We went to Crosshaven, then out along the cliffs to the harbor's mouth. It was the first time I had seen the ocean.

"There's two thousand miles of that stuff between here and America," said Terry. "Jeez, what a lot of water."

Then he said: "If your mother hadn't been put off the ship at Cobh, you would of been born in the Yew-Ess-of-Ay."

I was struck with a terrible sadness. I suppose I imagined that if I had been born in America, I would have been born whole, as if transportation across the ocean might have repaired the mistake in my genes. I had been so enthralled by Terry's tales of life in America that it did not occur to me there might be dwarfs in that place too. I turned away from Terry so that he couldn't see the tears welling up in my eyes.

In a pub in Crosshaven he let me drink from his pint of Guinness. I drank half the big glass of black stout and wiped the foam from my mouth onto my sleeve just like Terry. I wished it might have been him who made my mother pregnant—tall, lanky Terrycloth; grinning, crazy Terrycloth from Decatur, Missouri.

That night at ten o'clock Bernadette said to him, "You are always here anyway, you might as well stay."

His face worked furiously. He bit his lip. He flexed his long arms and cracked his knuckles. "Well, M'am, I, uh—"

"I'm going to bed," she said. "If you want to come, come. If not, lock the door on your way out."

She went to her room.

"Well, pal, whadaya think?"

"I think she wants you to stay," I said.

He stayed.

73

That was the summer of the fabulous auroras.

The sun went crazy, spewing charged particles into space. Protons and electrons flew across 93 million miles of emptiness and smashed into the atmosphere over Cork. Over entire northern latitudes, actually, but to me it seemed as if the show was for my benefit alone.

We had a stretch of cloudless weather, skies clear from horizon to horizon and illuminated with spectacular lights. It was all the talk on the radio. And in the newspapers. Every night I went to the roof and waited, hoping for a display. I was seldom disappointed. Yellow starbursts. Chartreuse curtains. Shimmering draperies of fuchsia light. During the best of these marvelous displays, I climbed back into the attic bedroom and stamped on the floor. *Come up and see,* I shouted. And Terry came, naked but for white briefs, and climbed with me onto the kitchen roof, folding himself like a carpenter's rule to get through the window. We sat on the tarred slope where I used to sit with Jack. But I didn't snuggle against Terry. I was too old for that now. And I didn't say a word. I just let him look.

"Jeez," he said.

"The particles come from the sun," I said. "It's the particles that make the air glow. They are blasted off the sun by magnetic storms. Some of them travel at close to the speed of light."

Terry's skin was gooseflesh.

"How do you know all this stuff?" he asked.

"I read books. Jack Kelly taught me lots of things. He's the one who first brought me out here."

The sky to the north of the city was a waterfall of color.

"Jeez," said Terry.

"The light is caused when the particles collide with air molecules. It usually happens near the north and south poles because of the earth's magnetic field. It's all just electricity and magnetism."

"Jeez."

Terry knew about motorcycles but I knew about the sky.

74

He took Bernadette for a ride on the bike. One cloudless day in May she climbed up behind Terry and they thundered off to Kinsale. Somewhere on the road between Kinsale and Begooly she became affectionate. Her hand crept down from his waist and worked at the zipper of his fly. Terry wasn't used to that sort of thing at forty miles per hour. He made the mistake of closing his eyes just as the road took an unexpected turn. The big Triumph 500 sailed across the shoulder, over a ditch, into a field of furze. Bernadette fell into the ditch unharmed. Terry ended up under the machine with a broken arm.

That was the end of their biking, but not of their lovemaking. Terry's cast was no deterrent. Bernadette found it provocative: something about the way his arm lay helpless in its heavy plaster sleeve.

75

And what about Roger? What about Roger Manning?

I suppose this is the time to raise the old question about whether a person can be in love with two people at the same time. In Bernadette's case the question is irrelevant. I'm not sure that she loved

Roger *or* Terry. I'm not sure that she loved anyone at all.

Bernadette was a romantic with no time for romance. In those days she was reading Daphne du Maurier, Norah Lofts, Anya Seton, that sort of author, good stuff and bad, all romantic. The *idea* of love, I think, appealed to her. But for Bernadette, it was only play-acting. She refused to be hurt. If she did not accept love, then love could not be taken away. She became intimate with two men at once because she was not committed to either one. She moved near the surface of their emotions, like a dragonfly on water, refusing to be ensnared by the sticky fluids of the heart.

Did she care that Roger or Terry might want more than games? Or that one of them might be jealous of the other? *Tu deviens responsable pour toujours de ce que tu as apprivoisé*, she had written in my copy of *The Little Prince*, but she felt no responsibility for either man. *I did not tame them*, she might have said, *they tamed themselves*. She was self-contained, a world unto herself. Roger and Terry entered her space at their own risk.

Terry accepted Bernadette's split allegiance with more equanimity than Roger. He was, after all, the intruder upon an established relationship, and he had won what Roger had not won, the occasional privilege of waking up in *her* bed. Terry was so struck by the forthrightness and spontaneity of Bernadette's lovemaking that he had not yet got around to feeling possessive. Roger, on the other hand, was frantic. As Bernadette's relationship with Terry revealed itself, he literally shook with fear that he might lose her. At Communion the eucharist trembled between his thumb and forefinger. The wine sloshed in the chalice. When he turned to bless the congregation, his hand cut a quavering cross in air. At breakfast the *Irish Times* rattled so forcefully in his hands that he could hardly read. The tic in his cheek became constant and violent. It wasn't as if she had changed. She came to him as before. She removed her shoes and pirouetted barefooted on his plush carpet. She sat cross-legged in the middle of the kitchen table dressed only in his gray clerical shirt while he cooked up rashers and eggs, and she was, he imagined, more beautiful than ever. She exhausted him in bed. On the face of it, nothing had changed. But everything had changed. The volatility of her affections oppressed him. He felt marginalized and murderous. He gave her poems, expressing his anguish, and she read them without understanding:

> . . . *your love is the curlew's cry*
> *on the high heathery slope*
> *in the first moment of waking,*
> *the beckoning of a bird not seen.* . . .

Roger was sick with jealousy, fevered, thin. What was worse, he felt himself morally sick, afflicted with unworthy emotions. His love for Bernadette was transforming itself into some monstrous manifestation of hate—for himself, for the intruding American, even for Bernadette. It was a metamorphosis he could not bear.

He laid upon a plan.

Did I inherit my mother's boiler-plated heart?

I was born and raised "in beauty's murderous blood." A crooked little man living alone in a crooked little house. They say there is a love in this world for everyone, that everybody has somebody somewhere. Can the crooked little man find his someone?

Only if he opens his crooked little heart.

I read the *Observer* review on the flight to Heathrow.

It is terrific. A smash. All I could ask for. *Nightstalk is a book for the solitary hours between midnight and dawn, full of dreams and equivocations, frightening shadows and night noises.* And on the same page a generous-sized advertisement from Penguin, including a photograph of the author and (already!) the blurb from the London *Times: Frank Bois's beautifully crafted memoir deserves acclaim.*

I pass the newspaper to Handy Paige. He squirms in the cramped economy-class seat of the Aer Lingus jet and enviously eyes the wider posher seats up front. His fingers drum the armrests. His knees twitch. Three little whiskey bottles rattle on his tray.

"Whatzit say?" He pushes the newspaper back into my hands.

I read a phrase or two: *Poised between poetry and natural history, between love and its absence, Bois's prose captures the essential loneliness of night . . . a melancholy pilgrim among the stars.*

"Fuk 'em," says Paige.

"It's a marvelous review."

"We don't need reviews. Reviews don't sell books. For Chrissake, Bois, *this* is what we need." He jabs his thick finger at my photograph in the advert. "*This* is what will sell your book. The fukkin' Irish leprechaun."

"You're not a nice person, Paige. In fact, you are distressingly obnoxious. It's hard to imagine how you manage to make a living as a literary agent."

"It was easy enough ta make a livin' when the business was run by men. In those days a deal was done with a drink and a handshake. Now with women runnin' all the big houses yer lucky to get a fukkin' letter. I'll tell ya, Bois, it's time for the likes of me to retire."

I nod affirmation.

"You don't have to like me, Bois. Just don't forget, I sold yer book. I know what people want, and you're it. The fukkin' LIT-ER-ARY dwarf." He jabs again at the photograph. "It makes 'em feel superior."

"Another endearing remark."

"If the publisher wants to sell your book, they'll sell it. If they don't want to sell it, it'll sink like a stone."

"But it's a good book, Paige. Surely good books succeed on their own merit. I would hate to be as cynical as you."

He tips the third of his Baby Powers into the plastic cup. The bottle is empty. He glances about for a cabin attendant.

"For Chrissake, Bois, you could write the fukkin' Bible and it won't sell if the publisher doesn't want to sell it. An' the opposite's true too. Put bare tits on the cover of the Cork telephone directory and it'll be a best-seller."

He rubs his hands together irritably.

"Good reviews *must* matter," I insist. I like Handy Paige. As obnoxious as he is, I like him.

He taps the *Observer* advertisement. "*This* is our ticket, Bois, the advert, not the review. This was dear, it cost 'em a pretty penny. Those London fukkers don't spend money unless they know they'll get it back. Jaysus, they're flying you over to the city. Puttin' you up in a hotel. They know what they're doin'. Selling books, that's what they're doin'. Do you think those editors at Penguin are fukkin' connoisseurs of literature? Do you think Jennifer Down gives a"—he jabs upward with his first and fourth fingers—"whether your book is Shakespeare or garbage? They've got a halfway good book by a fukkin' dwarf. Put those two things together and you've got dynamite."

We have been in the air for fifty minutes—barely time enough for Paige to gulp three whiskeys—and are making our descent into Heathrow.

"And why are *you* coming to London, Paige? They're not paying your fare."

"To keep an eye on you. To make sure my fukkin' dwarf doesn't crawl back under a rock. Look at yerself, Bois. You're forty fukkin' years old and it's only the second time in yer life you've been outside of Cork. Not since ya were a kid. If it wasn't for me, you would still be sittin' back there in that cave of a house with your head up yer arse."

"Paige, you miserable condescending bastard, I've been places you'll never go, places in the head, places in the heart."

"Fukkin' right, I'll never go. I don't know where you've been, Bois, but I don't want to go there. Just help me out in London. Do whatever Jennifer Down asks. Be charming. Play the congenial dwarf. Talk, for Chrissake, talk. Open your mouth and say things like 'This book is fukkin' wonderful.' Make us some money."

The wheels of the aircraft squeal on the tarmac. Engines roar in reverse. Handy Paige's bristly fingers are clamped to the armrests, knuckles white as piano keys.

"Make money, Bois," he hissed through clenched teeth. "I've got twelve percent of your lovable arse."

78

Jennifer Down and Walter Paige are waiting at the hotel, a modest establishment in Bayswater Road.

"François," she says, extending her hand and flashing a broad smile.

It takes a moment to realize that she is addressing me; I have almost forgotten my given name. I take her hand. I grin. I like her immediately.

I don't know why, but I had imagined that she would be younger. She is about my age—early forties—salt flecks in cinnamon hair, webs of tiny lines at the corners of her eyes and mouth.

Very stylish. Perfectly coiffed hair. Dangling gold earrings, Eastern looking, perhaps Indian. Eye shadow. A hint of lipstick. Trimly tailored linen suit and pink silk shirt.

"And this is Mr. Paige?" She extends her hand to my companion.

For once Handy is silent. He nods brusquely, avoiding her eyes. He glances at the bar.

Walter Paige knows what to do. "Come along, Uncle Handy, I'll buy you a drink. Jennifer and Frank will want to talk."

Handy's nephew is younger than Jennifer Down by a good ten years, and more casual. Rumpled cotton jacket. Black tie on chocolate shirt. Tatty plimsolls. No socks. He winks at Jennifer and takes Handy by the arm.

Jennifer's eyes sparkle mischievously. "I've heard lots about Mr. Paige from Walter."

"He *is* rather wearying," I say, "but he sold my book."

"Frank, there is one thing I should say right away. It may be true that your book came to my desk because of Walter. But that had nothing to do with the book being published. As soon as I picked it up, I loved it. Other editors at Penguin loved it too.

It's a marvelous book. We are very excited to be publishing it."

She deftly guides me to a table in a quite corner of the lounge bar, as far away as possible from where Handy and Walter stand drinking.

"The astrology is interesting," she says, "but what makes the book *really* work is the way you weave the personal stories together with the astrology. About your mother, for instance. That business in France. The mine exploding. It's hard to believe those things really happened."

"Astronomy."

"What?"

"Astronomy, not astrology."

"Oh."

A waiter appears. He does not ask for our preferences. He stands silently at Jennifer's side, waiting for *her* order, as if I didn't exist. Jennifer orders Perrier with a twist of lemon. I ask for Guinness.

"Are you often treated like that?" she asks when the waiter has gone.

"Very often."

"It is really unforgivable."

"One gets used to it."

"You are about to become famous, Frank, if your book does as well as we think it will. Have you seen the marvelous review in today's *Observer*?"

She extracts the folded page from her shoulder bag.

"Yes, I read it on the flight over."

"He calls you 'a melancholy pilgrim among the

stars.' Janke doesn't usually give himself over to superlatives, but he calls your book 'brilliant.' "

"It's all true."

"Yes, I know." She laughs.

"I mean the book is true, not the review. The things about my mother. The exploding mine. All the rest. You said it was hard to believe it really happened."

" 'Visionary yet intimate,' Janke calls it. And that man with the telescope, your mother's lover, the man who taught you about the stars?"

"Who is he?"

"The emigration person. With six daughters. Tadgh Cleary, I think you called him."

"No, I mean Janke. Who is he?"

"Oh, Janke. An Oxbridge type. An academic. He has written a few novels. Usually he has very little good to say about any book. More concerned with asserting his own opinions."

"Jack Kelly was his real name."

"Janke's?"

"No, Tadgh Cleary's. The person in my book. His real name was Jack Kelly. If it were not for Jack, there wouldn't be a book."

"Did you really do your stargazing from the roof-top?"

"Yes."

"I've been living with your manuscript for such a long time, I feel like I know you well. It's marvelous to meet you at last."

She brushes a sheaf of cinnamon hair from her eyes. Bangles tinkle on her wrist.

"They are often confused," I say.

"Tadgh Cleary and Jack Kelly?"

"Astrology and astronomy."

She laughs. "I have the feeling this conversation is tying itself in knots."

"I'm afraid I am not very practiced in the art of conversation."

The lemon twist lies at the bottom of her full glass. She has barely sipped her drink.

"Would you like another Guinness?"

I nod.

She jangles her bracelets to attract the waiter. Handy Paige is talking loudly at the bar, loudly enough, I guess, to embarrass his nephew. Jennifer Down pays no mind.

"I'll bet you are a Sagittarius," she says.

"A Leo."

She looks intently into my eyes, fingering the collar of her blouse.

"Yes, I can see that. Now that I think about it, you are definitely a Leo. Can you guess my sign?"

"I'm afraid I don't put much stock in any of that."

"I should have guessed. Astronomers are always skeptical of astrology. As for me, I'm afraid my knowledge of the stars is limited to the horoscope. I was terrible in science at school. I believe I set a record low on my science O-levels."

I find myself admiring Jennifer Down. There is something wonderfully—ah, *professional* about her, neither intimate nor condescending. In her presence I feel not unattractive, even a bit sophisticated.

A second Guinness is placed before me.

"I suppose if I added some astrology it would help sell my book."

She smiles.

I wink.

She reaches out and touches my wrist. Her nail polish matches the color of her blouse.

"Your book is perfect, Frank. You are perfect."

79

I have heard it said that the art of observing the night sky is 50 percent vision and 50 percent imagination. Nothing illustrates this better than the color of stars. Most people think stars are uniformly white, but I have observed a jewel box of colors. Betelgeuse in Orion is ruby red; Rigel is lapis lazuli. Albireo, in the Swan's beak, is a double star: topaz yellow and sapphire blue. I've seen garnets, opals, emeralds, and amethysts spilled across the night.

Tonight, the sky above London is pinkish-olive. Not a jeweled star to be seen in the interstices between the buildings, only the wan glow of neon and mercury. I am excited and depressed (which?) by the vibrant artificiality of the city. The hiss of electricity. The grind and purr of internal combustion. The cacophony of nocturnal commerce, the buying and selling of merchandise and souls. The sheen, the shabbiness, the aching reach from affluence to poverty; the plenitude of possibility is all-embracing. In these anonymous nighttime crowds I am

unexceptional, part of the ache, part of the plenitude, each of us grasping for a portion of the world's
happiness, happiness pared so thin there is little
hope that any of us will manage to obtain a sus-
taining share. But look, there, reflected in the windows of the trendy shops: the beautiful people
clutching their fistfuls of happiness to themselves.
In pairs and cliques they move along, holding
hands, arms linked; they lean into life, floating like
gorgeous angels in the glass. And my own image,
scuttling near the pavement.

You are perfect, Jennifer Down had said.

I watch the women in the glass, the glass mirrors
of Piccadilly. I am the practiced voyeur. Their skin:
honey, chocolate, blushed, tawny, sable. Their hair:
raven, sorrel, xanthic, flax. Their eyes: sky, sea, Indian, turquoise. I admire their clothes: the cottons,
wools, and silks, the clingy skirts and skin-tight
jeans. I love the way their jackets gape, revealing
glimpses of décolletage or breast; love the way they
move their hands to brush the hair from their eyes;
love the lanky stretch of their calves and thighs. I
slink through Piccadilly Circus under the eyes of
Cupid perched on the pinnacle of the fountain,
negotiate the hordes of beautiful children: back-
packers, punkers, skinheads, blond Americans.
Leicester Square. Charing Cross Road. I am master
of the art of averted vision (didn't Jack Kelly teach
me that the eye is most sensitive when it looks
aside of the thing it seeks), the surreptitious inspection. I lurk at the edges of respectability, mea-
suring out my voyeurism in inconspicuous doses.
I hate himself, hate the self I have let myself be-

come, the watcher, the dreamer of other people's dreams.

At midnight I am in Soho, poking with feigned nonchalance through porn-film houses, strip bars, sex shops, peep shows, having descended into a hell of whose existence I had barely guessed. *Chalk, zinc, rust, lead*: the colors of decay. Gases sizzle in glass tubes bent into letters and anatomical shapes—xenon, neon, krypton, argon—blinking, blinking, NUDE, TOPLESS, LIVE SEX, CUM IN. *Sallow, puce, absinthe, Pompeiian red*. Flushed skin, blue veins, breasts and bellies exposed in sags and creases, a grotty subculture of caked powder and greasy rouge. Beauty's stepsister.

And all the while a dialogue is running between my ears, a compulsion to fill the child's exercise book with exact description (the starless sky, *bloodless, ghastly, deathly pale*), the commentary of a conscience made frayed and ragged by rubbing too long against itself.

80

There is more. A chamber of horrors from midnight to dawn, including an astonishing proposition, but all of that is lost in a slurry of Guinness. When at 10:30 A.M. I meet Jennifer Down at the Penguin offices in Wright's Lane, I have somehow managed to restore myself, superficially at least, to the look of a man who has slept the sleep of the just.

Sunlight. Glass, chrome, blond wood, potted plants. Immaculate. Jennifer Down in pin-stripe suit, cream-colored blouse, pearls at the neck. Her coterie of colleagues, stylishly attired. And the author, Frank Bois, as spiffy as he can make himself in newly purchased turtleneck and rumpled corduroy trousers, his hobble-cobble shoes buffed to a big-city shine. Handy Paige is not to be seen; young Walter has been instructed to keep his uncle away from the day's proceedings.

But my self-appointed watchdog is not required. As Handy Paige requested, I am charming. Articulate. A PR person's dream. A winsome blend of naïveté and erudition, neither giddy nor grim. I am unprotesting as the house photographer snaps away. I smile with appropriate gratefulness into the beaming eyes of Penguin bigwigs. I blather with apparently practiced ease through an afternoon of Thoughtful Interviews. I am the well-behaved, eminently bankable Irish leprechaun.

What do the interviewers wish to know? They have not read *Nightstalk*, only the publisher's press kit. The book, according to the kit, is about the stars—the jacket is included, that dreamy starscape—so I am asked for my opinion on UFOs, astrology, black holes, space exploration, cities on the moon, none of which have anything to do with my book, being either silly superstitions or subjects beyond my competence. I do my best to steer the questions instead to the dark night, to the boy on the roof, and to Bernadette, Jack, Emma, Roger, and Terry in their fictional guises. One interviewer wonders about my title, *Nightstalk*, allowing me to talk, with

just the proper touch of frankness, about noctivagant walks and other rituals of solitude.

Any fair-minded observer would say that I acquit
myself well.

Jennifer Down included. Throughout the day she
watches and listens anxiously, as if at any moment I
might lapse into grim-lipped silence or speak some
embarrassment. When late in the afternoon we go
for a drink, just the two of us, to a posh little pub
called Nexus, she tells me why.

"You should stop feeling sorry for yourself," she
blurts, as I slip into the umbra of self-pity that inevitably follows my third glass of port (here measured
out in rather more parsimonious portions than I am
used to). We have been talking about the events of
the day.

Astonished, I look at her over the top of my specs.
Even after long hours of nervously ushering me
from place to place, she is—well, *impeccable*. Her
perfectly manicured hands clasp about a tall glass
of Perrier, the color of the nails transformed to
match the cream of her blouse, her fingers glittering
with rings. I pose the only relevant question by fur-
rowing my brow.

"I thought about it, Frank, as I read your book,
and I saw it in your attitude today. Very subtle, but
it's there. That measure of self-hate." She hesitates,
tries to read my reaction, then proceeds cautiously.
"You know, it is really the only unattractive thing
about you."

Her frankness is both distressing and refreshing.

"You should like yourself more."

She looks into her glass, perhaps embarrassed by her forthrightness. Then slyly smiles.

"Of course, it is really none of my business."

"No, it's true. I *don't* like myself very much. The reason I don't like myself is because I am *unable* to like myself. Does that make any sense? I look into the mirror and I see a person who is incapable of self-esteem, and I find him repulsive. You see, it's a circular, self-sustaining kind of thing. It's a Chinese puzzle I have not been able to undo."

"But you are quite a fortunate person, Frank. You were terrific today. I wish all of our authors conducted themselves with such effectiveness. Such aplomb. And your book—well, your book is terrific too."

"I think you are forgetting something."

"Yes, I know. But really—"

"Tell me, Jennifer, do you think that—hypothetically, I mean, I am speaking purely hypothetically— do you think that you could fall in love with *me*?"

"I'm already in love with someone, Frank."

"I'm only posing a hypothetical question. Let us assume that in every other respect I possessed all of Walter's fine qualities. All of the personable qualities, all of the intellectual qualities. But retained, of course, my own . . . my own *looks*. Could you fall in love with me?"

She is silent. She thoughtfully considers my question.

"No," she says, at last.

I shrug.

"But that may be *my* problem, Frank. I would like

to be the kind of person who could fall in love with someone like you. But I'm not."

"If it's any consolation, Jennifer, I don't blame you. I'm not that kind of person either. What is beautiful is always more desirable than what is not beautiful."

"But beauty is not just physical—"

"Oh, come off it, Jennifer. You have already said that you couldn't love me—someone like myself, I mean. And you have surely noticed how we skirt around *naming* the problem. Dwarfism. Listen to the word. *Dwarfism.* Even the word is ugly. The thing is ugly through and through. It is part of a vein of ugliness that runs through the whole universe, like woodworm or dry rot. It occurs to me now as we talk that *that* might be another meaning for the title of my book: those stunted plants that grow in darkness, photophobic, fungoidal, botanical dwarfs. And I'm not just talking about my particular deformity, Jennifer, not only about achondroplasia. Genes throw up all sorts of misshapen persons, twisted or broken in body and mind. It has nothing to do with morality or justice. It is ugliness, plain ugliness. Nature's built-in crown of thorns."

She shudders. "That's an ugly image, Frank."

"Q.E.D."

"But—"

"Look at yourself, Jennifer. You are beautiful. You are one of the beautiful people. I don't begrudge you that. I admire it. In fact, I am obsessed by it. It would be terribly easy to fall in love with someone like you, but there is no reciprocity. There is no reciprocity between ugliness and beauty. All of the energy flows one way."

There is a sadness in her eyes. I know that she is struggling bravely to escape the implications of what I am saying.

Finally, she says: "But you made something beautiful, Frank. Your book is beautiful."

"Yes, but how will you *sell* it, Jennifer? What about that photograph on the jacket? Tony Hanks's masterpiece? Handy Paige says that people will buy my book for the same reason they pay to see freaks at the circus. Can you honestly say there has not been some of that going on today as you put me on display? Step right up, folks. See the man with a dozen toes. Observe the Bearded Lady. The Fat Man. The Siamese twins. And for the first time in London, direct from Ireland, the dwarf author of the night."

"That's . . ."

"Yes?"

"OK, that's part of it, there wouldn't be a book if . . ."

"If you couldn't sell it?"

"Yes."

"I don't want that, Jennifer. I don't need it. If I take advantage of my ugliness, then I set myself even further apart from beauty. I . . ."

"Your book is full of it. Ugliness, that is. And beauty too. That's what the book is about. Ugliness and beauty."

"Yes, but the *book* is not me. The book is a *thing*. It belongs to *you* now, and to whoever wishes to buy it. I wrote it because I *had* to write it. I had to articulate what the world looked like from . . . Now I've done it. It's out of my system. I should go back to being what I was before, crawl back under my rock as Handy Paige would have it. You said the book might make me famous. What is it you are offering? Freak-show fame? I don't need it. I don't want it. It certainly won't help me to like myself."

"Frank . . ."

"You are a nice person, Jennifer. Don't worry, I'll help you sell our book. Just tell me what to do. I'll do anything you say."

I wink.

She pats my hand.

I am not unhappy. Oh, no, in Jennifer's presence I am not unhappy.

Roger Manning was another of the beautiful people. Delicate features. Soulful black eyes. Dark hair that fell across his eyes, perhaps just beginning to thin. *Yeatsian.* Yes, Bernadette was right to see a resemblance. And, like Yeats, he was irresistible to women.

It never occurred to Roger Manning to think of himself as beautiful. He seldom thought about his physical self at all. When women forthrightly offered themselves to him, he brushed the hair from his eyes and squinted blankly through wire-rimmed glasses, not quite comprehending. But Bernadette—with Bernadette he had fallen head-and-ears in love (only the cliché has the *force* of truth). She made him aware of himself, made him aware that he was beautiful. He sat on the edge of his bed peering at the palms of his hands, amazed to discover that they were parts of his body, connected with the rest of him (he wriggled his fingers) by bones and sinews that went right up the sleeves of his pajamas to connect with the shoulders (he hunched his shoulders, feeling their presence), torso (heaved his chest), legs, knees, calves, ankles, connected at last even to his feet (he saw them down there on the floor and wiggled his bare toes to confirm that the feet did indeed belong to him). At awkward moments—midstream in a sermon, talking to the choirmaster, instructing the sexton—he would suddenly be struck by his physical self, and all other thoughts would go right out of his head. He would continue speaking, perhaps, but the words were automatic. His thoughts were elsewhere. He felt himself fixed to the place where he stood, rooted like a tree. Physical. Beautiful. Sometimes he found himself staring into his convex shaving mirror, squinting one eye, straining to see himself undistorted, backing away, moving closer, seeking some focal point or distance at which the damn thing might cease to magnify and let him see plain what it was that Bernadette so admired.

She read his mind, perceived his fancies, anticipated his whims. It was uncanny—almost, well, *diabolical*. She acted out the things he dreamed. At night, alone in his bed, he felt her spirit moving under the sheets, causing . . . dear God, she intruded herself even into the fabric of his prayers.

What do you call such a spirit? Incuba? Succuba? He couldn't remember. If he had not been a Christian, a modern, rational Church of Ireland Christian, he might have thought her a practitioner of black arts, a witch, a trafficker with devils.

But he loved her. It was as simple as that. Loved her beauty, her spontaneity, her uncomplicated sexuality. And he was, he must now admit, jealous. Jealous of—of the American. After several visits to her house, it had dawned upon Roger that the American visitor—what was his name? Terry—was in residence, almost certainly shared her bed. It was more than he could bear. Compounding his jealously was his fair-mindedness; he knew his emotions were unworthy. He did not have any claim on her fidelity that would be recognized by church or state, no conjugal contract, not even the insubstantial verbal contract represented by those three words she had never spoken. What did Milton call jealousy? *The injured lover's hell.* Yes, hell indeed. Jealousy was devouring his soul, distracting him from prayer and work. Even his poems had begun to take on a morbid aspect. He posted them to her, and regretted his action the moment he had dropped the envelopes into the pillar box:

> . . . *a creature*
> *of nettles and thorns,*
> *a badger scuttling*
> *runnels of the heart.*

When he was away from her he rehearsed the things he would say, the chastisements, the recriminations, the renunciations, the indignant good-byes. But when she came around to his flat and pirouetted barefooted on his plush carpet, all of his stored-up bitterness and anger fell away. She cast her spells, spoke her incantations. She . . . yes, sweet Jesus, it was true, she *voodooed* him and made him terrified that he might lose her.

And that was when he decided upon Smerwick.

The Right Reverend Thaddeus Swift-Houghton, dean of St. Fin Barre's, owned a cottage at Smerwick on the Dingle Peninsula in county Kerry. Roger had often heard of it, listened to Swift-Houghton's enthusiastic accounts, seen photographs. The perfect country cottage. Daffodil paths. Sweet honeysuckle. Fuchsia. Bracing sea air. *You would love it, Roger,* Swift-Houghton had often said, never, however, actually inviting him to visit. But now the place—the place he had never visited, the place he had never been *invited* to visit—began to loom large in his mind. It would be an ideal, irresistible place to entice her into homey exile, into matrimony, to demonstrate to her the *desirability* of domesticity. He would take her there and woo her to his idea of connubial bliss, wedded and bedded, one bone and one flesh. The Smerwick cottage, Thaddeus Swift-Houghton's Smerwick cottage, would be the venue of his spousal seduction.

He could not, of course, simply invite himself to Swift-Houghton's holiday retreat. Nor could he apprise the dean of his plans. He was certain that Swift-Houghton would not be sympathetic to—to, well, the *unseemliness* of his tryst. So Roger would simply go, commandeer the place as it were, let himself in. And if the skeptic wonders that a man of Roger's propriety and restraint might resort to an action that was in fact quite illegal, even within the bounds of a . . . ah, friendship, then I have not yet successfully communicated the force of the affliction that had seized upon his soul. Roger was, after all—in his own understanding—bewitched, conjured, spooked, possessed. Love, sexual befuddlement, and jealously had cast their spell. He was addled, disordered, morally adrift.

What surprised him was how readily Bernadette assented. Yes, she would go. Yes, she would accompany him for the four days of the bank holiday weekend. Yes, *of course*. What he did not know—what he could not have known, because, unlike Bernadette, he was not adept at reading minds—was that Bernadette had begun to regret that she had admitted Terry Klout into her household and her bed. Yes, she fell asleep at his side in postcoital exhaustion; that was not the problem. The problem was that he was still in her bed when she awoke the next morning. She had surrendered, she now understood, a *territory* that might be difficult to recover. She had too quickly, needlessly allowed Terry Klout to occupy a portion of her independence. He had lodged himself tenaciously, taken hold, filled whatever space she allowed him. It was a situation that must be remedied. Four days away with Roger might provide her with the lever of time necessary to dislodge Terry from her bed.

It would be a mistake to believe that any of this was a conscious plan in Bernadette's mind. She was not a conscious person. Nor was she devious. It would not have occurred to her to *use* Roger. It was not her habit to form reasoned conclusions or draw up plans. She merely drifted—no, that is not correct; drift implies randomness, chaos. There was nothing chaotic about Bernadette's life. She was carried along by a story, as it were, by an unconscious narrative, the residue, no doubt, of long afternoons in the back pew of Fleurville's parish church with the *impropre* novels of Colette.

Roger Manning borrowed a motorcar, packed his valise, and collected Bernadette to his side. He marveled that she carried not a single accessory. Not a toothbrush or a comb. Not a change of clothes. No nightdress or pajamas. No bathing costume (they would be at seaside). Not even a handbag or a purse. She slid into the passenger seat of his motorcar with nothing more than the clothes she wore, a printed cotton dress that buttoned up the front, shoes and stockings, a heavy woolen pullover, and a rose-colored scarf wound round and round her neck. Under her dress she wore a new pair of white cotton panties, and in her pocket she carried a bright pink kerchief.

82

Roger Manning had graduated at the top of his class. As a divinity student at Trinity College he had outshone all his contemporaries. He excelled in debate with his learned professors on subtle points of medieval theology or modern philosophy,

leaping with an acrobat's agility from Clement of
Alexandria to Sartre and Camus. He had committed
to memory the works of the Church Fathers. Augustine was his bedtime reading. Asked to explicate
canon law, the doctrine of grace, or subtle points
of scriptural exegesis, he did so with effortless ease.
His essays were polished and lucid, his oral presen-
tations apt. He seemed not to be interested in
women or in frivolous social intercourse. He applied
himself with unceasing diligence to discovering
God's plan for the world as revealed in the Scrip-
tures, the Church Fathers, and tradition. It was assumed by his fellow students and teachers that he
was destined for a bishopric. It was only a matter of
time, they said. Now, at age thirty-seven, he was
jimmying open the kitchen window of Thaddeus
Swift-Houghton's holiday cottage. The irony of the
action was not lost on the curate of St. Fin Barre's.
Even as the casement splintered with a heart-
stopping *crack,* he held in his mind's eye the outline
of a promising career gone crazily awry.

Roger Manning was violating the property of his
dean.

His jimmy was a tire iron from the borrowed motorcar. But even after the wooden casement shattered, the window would not budge. He picked up a
stone and drove the iron under the window's frame,
then levered the thing upward with all his force.
Dear Jesus, let it open, he prayed silently. The glass
fractured, a large shard dropping like the blade of
a guillotine onto his burglar's hand.

Bernadette meanwhile had scampered down the
cliff to the crescent of pure white sand that curved

below the house. She doffed her shoes and stockings and plashed in the surf. Roger was not there to see her. Having at last gained entry to the house, he stood at the kitchen sink letting cool water from the tap run across his wound, an ugly gash on the back of his hand that disgorged an apparently unstoppable river of blood. Crimson water was spiraling down the drain when she appeared at the door, hair plastered on her forehead, wet dress clinging to her body, skin glistening.

"Come look," she said.

"I'm bleeding."

"Come look—the view. *Merveilleux.*"

And the view was indeed marvelous. Thaddeus Swift-Houghton's cottage was perched on cliffs above Smerwick Harbor. Across the water the little port of Ballydavid slept at the foot of Ballydavid Head. Fishing vessels rode at buoys. To the west, identical precipiced hills called the Three Sisters towered above the thundering Atlantic.

She grabbed his dangling braces and tugged.

"Come."

"I can't," he said plaintively.

"Come."

"Bernadette, I've sliced my hand. I've very nearly cut my hand off."

She looked. "It's just a little cut," she said. She tugged.

"I'll bleed to death."

"Don't be such a baby. Women bleed all the time. We don't make such a fuss of it."

He pleaded. "You don't seem to understand. I'm hemorrhaging. My lifeblood is going down the drain and you want me to—*see a view*. I should go to hospital, although God knows where the nearest hospital is. Dingle? Killarney? I'll be empty of blood by the time I get to Killarney. I can't drive a car in this condition. You can't drive."

She took a tea towel and wrapped it around his hand. "It's just a wee cut," she said sweetly, fixing him with sea-green eyes. "Put it into the sea. The salt will mend it."

She dragged him out of the cottage and down the cliff. She was as light-footed as a rabbit. He stumbled clumsily, spilling blood onto crumbling Kerry clay. On the strand she unbuttoned her dress and let it fall to her feet.

It was then that it dawned on him: *She is crazy. Certifiably crazy. Lunatic. Starkers. Off her head. Mad as a March hare. Cuckoo. Crazy as a loon.*

Briefly it occurred to him that he should run, that he was in danger of losing *his* sanity too, that she had infected him with her madness. Look! Consider the scene. An ordained cleric, a scholar, a man of God, standing in his shirtsleeves on some godforsaken beach with a half-naked girl, his braces down about his waist, a blood-soaked tea towel wrapped around his hand. He had wounded himself breaking and entering another person's house. He had committed a serious crime. He was bleeding to death.

All of this flashed briefly through his mind. It was the last brave squeak of reason.

An immortal soul. An immortal soul is the Believer's burden and Roger was a Believer. Or at least he had always assumed that he believed. It was, after all, the point and purpose of his life. He could muster, if called upon to do so, a dozen compelling arguments for the existence of God. Daily he invoked God's name. He prayed. And, for the Christian, a corollary of Belief is an immortal soul. The soul, he imagined, was like another self that enveloped his physical self, a vaporous Roger clinging to his flesh and blood like an odor. An airy, fairy thing. But sometimes, sometimes this other self—this other self for whom he was presumably responsible, responsible for this other self's eternity—sometimes this other self, this immortal self, went right out of his head.

Bernadette! Roger need only look into Bernadette's green eyes and his immortal soul evaporated. He wondered at this, wondered at the blow-away fragility of this thing that supposedly lasts forever. The immortal soul, he had been instructed, possesses eternal *lastingness* precisely because it lacks materiality. But when . . .

Bernadette was right. The salt water stopped the bleeding. She wrapped his hand with her pink kerchief and tied the kerchief with a knot. Then they made love on the sand, his braces and his trousers

down about his knees, watched (he imagined) by
God-knows-what gawping locals on the clifftops.

Roger Manning's weekend was not working
out. *The enterprise is doomed.* This melancholy
thought impressed itself upon his consciousness at
precisely 8:03 P.M., Saturday. He was looking at his
watch (his father's watch, actually, given as a gift on
the son's sixteenth birthday) when he realized that
things were not going as planned, and in fact would
never go as planned. Bernadette was—where? He
didn't know. In the bedroom? In the deck chair under the holly bush? In the sandy-floored cave at the
foot of the sea cliff? She had discovered among
Thaddeus Swift-Houghton's possessions a shelf of
Reader's Digest abridged novels, four novels to a
volume. For most of the day she had been reading,
stopping only to eat, or to tease Roger, or— Dear
Jesus, what did she imagine him to be? He was no
longer capable of performing (what a word!). He
was depleted. Expended. Dribbled away. A derelict
vessel cracked at every seam. Desiccated. Dry as a
bone. And what of his dreams of domesticity? Did
she, sweet Bernadette, busy herself in the kitchen
while he, in his study (Swift-Houghton's rusticated
study), wrote out in longhand (on the dean of St.
Fin Barre's high-quality but slightly damp bond paper) his sermon for Sunday week? Not at all. She
showed not the least inclination to participate in

feathering their borrowed nest or making permanent their weekend tryst. The two of them would have starved had *he* not fried up eggs and tomatoes, brewed coffee, boiled potatoes, buttered bread. And when they had finished their meals (she reading all the while), guess who was required to do the washing up, one-handed (the other bundled in a bandage)?

Roger glanced at his watch again: 8:03. But surely a minute had passed. The sweep hand—stopped! He shook his wrist. He put the thing to his ear. He shook his wrist again. Stopped! It had never happened before. His father's watch. Stopped. Stopped, he knew—he guessed, with sand in the works. A cold fear came over him, as if a cloud had covered the westering sun, his father's reproving stare, his mother's timorous voice whispering in his ear *Roger, what have you done? What will your father say?* He shook his wrist and listened to the silent mechanism. And groaned silently. It was ridiculous. This upwelling of guilt. It was unwarranted. He was thirty-seven years old, he was not a child. The watch was his own. His father, for God's sake, was in the grave for a dozen years, and his mother beside him, laid out side by side in St. Columba's churchyard in Donnybrook, Dublin, as formally paired in death as in life they had shared the big double bed in which Roger was born. Well, enough! He would have the watch repaired when he returned to Cork. In the meantime he had other problems.

Roger was no fool. He knew the problems he faced were not amenable to a reasonable solution. He might sit here on this marvelous cliff above the

green sea and marshal a thousands reasons why
. . . Why? No good. The thing was in motion. There
was no going back. It was easy enough to say *I
should, I shouldn't*, but the sorry fact—the blunt
irreducible fact of the matter—was *he loved her.*
Admitting that, it was only natural to ask *Why do I
love her?* Yes, she was beautiful, achingly so. Yes,
he was hopelessly in thrall to her sexual resourceful-
ness. No, he did not really know her in any intimate,
personal sense; of her secret self she had revealed
nothing; she had never even spoken his name, and
certainly never spoken those three words he so often wished to hear. But . . . Suddenly it became
clear to him. Yes, why had he not thought of it before? He was in love with her *freedom.* She was free.
As free as the sea that pulsed on the white strand
below the cliff. As free as the cormorants and gan-
nets that dove for fish in the harbor. As free as the
fish themselves, all slippery and silvery in their blue-
green medium. He was in love—miserably—with
what he could not have.

A lump of anguish rested in Roger Manning's
heart as he sat on the clifftop by Smerwick Harbor
watching the sun's slow decline beyond Sybil Head.
He was burdened. With a crushing weight of baggage. First of all, the Past, which he dragged behind
him like a weighted lorry. And then, that cumber-
some portmanteau that could not be put down,
Conscience. And—he shook his wrist and listened
for the tick—Guilt. He, who would have been a
bishop. He, who could quote letter and verse from
Augustine's *City of God* and who had once published in the *Church Review* a forty-seven-page

monograph on Clement of Alexandria's doctrine of grace. *Dear Jesus,* Roger prayed, *the list of my burdens is as long as my arm.* But—and this was the gist of it—when she swept him into her erotic games, into her loony spontaneity, when he became indeed her plaything, he was in those moments free, as light-headed and lighthearted as a child. And then—while her beauty (and *his*!) made him dizzy with lightness—then that most burdensome baggage of all, that infinitely weighty whiff of eternity, the Immortal Soul, was momentarily lifted from his frame.

She would not be domesticated, and he could not shake off (for more than a few moments stolen out of time) the constraints of the past. The equation could not be factored. He thought—since he was alone—to write a poem on this theme. He tried out phrases in his head: *the cormorant's heedless headlong dive . . . the beckoning gannet sea . . . to rise on silver spume like an airy stone.* It was no good. The words stuck. His pen could not find the music. His hand ached. His watch was dead. Somewhere inside or near Swift-Houghton's holiday cottage, *she* was curled up with Thomas Costain, Samuel Shellabarger, Daphne du Maurier, Frances Parkinson Keyes—four in one. And then the shattered window casement and broken glass began to intrude their necessary repair and replacement into his conscience.

According to the quantum theory, events in the atomic realm occur not deterministically but according to a system of probabilities. For example, when it is time for an electron to change its position, the laws of nature decree a 50 percent chance (say) that the electron will jump to the left, and (therefore) a 50 percent chance that it will jump to the right. Both outcomes are possible. Whereas in classical physics the direction of the electron's jump is fully determined by the electron's past, in quantum physics exact prediction is impossible. The past does not rigorously constrain the future. Left or right; anything is possible. Certain speculative philosophers take this a step further. Not only are both events possible (they say), but both events occur. The electron jumps to the left, *and* the electron jumps to the right. Reality forks. Time divides into two streams, so that at every moment in each of a myriad of quantum events the universe fragments into an ever increasing number of universes endlessly forking, and *this* universe, *this universe that we are aware of*, the universe in which our consciousness resides, is just one of many parallel universes fingering their way into the endlessly fissioning future. Yes, think of a tree. The trunk divides, and this division can be taken to be a single event in a certain person's life—say, for the purpose of discussion, Roger Manning's life. The trunk divides. Then each branch of the bifurcated trunk divides again. Two become four, four become eight, eight become sixteen. At some later moment in time there is not *one* Roger Manning, but as many Roger Mannings as there are twig tips on this tree of universes, and each of those many Roger Mannings is conscious only of himself.

This curious theory of endlessly fissioning universes is both melancholy and consoling. Melancholy because it emphasizes the hopelessly random character of a life. Consoling because it suggests that if _this_ life is not satisfactory, then there are other lives, in other parts of the bifurcating space-time manifold, that are more satisfactory. So, let us say that the shattering of Swift-Houghton's window was an event so _iffy_, so delicately balanced between happening and not happening, that only a tiny cascade of quantum events sent the thing one way or another. Then, although Roger Manning (groaning at his fate) might wonder how he will repair or explain the shattered casement and broken glass (for that he should just let it lie to be discovered later by Swift-Houghton and accounted an act of local vandalism was, he knew, although certainly an option, altogether impossible, considering the tender nature of his conscience), he might nevertheless take some small measure of consolation in the knowledge that along _other_ tracks in space-time there are _other_ Roger Mannings (himself and yet not himself) for whom the window did not break.

And now we come to a turning point where there occurred an event so chancy, so altogether unpredictable, that one might reasonably conclude that the jog of a single electron (to the left or to the right) might have determined the outcome, an event that nudged a life onto an altogether different course, so that thirty years later Roger Manning (yes, it is _his_ life we are considering) might look back and wonder how wildly iffy it all was.

Roger Manning went looking for his weekend

companion, and—here is that *tick*, that quantum jump at the back of his brain—quite spontaneously, without conscious reason, opened a cupboard door in the hallway between the kitchen and bedroom of Thaddeus Swift-Houghton's holiday cottage and saw there, on a shelf at the back of the cupboard, a bottle of Jack Daniel's Tennessee whiskey.

Roger was not a drinker. Apart from the eucharistic wine, not a drop of alcoholic beverage passed his lips. But he *was* a philosopher, and he recognized in the bottle of Jack Daniel's whiskey the possibility of an experiment in—ah, shall we say, the amelioration of existential angst.

Bernadette Bois was not a philosopher. Bernadette Bois, it is fair to say, did not have a philosophical bone in her pretty body, unless the reader wishes to account her intuitive touch-and-go nihilism as a kind of philosophy. So when she found Roger collapsed snoring across the kitchen table with a half-empty bottle of Jack Daniel's by his hand, she did not meditate on human folly or wonder at the ways that whiskey might lubricate the slippery slopes of probability. She went to bed.

But not without a certain twinge of conscience. And when, in the middle of the night, she heard him slip from his chair and fall to the floor, she roused herself from bed (Thaddeus Swift-Houghton's big goose-down bed) and placed a pillow under Roger's head. She did not know, nor did unconscious Roger know, that the short straw had been drawn, the two-of-diamonds turned, the space-time continuum pared once again on the knife-edge of quantum chance sending Roger (*this* Roger, the one we know and love, who is today nearly seventy years of age, a tippler, and the vicar of a depopulated parish in the Midlands) into the genteel but addled company of grain spirits.

He woke in pain. Pain in the head from the whiskey, in the shoulders from sleeping on the hard wooden floor, and in the hand from the cut, which now throbbed with the insistent drumbeat of infection. It occurred to him, finding no medicines in the cottage, that he should set about securing aspirin for the headache, balm for the sore muscles, and—most urgently—antibiotics for the festering wound. This meant driving at least as far as Dingle and rousing a chemist from his bank-holiday-weekend Sunday leisure. But first he left a note for the sleeping Bernadette on the chair next to the bed: *Gone to Dingle for medicine. Back few hours. Rashers and eggs on table. Butter and milk on porch. Gas*

*cylinder is turned on. Matches in box on shelf by
cooker. R. P.S. Careful with burner on cooker, it
tends to light explosively.*

Bernadette woke with sunlight streaming in the
window, found Roger's note and read it with bemused detachment, crumpled it with her hand and
tossed it onto the bed. Lifted her dress from the
chair and decided, feeling the warmth of the sun on
her skin, to wash it. Took the top sheet from Swift-
Houghton's bed and wrapped it sarong-fashion
about her, tucking the loose end between her
breasts. Pattered barefoot to the kitchen. Lit the
cooker and boiled up the full kettle, a cup for tea
and the rest into the enamelware basin in which,
with a frothing bar of brown soap, she rinsed her
dress and panties. Stepped onto the sunny clifftop
where she draped her washed garments on a fuchsia bush to dry. Tipped back her head and let the
sun fall full on her face. And remembered the blood-
soaked pink kerchief.

In its drumroll rhythm the previous paragraph
evokes the run-up to a Moment of Consequence.
And indeed the separate pieces of the dénouement
are all in place. The pink kerchief lies on the porch
floor, brown and stiff with Roger's dried blood.
Roger is on Green Street in Dingle town, hammering
on the door of W. Sheehy, Chemist. A black Ford
motorcar, not Roger's, moves along Green Street,
passing unnoticed at Roger's back. If history does
indeed fork at every instant, branching into different
but equally real futures, then, at *this* moment there
are potentially a myriad of stories that might unfold,
corresponding to the myriad separate futures that

will happen according to quantum chance, a plenum of universes. An electron jumps, setting off a cascade of cosmic events, an avalanche of ever-gathering historical force, a chain-reaction of consequence. Depending on the path we follow, Bernadette, searching earnestly about the cottage, may or may not find the blood-brown kerchief. W. Sheehy, Chemist, may or may not respond to Roger's impatient hammering. At Ventry Junction outside Dingle town, the black Ford motorcar may turn left toward Slea Head (the long way round) or right toward Ballyferriter (the short way to Smerwick). Of the possible futures that might emerge from these multiple forks we can know only one, the one that carries *us* along in its course, for the historian (or even the amateur chronicler who compiles because he *must* compile, filling notebooks with his scribble) can only look backward, along the path from whence he came. Those other stories, those other universes, are known only to an Omniscient Deity, perhaps the very deity to whom Roger Manning, standing on Green Street, earnestly prays, *O Lord, please God, dear God in heaven, let him answer my knock*.

The knock is not answered, and Roger, head aching, hand throbbing, stumbles down Green Street searching for another chemist. The black Ford motorcar turns right on the short road toward Smerwick. Bernadette finds her kerchief and rinses it in the enamelware basin. As she wrings it dry, she hears the approaching motorcar and thinks—kindly, affectionately—of Roger. She remembers how prettily he slept on the kitchen floor. She remembers his poor wounded hand. Untucking the sheet from between her breasts she lets it fall to the floor. She ties the wet pink kerchief as a blindfold around her head. The door opens. Roger (Omniscient Deity, observe: a concatenation of chance creates the illusion) enters. Bernadette turns and turns, round and round, hands spread out before her, moving carefully across the room, a room suddenly made dusky by an overcast sun, pirouetting, stark naked except for the still slightly bloodstained pink kerchief tied about her eyes, toward Roger. Her outstretched fingers touch his breast. Her fingertips ascend across his chest, his collar bones, his neck, to caress his cheeks, to—

"Mon Dieu!"

With her pinky finger Bernadette pulls the blindfold down from over one eye, confirming visually the discovery she has made with her hands. The man who stands before her is not Roger. The man who stands before her is barrel chested, thick necked, jowly, flushed red, and clothed in clerical garb.

The dean of St. Fin Barre's, the Right Reverend Thaddeus Swift-Houghton, dryly observes, *"Non pas le bon Dieu, ma jolie fille, mais le maître de la maison."*

87

On my second morning in London I go to the Science Museum in South Kensington to see an object described to me many years ago by Jack Kelly: the seventy-two-inch specular metal mirror that was the light-gathering agent of Lord Rosse's giant telescope at Birr in Ireland, the telescope that provided the first unsettling hint that this world of stars we inhabit, the Milky Way galaxy, is just one of—tens or hundreds of billions—who knows, perhaps an infinity—of galaxies. Not more than a quarter-hour's drive from Lord Rosse's estate at Birr is the village of Ballymahon, once the commercial outlier of a prosperous Anglo-Irish demesne (supporting a generous complement of bailiffs, agents, soldiery, constables, magistrates, and hangers-on, all of whom gathered of a Sunday in the tiny but architecturally distinguished parish church that still occupies pride of place in the village square), today no more than a slowdown on the road from Athlone to Birr. The demesne has been disassembled and parceled out to its one-time tenants, the human apparatus of the ascendancy dispersed. The ancient Roman Catholic chapel on the outskirts of the village has been replaced by an ample barnlike structure of yellow brick and plate glass (Our Lady of the Angels) and is—between half-ten and noon on Sunday mornings—the scene of teeming activity. The Anglican parish church in the village square (St. James the Apostle) languishes.

As does its parson.

For it is here that Roger Manning tends a relict outpost of his faith, not because the parish church of St. James the Apostle any longer requires tending (the occasional tourist is his only congregation), but because—let's put the best face on it—Roger Manning is a preacher of considerable eloquence, a poet, an amateur archaeologist, the chairman of the County Offaly Historical Society and editor of its newsletter, and a tippler. Banished from Cork to Tipperary for an indiscretion involving a naked young woman and an improperly requisitioned holiday cottage, he has subsequently tippled himself into the most resolutely solitary corner of the Church of Ireland's still not inconsiderable ecclesiastical establishment, from where, once each year at Christmas time, I receive a card bearing the message *Greetings of the season, I think often of your mother. Roger Manning.*

I have no doubt that Roger Manning thinks often of Bernadette. Such is the power of beauty that its wounds are incurable. The gash that Roger Manning acquired on his hand as he jimmied open the window of Swift-Houghton's cottage quickly mended; the gash on his soul delivered by Bernadette's beauty is (I have no doubt) as fresh and hurtful today as on that evening of evensong so many years ago when she rose from the back bench of St. Fin Barre's (with her dwarf child) to leave the church, and Roger (standing with his back against the notice board) was stricken by her unconventional beauty. I know. I know of what I speak. I have spent a lifetime studying the pathology of Beauty. The morbidity of its wounds. The pharmacology of its purported cures. Its failed antidotes and ineffective prophylactics. I have been given a special dispensation for this study by the circumstances of my birth: the possibility, shall we say, of a certain clinical objectivity. For ugliness is not the mere absence of Beauty. Nor is it Beauty's opposite.

"It's no good, Jennifer, arguing that beauty is only skin deep."

I have met her for lunch at the Bunch of Grapes in Berwick Street. On our afternoon's agenda is a book signing at Foyle's, an interview with someone from *Vogue* magazine (ah, *that* should be interesting, the archetypal fairytale, the Little Man—Thumbkin, Rumpelstiltskin—in Beauty's boudoir), then the flight back to Cork. Still in my mind is the seventy-two-inch metal disk that enabled William, Third Earl of Rosse, to peer deep—35 million light-years deep—into the space of the galaxies.

"I refuse to admit, Frank, that looks are as important as you say." She pokes inconclusively at her salad with her fork.

"Looks are not only important, they are everything."

"Nonsense."

"Don't mistake me, Jennifer. By 'looks' I don't just mean superficial glamour or voguish prettiness. I mean the whole of what presents itself to the senses, the totality of physical sensation. And *of course* it is more than skin deep. It exudes from the skin, pours out of the eyes, emerges from the mouth like breath. It is movement, scent, touch—ah, yes, touch, should one be so lucky—even sound. It is an active thing, beauty, more than the sum of its parts. And it can wound mortally."

"It sounds to me like you're talking about sex, not beauty."

"Yes, of course I'm talking about sex. I'm not a psychologist, Jennifer, nor an evolutionary biologist. I don't know all the ways that sexual attraction is bound up with beauty. The brain, after all, is an organ of the body, and what happens in the brain— the apprehension of beauty, the stimulation of desire—is surely no more or less physical than—"

"And what about the soul, Frank?"

"The soul?"

"Yes, the soul. Surely the soul can be beautiful even if the body is—"

"Ugly?"

"Yes."

"Do you *believe* in souls, Jennifer? If you do, then you are lucky. I don't. I don't believe in souls. I only believe in what I see."

"I believe in lots of things I don't see."

"Like souls? Like the astrological influence of stars?"

"Well, yes."

"Look at you, Jennifer. You *look* spectacular. Your hair. Makeup. Clothes. Jewelry. Everything—absolutely perfect. Nibbling at your healthful salad. Sipping your Perrier. I would guess that you probably belong to a posh health club, one of those places with shiny high-tech equipment and beautiful people in sexy work-out outfits, that sort of thing. How long did you spend getting dressed this morning? How large *is* your mirror?"

"I . . ."

"You *know*, Jennifer. You *know* that looks matter. You *know* that beauty is more than skin deep. Beauty soaks *your* life like water soaks a rag. You are steeped in it. You have it all."

"You sound bitter, Frank. Envious, even. You shouldn't be." She speaks gently, not meanly.

"No. I am not bitter—nor am I envious. I love being here. I love sitting across from you, looking into your eyes, smelling your perfume, listening to your voice, enjoying your frankness. Do you know what color your eyes are? Cerulean. No, Rigelean." I laugh.

She smiles faintly, not comprehending.

I ask: "May I tell you about something that happened on Sunday night. My first night in London. Do you mind? May I make a rather, ah—plain confession?"

"Of course."

"I went for a walk. Ended up in a bar in Soho. A sleazy place. A girl was dancing in a cage behind the bar. In a cage like an animal might be kept in a zoo. She was naked except for . . . Anyway, I sat at the bar and I watched the girl dance. *You*, Jennifer, would not think her beautiful. You would think her tawdry, even ugly. But she possessed a kind of beauty. The place was just dark enough and I was just drunk enough to imagine that she was beautiful. What I discerned as beautiful was not actually the girl but the *idea* of . . . Can I be blunt?"

"Of course."

"Sex. The idea of sex with *that woman*, something . . ."

"Go ahead. You can say it. If you must." There is in her voice an honest solicitude, sorrow, perhaps pity.

"Something I have never experienced. As I

watched, watched the girl dance, this guy comes up
to me and buys me a drink. No, he doesn't *buy* the
drink, only motions to the barman and the barman
supplies another of what I am already drinking."

Jennifer pokes at her food, separates bits of salad
with her fork and nibbles the chosen bits. She is
listening but she is looking into her salad. Evasively.

"No, it is not what you think. I'll tell you straight
out. This guy—big guy, expensive shiny black suit,
silk shirt—wants me to—he offers me a hundred
quid to—to be in a pornographic video. Something
explicit. With a woman . . ."

She looks up. Looks into my eyes. She is suddenly
frightened.

"He writes down an address and tells me to come
back, today, in fact, Tuesday. This afternoon at
four o'clock. So what do you think, Jennifer? Will
you let me off the hook for that interview with
Vogue? This is my chance to be in the movies. My
first chance to have sex, real sex"—I laugh—"and
get paid for it."

"Don't joke, Frank. It's not something to joke
about."

"Think about it, Jennifer. Why does this guy want
to put me in a video? A dwarf? Having sex with
an attractive woman? Well, let's *assume* that she's
attractive. Attractive like the dancer in the cage.
Beautiful even, if one is drunk enough, or the
light . . . Who will he sell these things to? This video
of Beauty and the Beast?"

"It's a perversion, Frank. There's a market for any
sort of filth."

"But why me? Why the juxtaposition of the Little

Man and Beauty. Presumably men buy this stuff. Tell me, Jennifer, what need does it satisfy?"

"I don't know, Frank. I don't even want to talk about it. It is ugly."

"Yes, that's it. That's it exactly. If a woman—this woman in the video—can have sex with a dwarf, the epitome of brokenness, then—well, then even the sleaziest of men might feel himself . . . attractive, desirable."

"Frank, please. I appreciate what you are trying to tell me, but it's not—"

"Beautiful?"

"No, it is not beautiful."

We are silent. For a long interval we are silent.

"Jennifer, I know that this—that this is not pleasant, but I appreciate that you are listening, that you are taking me seriously. I have never had a chance to talk like this with anyone before. I feel comfortable with you. You value honesty."

"I try to."

"Let me ask you one more question. And it's not a rhetorical question. I honestly don't know the answer."

She nods. Her eyes give assent.

"What's the connection, Jennifer? What's the connection between the pornographic video and the thing I will be doing at four o'clock this afternoon? With the person from *Vogue*?"

88

History is replete with the stories of individuals who despite wretched physical defects—twists of fate far worse than mine—have accomplished much and achieved happiness. Found love even. But so what? It is the business of historians to generalize. Philosophers generalize. Frank Bois is neither a historian nor a philosopher. Frank Bois has never been able to weasel his way out of the particular. And the particular is this: Frank Bois is in love with Beauty. And Frank Bois is horny.

"Let me ask you about an episode in your book."

The interviewer from *Vogue* magazine (blond, svelte, articulate, Beauty's flawless emissary) leans toward me. "Let me ask you about the thing that happened when you were ten years old, on the morning of the meteor shower. With the girl Fiona."

"Emma."

"Emma?"

"Of course. Fiona."

I keep forgetting Jennifer's fictional names. Why? Why the aliases? Because . . .

"You call it"—she holds the book in her hands, the handsome hardcover, glittering stars on a purple field—"a 'religious experience.' Could you expand on that. It seems extraordinary to me, a woman, that what is essentially an act of voyeurism should be called a 'religious experience.' "

I laugh. "Now, really," I ask her, grinning, "do you think a ten-year-old boy can be called a voyeur?"

She shrugs. "Of course."

Over the tops of my specs I look into her cool brown eyes and see that she is serious. Very serious. There is a nervous giddiness about her, but also a tenacity.

I answer: "Well, I suppose, yes, technically he *is* a voyeur in the sense that the young woman washing herself at the basin does not know that she is being watched. But the boy does not feel himself to be a voyeur. He has been watching a sky made luminous with shooting stars. A night of exceptional beauty. Then, a pink and yellow dawn seeps into the sky, as if by capillary action, pure liquid color. He turns from the roof to go into his room and stops at the window—"

"The woman is naked."

"—and sees the partly naked woman."

"Exactly. And this is a 'religious experience'?"

"I suppose it is in the nature of a religious experience that it is untellable. And it is in the nature of a writer that he tries to tell the untellable. I tried to describe the experience in my book, as best I could. The business of being suddenly struck—paralyzed—by the recognition of—of something that the boy had not known before. Something about— may I coin a word?—something about the *isness* of the world. The boy perceives a world that exists without any sort of cosmic distinction between good and bad, fair and unfair, right and wrong. A world—"

"And this, all of this, when he sees—"

My interlocutor's moist lips. Her eye shadow. Cheek blush. Nails. Cosmetic colors. *Florentine Pink. Raphaelite Rose. Venetian Brocade. Sweet Sienna.*

"Yes, when he sees the girl, the young woman. She is beautiful, you see. The aura of her hair, that marvelous wispy coppery hair that she shares with her sisters, the thin white neck, the pale blue veins, the shoulder blades like nascent wings, the—"

And then, as I respond to the interviewer from *Vogue*, I remember something. A part of the experience that I had forgotten. *There was a mirror.* There was a tiny oval mirror on the wall above the basin. As I watched—as I watched Emma at her bath, I glanced at the mirror and saw her eyes. And this is what I did not recognize or chose not to recognize— *she saw me*, at the window, saw me reflected in her mirror.

"But this thing you call a 'religious experience,' Mr. Bois, it seems, essentially, that it caused you to *abandon* God. It is a curious sort of religious experience that causes a person to abandon God."

I close my eyes and fish about in the pool of memory for details of the image. Emma's eyes, bright in the mirror, fixed upon me. But—the fragment of face in the glass is not Emma's. I have only a momentary glimpse of—of whom? Emma is this other person who stands before the basin with her nightdress down about her waist. Her hands move to her breasts, to cover them. I see the tips of her fingers exert *the slightest pressure* upon the skin. Then she takes her hands from her breasts and draws up her nightdress to cover her nakedness.

I say: "Perhaps the boy *discovered* God."

"That sounds rather far-fetched."

I shrug. "We are all God's voyeurs. We are all of us forever sneaking a look at his private doings, hoping to catch him out in something that will—confirm our prejudices, give meaning to our lives. You would perhaps think it more likely that the boy would have found God *outside*, among the stars—infinity and all that. But infinity is such an abstraction. The stars are too remote to touch us deeply. Remote and terrible. But her fingertips—"

"Fingertips?"

"Her fingertips, so delicate, intimate, yes, the *lightness* of the pressure against the skin. I had caught him out—the boy, I mean, the boy had caught God out, seen something he was not supposed to see, something—"

"Revelatory?" There is an unpleasant irony in her voice.

"Yes, but damaging too."

"Damaging? How?"

How? Yes, how? Skin deep? How thick is the skin, Jennifer Down? Was what the boy saw that morning skin deep? It certainly got under *his* skin, didn't it? Got under his skin in a way that couldn't be rooted out. Look, Jennifer, look at this person from *Vogue* magazine, this journalist friend of yours, this ambassador from the world of glamour, this person who wants to know about religious experiences. She works in a world that is premised on Beauty. She is beautiful. The photographer who accompanies her is beautiful. He tries, Lord knows he tries—like that other photographer, Mr. Tony Hanks—to make the dwarf-author beautiful. But not *too* beautiful, for that's the point isn't it, Jennifer, not *too* beautiful. We know what our readers *want*, don't we? They want the Frog Prince. *Almost* beautiful because of the beauty he has created in his book. This stubby pencil of a writer will be adopted by the Beautiful People—why? Is it because his froggy little body makes *their* beauty all the more fetching? Or because—*see*, oh, see how Beauty can be generous, Beauty is not skin deep, she reaches out and clutches the froggy Little Prince to her bosom? Or is it something else? What? What, Jennifer? You tell me.

But the Frog Prince has an ace up his sleeve—or up his pants leg, I should say—as frog princes always do. Does that have anything to do with it, Jennifer? That thing that reaches halfway to his knees? Does Miss Vogue care about that? Or is *that* the Frog Prince's own dirty little secret?

"Can we talk for a moment about sex, Mr. Bois?"

"Ah, sure, of course. But what about the stars? After all, my book is about the night. We could talk about stars."

"I know. But our readers will be more interested in hearing about *you*, Mr. Bois. How you came to write the book. Your motivations, that sort of thing. What it's like to look at the world from . . . Our magazine feature will be more a personality profile than a book review, if you take my meaning."

"Oh, I do."

"And quite frankly, Mr. Bois, it is the fact that you are—a dwarf that will interest our readers. People do not usually associate *little persons* such as your-self with the world of literature."

"I know, ah sure, I know that most people will assume that a person such as myself is—how should I say it?" I tap my forehead with a stubby finger.

"There is, of course, the example of Toulouse-Lautrec."

"The little teapot with the big spout."

"I beg your pardon?"

"That's what he called himself. The little teapot with the big spout. You wanted to talk about sex. Toulouse-Lautrec was normal, sexually I mean. If anything, he was oversexed. And certainly he had his share of women. Normal women. Pretty women."

"Ah, but that's a problem, isn't it, for—"

"You must remember that Toulouse-Lautrec was wealthy. And extremely well connected. He was de-scended from one of the most famous noble fami-lies of France, the Counts of Toulouse. But even with all of that—the wealth, the status—his love affairs were mostly—perhaps entirely—with prosti-tutes. He paid for sex. There was no love."

"There is an episode in your book where you try to pick up a prostitute."

"Yes."

"Could you say more about that?"

"What more is there to say?"

"It seems to have been—a turning point."

I smile at my journalist from Beautyland. *Roman Red. Tuscan Earth. Botticelli Blush.*

"Do you recall what the prostitute said?" I ask. I answer my own question: "Be gone, ye little dork."

"Ah—"

"It was an interesting response, you see."

"You mean?"

"Skin deep."

"What? I beg your pardon?"

"Skin deep. Skin trade. Skin flick."

"I . . . ?"

"*Dork.* The Dork of Cork."

Noctivagant. *Nighttime vagabond. Darkness stalker.*

But not from the roof of my mother's kitchen. Not anymore. When Jack Kelly first took me through that magical window into the universe, the sky above Cork could be—if the clouds were kind enough to part—spectacularly dark. Now the night sky above the city is a pool of light. Jaundiced light. The garish cast of sodium and mercury. And getting brighter all the time. Flying from London to Cork, I look down on merging blotches of luminescence. Bristol. Cardiff. Waterville. Youghal. Cork. Spreading like a blight over the land. Soon our nighttime commerce will swathe the planet with an unbroken skin of light. The stars will vanish, lost in the sickly glare of artificial illumination.

At Cork airport I ask Handy Paige to carry my small bag into the city by taxi. I walk home, detouring through the hills south of the city, on an all-night ramble along familiar paths. With familiar companions. Foxes. Badgers. Hedgehogs. Barn owls. Long-eared bats. And—a generous sprinkling of stars. The Swan. The Lyre. The Eagle. The Dolphin and the Dart. According to astronomers, every atom in my body was forged in a star. I am made, they insist, of stardust. I am stardust braided into strands and streamers of information, proteins and DNA, double helixes of stardust. In every cell of my body there is a thread of stardust as long as my arm. And in every cell, in every arm's length of double helix, is contained that same damaged twist, that pinch of disarranged stardust, that kink in the plan. *Yes, Jennifer, we are all stardust, but your stardust is arranged more felicitously than mine.*

South along the Kinsale Road, skirting the airport runway, then west, crossing the N71 at Ballynagrumoolia, fuchsia lanterns hanging in the hedgerows, puce and scarlet, yellow flags in green scraw, foxgloves in the ditches, returning to the city through Curraheen and Bishopstown just as dawn erases the last stars and daubs the River Lee with color where it slows to the tide. Above the river, swans wing westward. *I lied.* I lied to Jennifer Down about the video. No, not about the proposition. Not about the man in the expensive black suit, open-neck silk shirt, gold chains, pallorous skin. Not about the proffered drink or the one hundred quid. I lied about *the time* of the assignment. Not Tuesday at 4 o'clock (". . . more of a personality profile than a book review . . ."), but Monday evening at half-eleven. I lied about the time. Lied because I—

I went to the address on the slip of paper.

A mews flat in a maze of narrow lanes behind the V & A Museum. Cobblestone paving. Posh cars. Rollses. Jags. The unmistakable smell of money, but classy too. Yes, very upper-class. The last place you would expect to find the silk-shirted sultan of sleaze. Or, for that matter, Penguin's voguish new author, Peeping Tom Thumb, skulking along the walls, slithering from shadow to shadow, feigning propriety, a much-fingered slip of paper in his pocket: 7, *victoria place mews, 11:30*. His ticket to—to what? Make no mistake, the author of *Nightstalk* has not come to fetch his hundred quid or submit himself to the degradation of a porn video. He has too much pride for that. Too much—ah, integrity. He . . . What then? What is his motivation? Curiosity. Morbid curiosity. Wants to know what he's missing. Wants to sniff the seamy underside, catch the pornographer at his tricks, peek under the rug where the dirt is swept. Have a look-see in the land of the moral midgets. No. 7 Victoria Place Mews is no different in outside appearance from any other house in this stylish neighborhood. But inside, a camcorder whirs. Lights! Camera! Action! Gentlemen, observe. Captured for your amusement on videotape. The Princess and the Frog. Beauty and the Beast. All explicit, nothing faked, quadruple-X entertainment: the Mistress of Sin and the Dork of Cork.

90

The River Lee runs through my story like a silver thread.

It rises in a horseshoe of heathery hills on the Cork-Kerry border at Gougane Barra, St. Fin Barre's rock cleft. Cold mountainy water pools behind a glacial moraine to form a silvery lake where the seventh-century saint had his island hermitage (and where the shivery silence was shattered in the summer of 1959 by the roar of a Triumph 500 motorcycle and the booming voice of a lanky American bouncing echoes off the precipitous valley walls for the amusement of his diminutive pal). A trickle of water spills from the lake, tumbles through a wild mountain valley, gathers volume from tributary streams leaping down sandstone ledges of the Shehy and Derrynasagart Mountains, meanders past the stumps of castles and sedgy pools to the lively market town of Macroom, which commands the junction of the Rivers Lee and Sullane. The joined waters flow through the gorge at Inishcarra (past Hans Scrieber's charmingly rusticated cottage) into the valley of the River Bride, which the Lee adopts as its own. Now the river's run into the city is unimpeded, past broad meadows where gypsy horses graze, to the salmon weir and waterworks, dividing into two channels to embrace the city. The south channel flows past the Protestant cathedral (where Roger Manning, standing one Sunday evensong with his back against a notice board, noticed a strange young woman with dwarf child), and thence beneath the foot of Elizabeth Fort and—green and murky now with the sluggish residue of tide—near to the foot of Nicholas Road (where from the roof of his mother's kitchen the dwarf child Frankie Bois was shown the stars by Jack Kelly). At the Custom House the north and south channels converge, becoming sufficiently capacious in their combined volume to support oceangoing vessels (and to carry, when my story has reached its climax, one last melancholy cargo). The restored Lee turns south into Cork Harbor (where the USS *California* waited at anchor while being reprovisioned, and discharged an uninvited passenger), slices a last sandstone ridge, and spills into the sea.

The sea. Two thousand miles of water between Cork and America. A volume of water infinitely diluting Fin Barre's stream. Two thousand miles of water and then another two thousand miles of mountains and prairie separating Cork, Ireland, and Decatur, Missouri.

Terry Klout's Decatur.

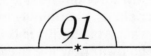

DEE-cate-er, as Terrycloth says. *DEE-cate-er, Mih-zur-uh.*

We were sitting at the edge of Fin Barre's lake in the sandstone bowl of Gougane Barra. Terry's big cycle leaned on its kickstand, its nose grazing the grass, blue vapor rising from chromium exhausts. On the opposite side of the lake a sleepy hotel, apparently unoccupied. Terry skipped a sandstone flake across the smooth water, his left arm, still not fully healed, held gingerly at his side.

"Do you think your mother would come with me to the States?"

"Ask her," I said.

"And what about you, Pug? Would you come? Would you like to see Decatur? And not just Decatur, but Kansas City and St. Joe. St. Louie, even. We could take a look at the Mississippi. That's a hellava river, pal. It took us a couple of hours to get from one end of the Lee to the other, but to ride a bike from New Orleans to the source of the Mississippi would take a couple of weeks. We could do it, you know. We could hop on my bike and ride from Decatur to New Orleans, then turn around and go right up the river to its source. That'd be sumthin'. "

Terry's arm swung a pebble out across the lake, slicing the air like a whistling scythe. *Plip, plip, plip, plip, plip, plip.* Six long skips. *A couple of weeks* to reach the source of the Mississippi! Everything seemed stretched out in America.

"Sure," I said. "I'll go."

But I was skeptical. I knew, even then, that places are unimportant, that the only geography that really matters is—

"Are the stars bright in Decatur?" I asked.

"Are the stars bright! Holy Toledo, Pug, the stars in Decatur are so big we hardly have any night at all. Zillions of stars. You can reach up and grab 'em right out of the sky. And the sky! There's more sky in Decatur than in all of Ireland."

But I knew more about the stars than Terry knew. I knew how far away they are, and I knew that the stars in Decatur are no closer than the stars in Cork. Maybe there aren't so many clouds in Decatur, but the stars aren't any closer, that's sure.

Terry said: "The thing is how to talk your mama into going. I'd marry her, Pug. I'd marry her if she'd have me. 'Course, I'd have to get a divorce from Marcia. But I don't see that'd be a problem. I'd get a divorce from Marcia, then marry Bernsie. And I could adopt you. You can be my son, Pug. We'll live in Decatur. Go fishin'. Ride bikes. Race cars."

He got up to collect more pebbles. Unfolded his body.

"Are there dwarfs in America, Terry?"

Terry stopped, turned, his blue eyes alight.

"Gee, I guess so, Pug. Sure. There's dwarfs everywhere. Just can't think of any right now. Not in Decatur. But sure. Sure. There's dwarfs."

"Tell me about your children, Terry. Tell me about Lisa and Charlene."

He came back from foraging along the lakeshore and sat down, his hands full of sandstone flakes. He dropped the stones between us, then divided them evenly into two piles, one for him, one for me. I watched his face. I knew I could tell what he was thinking about his girls if I watched his face. His eyes got watery. He chewed his lip.

"Lisa's 'bout your age. Pretty as a picture. Blond like her mother. Big blue eyes with long lashes. Just turning into a little lady. Just startin'—you know, fill out, be a woman. There's not a girl in Decatur that's half as pretty. Charlene, well, Charlene's the smart one. Maybe not as pretty as Lisa, but she sure is smart. Gets nothin' but A's in school. I give her a dollar for every A and she's collected a little fortune."

I tried to imagine Terry's girls. I tried to imagine girls who looked like Terry. What came into my mind were girls who looked partly like Terry and partly like Jack Kelly's daughters.

I asked: "Do you think Lisa and Charlene would like me?"

"Sure, sure they'd like ya."

But I detected a note of doubt in Terry's voice. An instant's hesitation. A withholding of assent in the eyes. He cocked his head away from me. He swung a pebble out into the lake. *Plip, plip.*

"Do you think my mammy likes me, Terry? Does Bernadette like me?"

He looked at me, eyes wide, arms flopping at his side.

"Jeez, Pug. Of course she loves you. All mothers love their kids."

"Do you think she *likes* me, Terry?"

"You're a crazy kid, Pug."

His pile of stones was depleted. He took one from my pile.

"Crazy kid." He shrugged. "I don't know, Pug. Don't know who or what Bernadette likes. But I think I know what you mean, though. Bernadette's funny."

He tossed a stone, his wrist snapping like a bullwhip. A necklace of circles expanded in the silvery water.

He said: "Sure is pretty, though. She sure is pretty."

And her son, Terry. Is he pretty?

"Come on, kid. No point sittin' around worrying about things like whether your mama likes ya. Let's go for a ride."

But first we pissed. We stood on the gravelly shore and pissed into Fin Barre's lake. Sent our water on its way to the sea. Two silver streams arching far out into the lake. Two equal parabolas. I glanced at Terry's thing.

It was the same size as mine.

92

OK, Jennifer, let's talk about *things*. Cocks. Dicks. Pricks. The one thing about me that's not stunted, the same as everyone else's. What? No? The topic is vulgar? Size doesn't matter? OK, then let's talk about—

93

Motorbikes and leather.

Let's talk about flying down the Macroom–Coachford Road at sixty miles per hour. The wind in our hair. A deafening roar. Billowing blue clouds of hydrocarbons. Road chips spraying. Cattle starting from the fences. My arms tight about Terry, my face buried in his leather jacket.

I love you, Terrycloth. I want to be your son.

Terry Klout had reason to be encouraged. Roger Manning was out of the picture. Roger Manning had been banished to the diocese of Offaly and Tipperary (where he filled his time ministering to a vanishing flock and composing frankly erotic verse dedicated to my mother). Roger Manning had left Cork without even saying good-bye. For Terry Klout the field was wide open. Bernadette's heart was his for the taking.

Except that Bernadette's heart was not easily taken. Bernadette's heart had been taken only once in her life. By a boy named Charles. Who touched her hand as it grasped a strand of barbed wire. Who kissed her cheek. Who, to please her, threw a stone.

When, Jennifer? When has the beginning of love been followed so abruptly by its laceration? Picture this: A twelve-year-old girl stumbles dazed on a sandy foreshore, her dress blown from her body by a wind more powerful than any storm from the sea. In her hands, a six-foot strand of barbed wire. On the sand, bits and pieces of her friends. Bits and pieces of the boy who had kissed her cheek. *She had seen inside the mine.* Seen the evil lurking there. Seen the gelatinous mass of explosive that

curled within the black sphere like a monstrous mal-
formed embryo. Knew, even as the boy hurled the
stone, that the monster would awaken.

What are we to make of this, Jennifer, this business of visions? Of second sight? We are rational
persons, are we not? No? Not you? You are willing
to entertain the possibility that certain gifted people
can foresee things before they happen? Well, not
me. I have looked into the sky. All my life I have
watched the heavens. I have kept an ear cocked for
God's whispery voice. And I've heard nothing. The
heavens are silent, Jennifer. The gods are speechless. I know. I've listened. I've listened from places
so dark and silent that I could have heard the faint-
est murmur. Nothing. No voice in the burning bush
of the galaxy. Astronomers turn their radio telescopes to space and convert the received radiation
into audible sound. And what do they hear? The
random crackle of elements. The static of electrons
fidgeting between energy levels in the atoms of stellar atmospheres. The hiss and sputter of interstellar
hydrogen. Random, statistical, indifferent noise. No
visions, no voices. It's all the roll of dice. The universe is a game of Russian roulette. A stone is
thrown at a sphere washed up from the sea. An
inch to the left or an inch to the right and nothing
happens. But *this particular pebble*, carelessly
tossed to impress a girl, hurtles through the air and
strikes precisely at the place that will trigger the
explosion. Chance. Pure chance.

But if the gods are silent, then how do I explain
Bernadette's premonitions? Easy. *Coincidence*. You
laugh? OK, then, *intuition*. A knack for anticipation.

Perhaps the clairvoyant gives events a nudge so that they tip in the direction already "foreseen." I don't know. I can't be expected to explain what the collective wisdom of science fails to understand. The human mind is a thing more complex than any star or any galaxy. I can't explain Bernadette's gift. But I know that when the mine exploded on the beach at Fleurville, the detonation extinguished a flame that had been ignited in her heart only a moment before. And I know that if the stone had struck an inch to the left or an inch to the right, my story would have been different.

Or perhaps there wouldn't have been a story at all.

Another mystery. A tall ungainly boy from Missouri, not a virgin but not all that experienced, watches a girl give herself to other men. Envying, but hurting too. He stands away. He has watched her since Le Havre. Watched her since the clique of young GIs took it upon themselves to help her get to America, smuggle her aboard the USS *California*, hide her, feed her, and when the opportunity presented itself, accept her freely proffered sexual favors. He watched her—and he loved her. Ah, Jennifer, it's that greatest of mysteries: *falling in love. Falling.* An accurate word, suggesting as it does something that occurs independently of the will. The irresistible pull of gravity. A man falls from the roof of a building; he cannot *by willing it* impede his progress toward the ground. A man falls in love; he cannot check his descent. While Terry's pals sought to impress the girl with displays of bravado and braggadocio, he hung back. While the others took her one by one on a government-issue mattress on a lower deck of the USS *California*, he felt his heart break, a hairline fracture that did not heal for thirteen years, so that when—

He was out of her house now, but not out of her bed. Bernadette liked having Terry around. He wasn't as pretty as Roger, or as pliant a participant in her sexual games, but he was less complicated. Made fewer emotional demands. He didn't have Roger's hangdog, tragicomic, befuddled-poet pout. And—ah, this is the unexpected twist—he liked *me*. He was the first person who had befriended me since Jack Kelly went to Rosslare. I'll pose a hypothesis: Bernadette liked having Terry around because Terry took young Frankie off Bernadette's hands. But when Terry sprang his proposal about going to America, well, that was something else.

Terry might not have been as smart as Roger Manning, but he was no fool. He knew he couldn't stay much longer in Ireland; for one thing, his money was running out. But he did not want to leave Bernadette. He didn't ask for love. He didn't ask for Roger's dearly imagined connubial bliss. He just wanted to have her about, watch her do nothing. "Darn it, Pug," he said to me, "I get a kick outta just watchin' her read a book."

Once he had picked up a book she had left lying about. It was Yeats's poetry. He read at the place where the book was marked with a dog-eared page. He read the poems about Crazy Jane. And he couldn't make head or tail of them. He furrowed his brow and screwed up his lips and read them one more time, and then again. The words were familiar, but he couldn't make much sense of the way the words were put together. What meaning he surmised seemed harsh. *Love has pitched his mansion in the place of excrement.* What did that mean? He puzzled on it. *Love is like the lion's tooth.* Lion's tooth? What kind of love was this? When next she had the book in her hands, he watched her read. Watched her green eyes burn along the page. Watched her lips silently shaping the words. She was curled up in her favorite chair, the book cradled in her lap.

You will know the line, Jennifer, the line that follows *Love has pitched his mansion in the place of excrement.* You remember? *For nothing can be sole or whole that has not been rent.* One could poke about those lines all day looking for Bernadette. She was rent—oh, indeed, she was rent. When the barbed wire went through her chums, she was rent. Shredded. Diced. They collected her friends in wicker baskets and buried them in a common grave because it was impossible to sort out the pieces, but no one helped Bernadette collect the fragments of her soul. Terry knew that the poems meant something to her, and asked Bernadette to read them aloud to him. And she did. Sitting naked on the bed she read *The more I leave the door unlatched the sooner love is gone, for love is but a skein unwound between the dark and dawn.* He watched her, searching for the meaning of the words in the way her mouth spoke the sounds. He decided: *I could sit all day and watch her read.*

And then he said, "Come with me to America."

She looked up. Looked at the impossibly articulated person in her bed, his arms and legs bent and folded this way and that, his arms covered with yellow down, his face grimacing in anticipation of her answer (her son, above in his bed, thinks: *Mammy, if he asks, say yes*). She closed the book of poems. Pulled her knees to her chin. Considered this man who would have her go across an ocean. His beaked face. His scraggy hair. The body that seemed to have lost its bones.

He grinned. His face unzipped from ear to ear.

Terry was right about the stars in America. The sky is bigger and the stars are closer. In Ireland the sky is a wet drapery hung between earth and heaven. In Decatur, Missouri, the sky is a crystal bowl turned upside down on the prairie. My first night at Terry's house, I went out into that starry darkness, climbed the fence at the back of the yard, and walked through acres and acres of corn to a creek bank far from any house. I lay down on my back and gaped. Fireflies flickered in the corn rows ("lightnin' bugs," Terry had called them). A mysterious light glimmered on a far-off horizon ("heat lightnin'"). And so many stars that it was difficult to recognize constellations, except in the south where Antares flickered alone in the pink glow of Decatur. If I stood on the concrete dam that blocked the stream (and formed a muddy pool for cattle), I could just make out the lights of Terry's house.

Where already Bernadette rued her decision.

This was not the America Bernadette had imagined. It would be difficult to say what sort of America she had expected, but Decatur was not it. A Chevrolet dealership at one end of town and a Ford dealership at the other, and in between, tucked into a half-mile "downtown" of three-story buildings: the First Citizens Bank, faced with limestone, where Terry used to work and hoped to work again; the White Castle hamburger shop, wrapped with shiny metal, where Marcia met Tobin; and the Greyhound Bus Depot, papered with adverts for Coca-Cola and Holsum Bread, where Terry, Bernadette, and Bernadette's son alighted from a coach after a long hot ride from St. Louis. As their taxi moved along Main Street past the bank, the White Castle, and Jimmy Clark's World of Fords, she put her head against the window glass, regretting that she'd come. When the taxi deposited them in front of Terry's house (white, asbestos sided, all by itself on a country road, waist-high weeds in the lawn), she knew she had made a terrible mistake. And when Terry opened the door of his boxy bungalow, dropped their bags on the floor, and turned on the telly, she went into the bathroom, closed the door, and banged her fists against her forehead.

Sitting on the floor in Terry's bath, Bernadette realized the enormity of her mistake, a mistake that could not be easily remedied. Terry had spent the last of his money. Bernadette had none. Their flight from Ireland had been on one-way tickets (with hastily arranged passports and visas). When she emerged from the bathroom, Terry was stretched out on the sofa, his feet aimed at the telly, a can of beer in his hand, and a split six-pack on the floor by his side. On the telly was a sports event that she supposed was American football.

"Where did you get the beer, Terry?" It was the first time she had used his name.

Terry recognized, when he heard those two syllables, that something had changed.

"Would you believe it, I found a six-pack on the back porch? Marcia must have left it there. Not cold, though. Want one?"

"Terry, I'm going home. I'm taking Frank home."

He swung his legs around to the floor and patted the cushion next to him. She sat down where he indicated, slumping back against the cushions, arms clenched across her chest. She was wearing his favorite blue cotton dress. She pulled her knees up onto the sofa and tugged her skirt down over them. Something was different, he could see *that*. She was closing into a shell. He was losing her.

She was pretty. That was the thing. He just sat there looking at her and thinking, *Sweet little Jesus, she sure is pretty*. His heart swelled against the cage of his chest. He didn't ask for much. He just wanted her to stay. To sit on the sofa looking pretty. He knew by now that she would never return his love. That was OK. She could be herself. She could come and go as she pleased. As long as she was there now and then, that's all he wanted. He would wait on her hand and foot. He would give her anything.

He saw that her green eyes had darkened. Some little light had gone out.

He was thinking, *Give it a chance, sweetheart, you just got here*. He said: "We'll have to get the money. We'll need—jeez, I don't know, maybe two thousand bucks to get you two home."

She worked her lips. She thought, *He is a good man*.

"I'll go to the bank tomorrow," said Terry. "I'm hopin' they'll give me my job back. I'll ask for an advance. Maybe I can get a loan. Maybe we can use the house for collateral."

He chewed on the tip of his thumb.

The telly was flickering beyond his shoulder, the sounds of a stadium surging with excitement. He didn't notice. She thought, *He doesn't notice*.

Then he said, just said it flat out: "I love you, Bernsie. I love Pug, too. I'm glad you came here. I'm—"

She shook her head. He flopped his long arms trying to find a place to put them. He wanted to touch her. He wanted to put his arm about her shoulder. He wanted to pat her hand.

She said: "Show me the bedroom."

He smiled, his corn-row grin.

"Does that mean you'll stay."

"No."

"Oh."

She picked up the five-can six-pack.

She said: "I have to go home, Terry. I'm sorry I wasted your money."

96

But Terry didn't go to the bank the next day. Terry took me hunting. He walked a half mile down the road to the house of a friend and borrowed a pickup truck and twenty bucks. And took me hunting.

I wouldn't say that Terry was devious. He probably never thought much about it. He just figured that maybe, if Bernadette's son wanted bad enough to stay, then Bernadette would come around. But he also wanted me to have a good time. He never had a son of his own to take hunting. I think he was glad to have my company.

We drove south from Decatur, thirty or forty miles. The distance would have taken us halfway across Ireland, but here it seemed not very far ("A skip and a jump," said Terry). He drove very fast. The needle on the clock pushed the top of the scale. He paid no mind to the posted limits. He drove as fast as the pickup would move to where the land began to rise in wooded hills.

We parked at the side of the highway.

"Squirrels," said Terry.

"You kill squirrels?"

"You betcha, Pug. We'll blow the little suckers' heads off."

He had a rifle. A .22-caliber single-shot. He balanced it on his palms and passed it to me.

"Just right for you, Pug. Not too heavy. Not much

recoil. When you're bigger, you can use my shotgun."

He reached into the pocket of his hunting jacket and pulled out a handful of shells, tiny shiny things like gold teeth, and slipped them into the pocket of my trousers. I could feel the cold weight of them sagging as we walked into the trees.

"Weren't never here that there wasn't squirrels," said Terry, bobbing and ducking to dodge the lower branches of the trees, tall spindly oaks and evergreen pines. "Red squirrels, gray squirrels. Easy as pie. It's like a shootin' gallery."

The trees almost closed off the sky. The woods were silent and beautiful, like being in a church. I was content to walk at Terry's side, shuffling my shoes through the leaf litter on the forest floor. And did so, happily, until he touched my shoulder and pointed upward—a gray squirrel high in an oak. Terry took the rifle from my hands, drew the bolt, inserted a shell. Then he reversed his actions, removing the shell, and handed the gun to me. I copied him. I drew the bolt, slipped the shell into its chamber, pushed the bolt home. There was something satisfying about the snug fit of shell in chamber, and in the lubricious slide of the bolt. The gun had a pleasurable heft in my hands. Terry tipped the barrel upward and placed the stock squarely against my shoulder.

"Don't jerk," he said. "Take your time. When the animal is in your sights, squeeze gently."

It did not occur to me that I might actually hit the squirrel. I lined the animal up in the sights and waited until it was still. Then I squeezed. The report startled me. The gunstock smacked backward against my shoulder. The squirrel came tumbling down.

"Hey!" Terry shouted. "Holy Toledo! First shot!"

The squirrel writhed at our feet, a gaping scarlet hole in its rear leg. It tried to rise and run, but collapsed, spinning in circles.

Terry was ecstatic. "You did it, Pug! Jeez, you're a helluva shot. The first time you pulled the trigger! I don't believe it!"

I was pleased that I had pleased Terry, but my happiness was tempered by the plight of the animal on the ground. A glistening ruby grew on its pierced leg.

"It's not dead, Terry."

"You can't let it suffer, Pug. Ya gotta put it out of its misery."

I looked at him confused.

He took the rifle from my hands and smashed the squirrel with the stock, square across the neck.

"It's unsportsmanlike to let it suffer."

"What about shooting it, Terry? Wasn't it un-sportsmanlike to shoot it?" I had decided I didn't like hunting.

"It's only a squirrel, Pug. There's a million of 'em."

Maybe I was just closer to the ground than Terry, but I could see the growing bubble of blood on the squirrel's leg. And the glassy eyes, clouding over. The velvety smooth fur. The luxurious tail. And the tiny little paws, outstretched like grasping hands.

I looked up at Terry. He seemed to be way up in the foliage of the trees. Looking down, he saw the confusion in my eyes.

"Jeez, Pug," he said. "It's only a squirrel."

I didn't shoot any more squirrels that day. Terry did, though. Terry picked off half a dozen squirrels. There wasn't any need to put them out of their misery. Terry's aim was dead on. All six squirrels had a keen round hole under the ear or between the eyes. *Ya get 'em in the head and they die quick*, he said. *Blow their brains out, that's the trick.* And he left them lying where they fell.

"Can't we eat them?" I asked.

"Too stringy. Not enough meat. Now, if they was rabbits. Next time, Pug, we'll go for rabbits. Make some real rabbit stew. I'll teach you how to skin a rabbit."

But there wouldn't be a next time. I had no stomach for hunting. Or for skinning rabbits. My shoulder hurt from the rifle's recoil.

"Let's take your mom a prize," he said. He produced a jackknife from his jacket and flicked out the largest blade. And cut the tail off our last squirrel. I heard the snap as the blade went through bone. There was no blood.

He drew the silky fur through a circle made by his forefinger and thumb, first one way, then the other, back and forth. "Look at that, Pug. Soft and pretty as a woman's pussy. Do ya think your mom will like it?"

No. No, Bernadette did not like it. Bernadette turned from Terry's gift with revulsion. She wanted to ask why he had not gone to the bank, but of course she didn't. She wanted to ask why she had been left alone in a house with no books, but she didn't. All day long she had been made sick by the smells of the musty house. If she opened the windows, the air became thick with road dust and pollen. All day she long had been rubbing dust and pollen from her eyes.

Terry saw her reddened eyes. He thought she had been crying.

He touched her cheek. He brushed her lips with his thumbtip and flashed his Terrycloth grin. The squirrel tail drooped from his other hand.

She turned away from him.

She knew that she was being cruel. She had seen the kindness in his eyes. She knew he meant well.

"I am going home," she whispered, to no one in particular.

Until that moment Bernadette had been like a ball of twine with the loose end tucked deep into the ball. You could turn the ball round and round in your hands and find no access to the twine. Roger, Terry, and even her son had searched for the place where they might catch hold of the loose end and unwind a bit, but Bernadette remained inaccessible.

All that day while Terry and I hunted squirrels, an airplane was crop-dusting fields near Terry's house. The noise of the machine was incessant, like an insect buzzing in Bernadette's ear, a fraying, shredding sound that snipped at the surface of her solitude. Soon she was a ravel of dangling ends, not so much unwinding as disintegrating.

And do not fail to take notice of the pilot of the airplane, who with his goggles and leather cap looks vaguely arthropodal. The man who with his right hand pushes the stick forward to bring his machine down to skim the endless rows of corn, and with his left hand pulls the shiny metal knob that releases the cloud of poison. The Insect Man, I'll call him. No, I will call him the Pilot. He will come into my story, too.

I know how Bernadette felt. How, after a long period of equilibrium, a decision is made, instinctively, without adequate consideration, to move toward something promising and new, only to discover that a balance, essential and painfully achieved, has been lost. For Bernadette, it was her decision to follow Terry to America. For me, it was a manuscript delivered to Handy Paige.

How say it? How do I describe the balance that has kept me sane? This is not an easy confession to make. I am a grown man. I am forty-three years old. I have the normal appetites of my gender. Since the age of ten I have been in love with women. Beautiful women. I watch them in the streets, in the shops, in the library. I fall in love. Sometimes I fall in love a dozen times a day. And the objects of my attentions are as far removed from me as if they were stars. If they notice me at all, they turn away in revulsion. What am I left with? The hurt. The aloneness. The sad little rituals of masturbation. An unceasing tension between mind and body: the mind full of affection, worship even, the body crushed like a clay manikin in a fist.

Beauty is not the opposite of ugliness; beauty is the opposite of death. To stay alive, I have sought beauty in the sky. The sky in all its nuances. Its shifting, shimmering subtleties: I am their connoisseur. The sky whispers: I listen. The stars speak sweet nothings: I am their paramour. Wind, rain, cloud, light: the permutations are endless. Stars, planets, nebulas: I have sought them. Once I observed the zodiacal light, the "false dawn" of Omar Khayyám. On a clear moonless night in late February, an hour after sunset, I saw the zodiacal light stretching up from the horizon along the band of the zodiac. The light is caused by sunlight reflecting from interplanetary dust. For twenty years I had sought it. For twenty years I had watched for a light so subtle that only the most perfect meteorological conditions would reveal it. And then I saw it. In the evening's first hours of darkness as I walked in the hills west of the city. A cold wind from the east had cleared the air, and stars fell to the very horizon. I saw the zodiacal light. I was overwhelmed by its beauty, which was more an aspect of its subtlety than its grandeur. I never saw it again.

Into such frail vessels have I decanted my love of women.

Night is the dangerous time, when the angels come visiting—whispering, whimpering, taunting, luring, pouting, smirking. They wear the faces of women I have seen in the street. They whisper phrases of that mysterious language that women speak. It is the time of madness. Or worse. And so I go into the night in search of noctilucent things. A lovely word—*noctilucent*, night-shining—usually reserved for certain high clouds seen in summer that catch the rays of the sun long after the surface of the earth has been plunged into darkness. Night-shining things: noctilucent clouds, the zodiacal light, the gegenschein, the Milky Way. I walk, I watch, I keep my journal. The pile of notebooks on the floor by my desk slumps under the burden of its own weight, a dozen dozen notebooks filled with nocturnal observations, with which I have attempted to armor myself against—

Ritual. Ritual is my shield against depression, insanity, death. The nighttime walks, the endless cups of tea, the black pudding and brown bread fried up every morning at eleven, the weather forecasts on BBC 4 at five till two and ten till six, the reading room of the Cork City Library at half-two, the glass of port at five. The writing up of the journals. The scribble-scribble. And the angels, fluttering there in the corner of the room, their wings luminous in firelight, held at bay.

And now my armor is at risk. *The book.* I have become a public person. Envelopes slip in under the door like windblown autumn leaves. Handy Paige badgers me into another excursion. Jennifer

Down's secretary sends notes and reviews. I hear myself on the radio, talking to an RTE presenter ("Would you say, Mr. Bois, that your book is as much about *inner space* as outer space." *Well, yes, I suppose.* "And the dark angels, could you tell us a bit more about that?" *No.*) The story in the Cork *Examiner*: "Small Man Publishes Big Book" (and the photograph: *Local author Frank Bois holds copy of new book*). So that now, when I walk in the street, people nudge their companions or jerk their thumbs in my direction. Shop clerks count out my change with blushing attention. Even in a pub on Albert Quay, where I am used to my solitude, a dockworker nominated by his friends comes up to me and asks, "Wouldn't you be the bloke we seen in the paper?"

The flat in Victoria Place Mews, London. No. 7. *Knock, enter.* My angel waits. She is dressed in— what? Leather, silk, black lace: take your pick. Her lips are scarlet. She kneels. She unbuttons my fly. *I squint into the glare of lights.* Behind the noontime brilliance other angels smirk and grin. *Cameras whir.* The tip of her tongue emerges from the scarlet hole of her mouth, a silky snake. *It is all recorded on magnetic tape, packaged, sold, a glossy video.*

Handy Paige arrives. Half-nine on a wet October evening, the fire has collapsed, the port is gone. I open the door to his knock. The angels scutter and hide.

The collar of his coat is turned up against the chill. He wears a gray fedora with a tiny green feather stuck in the band. His teeth are the color of tobacco.

"Fer Chrissake, Bois, put on some lights in here,

the place is a fukkin' cave. Jaysus, look at the mess. Ah, sure you live like a fukkin'—"

"Dwarf?"

"Ta, exactly. You live like a fukkin' dwarf."

"I *am* a fukkin' dwarf, Handy."

He pulls off his fedora and forks his fingers through the wild hair at the back of his head.

"What do you do in here—in the dark? Like a fukkin' mole in his burrow."

I flick on the desk lamp, a forty-watt bulb in a green glass shade.

"Christ, lookit the mess."

"I prefer the darkness, Handy. I feel comfortable in the dark."

He looks nervously for a place to sit. I sweep a pile of papers from the chair by the fire.

"Christ, it's cold in here. Yer a fukkin' rich author, man, put some coals on the fire. You can afford a few lumps of coal."

He picks up the scuttle and dumps coal into the grate, *tump, tump*, into smoldering ash.

"Jaysus Christ almighty."

"Have a seat, Handy."

He casts his badgery eyes about, then collapses into the chair. He attempts to clean the coal dust from his hands by brushing them furiously against each other.

The *Sunday Times Magazine* lies open on the floor, a full-page photograph of a French film star in a clingy gown. I tip it closed with my toe. Handy notices.

"Why are you here, Handy? You are not usually out this time of night."

"Yer fukkin' right I'm usually not out visiting dwarfs in their smelly little holes. This isn't any decent way to live, Bois. You've got money, fer Chrissake. Get yerself a nice flat, sumthin' bright and cheery. Buy yerself a television. Buy a car. Be out and about."

I screw my mouth.

He hammers his knee with his fist. "Yer a famous author, man. Act like one. Get yerself a girlfriend. Get yerself two or three girlfriends. Get yerself—"

"Why are you here, Handy?"

He slumps back into the chair. The fire sputters.

"Get yerself a telephone, for Chrissake. Yer editor, Ms. Down, called today. Asked me to get in touch with you. You're going to be signing books tomorrow at Waterstones. Ten o'clock. They'll have a special display. I was by there today. The window on Patrick Street is all Frank Bois. Fifty copies of *Nightstalk*. Like a fukkin' shrine it is. Yer the King of the Dwarfs, now, Bois. They'll be lining up to collect yer autograph."

"The Dork of Cork."

"What?"

"Handy, I'm frightened. I felt it very strongly tonight. You know what happened to my mother. And to her mother before her. It's dangerous. This whole thing is dangerous. I'm at loose ends. The—"

Handy leaps to his feet, eyes pricking the gloom.

"Christ, man, get a-hold of yerself. It's all in yer head. This whiney stuff is all in yer head. It's because ya sit in here in this rat hole yanking off. Buy yerself a television. Get a girlfriend. I tell you, Bois, there's nothin' wrong with you that a little contact with society won't cure. Sittin' on the high street selling books will be good for ya. Get you out and about."

"Beauty is only skin deep."

"What?"

"Beauty is only skin deep. That's what Jennifer said to me. And now *you* tell me that it's all in my head. It comes to the same thing. But Jennifer doesn't live in my body, Handy, and you don't live in my head. The two of you don't know what it's like to—"

"Yer fukkin' right I don't know what it's like. You think too much, Bois. That's yer fukkin' problem, you think too much."

He knits his fingers frantically, twirls his thumbs. His black eyebrows prick out from his forehead like hairbrushes.

"Books, Bois, books. That's what it's all about. Books mean money. Money means happiness. You got money, you can buy yerself any fuck in town."

"Are you sure of that, Handy?"

"Yer fukkin' right, I'm sure."

He slaps his fedora onto his head with such nervous violence that the tiny green feather flies out of the band and flutters to the floor.

"Ten o'clock, Bois. Ten o'clock sharp. Be there. And bring yer biro."

I am at Waterstones at ten, in what I call my author outfit—the black turtleneck sweater and brown corduroy trousers that I wore for Tony Hanks's jacket photo. I am greeted warmly by the store manager, Mr. Earnest Deasey, blond, blue eyed, and very young—thirtyish—to have a position of such authority.

His grip is firm and friendly: "Earnest Deasey, Mr. Bois. We are ready for you. I read your book last night. Loved it. We're all ready. Did you see the display in the window? The book is doing very well. Very well indeed. We generally do very well with local authors. In fact, the Irish author trade is really the staple of our business here. We are a British firm but we certainly cater here to the Irish market. Penguin's been very enthusiastic about your book. Did you see the poster they provided. Air-freighted overnight. Arrived by courier half an hour ago."

I am escorted to a captain's chair in the space between Travel and New Releases. There is a table piled high with *Nightstalk*. In the midst of the pile is a cardboard poster of Tony Hanks's photo blown up to triple size.

I sit. My legs stick straight out.

"Is the chair OK?" asks Earnest Deasey, with good-natured solicitude.

"It's fine."

Vivaldi's *Four Seasons* on the sound system. A

young woman arrives with a tray—coffee, milk, and sugar. Raven hair tied at her neck with a fuchsia ribbon.

"Coffee, Mr. Bois?" Her smile is touchingly sincere. *Perhaps Handy Paige is right; perhaps I think too much.*

Deasey beams. A few customers who had been browsing in other parts of the store drift to the tables near the front, but not yet to my chair. I sweeten my coffee and the woman departs with the tray, leaving behind a faint scent of perfume. Deasey clears a corner of the Travel table for my cup and saucer.

"John Banville is doing very well right now. And Dermot Bolger. But we expect you'll do very well, too. We do very well indeed with books of local interest."

"I'm afraid I forgot to bring a pen."

"No bother at all, no bother at all." Deasey pulls a felt-tip from his inside coat pocket. He forks back his blond locks. *Pin-stripe suit and spit-polished shoes.*

"Is this acceptable?"

"Perfect."

"I'll leave you to your fans."

My fans are slow in coming. The browsers who had drifted to nearby tables, once they appraise the situation, drift away. I sip my coffee and wonder what became of the attractive clerk. At last an elderly gentleman who has been hovering near Irish Interest picks up a copy of *Nightstalk* from the display and brings it to my chair.

Nervous. Big smile.

"May I have your signature, Mr. Bois?" He pronounces it *Bo-is*.

"Of course." I pop the top from the pen.

"Would you be kind enough to inscribe it to 'Arnie'? Just something like 'To my friend, Arnie.' "

I look up into his smile. Snowy white hair billowing about his ears, shiny pink skin on top. Cheerful blue eyes.

He says: "I have a collection of autographed books, you see. Quite a big collection. I never miss one of these sessions."

I sign, *To my friend Arnie, Frank Bois. May 29, 1990*. From the corner of my eye I catch a glimpse of the raven-haired clerk working the back desk.

The white-haired man takes the book from my hand. "I have a Maeve Binchy, you know. And a Frank O'Connor."

I pat the autographed book.

"Enjoy."

"Oh, I never read." He taps his specs. "The old eyes aren't as keen as they used to be. I just collect. Quite a collection, you know. I have a Maeve Binchy."

He backs away, bowing as if I were royalty.

Paige is right, I think too much.

By half-eleven I have signed three books and the raven-haired girl has twice refreshed my coffee. When next Deasey stops to pass the time I ask for the loo. While I am gone he moves my chair and the pile of books closer to the door. Now I am stuck between Local Interest and Irish Interest. Anyone who enters the store must pass directly by my chair.

I sign a book *To Tadg* for his wife, Flora.

"Tadg will love it," says Flora. "He's crazy on astrology."

"There's no astrology in my book," I tell her.

She is momentarily confused.

"There is astronomy," I say, "but no astrology."

Flora brightens. "Oh, stars is stars," she says, pleased. "Tadg saw yer pitcher in the *Examiner*."

At twenty past twelve I look up to see a woman offering me a book. Tall. Midfifties, perhaps. Short gingery hair, copper turning gray, wispy, uncombed. Blue eyes set in dark recesses above prominent cheekbones. Skin so pale and thin one might imagine it transparent to the light. She wears a beautifully worked lace collar over a pale blue cardigan.

I take the volume from her hands.

"Is there anyone particular to whom I should inscribe it?"

She doesn't speak, but shakes her head—*no, no*—in reply.

I sign, *Frank Bois, May 29, 1990*, and then, because I feel some curious affinity—what is it?—for this shy person, add a phrase from the book: *Listening and watching, waiting, always waiting, for the tingle in the spine*.

Earnest Deasey stands behind the woman as I return the book to her. She casts a nervous glance at him, then hurries to the door.

"Lunchtime, Mr. Bois." Deasey shoots his cuffs and tightens the knot of his tie. "You've had a busy morning."

He puts the best face on it. The pile of books appears undiminished.

"Things are always busier here in the afternoon. Miss O'Shea will take you for a bite to eat at Maguires next door."

I look over my shoulder. The raven-haired girl is waiting. She smiles. Her hand goes to her neck in a curiously familiar way. Suddenly I recognize the woman who has just left the store with an auto-graphed copy of *Nightstalk*.

It was Emma Kelly.

100
*

Terry got back his job at the bank, but only a single week's advance on his salary. With living expenses and the necessity of buying an automo-bile on credit, it would be quite a long time before there would be enough money to get Bernadette and Frank back to Ireland. This suited Terry. He hoped that as time passed Bernadette would settle in, become accustomed to Decatur, enjoy her new life.

He cleaned the house, made it sparkle. Packed the fridge and kitchen cupboards with TV dinners, sweets, snacks. Collected big bunches of field dai-sies and placed them in bottles and jam jars around the house. Purchased bright pink sheets for the big double bed. On their fifth day back from Ireland he set off for work at First Citizens, smartly dressed in a new blue polyester suit with wide padded shoul-ders, a white shirt with a cowboy cut, and string tie.

Bernadette had no intention of waiting months to return to Ireland. She despised Decatur and, against her will, began to despise Terry. She would gladly have exchanged Terry's fridge stocked with trashy food for an apple or a pear. The bread, thin sliced and wrapped in crinkly paper, was like paste. Smells of road dust and insecticide sickened her. To Terry's dismay she left his bed for the bottom bunk in the girls' room, Charlene's bed, with me above in Lisa's.

"Well, at least take the new sheets," said Terry. He folded them in half and used one to make her bed, the other to make mine.

With a fifty-dollar down payment (half his first week's salary), he purchased a 1956 Chevy pickup, "candy-apple red" and "clean as a whistle." On his second day at work Bernadette asked to be driven to town. She walked up one side of Main Street and down the other, from Jimmy Clark's World of Fords to Shiel's Chevrolet. She looked in at the window of the White Castle but didn't see anyone who might be Marcia. Then she explored the side streets of the town, the numbered avenues toward the grain elevators north of Main Street, and the lettered avenues reaching out toward the International Harvester factory in the south. At the C Street Bar and Grill she saw a hand-lettered sign in the window: Help Wanted. Ten minutes later she was a barmaid.

The proprietress of the C Street "took a shine to her." Angie Creech was a big Irishwoman in her sixties, with nicotine-stained fingers and a fag on her lip, a fret of fat red lines in her cheeks, and orange hair piled in flat loops on the top of her head. She had been managing the bar and grill since her husband died. There was no grill, really; ready-made sandwiches only. Angie liked Bernadette right away, liked her pretty face and charming accent, part French, part Irish.

"Nuthin' to it, sweetie. Take 'em their beer and take 'em their change. Thirty bucks a week an' tips. If they likes ya, you can do well on tips. The last girl cleared, oh, sixty seventy dollars. Always flirtin', she was. Went off with one of the guys to Kansas City. That's why I need a new girl. Y'can start tomorrow."

That night Bernadette cropped her hair to within half an inch of her scalp (she left the shorn tresses on Terry's kitchen floor; he swept them up but saved a pinch to put in the family Bible). The next afternoon she hitched to town and went to work for Angie Creech. The men who patronized the C Street Bar and Grill were mostly assembly-line workers at I-H. They had never seen a barmaid like Bernadette. The clothes she wore—well, they weren't Decatur. Even Terry was surprised at what she took to wearing. Her few cotton dresses, yes, of course, but now covered with layers of garments she found around the house, tee-shirts, baggy sweaters, Terry's work shirts, old football jerseys, a poplin hunting vest with lots of pockets. No matter how hot or how humid the day, she went off in layers. But even through her heaps of clothes, the men who sat at the counter or slumped in the booths of the C Street Bar and Grill could see that she possessed a fine figure. She wore no makeup or jewelry. She didn't speak. She stood by their tables and silently took their orders. She brought them their drinks without a word. She wore a vague, dreamy smile, and her thoughts seemed far away.

At first, because of the way she dressed, they thought she might be easy. But that perception soon changed. When they called her "sweetheart" or "honey-pie," she didn't respond. When they patted her bottom or touched her arm, she took no notice. She was a mystery, a riddle, and after a while they began to like her, more as a sort of silent pal than potential pickup.

And she liked them. Liked their coarse language and beefy skin, their beer bellies and tattoos. Liked the way they clasped their frosty mugs in ham fists. Liked the way they tapped their Camels and Lucky Strikes smartly from the packs. Like their up-front, what-you-see-is-what-you-get honesty. But mostly her thoughts were of Ireland, her flat in Nicholas Road, and the murky green waters of the River Lee.

One evening Terry said to me: "It's time to see about puttin' you in school, little feller."

"He's not going to school," snapped Bernadette. "He's going home."

"Well, unless you're makin' a lot more money at Angie's than I think you're makin', it's gonna to be a long while before we can buy your tickets." Terry didn't snap; he said it gently.

"He's going home," said Bernadette, and that was that.

Terry was more in love than ever. He could see that something strange was happening. Bernadette was drifting into dangerous waters and he wanted to help her. Wanted to take her in his arms, whisper comfort, sleep by her side.

"Your mama needs our help," he said to me as we sat in the glider in the backyard, looking at the stars.

"What's wrong?" I asked. I knew that something was amiss.

"Don't know," mused Terry. He kept the glider swinging slowly back and forth. "She was always unusual, your mama, but now she's actin' *really* strange."

"I wish she would marry you, Terry."

"Me too, Pug. But I don't think your mama's gonna marry anybody."

"If she goes back to Ireland, I'd like to stay here with you."

Terry took my hand. "I'd like that too, Pug. But a boy's place is with his mother. She won't leave you behind."

I wasn't sure of that. Wasn't sure about not being left behind. I watched my mother at night as she prepared for bed. Watched her come in from the bath in her nightgown, arrange her clothes in piles on the bureau, and lay down on Lisa's bed. She never took notice of me, never said good night. I could hear her breathing in the bunk below, like an anxious, feral animal, for a long time before she went to sleep.

Angie Creech, too, suspected that all was not well with Bernadette. She was surprised when the girl arrived for work on that first day with her hair chopped off.

"Oh, Lordies, girl, what happened ta y'hair?"

Bernadette smiled and stroked the stubble with her hand.

"Such pretty hair," said Angie, shaking her head.

She watched Bernadette with the men and worried what might happen. They were nice fellows, yes, but Bernadette was vulnerable. Or so Angie imagined.

Angie could see that the men couldn't make heads or tails of the new girl. "Jist off t'boat," she whispered to one of them. "Still a bit shy."

Angie knew that Bernadette's silence wasn't shyness. The girl was lost in her own little world. But she did her job. She learned the routine. Never made mistakes with the change. Helped keep the place spic and span. At the end of the first week Angie gave her three crisp tens from the register and asked about tips. Bernadette reached under the counter and removed a brown paper envelope from her string bag. She counted out the bills.

With Angie's thirty, she had ninety-three dollars.

That was the year of Comet Seki-Levi.

Early in the spring the comet had been discovered simultaneously on photographic plates by a Japanese amateur comet-hunter, Kiyomi Seki, and an astronomer at the Hamburg Observatory in Germany, Richard Levi. The comet was on an orbit that would take it very close to the sun. The predictions were that it would become very bright, perhaps as bright as the planet Venus. This was the first time such a potentially bright comet was discovered so long before its closest approach to earth. In Ireland the run up to the comet was subdued, but America went comet crazy. Seki-Levi became a media event. Newspapers ballyhooed its coming. Paperbacks appeared (*Seki-Levi: Visitor from Space*). Religious fanatics predicted the end of the world. The Franklin Mint produced "once in a lifetime" keepsake plaques in pure silver. Steamship lines offered comet cruises, complete with telescopes and lecturing experts.

Seki-Levi was a bust. The comet failed to develop its expected brightness. It was perhaps a virgin comet, approaching the sun for the first time, its early luminosity blown away by solar wind. While still in Ireland, I looked for the comet in the morning sky, unsuccessfully. In late June it slipped around the sun and reappeared in the pale pink sky of evening. Terry lent me the telescopic sight from his deer-hunting rifle and a borrowed pair of binoculars. With these instruments I found the comet. Night after night, while Bernadette carried drinks at the C Street Bar and Grill and Terry watched TV on the living room couch, I observed the comet from the concrete dam at the back of the cornfield. Watched it climb from the western horizon to a spectacular conjunction with Venus and Jupiter. At the end of the week it glided to a rendezvous with the slenderest of crescent moons.

Seki-Levi was a public disappointment, but for me

it was special, the first comet whose progress I had followed from discovery to departure. Never, in all the time that Comet Seki-Levi was in the sky, did it achieve naked-eye brightness. Even the binoculars and telescopic sight showed barely a hint of a tail. But somehow the elusiveness of the comet made it all the more exciting. The comet seemed to be mine alone. Delicate. Ephemeral. A thing of hints.

I took Terry out to the concrete dam. The wind whispered in the willows by the pond. Frogs *galomphe*d. Somewhere far off an owl hooted at the moon.

"Don't see a thing," said Terry, squinting through the borrowed glasses.

"South and west of the moon's horn," I said, indicating the position by pointing to a spot near my curved forefinger and thumb.

He looked and looked. "Don't see a thing."

"It's just a smudge, Terry. Just a faint little smudge near the horn of the moon. The moon's light makes it hard to see."

He peered again. "I'll try the telescope."

He swapped the binoculars for the telescopic sight.

"Don't see it, Pug. Sorry, but I don't see a thing."

"It's pretty, Terry."

"I'll take your word for it, Pug. I sure can't see what all the fuss is about."

High mare's-tail clouds moved in from the west, tinged with the last pink rays of sun. Cattle murmured in the stubbly field beyond the willows. Terry and I sat silently at the side of the dam considering the stars. The concrete was cool against my bare shins.

"It's just a smudge," I said.

At midnight Terry drove to Decatur and picked up Bernadette at the C Street Bar and Grill. He parked on the south side of C Street and watched through the plate-glass windows as Bernadette wiped up tables and Angie shooed the last customers from the bar. He watched the men swagger unsteadily into the street and realized that he was jealous.

When Bernadette emerged and climbed into the cab of the Chevy, he said, "Pug showed me a comet tonight."

She sat with her knees up under her chin, her string bag clutched to her shins.

"That's nice."

"Didn't see it, though." He laughed.

Bernadette opened her bag and removed an Indian cotton scarf. She wrapped it around her neck.

"You don't have to work, you know."

"I've always worked."

He turned the key in the ignition.

"Pug's happy here."

"I'm not."

He clicked on the headlamps and moved off down C Street.

He said: "I saw Marcia today."

"That's good."

"She wants to come home with the girls. I guess she's had enough of Tobin."

Bernadette shrugged. "I'll find someplace to stay."

"I want you to stay with *me*, Bernsie. If Marcia wants to have the house, then you and I can live somewhere else. But if you're goin' back to Ireland, then I guess that Marcia—"

"I'm going."

"I love ya, Bernsie. The thing is I miss my girls."

They had reached the highway out of town. As Terry shifted into third gear, his hand slipped off the stick to cover her hand on the seat. She didn't pull her hand away.

"You know, Bernsie, you're the prettiest thing I ever seen. Always was, always will be."

She looked at him. Saw the downy yellow hair on the back of his hand. Saw the affection flooding out of his eyes. He winked. His big sad mouth cracked into a grin. And she knew then more certainly than ever that she must go. If she did not go, his love would devour her.

103

The question was: How to get the money? Out of the blue, the wild blue yonder, an opportunity presented itself.

The Pilot was a regular customer at the C Street Bar and Grill. The crop duster. A bulky little man with stubbly beard and leathery skin. Oil-black eyes. A faint smell of gasoline and insecticide.

His eyes never left her as she made her rounds of the booths. She could feel them even when her back was to him. Every night he came in, took the booth by the door, ordered two ham sandwiches and a Miller's. Then another Miller's, and another. Some nights he stayed till Angie threw him out at midnight. Some nights he drank a dozen beers.

His eyes frightened her. They were like razors. What she liked about the Pilot was his aviator's jacket. Nut-brown leather, cracked by weather, with a lambskin collar. He never took it off. Even when the flies went dozy with heat and the other customers rolled the sleeves of their tees up over their shoulders, the Pilot wore his jacket.

He never spoke. When his beer was gone, he tapped the empty bottle with his forefinger and she brought another. One night as she returned his change and wiped up the table, he grasped her wrist with his right hand. With his left hand he smoothed a fresh $100 bill onto the wet Formica.

We were back in Cork by the end of the month. But not before a visit from Marcia and the girls.

On the morning of July 4th, Tobin dropped Terry's family off at the house, bags and all. They had come home.

Bernadette was in the backyard glider, reading a

magazine she had picked up at Angie's. I was in the driveway attaching the squirrel tail to the handlebar of Charlene's bike (it was Terry's idea that I should learn to ride the bike; I wasn't keen on bicycles). Terry was stretched out on the sofa in his jockey shorts watching a quiz show on television. When the car pulled up, he came to the open door and looked through the screen. His heart sank.

He ambled out to Tobin's car.

"They're all yours," said the manager of the White Castle hamburger restaurant, grinning good-naturedly. "She's letting me off the hook."

Terry looked at Marcia. She had dyed her hair a funny henna sort of color. Without makeup, her face was pasty white. A little fist of affection gripped his heart.

"I told you to wait till Bernadette and Frank were gone. This isn't a good time to come home, Marcia. You could'a waited."

"It's my house," said Marcia. "Our girls need a home. They're tired of bein' cooped up in Tobin's apartment."

"They's sweet girls," said Tobin, "but I can't say as I will miss 'em."

Lisa and Charlene hung near their mother, staring sullenly at me. Tobin dropped the last of Marcia's bags onto the lawn and started up his car.

"See ya round, sweetheart. It's been fun." He backed the car out of the drive.

Terry said: "I s'pose you're still goin' to work for that guy."

"Why not? You've got your own little thing goin'. I hear she's a real weirdo."

Terry glanced at the house but Bernadette was not in sight.

"Is this her kid?" asked Marcia, nodding toward me. She folded one arm across her chest and propped her chin on the other fist, looking sidewise at Terry as if to say—

"Pug's a great kid," said Terry. "Smart as a whip."

"Ain't very big, though, is he? I'm sure you'd love to have a whole bunch of littl'uns like that runnin' round."

"Cool it, Marcia. This is Pug's house now. You could have waited before coming home. I told ya they'd be goin' soon."

Terry took Lisa and Charlene by the hands and led them to where I stood by Charlene's bike. He said: "Kids, this is Frank Bois. I call him Pug."

I didn't want anyone but Terry to call me by that name. That was a special name, just for Terry.

Terry held out Lisa's arm to me, then Charlene's. I shook their hands.

"It's my bike," Charlene whispered to Terry, "and I don't want that dirty squirrel tail on it." She wiped her hand on her blouse.

Terry ignored her. "Pug knows ever'thing there is to know about the stars."

"Movie stars?" smirked Lisa.

"No," Terry laughed. He threw back his head and pointed up at the sky. Huge stratocumulus clouds were heaped on every horizon, black as night but lined with silver. "Real stars, Lisa. Galaxies. Constellations. That sort of stuff. This kid knows it all."

Lisa rolled her eyes. Charlene shrugged. I detached the squirrel tail from her bike.

Terry turned to Marcia. "Ya can't stay here, Marcia. Not yet. There's not enough room."

Marcia fluffed her hair and tucked her pink blouse into green slacks. She undid the top few buttons of her blouse.

"It ain't her house, Terry. It's my house. Let *her* find somewheres else to stay. Of course, you can go with her if you want." She pushed up onto the toes of her pink sneakers and surveyed the house. "Where is she, by the way? Where is this little Irish *col-leen*? I'd like to see what you think's so special. I hear she's a real *bo-hee-mian*."

Terry's nose wrinkled. "She's in the backyard. And she's not a bohemian."

Marcia marched off around the side of the house.

The girls stood for a moment nervously in the driveway, then ran to follow their mother.

Terry looked at me. "Well, Pug, I sure got my foot in it this time."

"Both feet, Terry," I said. "You've got both feet in it."

Bernadette cleared out of Terry's house. She tossed her few clothes into the string bag with the money envelope and the magazine and walked to town.

"At least let me drive you," pleaded Terry.

"I'd rather walk. Thanks for letting Frank stay."

"Where will you live?"

"I'll find someplace. Maybe I'll stay with Angie."

She hiked the four miles into town, arriving just in time for the Independence Day parade. Main Street was festooned with red, white, and blue bunting. The high school band was drawn up in front of the memorial monument by the courthouse, playing what sounded like *God save our Queen*. People with balloons and candy floss were jammed on the Courthouse lawn. She passed the festivities by. She went directly to the boarding house on E Street where the Pilot had a room. She had been there twice before. He was sitting on the front stoop smoking, in a black tee-shirt with rolled-up sleeves, the aviator's jacket across his lap. A tobacco pouch and pack of cigarette papers lay beside him.

His eyes flared when he saw her.

"What'ja doin' here?" He crushed out his cigarette on the cement step.

She planted herself before him, folded her arms, and said: "I'll stay one week for seven hundred forty-six dollars." That was exactly the money she needed for the tickets.

He laughed, a tobacco-stained *hee-haw*. "Now where would I get money like that?"

"You've got the money. I've seen you have the money."

He squinted.

She said, "Take it or leave it."

He sat up straight as a board. "Listen, lady. I've been with lots of women and never paid money like that."

She folded her arms. "You've got thirty seconds to make up your mind. And I want the money now."

He leaned back against the steps and considered her proposition.

The next morning Bernadette was at the door of Sunfare Travel when it opened at nine.

No, Jennifer, I did not include the things that happened at Terry's house while my mother was with the Pilot.

Why not? I don't know. It was personal, and—no, really, humiliating too. It was not a pleasant week, although it had its memorable moments. Maybe if I write a second book. Maybe the second book will include what happened in America. God knows, there would be enough to write about.

Lisa, for instance. I could write about Lisa.

When Marcia and the girls moved back into the house, I was displaced to the back porch. Terry made me a bed out of two sleeping bags. I was out of the house now; banished, so to speak. The new sleeping arrangement pleased me. I exulted in my banishment. Even then, you see, I was fond of solitude. I loved to lie on my soft bed and watch the fireflies—*lightnin' bugs*—blinking on the lawn like constellations of movable stars. And cicadas, and crickets; their music was beautiful. Except for the mosquitoes. The porch was screened, and I tried to block all the rips in the screening with little bits of paper, but mosquitoes found a way in. They feasted on my flesh. I scratched the itchy bites. By the end of the week my legs and arms were covered with scabs.

Once I was awakened by the beating of wings. I woke in a fright. It was a polyphemus moth, the size of my hand, fluttering helplessly against the wire screening by my bed. A great lamp-eyed gaudy thing, fern fringed and furry. I had never seen such an insect. Terry had given me a penlight to use in the night. I turned the beam on the moth. The moth thrashed against the wire. A powdery dust fell from its wings. I caught the moth up in my hands and carried it outside. When I opened my hands it fluttered upward, ascending on heavy strokes. A velvet-soft wing brushed my cheek and the moth disappeared into a universe brilliant with stars.

Marcia called me "Shortie."

"I'll not have Shortie at the table," she said. "He can eat where he sleeps."

"Pug will eat at the table with the rest of us," insisted Terry.

"Not while I'm the cook." Marcia was adamant. "It's not that he's—you know, *like he is*. It's just that I won't have *her kid* at *my* table." She pulled her housecoat closed at the neck. "And I can't stand to have him looking at me. Do you see the way he looks at me? It gives me the creeps."

We ate in two shifts: Marcia and the girls, then Terry and me. While the women ate, Terry and I sat in the glider in the backyard and talked about the automobile he was going to buy and fix up. The souped-up Chevy. The triple-baked tangerine-flake paint job. The moly-chrome hubcaps. The quadruple overhead double-cam whatever-it-was. It was like a foreign language. "I'll blow 'em away," confided Terry.

After a few days Lisa took to sitting for dinner on both shifts. Lisa liked her daddy.

And I liked Lisa. She was only a year older than me, but she seemed very grown-up, with summer-blond hair tumbling to her shoulders and pubescent breasts swelling under tees and tube tops. As soon as her parents left the house in the morning she slicked on shiny red lipstick ("It's OK with Mom, but Daddy hates it"). It was high summer and the girls were on school holidays.

Charlene had nothing to do with me. Charlene was loyal to her mother. Charlene recoiled from my presence. But Lisa was curious. Lisa came to sit beside me in the backyard glider. Lisa asked questions.

"Why are you so short? Didja have a disease or sumthin'?

"Do ya go to school? What do the other kids say when ya come to school?

"Where'd ya get those shoes? I never seen shoes like that before."

We pendulumed back and forth in the summer sun, and I answered her questions as best I could, always conscious of the nearness of her thin bare arms and her bare toes sweeping the grass.

Sometimes we saw Charlene watching from the kitchen window.

"Don't mind Charlene," said Lisa. "She thinks you're a freak or sumthin'."

"What do you think, Lisa?" I wanted to know.

The glider came to a stop. She plucked out a

dandelion with her toes. The toenails were painted a glossy red that matched her lips.

She said: "I don't know. You *are* a freak, I guess. I guess you're just unlucky."

"Unlucky?"

"Yeah. Your egg got all squashed or sumthin'."

My egg got all squashed. She wasn't a bad girl. She just wasn't used to having someone like me around. She tried to be friendly. She talked. I think she was lonely.

"All Charlene does is pout," moaned Lisa. "She's such a goodie-goodie."

At the back of the yard there was a see-saw that Terry had made from a two-by-six. I climbed on one end and Lisa on the other. She weighed more than me. Up and down we went, Lisa springboarding on the grass, my legs never touching the ground. At the top of every ascent she gave me a bounce by thumping her end of the board hard onto the ground.

She tried to dislodge me.

"I'll getcha," she laughed. Her white knickers showed in the gaps between her shorts and her legs.

You see what I mean, Jennifer. It's not exactly the sort of thing one puts in a book about the beauty of the night. The white knickers, I mean. OK, so it happened. So what? Not everything that passes through a twelve-year-old boy's mind should be put on paper. There's such a thing as reticence. And sure there's not much that's attractive about the thoughts of an adolescent boy, especially if the girl he is dreaming about thinks he's something of a freak. Or *unlucky*. That was her word: *unlucky*. What do you think, Jennifer, *am* I unlucky? Could what happened to me have happened to anyone? Could it have happened to *you*, for instance? Think about it, Jennifer. What if achondroplasia had happened to you? That damaged little snip of DNA floating around in the gene pool like a mine adrift in an ocean. Waiting to explode. No, don't cringe. If I was *just unlucky*, then it might have happened to you.

Or to Lisa.

That's what I said to her. "It's just something that happens," I said. "It could have happened to you."

"No, it couldn't." She answered quickly. "There must have been something wrong with your mother. Or your father. Something yukky. My daddy and mom are OK."

Something yukky. Not a pleasant thing to remember, is it, Jennifer? Not a pleasant thing to dredge up out of memory. Not a pleasant thing to write down. That's why I left it out of my book. And there was more.

There was the thing that happened on the concrete dam.

A sweltering, still, sultry day. My body ran with sweat under my long-sleeved shirt and corduroy trousers. Lisa wore cotton shorts and a sleeveless tee. We walked to the concrete dam behind the cornfield.

"Why don'tja wear summer clothes?" she asked.

"It never gets hot in Ireland. These are the only

clothes I have." To tell the truth, I was glad to be covered up in Lisa's presence. Especially with all the mosquito bites. I would have been gladder yet to be invisible. Watching, but invisible.

The air crackled with electricity. Distant thunder rumbled.

We sat on the pond side of the dam. Lisa removed her sneakers and dipped her feet in the muddy water. Her red-glossed toes broke the surface like the watching eyes of a partly submerged many-eyed monster.

My feet didn't reach the water.

"Where'd ya get those shoes?" she asked.

"They're made especially."

"Can I see your feet?"

"Why?"

"I just want to see them."

I shook my head.

"I'll show *you* somethin'." She was making a deal.

"What?"

She touched her breasts.

I blushed. I stared into the pond.

"Why do you want to see my feet?" I was almost whispering.

"Don't know. Just do."

Dragonflies darted on the surface of the pond in linked pairs. Whirligigs skittered in crazy circles.

I unlaced my shoes. Pulled them off. And the socks.

Like fists.

My feet looked like fists. Lisa glanced quickly and squinched up her nose.

"Let's go swimming," she burbled. She jumped to her feet.

"I can't swim."

"Oh, come on. It's not deep. Anyone can swim." She pulled her tee off over her head.

"Go on, *look*."

I glanced, embarrassed. Her breasts as pink as peaches.

She slipped out of her shorts and stood at the edge of the dam in her knickers.

"Come on, sissy."

And while I was still trying to comprehend what was happening, she placed her palms together in front of her nose—as if saying a prayer—and dived.

Into opaque water. Scattering whirligigs and water striders. Dragonflies zipped for the greasy grass at the water's edge. She was gone.

And then, her bobbing head, the blond hair splayed on the brown surface of the pond. She turned. Licked her shiny red lips.

"Come on."

I shook my head.

She swam to the dam and held up her arm.

"Give me a hand."

I pulled her up, trying to avert my eyes from her breasts.

"Come on, then, you too."

"I can't swim."

"You can swim in your underpants. It's not deep. It's not over my head. It's not even over *your* head."

"I can't."

"Fair's fair."

Fair's fair. Tell me, Jennifer? Is fair fair? What was I to do? I had no desire to expose my body to Lisa. And there *was* something else. There was a bothersome swelling in my shorts, the boy-part, now in full extension.

I unbuttoned my shirt and slipped it off. Lisa watched studiously, as if my disrobing were a science experiment at school. Her wet hair was slicked back, her breasts covered by her knees. I pulled my vest off over my head. And dropped my pants.

I stood as if on public display, as if I were an illustration in a medical book—*the achondroplastic child*—Lisa watching. And then the most astonishing thing happened. She reached out her hand and, with the tip of her finger, touched the tortured, bent excrescence that strained against my cotton shorts, as if to convince herself that it was real.

I could hear my breath. And the eerie stillness of the afternoon.

"Maybe sumthin' happened to the egg," she said, absentmindedly touching her scarlet lips with the magical fingertip. "Maybe it got squashed."

She jumped up. And pushed me into the pond.

I fell into a night without stars.

My eyes, gaping wide, saw nothing. My mouth opened to cry out, and accepted instead a rush of muddy water. Sank. Sank to the bottom of the pond. Feet first into soft mud. Falling backward onto my bum. Then my hands into the silt. A squishy, bottomless, accepting darkness.

It's not important.

Not important to the book? OK, OK, it was important to me. And I know what you are going to say, as an editor, I mean. About how it connects with Bernadette's fate. Prefiguration, and all that. Very novelistic. Yes, I suppose you are right. But remember, Jennifer, my book is not a novel. The last thing I set out to do was to write about—

Do you know what she said? What she said when she pulled me out? When I was standing barefoot among the cow plops on the muddy bank of the pond coughing up silt? As she stood there very prettily, each of her thin white hands cupping a breast as if she were— She said, *Looks like somethin's not so big anymore*. Yes, I suppose it's funny. But it wasn't funny then, and to tell the truth, it's not funny now. And I'm not talking about the deflation of my— What's the right word to use with a classy woman such as yourself, Jennifer? Member? That's very literary. Not the deflation of my member. I was too scared and sick to think about *that*. No, deflation of my ego; that's what I'm talking about. It wasn't so much *what* she said as *the way* she said it. Dismissive, like. She'd had her fun. She had teased me into doing something I had not wanted to do, something humiliating, and now she was finished.

There would be no more teasing from Lisa, ever. I was left to be a watcher, again, but now—*the touch of her fingertip, as delicate as a dragonfly dimpling the surface of the pond*—with one more reminder of what I would never have.

Don't make that face. I know, I know, you've said it before, again and again: Lots of people like me get on without all the whining, without the mawkishness. But that's what I have been trying to explain to you, Jennifer. It's, well, it's *almost religious*. You see, I had to get on with life. So what I did was—I suppose I turned watching into a kind of religion. And, yes, of course Lisa was important—that's it, *as if she were holding a peach in each white hand*—but it's more than Lisa, more than any single attractive person. Let's call it Beauty with a capital *B*, pure abstract Beauty, a kind of charge that runs through all things. It's hard to explain, Jennifer, but it's the one thing I have followed all my life, like an Ariadne's thread that will lead me out of brokenness into—what? I don't know. Does any religion have a clear view of the thing it seeks? In school they called it the Beatific Vision. When we die and go to heaven, we are rewarded with the Beatific Vision; that's what they told us. Of course, you and I don't expect anything after death. You wrinkle your brow? You're not sure? Well, *I* am sure, as sure as I can be about anything. Death is final, and *empty*, like the muddy absence of light I found at the bottom of the pond. Still, it is something like the Beatific Vision that I seek. Not a thing to be enjoyed eternally, but caught in glimpses, *now*, day by day, catch as catch can, flaring out—what was Hopkins's phrase?—*like shining from shook foil.* Like what I saw on the morning of the Perseids, do you remember? Like what I saw on the night of the day that Lisa pushed me into the pond.

Admittedly my imagination was excited by the events of the day—the touch of Lisa's fingertip, the almost drowning. I was keyed up. I couldn't sleep, rehearsing in my mind the things that had happened. Anyway, I abandoned my bed on Terry's porch for the backyard glider. It was past midnight. The house was dark except for the light that Terry always keeps on in the bath. In the gaps between gray clouds stars slipped westward, but of course it was actually the clouds moving to the east. Fireflies flashed. I watched. I counted flashes. I counted the times between flashes, tapping my hand on the glider. It seemed as if the insects used a kind of code, a semaphore of blinking lights. The male firefly flashed, and then a few seconds later came the female's answering response. Or perhaps it was the other way round. It doesn't matter. I sat very still and flashed my penlight, intruding myself into the rhythm of their luminous code. And, yes, they came, came in answer to my beseeching light. For an hour I held a teasing conversation with a constellation of insects, the glider enveloped in a galaxy of fireflies, blinking, blinking, and the sky scudding stars.

Then the wind picked up and the insects disappeared.

I walked to the dam, down a long row of wind-rattled corn, and lay down on my belly on the concrete at the place where Lisa had pushed me in

(*He fell into the pond, Daddy, I had to pull him out. He's such a clod. Have you seen his feet? They're like a chimp's*). The dam was wet with dew and soaked my undershorts and vest—I wore nothing else. I slipped my chin over the edge of the dam and looked into the dark water. The water of the pond had cleared; it was no longer muddy but black and deep. I thought, *If I roll over, I will tumble off and fall, as lightly as a feather falling in air, into the soft enveloping silt at the bottom of the pond*.

It was not the only time in my life that I have contemplated death, but it was the only time I considered taking my own life. And now that I think about it, that phrase—*taking my own life*—does not accurately describe what I felt at the dam. Better, *giving my own life*. It was like—I would be handing over something to an impatient receiver, as one might return an overdue library book. It seemed—as I lay on the dam—that my life was a shabby sort of thing, in urgent need of mending. Lisa's shiny red lips and painted toes: that's the way life should be. Pretty. Everything pretty, like fireflies flickering in unison. *Gloss*, she called it, *lip gloss*. Roll over, fall into the soft darkness.

I don't want to sound metaphysical. You're the superstitious person, Jennifer, not me. But that's when it happened. One of those—what shall I call them?—beatific visions with lowercase *b* and *v*. A shining from shook foil. I was quite literally poised at the edge of oblivion when I saw something in the water, a point of light that seemed to be shining from the very bottom of the pond, no, from somewhere *beyond* the bottom, blinking, beckoning, a firefly light or will-o'-the-wisp. You know how it is. Something happens that's out of the ordinary, apparently inexplicable. You know there *must* be a perfectly natural explanation, but no explanation presents itself. That blinking pinprick of light, shining up out of the pond, on, off, on, off. Almost supernatural. The light seemed to be inviting me to—to enter the pond. Then, quite suddenly, *I knew what it was*. I rolled onto my back. Yes! Arcturus, nearly at the zenith, was shining through scudding clouds.

I had seen Arcturus reflected in the water of the pond.

At that moment, Jennifer, I felt as if my body was a kind of—a kind of interface, between the very high and the very deep. As if my body, the dam, the dark water, the distant house with its one faint light, all of that, were just a thin membrane stretched in space, utterly transparent. A film through which beauty simply shines. Do you know how far away Arcturus is? how many light-years? how many miles? It's hard to explain, but at that moment I felt—how shall I say it?—precious.

But I'm prattling on. It's your turn to talk, Jennifer. You tell me. Tell me what it's like to be beautiful and whole, not just at certain special moments, but day in and day out.

Arcturus. The fourth brightest star in the sky. Forty light-years away, 240 trillion miles. The light I saw reflected in the water of the pond had left the star before Terry or Bernadette was born. And here's the funny thing. Arcturus is getting closer. As the sun goes whirling around in the pinwheel stream of the galaxy, Arcturus is on another, crazier course that brings it crashing down through the pinwheel. The star became visible to the naked eye half a million years ago. It is getting brighter as it approaches. In a few thousand years it will pass us by, and then retreat, fading to invisibility.

An ancient name for Arcturus was the Watcher.

Jack Kelly told me these things. Jack Kelly taught me a lot about watching.

I wrote to Jack. I asked about Emma.

A letter came by return post:

Rosslare, 17 June, 1990.

Dear Frank,

I hope you do not mind that I am writing in answer your letter to Jack. Jack passed away six weeks ago. I have been meaning to write and tell you. It was his heart. I woke up one morning and he was lying there besides me dead. He cannot have suffered, thanks be to

God. His heart just stopped in his sleep. He had
told me once that when he was gone you were
to have his astronomy books, of which there is
a good number as you will know. I will try to
get these posted to you as I am able. The book
which you have written arrived here after Jack
was gone. He did not see it. I see that it is
dedicated to him. "To Jack Kelly, for the stars."
That is very kind. I am sure he would have been
happy to receive it. About the stars, is it? I hope
to read it when I have the chance. In answer to
your questions about Emma. Yes, it was very
likely her you saw. She lives in Cork. Her trou-
bles are passed, thanks be to God. She is as
well as you or I. Her address is St Teresa's Villa,
Lough Terrace. Sure she would be glad to see
you. Sarah is in England she is a schoolteacher.
Una and Orna are in America they are married
and have children Una three Orna two. Caitlin
is a Presentation Sister she is in Roscommon.
Deidre is married here. It is with her I live. I am
as well as I can hope to be and think of you
often.

> With kind regards,
> Effa Kelly

So it *was* her. It was Emma.

110

"Tell me, Emma. Why didn't you introduce yourself when you came into the bookstore? Something struck me about you, instantly. But it wasn't until you had left the store that I realized it was you."

She shrugs. "I was afraid. Afraid about the dog. About what I did to your dog."

"Have you read the book? Have you read *Nightstalk*?"

"I have."

"Then you will know very well that you have nothing to fear on that score. It was a crushing loss, I will admit, but I forgave you immediately. I could not have done otherwise. You've read the book, so you know—"

She blushes. She stirs her tea, the spoon going silently round and round.

"But of course that was all a long time ago."

She has dissected the food on her plate into bite-size bits.

"I'd not read the book when I had you sign it."

"And you've read it now?"

"I have."

"Do you mind—do you mind that I told your story, or at least the part of it that I know? Do you mind that I put you in my book?"

"Fiona?"

"Yes, Fiona."

"No, I don't mind. Very few people who might

read the book know me at all. I live pretty much on
my own. There are some of the staff at the Art Center
who know about—who know something about my
past. If they read the book they might guess that
Fiona is me, but I don't care if they do."

"I am afraid that I left Fiona in a rather unhappy
state. The last thing I heard of you, Emma, was that
you had left the hospital and gone to live with your
parents in Rosslare. They were still very concerned
about you then. Now your mother tells me you're
well."

Her eyes meet mine.

"And you don't mind that I mentioned—your ill-
ness?"

"I don't mind. It was something I had to work my
way through. The staff at Our Lady's Hospital were
very helpful. I had some shock treatments. My parents were supportive."

"I am sorry to hear about your father. I suppose
you could say that Jack was the closest thing to a
father I ever had. You noticed, did you not, that the
book is dedicated to him?"

"I did."

"It was Jack who gave me the sky. It is the thing
that has kept *me* sane all these long years. I will tell
you frankly, Emma, it could have been me that went
into Our Lady's. There were times when I was close
to the edge."

"I'm glad you wrote to me, Frank. That you invited
me to tea."

"Why is that?"

"It's good to know someone from that time.
Someone who understands. There's a tendency to

brood on it, to sink back into it, to fall back into that old depression. There's always a downward slope at my back. It is good to know that you don't hate me. I have often thought about that poor dog. I don't know how it was I did it—"

"Don't think on it, Emma. You were not responsible. You were ill. You had been through a terrible experience."

"Scrieber."

"Yes, Scrieber."

"You know, Frank. It needn't have been such a terrible thing. If I'd been stronger. If I'd been as strong as him. The thing I'm most ashamed about now is not what I was 'shamed of then. Then I was confused, about—about committing a sin. Now I'm ashamed to have been exploited. To have been used by him."

Her eyes are perfectly still, not fixed on anything in particular. Her skin is limpid, almost transparent. And—the aura of coppery hair that once wreathed her head is subdued now, gone gingery, flecked with gray, shorter, thinner, wispier, but still resisting comb or brush. It is her voice that is most changed. I hear the voice I have from memory and compare it as she speaks.

She is whispering. "God, too."

"God?"

"God used me."

"What do you mean?"

"God took advantage of my weakness. Placed me in a position of—humiliation. It was all so confusing. He—"

"He?"

She laughs. It is the first time I have seen her laugh.

"Oh, yes. Definitely *he*." She nibbles a bite of boiled ham. Lifts her eyes. Her eyes twinkle. "He looked a bit like Tyrone Power, you know."

"Scrieber?"

"No, God. It was God who looked like Tyrone Power." The corners of her mouth dance upward.

"Then do you not believe anymore?"

"Oh, I believe. Surely I do. If I didn't believe in God, I would be completely alone. I don't want to be alone, Frank. I need God. But I don't worry anymore about what he wants of me."

"It seems to me that religion does people a lot of damage. Sometimes it seems as if I have lived all my life among the wreckage of religion."

"It isn't religion does the damage, Frank. 'Tis ourselves."

"I wish that I *could* believe in God. It would be good to think there was some point or meaning to it all. But I can't, Emma. If I truly believed in a God who is responsible for everything that happens, then I could do no less than despise him."

"Then what do you believe in, Frank? Everyone must believe in something. Something bigger than themselves."

I believe in you, Emma. I believe in you.

"Do you remember, Emma, the bit in the book about the polyphemus moth? How the boy was awakened by the thrashing of the moth's wings about his head? How he caught it up in his hands and took it out into the night? How it flew up into a velvety canopy of stars, trailing the powdery substance of its wings? *That's* what I believe in. I believe in the polyphemus moth."

"But, Frank, the moth is just a *thing*. Surely, whatever you saw in the moth came from within yourself. It is yourself that is the godly thing."

"No, Emma, I don't agree. It is the moth that is godly. If you insist on using that word—*godly*—then the moth is the godly thing. *Godly* isn't a word I would use. I would never suggest that the moth was divine. At some other moment, in some other person's hands, that same creature might have been—just an insect fluttering its wings in a futile attempt to escape. But *then*, at that moment, under those stars, that particular child saw something that was there *in the moth*, something outside of himself, something that is there all the time residing in things, but usually hidden—something that revealed itself."

"And what would that be?"

I shrug. I cannot name it.

"It would be God, maybe."

"Perhaps. Perhaps after all it is only a matter of words, only a matter of attaching an arbitrary label to something which should not be named. But your word—*God*—carries too much theological baggage to suit me, drags too much human wreckage behind it. I would prefer not to name the thing that resided—so briefly, luminously—in the moth. The thing that flamed out. The moth was a vessel. A fringed and powdery vessel."

As once, Emma, you were the vessel.

"As once, Emma, you were the vessel."

Again, she blushes: "I suppose I should be embarrassed to find myself described so intimately in a book."

"You have nothing to be embarrassed about. You were—you *are* beautiful. The morning was magical. Do you remember that morning at all, Emma, when I watched you at your bath?"

"No, Frank, I have no memory of it. So you see, perhaps it was what *you* brought to it that mattered. The thing within yourself."

"No, Emma. Beauty is not in the eye of the beholder. That's a Christian heresy. I prefer to be pagan about this. I prefer to believe that beauty resides in *things*. In a polyphemus moth. In a night of shooting stars. In a woman at her bath."

"I am not a 'thing,' Frank."

"We are all 'things,' Emma. We are no more nor less 'things' than is the rest of creation, except in our inflated self-esteem. It is Christianity that tells us we are more than things, that there is something in us that will survive our thingness, an immortal soul and all that. But if I am more than a thing, then when did I become so? Was it at the moment when the embryo in my mother's womb became recognizably human? Or was it in the fusion of the sperm and egg? Or earlier still? Was it in the *egg* (for—oh, yes—I know now that it was *the egg* and not the sperm) with the twisted gene, that little bit of flawed chemistry—molecule A instead of molecule B—that jumbled, misspelled egg, waiting, as my father's sperm propellered its way through the dark night of my mother's womb—was *that damaged egg* more than a thing?"

Her hands lie flat upon the table, perfectly still,

but seem—so lucid is her skin—to float a millimeter above the varnished wood. There is a delicacy, an *insubstantiality* about her, as if, if I clapped my hands, she might vanish. A phantasm, a beautiful illusion. She is silent a long time, then she says: "But there is something you are leaving out, something you haven't mentioned at all. Something that is missing from your book. With all this talk of stars and moths—with all this talk of *things*—there is one thing you have left out."

111
*

Oh, you are wrong, Emma. *Nightstalk* is full of love. Full of love by its absence.

As this dark little room—my cave, Handy Paige calls it—is full of light. As the glass now standing empty on the armrest of my chair is full of port. *Full by the absence of the thing it is meant to contain.*

A paradox? Yes, but, dear Emma, it is a paradox at the heart of all creation. Even God, they say, reveals himself by his absence. *Deus absconditus*, isn't that what the theologians called it? It's the oldest paradox in the world: that emptiness is fullness, that black is white, that love in its absence is love revealed. Roethke has a line: *In a dark time the eye begins to see.* Isaiah has it too: *The people who walked in darkness have seen the light.* It's the oldest paradox in the world.

I fill my glass—the dregs of the bottle, a tumbler

half-full of simmering firelight, ruby red. If I were a
seer, I could read the shadows in the glass. The
books, the clutter of manuscript pages, the piles
and piles of journals, thirty-seven years of darkness,
dark hours on country roads, dark solitude. How
can you say, Emma, that *Nightstalk* contains no
love? Are you forgetting the boy who watched you
from his bed, pretending to sleep, watched as you
prepared yourself for sleep by candlelight? You pulled
on the nightdress over your head, then slipped off
your underthings. Your undergarments fell to the
floor, you stepped out of them and left them lying
there on the unvarnished boards. And when you
had pinched out the candle and turned your face
into the pillow, the ten-year-old boy's gaze remained fixed upon those cast-off garments (watching through a fold of his blanket, like an astronomer
with his eye to a telescope), those fragments of
cotton cloth perfumed by your body.

Voyeurism? Fetishism? That's too easy, Emma. It
was love. Plain and simple. There's no other word
for it. If at that moment you had asked the boy to
sacrifice everything to those few fragments of cloth,
he would have done so. Does that shock you? Wait,
let me tell you a story, a story your father told
me, the story of Orion, the giant star-spangled
hunter, the most ancient of the constellations. This
is the story, or a part of it: *After many adventures,
Orion came to the island of Chios, where he
glimpsed Merope, the daughter of King Oenopion,
and fell instantly in love. The king agreed that Orion
should wed his daughter but insisted that the giant*

*should first prove his worth by accomplishing a
series of difficult tasks. As Orion completed each
assignment, the king imposed another, each more
demanding than the one that went before. At last
Orion began to suspect that Oenopion had no intention of giving up his daughter and that the tasks
would have no end. He decided to be done with it;
he would carry Merope away by force. But Orion's
plan was discovered by the king, who had the giant
seized and blinded. Sightless, the disappointed
lover was cast from the island to wander the earth
in darkness.* You see, Emma, what led to Orion's
blindness? Beauty. A woman's beauty. And please
don't tell me, as Jennifer Down insists, that beauty
is "skin deep." Beauty strikes through and through
a thing, permeates to the core. Orion was stricken
by Merope's beauty and fell in love. For his love he
was willing to endure an apparently endless succes-
sion of hardships. And what was it that sustained
him through his trials? *A memory.* He had seen her
at her bath, her bare feet on the polished marble
of the palace floor, her cloth-of-gold gown draped
down about her hips, a glimpse—only a glimpse,
of the shadowed declivity at the base of her spine?
For that glimpse, Emma, Orion was condemned to
walk in darkness.

From that morning when I saw you at your bath I
was condemned too to be unsatisfied with anything
except perfection, and therefore to live alone in this
dusky house, drink port, poke the fire, stalk the
night, scribble endlessly in my journals. I am seven
dwarfs in one. But where is Snow White? If she appeared, here, out of the blue, we know what would

happen, don't we? Oh, yes, if Snow White were a nice little girl, like your lovely sisters, or Jennifer Down, she'd tickle Bashful under his chin, stroke Grumpy's hand, tuck Sleepy between the sheets. But in the end it is Prince Charming that she loves. And you, Emma, you say there is no love in *Nightstalk*. Dear God, this dank little room reeks with love; love stains the walls, mildews the carpet, and infiltrates the pages of my manuscript like an army of silverfish. A huge and yearning absence of love.

112

*

As they say in America, Emma Kelly and Frank Bois have become an item.

An unlikely couple: she five foot ten, he not four feet tall. Rapunzel and Rumpelstiltskin. She a receptionist at the Trickle Art Center, he the locally famous writer. No longer is Frank Bois one of that ragtag band of broken and disfigured people who walk the city streets; nowadays people nudge their neighbors, glance at him over their shoulders, point him out to their children: *Do you see, it's the fellow who was on the telly. Look, it's the wee man who wrote the book. Sure it's him, the dwarf whose picture we saw in the window of Waterstones.* He meets her in the Grand Parade at half past five when the Center closes. They have a Guinness and a cider in the Mutton Lane Inn and dinner in one of the bistros off Paul Street. He walks her to her flat at the Lough, to a house called St. Teresa's Villa.

"Frank Bois has a lady friend," observes Handy Paige.

"And she is just that, Handy. A friend. Surely you can imagine that I am capable of ordinary friendship?"

"And it's about fukkin' time, Frank, about fukkin' time. Didn't I tell ya? Didn't I tell ya that when ya had a bit of money the ladies would crawl all over ya? Do you think they care if yer three foot tall with a mouse's dick. All women care about is—" He rubbed his forefinger against his thumb.

I've come to Handy's place for news of the book, to the one-room office at the front of his flat. *Nightstalk* is off to a successful start. A second printing is in the works. The Americans are interested.

"Don't be crude, Handy."

"Jaysus, Bois, don't be so fukkin' naive. Yer business is writin' books, my business is—" Again the finger against the thumb. "I know what I'm talking about."

"You don't know anything, Handy. You certainly don't know Emma. You've probably never had a real honest-to-goodness friendship with a woman in your life."

"Christ, look who's talkin'. This is the dwarf who's spent thirty years jackin' off with underwear ads in the magazines. You forget, Bois, I know you, I've been into yer smelly little cave, I've read yer secret thoughts. Let me tell ya: while you were holed up in that dark little house, I've been around with lots of ladies. And let me tell you, I know what they want."

"For the life of me, Handy, I don't know why I gave you my book. You are crude and offensive. You take perverse pleasure in insulting your clients. Your notion of women is atavistic."

"Atavistic, smatavistic. Don't use big words on me, Bois. You fukkin' well know why you gave me yer book—because there fukkin' wasn't anyone else to give it to. And I sold it—to the best house in England. Meetin' up with me was the luckiest day of yer life."

"I will admit, Paige, that you do have a kind of obnoxious charm, and I am grateful for the attention you gave to my book. But maybe the real reason I like you is that you make me feel positively attractive."

"You want to be attractive, Bois, then stick with me. I'll make you fifty thousand pounds attractive. You'll have a dozen women on yer arm."

Paige bobs and twists in his swivel chair. Twiddles a pencil. Scratches his neck.

Do I want fifty thousand pounds?

"She's an artist, Handy. She paints on silk"—I indicate a circle with my hands—"circles of silk. She has shown them to me. They are extraordinary. Very beautiful. Magical colors. Like fairy paintings."

"Whatever she is, the two of you are the talk of the town. I haven't seen her, but I hear she's tall. And old. Older than you. What you need, Bois, is a young woman. Someone that'll make you feel frisky again. Let me put you on the telly; when yer famous, you can take yer pick."

"Handy, you haven't the least notion of my relationship with Emma. I've known her since I was a kid. We are friends. We talk. She is interested in my writing. She lets me see her paintings. I think I'm the only person who has seen them, dozens of beautiful paintings. We enjoy each other's company. Can you imagine that, Handy? Does that compute in your simpleminded view of the world? And most extraordinarily, I feel completely at ease with her, even in public. I know that people are observing us, taking note of the dwarf who accompanies this striking woman, but she makes me feel completely at ease. I don't think my physical condition enters into her thoughts at all. She doesn't care what people think. It's remarkable, Handy. She's the first real friend I've had since Terry Klout."

"The American? In your book?"

"It doesn't matter."

"Well, I'm glad you have a friend, Frank. And I'm glad yer out and about in the light of day. I'm glad for ya. This lady friend of yours is the best fukkin' thing that ever happened to ya."

"You are right, Handy. She's the best fukkin' thing that ever happened to me."

"It's for you, Frank. Happy birthday."

Emma passes a flat package across the checkered tablecloth. A guttering candle flickers at our elbows, igniting the inch or so of amber liquid in the bottom of the wine carafe.

She is wearing the white lace collar that she wore when she came to the autograph session at Waterstone's, with an attractive olive dress. I have not seen the dress before. It occurs to me briefly that she might have bought the dress especially for me.

"How did you know it is my birthday?"

"I have my ways."

"I'm not sure that I want to be reminded."

"Take my word for it, Frank, the best years are yet to come."

"It's been a long time since I've had a birthday present. Not since—" *Not since Bernadette's death.*

"Open it."

I peel away the cellotape and fold back the crisp tissue.

It is a framed painting, one of Emma's paintings on silk: a river flowing between hills that vaguely evoke the body of a woman—fluid hair, sinuous limbs, milky colors of pink, mauve, and violet.

It is beautiful.

"It is beautiful. Thank you."

"One of the staff at the gallery framed it."

I examine the painting. "It is extraordinary, Emma. You are very talented."

She shrugs away the compliment, but the corners of her mouth betray her pleasure.

Details of the painting slowly reveal themselves. The composition is as intricate and artfully arranged as a page from the *Book of Kells*, but soft, delicate. Colors bleed through the lustrous cloth.

"There is something magical about it. What were you thinking as you painted it."

"I was thinking," she says very quietly, "of Berna-dette."

114

As Bernadette Bois, with her twelve-year-old son by her side, winged her way from St. Louis to New York's Idlewild airport and then to Shannon, she became aware that she was pregnant. She was looking out the window of the TWA Jetstream 707 onto an unbroken expanse of cloud when she suddenly knew. And it didn't matter who the father was, Terry Klout or the Pilot, because even as she sensed the presence of the creature growing inside of her, she remembered something that had happened when she was a child, in the years before the war, something she had forgotten. She was three, perhaps four years old. Her father's relations had come for a visit, motoring from Le Havre to Fleurville in a shiny black motorcar. While her father, mother, uncle, aunt, and three young cousins visited in the kitchen, Bernadette wandered into the yard. The shiny black car was parked near the cow-shed gate, its engine popping and pinging as it cooled. She walked to the car and pulled herself up onto the running board.

Inside was a little man.

And now she realized—somewhere over the North Atlantic—that the person she had seen sitting in the back seat of her uncle's car was a dwarf. Which meant that it was *her* body that bore the debilitating gene. And now there was another broken child growing inside of her.

What I say of Bernadette's terror must be mostly conjecture, but she did leave clues to her state of mind. It wasn't long after we had reestablished ourselves in the flat in Nicholas Road that she circled the following lines in her leather-bound copy of Yeats's poem—

A mound of refuse or the sweepings of a street,
Old kettles, old bottles, and a broken can,
Old iron, old bones, old rags, that raving slut
Who keeps the till. Now that my ladder's gone
I must lie down where all ladders start
In the foul rag and bone shop of the heart.

—and in the blank pages at the back of the book she began to scribble the frenzied fears that give me access to her thoughts.

She did not go back to work at Cash's but lived on Mrs. Brosnan's generosity, eating very little, sleeping hardly at all.

Nor did she pay me any mind.

When after two weeks she missed her period she went to the hospital in Angelsey Street and demanded an abortion.

"You cannot take the life of your child," said the nurse, adamantly but not without concern.

"It is not a child," whispered Bernadette. "*Un nain. Un monstre.*" She shuddered.

"I do not understand, *non comprendre.*"

"It is a dwarf."

The nurse took Bernadette's hands into her own. "My dear child. You cannot be sure of that. There is no reason to expect that your baby is a dwarf."

"*Un nain,*" breathed Bernadette. She was certain. She retrieved her hands from the nurse's grasp.

"Even if the child *were* deformed, you cannot take its life. It has a soul, dear, an immortal soul. It is as much a human being as you or I. Sure, to take a life is murder."

Bernadette looked deep into the nurse's eyes, which were not without compassion. "Please," she whispered, "*je vous en prie*. It is not yet a child. *Un excroissance. Un champignon.*"

No abortion was forthcoming at the Angelsey Street hospital, nor anywhere else. She felt the thing growing, becoming demonstrably human, although stunted, a homunculus, like the little man in the back seat of the shiny black car.

Like her first-born son.

I'll not judge her. She did not abandon me that night when she let herself slip from the Albert Quay into the waters of the Lee (an iridescent oil slick broke to let her enter, shimmering in starlight, a thousand thousand welcoming stars). She had abandoned me long before she gave herself to the Lee; I had never managed to secure for myself a place in her heart. See, here is an old photograph from Jack Kelly's time: Bernadette and her son on the Merchant's Quay. She sits on the parapet, her hands pressed between her knees. Her head is cocked to the side. She is pretty. She is aware that she is pretty. Her eyes are attentive to Jack's camera, to the camera alone. Her son eases himself into the frame; he knows he is intruding. He is the raveled edge of her beauty, the usurper.

Was it murder, then? Of my half-brother or half-sister? When they found her body on the shingle at Ringaskiddy, no one guessed that she was pregnant. There was an autopsy, of course, to determine the cause of death (asphyxiation by drowning), but even if the pathologist's blade had more carefully probed the lining of her womb and found the fissioning cluster of cells, it was too soon to tell if the embryo was normal.

Her mind had given itself up to morbidity, but she was not rag and bone, no, certainly not. The autopsist could not have been so inured to death's waste that he did not pause, his scalpel poised above her flat white belly, and whisper a prayer, perhaps a another verse of Yeats's:

> Here at life's end
> Neither loose imagination,
> Nor the mill of the mind
> Consuming rag and bone,
> Can make the truth known.

115
*

Praise the world to the Angel, says the poet Rilke. *Do not tell him the untellable. Tell him things.*

No, I cannot praise *your* God, Emma. I cannot speak with any confidence of the Alpha and the Omega, the omniscient and the omnipresent. Space and time extend too far beyond the tip of my tongue. The galaxies go tumbling off the precipice of my speech. I have looked into the Pleiades, the

Seven Sisters, with binoculars and seen a dozen dozen stars; I have looked with a telescope and seen thousands. The world is deep beyond our inspection. We look into the pool and see only the surface. And seeing there in the surface of the pool our own reflection, we call it God. But perhaps it is as Rilke says, we are here only to say, *house, bridge, fountain, gate*. For me, Emma, it is enough. Look, says the Angel, this is a house. *House*, I repeat, praising. And a bridge. *Bridge*, I say. And a fountain. *Fountain*. And a gate. *Gate*.

Look, says the Angel, look here upon the shingle at Ringaskiddy. A young woman, thirty years of age. Her green eyes agape at the stars, but clouded and unseeing. A froth of yellow foam at the corners of her mouth. Someone has been kind enough to arrange her blue cotton dress—tiny violets on an azure field—so that it modestly covers her legs. One of her feet is shod in a soft black slipper, the sort a dancer might wear; the other foot is bare, a skein of green algae is tangled in her toes. On the turf bank above the foreshore stands a cluster of observers, men, women, children even. One by one they step down onto the shingle for a better look, then quickly retreat to the solace of the crowd. They communicate in whispers, out of respect for the drowned woman.

There is one word on all their lips.

Beauty.

She might have been sleeping, or in suspended animation like Snow White or Sleeping Beauty. You see, Emma, even in death she was beautiful. That ghostly insubstantial thing, the soul, had departed, but not beauty. Not yet at least. Later, yes, later, but not yet—listen, listen to what they are saying: *Glory be to God, she is beautiful. Faith, she is. Ah, sure 'tis a waste.* Make no mistake: it is a *thing* they are praising there upon the shingle. So let us not speak to the Angel of invisible spirits and unspeakable essences. Let us speak to the Angel of things. Let us praise what we *see*.

I have hung Emma's painting on the wall by the hearth. More than that, I have painted the wall—I have painted *all* the walls of the flat—a light cream color that complements her gift. Her colleague at the Trickle Center who framed the painting asked to see more. Reluctantly, she brought a dozen of her silks to the Center. An exhibition has been arranged. Soon the artistry of the Trickle Center's receptionist will be on display in the gallery upstairs.

I have discovered something else about Emma: she likes to walk. On weekends she joins me for walks in the country, in the light of day. We have ranged as far as Crosshaven and Fota. We are an exceptional couple striding along country roads; I take two quick steps for each of her strides. We talk unceasingly. About God. About the past. About ourselves.

I teach her what I know of nature—the names of plants and animals, their habitats, their modes of life. And she, in her turn, teaches me to see these things in her curiously holistic way. *Look, there*, I say, *it's the caterpillar of the green hairstreak butterfly, feeding on gorse*. She looks and sees a humpbacked thing that flows with a sea of green into all the countryside. She stores up images for her work. I see boundaries; she sees continuity. I see a material thing that stands out from the background; she sees the entire canvas charged with light.

"Do you mind," I ask, "being seen with me? Surely we must be the oddest couple anyone has ever observed walking along these roads."

She shrugs. She hasn't thought about it. She doesn't care.

There are springs in my feet. I am like a spaniel trotting at her side.

I ask, "Do you remember how it started?"

"How you watched me when I shared your room?"

"No, earlier."

"Earlier?"

"Your father and my mother. Jack and Bernadette."

"It was me who brought their affair to an end."

"Yes."

"The thing I saw when I looked in Bernadette's window stayed with me for a long time. But I can't remember now. I can't remember what I saw. I remember climbing onto the coal bunker and putting my face to the dusty glass. I can even remember what I was wearing. But— It's funny, there are lots of things I *can't* remember from that time."

"Perhaps it's a blessing."

She is quiet. Then she says: "No, remembering would be best. I think I need those memories now, *all* of them, even the hurtful parts, in order to understand who I am. It is like certain pieces of the puzzle are missing and I don't know if they are important or unimportant." We step to the side of the lane to let a tractor pass. The farmer turns, looks over his shoulder. She says: "But perhaps you are right. Perhaps it was necessary to forget—to become well. My head was full of such rubbish."

"I admire your strength, Emma. You seem exceptionally sane. I admire the way you are able to live life on your own terms."

"I'm not strong, Frank."

"You seem very strong. I suppose I am most impressed by your honesty with me. You are at ease, and you make me feel comfortable in turn. It's—you see, most people are uncomfortable, nervous, even those who like me. There's always this—emotional charge."

"And why is that?"

"I don't know. I have always supposed it's because they don't want to be reminded that the world is broken."

"I was like that once."

"Like what?"

"Not wanting to believe that the world is broken."

"What do you mean?"

"Sure, you remember, Frank. I lived in a world of movie stars and saints."

"Yes, I remember."

"What?"

"I remember the movie magazines. How you read

them before you went to sleep. The pictures of Hollywood stars that you cut out and pinned to the wall. And the holy pictures. And the scapular—I remember the scapular."

"I still wear it."

"Why?"

"I still believe, Frank."

"Why? Why, after all that's happened, do you still believe? All the waste, the death, the brokenness?"

"We *have* to believe, Frank."

"What do you mean?"

"We have to believe that there is at least one unbroken thing. I've thrown away the holy pictures, except for the scapular. I don't know why I keep the scapular, unless it's because no one sees it." She reaches into the collar of her jumper and retrieves one of the little stitched rectangles, two soft holy pictures sewn into a plastic casing, on brown strings. She turns it over from side to side. "Jesus and St. Francis, my two little movie stars."

I laugh.

"It is my way of believing, you see. And *you* believe too, Frank. You just don't choose to call him God."

"No, I don't believe."

She shrugs.

"Do you pray, Emma?"

"Not like I used to. Sometimes when I'm painting I sit very quietly with my eyes closed. I suppose it's a kind of praying. I'm happy then. I sit very quietly and—it's like I fill up, like water being poured into a glass."

Our road descends into a shaded glen, trees

twined with ivy, a clear stream tumbling in a mossy channel. We catch our breaths as a stoat flashes across the road from ditch to ditch. The sleek brown animal pauses, turns to look at us, displays a glimpse of white belly, dives into the undergrowth.

I ask, "Are you ever lonely?"

She has been fingering the scapular. Now she slips it beneath her collar. We are moving along the road again. Her voice is subdued. "I don't know. I suppose I never think about it."

"Is it bold of me to ask?"

"'Tis."

"Emma—" I consider how I might apologize.

She jams her hands deep into her pockets.

She says: "But I don't mind."

117
*

Emma's opening is a great success. Two dozen of her best paintings are displayed with simple elegance on white mats in natural wood frames. A table at one end of the gallery is spread with wine, cheese, and biscuits. There is a floral display for Emma from the Center's staff. The city's art crowd is here. A stringer from the *Irish Times*. A photographer from the *Examiner*. A preview of the show appeared in the morning paper: *Paintings on silk tend to be prettified and artsy-crafty. There is something about the ink-silk medium that encourages sentimentality. But Emma Kelly transcends the limitations of her medium. Her images are powerful, haunting. By some magic she conjures from lyrical line and luminous color intimations of fear and trembling. The viewer comes away uncertain of what he has seen, but transformed and deeply disturbed.*

The artist reluctantly presides. She has invited me to be her escort. *Please be with me, Frank, I could never do it alone.* I think her radiant in her new olive dress and lace collar. I bask in her glow. I won't deny it: I am head over heels in love with her. Any fool can see it. Emma, too, must surely know. She is asked to pose for photographs, standing before her paintings with Cork's most recently successful writer, holding the long-stemmed red rose which was my gift. She is awkward, a little frightened, but not unhappy. She nods as gallery-goers offer appreciations, comments, congratulations. Red-dot stickers begin appearing at the corners of her paintings, indicating sales, at prices—£100, £140, £160—suggested by the gallery director. Just one red dot represents more than her week's salary.

My wine glass seems to stay miraculously full. I have grown a little unsteady. I graze the crowd, placing myself in positions to hear remarks on Emma's work. *These things are amazingly sensual*, a woman says. I look, and yes, I see that they are sensual. Human forms, especially, are used by Emma to great effect. *They are like optical illusions*, says someone else. *You think you are looking at one thing, and then realize that you have been looking at something else all along.* I look and I see that what I had imagined to be a stoat curling in a pool— is, well, vaguely anatomical. *They frighten me*, a man says. *Well, they should*, replies his female companion, laughing. I drift along the wall, eavesdropping, seeing things I had not seen before. I am startled by the complexity of Emma's work and by the intensity of the crowd's reaction to it. No one seems to know what to make of it. *Do you know what these paintings remind me of?* a young woman says to her friend. *Christina Rossetti's "Goblin Market." The poem I mean. That same spooky sense of innocence and menace.* I look; I don't see it. I look again. Well, perhaps. Someone asks, *What's she up to?* and is answered, *Christ, I don't know.* People look from the paintings to the artist and back again to the paintings, trying to make a connection, searching for clues to the meaning of her work. I look too, through a forest of elbows and handbags and lipstick-rimmed plastic glasses, to where Emma stands at the far end of the gallery talking with four elderly people. She towers over them. In the intense artificial light of the gallery, her hair is charged with the old flame. Her presence is commanding, yet she seems almost immaterial, as if she were a hologram that one might pass one's hand through. I think: *I don't yet know this person.*

My glass is filled again. The *Irish Times* reviewer sidles up to me.

"I take it you are a friend of the artist, Mr. Bois?"

I nod.

"Would you mind if I ask a personal question? Are the two of you—romantically involved?"

"Just friends."

I wolf down a handful of crispy crackers to moder-

ate the effect of the wine. *What Frank Saw.* I look
again. The title of one of Emma's paintings is *What
Frank Saw.* I hadn't noticed it before. Blacks and
grays on silvery silk. I push up on tiptoes to study
it. What is it? A sky of stars. But not stars, more like
fountains. Or eyes, weeping tears. Into a pool, or is
it cupped hands? There are flowers in the pool. Or
are they—? Tipsy, I stagger and fall against a young
woman, punkishly attired, her hair dyed a hideous
fuchsia, dozens of bangles on her arms. She jangles
from the impact.

"Jeez," she says.

I apologize meekly.

But it is the painting she is referring to. "Jeez,
what is it?"

"It's a dog," I say.

"A dog?"

"A dog."

"Jeez, I don't see a dog."

My head is spinning. The gallery director approaches me. A young man, white linen jacket, a red
silk handkerchief jammed casually into the breast
pocket.

"I think our visitors appreciate Emma's work," he
says. "Half of her pieces are already sold. That's
extraordinary for an opening."

"I'm not surprised."

"Did you see the review in this morning's *Examiner*? Tip-top. Absolutely tip-top."

"I did."

"I'll be honest and say that I never guessed her
talent. She is such a reticent woman. If she hadn't
asked us to frame one of the paintings, we might

never have known. Thanks for lending us *that* one, by the way." He points.

I glance across the gallery to Bernadette's birthday gift. The red dot is me.

"I read your book. Loved it. I was particularly drawn to the character Fiona."

He is fishing. "Yes."

He smiles slyly. "Fiona seems familiar."

I say: "Oh, it would be a mistake to try and identify anyone in the book. All of the names are fictitious."

"We are very proud of Emma."

"Yes."

I edge away. I need fresh air. I leave the gallery and sit on the stairs to the lower floor. The punk young woman comes out and sits down beside me, jingling. A gold ring in her nostril. Lips painted black. She props her cheek on her fist.

"You're the guy who wrote the book?"

Her waxy odor makes me dizzy. I nod.

She grins: "I never read books."

I shrug.

She asks: "Do you guys fuck?"

"Pardon me?" *Dwarfs? Writers?*

"You and her. The artist lady. I seen you together. I seen you together a couple of times, you know, in the street."

Her ankle socks match her hair.

"I really don't think that is any of your business."

"Yeah, I know. But I was just thinking about it. It's crazy and all. You know, you being so, you know, little. An' her bein' so, you know, tall. I was just thinking about it. That, you know, like you're a gorgeous couple."

"Gorgeous?"

"Yeah, you know, like sexy. I was just thinking about it."

"I—" *I was just thinking about it too,* I almost say.

She pats my knee. "Hey," she says. "Good luck." She hops to her feet and jingles down the stairs, black as death except for the fuchsia hair and socks. And the jingling silver bangles.

Thanks.

It's past ten when we leave the Trickle Center. Venus blazes in the purple twilight, low on the western horizon.

"A success," I say. "A smash. You made lots of money tonight."

"It's rather scary."

"People asked me where you get your ideas. I didn't know what to tell them. Your paintings seem to slip in under their skin."

She shrugs. We walk along the Grand Parade toward Nano Nagle's Bridge. "I don't know that I 'get ideas.' I just paint. It's something they started me on at the hospital—as therapy. Just paint, they said, don't think about it, just paint what you feel."

"Whatever it is that you do, it works."

"It's funny."

"What?"

"That people want to buy my things. I never thought of myself as an artist."

"You are."

"What?"

"An artist."

"Hmmm—"

"Coffee?"

"OK."

"Emma—"

"What?"

"Marry me."

119
*

"I like her, Frank. She is a lovely woman."
Jennifer Down sips from a tall glass of Perrier.
Two hands enclose the glass; her nails are a pink
that matches her suit, although a slightly darker,
complementary shade. A few more flecks of gray in
her hair.

"She is," I agree. "And quite a talented artist.
She had a show recently at a gallery here in Cork.
It was very well received. She sold everything on
display—except for one painting, which was
mine."

We turn to look at Emma, who stands across the
room in a cluster of well-wishers, mostly people
from the Trickle Art Center. She is wearing a yellow
dress and a circlet of daisies in her hair. *God, she's
beautiful,* I say to myself.

"She is stunning," observes Jennifer. "So—unaffected. And yet—there's a striking presence about
her."

"She hardly gives her looks a thought."

"Well, whatever she does do or doesn't do, it works. I wish I looked half as good."

"You look fantastic, Jennifer—and you know it." She might have stepped out of the pages of *Vogue*.

She laughs. "But I work at it, Frank. It comes naturally to Emma."

"I'm glad you are here, Jennifer. And Walter, too." Her young companion is drinking at the bar with his uncle. "It's—well, I know it was expecting a lot to think that you might come to Ireland for our marriage, but I like the sense of completion, of tying up loose ends. We invited everyone we know, which is not a lot of people. Having you all here brings everything together."

"I wouldn't have missed it, Frank. After all, you are my most successful author. I looked at the computer yesterday afternoon. The figures are holding up nicely. An American edition is in the works. I wouldn't be surprised to see a few European translations." She touches my shoulder. "We're expecting you to make another visit to London soon."

"Too bad we didn't wait a year before publishing the book, it would have had a happy ending."

Thoughtfully, with the tip of her pink-painted pinkie, she stirs the lemon wedge that floats in her glass. "No," she says at last. "From the strictly commercial point of view, I think it's well that we ended the book with your mother's death. Very poignant— in keeping with the melancholy spirit of those nighttime walks. What's that word you use? *Noctivagant?* That's it. I think the reader would have felt cheated by a happy ending."

"So what do you think, Jennifer? Did Emma and I make a handsome couple at the Registry?"

Lines explode at the corners of her mouth and eyes. "I assure you, Frank, the likes of it have not been seen before and will probably never be seen again. Emma is a beautiful bride, and you—you look positively dashing in that suit. Very—ah, *author-y*."

"It cost a few quid, I can tell you. I spent more on this outfit than I spend in a year on drink."

"I hope that now you won't drink so much. A Leo shouldn't need drink, you know."

"And Virgos shouldn't need astrology. Drink, horoscopes—it's the same thing really. Escape from reality."

"I suppose I left myself open for that. Anyway, you are indeed a handsome groom."

"Do you remember, Jennifer, that once I asked if you could love someone with my disability? I must say that I appreciated the honesty of your answer. It was very important that you didn't hedge. It's hard to explain, but when you answered me the way you did, I felt very grown-up—for the first time."

"I thought about my answer afterward. I suppose I was a little ashamed that I couldn't say yes. I like to think of myself as—" She is thoughtful for a moment. "I suppose that appearances are important to me, maybe too important." She glances wistfully toward Walter Paige, who has left the bar to chat up Deidre Kelly.

She says: "Perhaps I care too much about what people think."

I follow her eyes to Walter. "You needn't feel

ashamed, Jennifer, because you are attracted to a beautiful person. I'm exactly the same, and with far less right."

"Who is the woman Walter is taking to?"

"Deidre Kelly. Emma's sister. I'm afraid I don't remember her married name."

"She is attractive."

"All of the Kelly women are attractive, of that I assure you." I grin. "I was like their doll when I was a kid. All of that petting and cuddling from the Kelly girls probably scarred me for life."

"Let's hope that—what's her name? Deidre—let's hope that Deidre doesn't have the same effect on Walter."

Walter senses our attention. He excuses himself and comes to join us.

"Well, Frank, you're in the clover now."

"I am."

"Your bride's a stunner."

"She is."

"Who were all the photographers at the Registry?"

"Your friend here, the editor, has made me into something of a local celebrity. It was probably she who tipped off the press."

Jennifer feigns indignation. "Not me, Frank. But I think I can guess who the real culprit is. Your endearing agent, Mr. Paige. Scoundrels seem to run in Walter's family."

Walter takes her meaning. "For Chrissake, Jen. She's Emma's sister. Married with three kids. We were just talking about Frank."

"Hmmm."

"And Handy may be bumptious, but he's not a scoundrel. He doesn't pass a chance to turn a few bob."

As if beckoned by his name, Handy Paige joins our circle. He is deep in his cups.

"Jaysus, Bois. Yer look a right eejit in that suit."

Walter says, "Not at all, dear Uncle. He looks quite smart."

Handy gravely examines his nephew up and down, the cotton suit, dark shirt, cream tie, plimsolls. "Ye look a fukkin' eejit too. What kind of shoes are those? Kid's shoes."

"Your nephew is the most beautiful man in London," says Jennifer, smiling sweetly.

"He fukkin' well better be," roars Handy Paige. "It wasn't off the wind he took it."

Jennifer touches Handy on the sleeve. "Do you have any more best-sellers for me, Mr. Paige?"

Handy slaps my back, spilling Guinness from my glass. "Depends on my little friend here. I 'spect he isn't scribblin' much a'tall these days. Too busy"—he winks to Jennifer, a broadly suggestive wink—"tiddling his lady friend over there."

I say: "Handy, you are reliably obnoxious."

"Sure, and would ye rather I was mealy-mouthed like those stiff-assed ponces from London? My nephew here used to have a mouth on him until he took up with yer lady editor." He winks again at Jennifer. She excuses herself and moves away.

Walter says, "Give your tongue a rest, Uncle. If you want to sell another book to Penguin, you would do well not to insult her."

"Who's insultin', fer Chrissake? Jaysus Mary and Joseph, I never met such sensitive souls. Like a bunch of fukkin' priests you are."

"This is a special occasion, Uncle. It's Frank and Emma's day. I'm sure Frank would appreciate your best behavior."

"I'm used to Handy's extravagances, Walter."

"Yer fukkin' right he's *used* to me. When this poor bolloksed divil walked into my office he was a trog without a pot to piss in. Now look at 'im." He scans my new togs up and down. "Marryin' the fukkin' princess he is."

"It's true enough, Handy, if it wasn't for you, none of this would have happened. I might not have met Emma again."

"An' didn't I tell ye, me boy-oh, didn't I tell ye it doesn't matter if yer a fukkin' dwarf, it doesn't matter if ya got three fukkin' heads, if ya got the"—he jingles the change in his pocket—"the ladies will think yer the King of Spain."

"Handy's ready for another drink, Walter. Would you mind if I—?" I give my agent a pat on the arm and move off.

"Another charming conversation with Handy," I say to Emma as I join her companions.

"I was just telling Emma that I have a sheaf of poems I might submit to Mr. Paige," says Roger Manning. "Perhaps he could place them with a publisher."

"I once read a volume of your verse," I say. "It was among my mother's books."

"Oh, my goodness, you don't mean—?"

"*Gargoyle*, I believe the title was."

"Oh my goodness, yes. I wouldn't want it to get around that I am the author of *that*." He laughs.

These many years later it is easy to see what my mother found attractive in Roger Manning. He is tall, thin, gloriously white maned. Wire-rimmed spectacles perched on his nose. His delicate hands clasp a cup of coffee (to which the barman has added, at the clergyman's instruction, a measure of Jameson's). Emma's mother, too, is taken by Manning's charm; she gazes into his eyes with bewitched amusement.

"I used your poems as a source for my own book, for reconstructing that part of my mother's life. I will admit that it was often necessary to read between the lines."

Manning glances from Emma to Effa with a puckish grin. "Oh dear, I'm not certain we want to talk about *those things* now."

"Have you read Frank's book, Reverend?" Emma asks.

"Oh, indeed I have. It certainly isn't difficult to recognize my own small part. Perhaps Mr. Bois didn't get it all entirely right, but oh, yes, indeed, it was—" He drifts into reverie, his spectacles sliding down his nose. Then he says, "You know, Mr. Bois—"

"Please call me Frank."

"You know, Frank, my career as a clergyman certainly had its ups and downs, but nothing in my life was so, ah, *eventful* as my—*relationship* with your mother. She was quite a remarkable woman. Not a day goes by that I don't think of her. My goodness, I could tell you stories—"

I tease: "Effa hasn't yet read my book, Roger. Shall we tell her about the episode at the dean's cottage in Kerry?"

"Great heavens, no," exclaims Roger Manning, blushing. "*That* story, by the way, has become part of church history. The dean was not discreet. It seems that *everyone* knows. I'm afraid it is the only thing I shall be remembered for."

"I didn't know the story was widely known. Was it wrong of me to use it in my book?"

"Bernadette—" His thoughts drift away from us. He takes a long sip of coffee.

Effa has been puzzled by our conversation. I say to her: "Reverend Manning knew my mother."

Emma's mother is seventy-six years old, but spry and alert. She takes Manning by the arm and leads him toward Handy Paige. "Let's just see about those poems," I hear her say.

Emma and I are alone. "She misses Jack," I say.

"Yes, she and Daddy were very close."

"I was always impressed with the way Effa forgave your father's infidelity. And with how she took me, and even Bernadette, into your family. She is a generous woman."

"It was not as easy for *me* to forgive Da."

"It's natural for a daughter to feel protective of her mother."

"I was terribly confused. I felt guilty—for spying, *for seeing what I saw*. It was as if I were the one who had betrayed my mother."

"That's all in the past."

"Do you think Bernadette forgives me?"

"Bernadette? Why should—"

"HOLY TOLEDO!" A big American voice booms across the room.

"Good lord, it's Terry Klout. I don't believe it. This is really too much." I take Emma's hand and we go to greet him.

Terry Klout shambles into the room, swinging his arms like lassos. The same old Terrycloth. Cowboy boots and polyester suit. String tie. Marcia tripping behind in stiletto heels.

"PUG! JEEZ!" He shakes my hand as if he were driving water from a pump. "Jeez-Louise, who'd a thunk it?"

I grin. "You're the last person I expected to see."

"When we got your invitation, I says to Marcia, hell's bells, we haven't had a vacation in twenty years. Let's pack up and go. We can combine Pug's weddin' with a trip to Europe. See gay Par-ee, have tea with the Queen."

"This is Emma, Terry. My bride. Emma, Terry Klout and his wife, Marcia."

Emma smiles sweetly. She is nearly as tall as Terry. His jaw hangs open like a broken hinge.

"Frank has told me about you," says Emma politely. "And of course I read about you in Frank's book."

"The kid was like a son to me," says Terry. "But— jeez—lookit 'im now."

Marcia steps past Terry to take Emma's hand. "Pleased ta meetsha." Her dress is the same color as Terry's suit, sky blue—that old Missouri sky. Her tight-fitting jacket gapes at the throat, revealing ample décolletage. From memory I retrieve a sickly scent of lilac-sweet perfume, inextricably mixed with the odors of dust, cow pats, DDT.

"Jeez-Louise," says Terry at last. He gazes straight into Emma's eyes, then down at me. "Well, whadaya know!"

"I can't believe you're here," I say again. Terry appears much the same as thirty-one years ago. Lanky, as flexible as string. Bald on top, but the same shag on the sides, straw yellow. Marcia is plumper, blowsier, blonder. I repeat, "I don't believe it."

"Glad ta meetsha, M'am," says Terry to Emma, pumping her hand with such vigor the wreath of daisies slips down over her eyes.

"She's a real looker," he whispers aside, a little too loudly, winking at Emma. "Jeez, whadaya know."

Terry goes up on tiptoes and casts about the room. "Where's Bernsie?"

The old affection is still in his eyes.

"Bernadette is dead, Terry. I'm sorry. I should have written."

His face collapses like a wrung rag.

"And you?" I ask. "How are you?"

"FAN-tas-tic! Couldn't be better. Marcia and I have a chain of fast-food restaurants, barbecued ribs is our speciality. Adam's Honey-Baked Ribs we call 'em. A franchise operation. We jus' set back and cash the checks." Marcia jabs her elbow into Terry's ribs. He corrects himself. "Well, maybe it's not as easy as all that. But Marcia here does all the work.

I race cars and bikes. I don't actually do much of the drivin' anymore"—she jabs him again—"*any* of the drivin', but I—"

"The kids?"

"Lisa's in California with husband number four. Charlene lives in Tulsa. Married to a man in the oil business. Sells moly-carbide drill bits. Money? You'd better believe it. You could stick this hotel into Charlene's living room and still have room fer—" He casts about wistfully. "I was sure hopin' to see Bernsie."

"Terry never forgets his old girlfriends," says Marcia. She jingles her charm bracelet at a passing waitress.

"Jeez, Marcia," Terry whines, "who could forget Bernsie?" He turns to me. "Sorry about your mama, Pug."

"Thanks, Terry. It's been a while."

"Frank's an author, now," interjects Roger Manning. He has slipped into our circle to greet his old rival. "Frank's book is on the Irish best-seller list."

"Hell's bells!" Terry exclaims. Then, toward Emma, "Sorry, M'am, no offense."

"The Reverend Manning," offers Emma politely.

Terry appraises Roger, looks the priest up and down—trimly tailored Anglican-gray clerical suit, crisp starched collar, and handsome thatch of silver hair. A big grin splits his face. He pulls Roger's hand. "She was some lady," he whispers conspiratorially, cheek by jowl with Roger.

"She was indeed," says Roger Manning, a bit abstractly.

"Yep, the prettiest thing I ever saw. How about a toast, Reverend. How about a toast to Frank here and his lady friend."

"I am not Frank's 'lady friend,' " says Emma quietly.

Terry corrects himself. "To Frank and his bride. So how 'bout it, Reverend? Gimme a drink. I wanna propose a toast to Frank here and his lady friend." He lopes toward the bar.

Marcia acknowledges me. "Looks like ya done OK, Frank."

I wink. "Not bad for a shortie."

She bats her lashes at Emma. "Takes all kinds ta make a world," she offers philosophically.

"We're glad you came," says Emma.

"Sorry we missed the service. Got hung up at Kennedy and was late for our flight outta London."

Emma embraces Marcia. "It was Frank's idea to send you an invitation. He's very fond of Terry. But it's been so long. He didn't know if Terry was alive or dead. And I'm certain he never expected you to come all the way from Missouri."

A three-man band has been setting up their equipment at the far end of the bar. Now they belt out a jazzy *Stardust*.

Terry bangs his glass with a spoon. "Let's have a dance! Bride and groom onto the dance floor!"

The *clang-clang* is taken up by the Trickle Center crowd and by Deidre's kids. Car keys, coins, flatware clanging on glasses.

"Dance! Dance!"

"I've never danced in my life," says Emma.

"Nor I."

"Do you suppose we should try."

"I don't think we have a choice."

I guide Emma onto the hardwood square near the band. There is a moment of general hilarity as we figure out what to do with our hands and arms, then a thunder of applause as we stumble around the floor.

"God moves in mysterious ways," observes Roger Manning.

"God ain't got nothin' ta do with it, Rev'rend," says Marcia, missing his irony. But she catches the twinkle in Roger's blue eyes. "Hey," she adds, giving his ribs a nudge, "save me a dance later, willya?"

"Indeed I will, madam."

Terry introduces himself to the Kelly clan. "You must be the mother of the bride," he says to Effa.

"I am," says Effa Kelly.

"She's a knockout."

"Sure if only Jack were here to see it." Effa dabs at her eyes with a wet serviette.

Deidre explains to Terry. "Jack was our father, Emma's dad. He and Frank were friends."

"If only Jack could see it," Effa sniffs.

"A hellava couple," observes Terry Klout. "I'm gonna give 'em a motorcycle for a wedding present."

A tear etches a line through the makeup on Jennifer's cheek. "I think they're beautiful," she says to Walter Paige.

Walter grins. He turns to Handy. "What do you think, Uncle?"

"I hope they fuck better than they dance," mumbles Handy Paige into a froth of Guinness.

"What's that?" asks moist-eyed Jennifer Down.

Handy Paige takes a gulp of stout and tugs at his ears. "A fukkin' miracle," he says.

On the dance floor the bride and groom begin to catch the rhythm.

"What did you say?" asks Jennifer.

Too loudly Handy Paige repeats, "A FUKKIN' MIRACLE."

I don't ask for miracles. I will settle for Emma Kelly sitting on the edge of the bed in our flat in Nicholas Road—in her yellow wedding dress, her gingery hair in disarray, the circlet of daisies in her hands.

Outside, a cloud-garnished Irish night. Summer stars have climbed to culmination, Vega and Altair, the Herd-boy and Weaving-girl, and the intervening river of light. *I think the reader would have felt cheated by a happy ending,* said Jennifer Down. By sheerest coincidence it is the seventh night of the seventh moon. Listen! Do you hear the rush of wings? The flight of swans sculling the air on their course up the Lee, wingtip to wingtip, a bridge of birds across the severing stream.

I don't ask for the Beatific Vision. Moonlight fills the window in the yellow wall. Emma turns the circlet of flowers round and round in her hands. It is enough. She places the ring of daisies on the bed's coverlet. Her thin white fingers go to the buttons at the top of her bodice.

Let beauty flare out now and then. In hints and traits. A powder of tiny stars winking from the Pleiades. Orion steeped in a pink aurora. The velvety dusted wings of a polyphemus moth flapping up into the night.

Her eyes are full of uncertainty. "Frank, be patient with me, I don't—"

I sit beside her on the bed.

"—have much experience."

I touch her hand. "Dear Emma, you have married a forty-three-year-old virgin. In matters of love you must be my teacher."

We laugh.

I volunteer, "I'll undress first." I stand. I undo the buttons of my shirt.

Emma says, "I've only seen two men naked before. My father—with your mother. And—"

"That was a long time ago. Tonight we begin new lives."

I drop my pants. I drop my shorts.

She observes, "It's so big."

"I've always heard that size doesn't matter."

"Frank."

"Yes."

"Lie beside me on the bed."

She drops back against the pillow. I lie beside her. I place her wreath of flowers on my head.

"Do you mind," I ask, "that I'm not beautiful?"

She touches my cheek, as briefly as the stroke of a moth's wing.

We are silent a long time. Moonlight puddles in the corners of the room. Shadows drift on the yellow walls. Her wedding dress is soft against my skin.

"Frank."

"Yes?"

"Hold me."